To Theodore Hu...
Dec. 25, 1964
From Tommy Hvale

BRET

THE LUCK OF ROARING CAMP

and 16 Other Exciting Tales

of Mining and Frontier Days

❧

Each Story Complete

PLATT & MUNK
GREAT WRITERS
COLLECTION

≈ Bret Harte Stories

HARTE

❧

❧

❧ *Stories*
of the Early West

Foreword by WALTER VAN TILBURG CLARK

PLATT & MUNK, *Publishers* • NEW YORK

∾ Contents

M'LISS: AN IDYLL OF RED MOUNTAIN

Bret

∾ Harte

A FOREWORD *by Walter Van Tilburg Clark*

AT the height of his career, from the late 1860's to about 1890, Francis Brett Harte, better known by the shortened name he signed to most of his work, Bret Harte, was one of the most popular writers in the world. Indeed only three other American writers, Mark Twain, O. Henry and Jack London, all of whom had a good deal in common with him, have ever been anything like as widely read and as constantly sought after as he was then.

Single stories of his, such as "The Luck of Roaring Camp," which won him his first national renown, could be found in expensive, illustrated editions on the living-room tables of all the reading families in America. They were reprinted in England and, in translations, all over Europe. Editors and publishers vied for his new work. Theatre men pressed him to make plays out of his best known gold rush stories and out of new subjects drawn from the same world. He was invited everywhere to make lectures on California life.

7

His precise ironical, little poem about the superior wiles of a Chinese gambler, which he called "Plain Language from Truthful James," caught the popular fancy under a title someone else pinned on it, "The Heathen Chinee," and swept the country as not even the best-selling of best-selling popular records can sweep it today. It was reprinted in thousands of newspapers and magazines and cut out and pasted up in store windows, hotel lobbies and street-cars. It was recited at all sorts of gatherings and quoted and misquoted in connection with everything under the sun. It was even set to music and sung in the streets.

Nor was his fame entirely a popular one, by any means. When he finally left California in 1871, he became the welcome guest of the best-known literary figures in the east, such men as Longfellow, Emerson, Lowell, Holmes and Howells. *The Atlantic Monthly,* then the foremost intellectual magazine in the nation, made him an unprecedented offer, a "salary" of ten thousand dollars, the equivalent of thirty or forty thousand today, for whatever, much or little, he might write in the next year. The great English novelist, Charles Dickens, the living writer he himself most admired, invited him to contribute to the London magazine of which he was the editor.

The most trusted reviewers and critics spoke highly of his work, particularly of his stories. They found them dramatic and convincing, and pointed out that many of them, such as "The Luck of Roaring Camp," "The Outcasts of Poker Flat," and "Tennessee's Partner," by way of their combination of human responsibility and the operations of blind Fate, attained a tragic power comparable to that of the classical Greek tragedies. They praised him for his moral themes demonstrating the natural goodness circumstance could bring out in even the roughest and most hardened people. They called attention to the new realism of his background portrayals of the tough and even sordid gold-camp life, though sometimes they felt that he went too far in this matter, was too particularly and grimly realistic. They found his characters, even the minor ones, equally real and convincing.

His writing, in their opinion, was as new as his themes and scenes and people, and perfectly suited to them. It was, they said, remarkably clear, simple and economical. It was quietly controlled, even understated in its narrative passages, precise and suggestive in its descriptive passages and daringly true to life in its illiterate, jocular dialogue, full of the colorful metaphors of mining and gambling, and at the same time careful and accurate in its preservation of individual differences. More than that, they felt that he managed, by way of a graceful, rhythmic modification of all the elements, to blend them into a pleasing uniformity. He was, in short, as highly thought of by the literary professionals as he was widely loved by the common readers.

Thousands of people, young and old, still read and reread Bret Harte with pleasure every year, and every new history of American literature still gives him a place. Very few of those thousands of readers, however, know as many as ten of his nearly two hundred stories and sketches, and most know only three or four, always "The Luck of Roaring Camp," "The Outcasts of Poker Flat," and "Tennessee's Partner," all early stories, and sometimes "M'liss," an even earlier story which drew heavily upon his own experience as a school teacher in California. If any of them know even one of his many poems, it will almost certainly be that same unconquerable "Heathen Chinee."

Though his place in the histories of American literature is secure, it is also generally small, and the emphasis is always placed on those same few early pieces. He is invariably described as an "early, influential local-color writer," in a way which suggests that local-color writers are not quite the best sort, and that early local-color writers, no matter how influential, are not likely to be quite as good as later ones.

Contemporary critics, moreover, seem to have come around to a view which is almost exactly opposed to that of the critics of his own time. They find his plots artificial and contrived and far too often dependent upon mere chance for their working out, even, as in "The Luck" and "The Outcasts," a completely external chance, such as a change in the weather. They do not find his people convincing either. On the contrary, they speak of them as exaggerated and over-simplified types, like the characters in an old-fashioned melodrama: the impossibly young and lovely heroine (Piney in "The Outcasts" and Polly in "An Ingenue of The Sierras") who is able, by simply making an appearance, to move a cold-eyed, laconic gambler (Oakhurst) into fatal self-sacrifice, or lead a lordly, all-knowing stage-driver (Yuba Bill) into error. Then there is the tough, bearded, profane, hard-drinking miner (Kentuck of Roaring Camp and Dick Bullen of Simpson's Bar) who is yet so tender-hearted that he will risk his life for a child, or the equally tough and veteran miner who nonetheless pines away like a sickly romantic maiden when he loses a scapegrace partner (Tennessee's Partner), or the poor orphan babe whose mere presence reforms the disreputable Roaring Camp, and so on and so on.

These critics feel also that with his contrived and chancy plots and his improbable characters, Bret Harte is more often an embarrassing sentimentalist than a realist. Nor do they admire his style. The narrative and descriptive passages, they say, are self-consciously "literary" and quite out of keeping with his subjects. The dialogue is just as self-consciously illiterate and folksy, and the two simply don't get along together. They add that at times the too consciously literate and illiterate are even combined, as in the conclusion of "Tennessee's Partner," in a quite impossible way. No such slow, crude, unimaginative man as the partner, they maintain, ever beheld such a vision or spoke such lines as Bret Harte made him behold and speak in that final scene.

For such melodramatic excesses, and for similar descriptive excesses, such as the participation of even the forest in Tennessee's funeral procession, they call him "an incurable romantic," in a tone of voice which suggests that romanticism is over and done with.

All this adds up to a considerable shift for Bret Harte, both popularly and critically, from the tremendous fame of his best years. We cannot help but ask what has brought about so great a change in what is, literarily speaking, so short a time?

Well, for one thing, Bret Harte never went back to California after he left it in 1871. He lived for some years in the east, then for a time in Germany, and finally, for the rest of his life, in Scotland and England. During that time, nearly half his life, he quite lost touch with California, and even lost a good part of his desire to write about it. He was forced to continue writing about it more than about anything else, however, because that was what his publishers and readers most wanted from him. As a result, much of his late work *was* contrived and artificial and even repetitive, so that his reputation had already lost a good deal of its earlier luster before he died in 1902.

In addition, his own considerable influence has worked against him. A great many writers who came after him imitated him in one way or another. Others, moved by his example, began to write local-color stories about different regions of the country, making use, as he had, of the ways of life and ways of speaking peculiar to those regions. Still others, like Mark Twain, who said that Bret Harte had taught him a great deal about how to write a story, and particularly about style, while they were both working for an early San Francisco magazine, *The Northern Californian,* and O. Henry, who fashioned his plots in much the same way Bret Harte did, continued his tradition along lines of their own and became even more popular than he was. So, by the end of the nineteenth century there was no longer anything very new about Bret Harte's kind of writing.

Besides, literary taste, like every other kind of taste, changes with the passage of time. Thanks largely to an increasing recognition of the methods of more complicated storytellers like Stephen Crane, Henry James and Joseph Conrad, it has changed even more rapidly and more radically in the United States since Bret Harte died.

Somehow, though, it doesn't seem as if all these literary changes put together add up to quite enough to explain why the present view of Bret Harte is so very different from the view taken in his own time. We cannot help but wonder, for instance, how Bret Harte, who had good eyes and good ears, who lived in California for seventeen years and took part in every aspect of its gold-rush life, and who, according to all kinds of literary friends of his, including Mark Twain, always took great pains with his writing, could have presented his chosen world as badly as the contemporary critics think he did.

We cannot help but wonder, also, even granting a marked change in literary taste between then and now, how the readers and critics of his own day, many of whom knew his California at first hand, and all of whom had at least heard a great deal about it from friends who had been out, or read about it in the newspapers and magazines, could have been so wrong in their estimate of his work. These very wonderings, in turn, seem to suggest that there must have been other, and possibly even more important changes at work along with the change in literary taste, since Bret Harte's day.

There have, of course. Taste, of whatever kind, is far from being the only thing that changes with time. Ways of living, feeling, thinking and behaving change with time too, and changes in taste come about very largely because of them. These fundamental changes have been even greater all over the world, and particularly in America, since Bret Harte's time, than the changes of taste. To say nothing of the fact that even within Bret Harte's time the gold-rush world was a very special one. Perhaps, then, what will help most to bring our view of Bret Harte's stories closer to the view taken by the people of his own time, is a clearer sense of what the California gold-rush world was really like:

The California gold rush did not begin, as many people still believe, just because a man by the name of James Marshall happened to find a little gold at Sutter's Mill in January of 1848, and the news leaked out.

Gold had been found in California a good many times before that, and at least as long before that as 1690, and it had been found and mined in a great many other places in the world ages before Christ was born, and none of those earlier discoveries had brought on a rush. What really brought about the rush to California was the fact that for the first time in human history a treasure hunt was open to all comers. Always before, any kind of treasure, including gold, found anywhere had always been the property of the rulers of the country in which it was found, or of the rulers who had sent out expeditions to rob the countries which had it. That had been the case in California under the Mexicans, and under the Spaniards before them.

But early in 1848, at just about the same time, in fact, that Marshall made his little discovery, the United States took California away from Mexico, and under the laws of the United States anyone who found gold could keep gold. That made all the difference. The world had never before seen anything to compare with the stampede which ensued, and it has never seen anything like it since, not even in the Alaskan gold rush. Tens of thousands of men poured into California from all over the world. They were all after the same thing, gold, and they were all excited by visions of big fortunes and long ease, so the competition was lively.

For some time there was no law to control the competition, since Mexican law was out and American law was not yet effectively established. Often, when the greedy competitors were too close to each other, and particularly when they had come from different nations, the competition got beyond mere liveliness. There was claim-jumping at gun-point, beating, robbery and murder. Majority groups of miners, usually American, tried to set up their own local laws and enforce them, but often the workings of their "courts" were no prettier than the activities they punished ("The Outcasts" and "Tennessee's Partner").

Racial antagonism, particularly that between the Americans and the Mexicans, sometimes swelled and spread until it took on the proportions of organized banditry and even of small-scale warfare. Needless to say, under such conditions every man went armed, and many were more than a little trigger-happy or sudden with a knife. The fact is that the dominant American element for some time was made up of various explosive types of men: rough, illiterate, quarrelsome midwestern frontiersmen; Oregonians for whom shooting Indians had become a pastime; and self-styled "southern gentlemen"—gamblers and others of doubtful or shady past—who were touchy upon "points of honor," habitually condescending to all colored races, and given to settling all differences of opinion with pistols. These men made things no easier for those elements, of whatever race, whose intentions were more tolerant and peaceful.

Besides that, the mining itself, even when there was no trouble to go with it, was extremely hard and often dangerous labor. There was a great deal of sickness in the flimsy, unsanitary camps and in the often-flooded valley supply-towns such as Sacramento, Stockton and Marysville. With very few able doctors to cope with it and very little medicine to use against it, hundreds of men died of dysentery, malaria, typhoid fever and cholera, and thousands more were crippled by them.

It was years before there were any women in most of the camps except a few of the toughest kind (the Duchess and Mother Shipton) and there were never many until the excitement was all but over. Children were even fewer. As a result, the miner's play was as rough as his work and politics. He danced wild *fandangos* in his heavy boots, drank quantities of whiskey and gambled, and the combination of liquor, poker and the practically universal tradition of every man for himself often produced fatal quarrels, even between men who had been good friends. Nobody cared much what he looked like, either, in this wholly masculine world.

In addition, none of the treasure-seekers had come to California to stay. Every man was there to make his pile, whether by mining, storekeeping, hauling supplies or gambling, and then get out and go back home to spend it. So even when they could have fixed them up, these men didn't much care how flimsy and ramshackle their cabins were, as long as they were protected from the weather, or how much they tore up the land with their mining, or hacked down the forests for building or firewood. They slaughtered game and even ranchers' stock with the same indifference. If they left a shambles behind them when they went home rich, what difference did it make? If they left bad reputations behind them, what difference did that make either? California was a long way from home.

Needless to say in such a comfortless, temporary, hazardous, reckless, wilderness world, where seeking gold was the chief occupation, where making a big strike which would get you out was the chief hope, and gambling and betting the chief amusement, and where former beliefs and moralities lost their power all too rapidly, chance or luck, whether good or bad, did become the deepest and most constant concern. It *did* assume, that is, something very like the consequence the great Greek tragedians gave it under the name of Fate, or in the form of the arbitrary and interfering activities of the gods. To have luck was everything. "Lucky" was a nickname to be envied. On the other hand, if your luck ran out beyond recovery, you accepted that fact too, as fatalistically as the characters in a Greek tragedy accepted a curse from the gods or the doom pronounced by an oracle. You were done, and you knew you were done. The only thing left that mattered then, courage being the most important, if not the only, virtue left in such a world, was to make "a good end," even to finish with a joke, if possible, as do Oakhurst and Tennessee.

Furthermore, in that wilderness world of the Sierra

Nevadas, changes of weather were far from being the least important gestures of Luck or Fate. The mining depended upon them entirely. No water and you couldn't wash your gold (or yourself either, for that matter). Too much water— and the seasonal rains of California are usually torrential— and you not only couldn't hunt for the gold, but you might even find, as the miners of Roaring Camp did, that once the floods had passed, the rich deposits you'd been working had vanished. Even staying alive depended on the weather. When the rains were heavy the big supply wagons bogged down in the valleys, and the river-crossings became impassable for stagecoaches and even for men on horseback ("How Santa Claus Came to Simpson's Bar"). Floods often washed the camps, or parts of them, away along with the gold-bearing sandbars too, as in Roaring Camp, because most of them were built as close to the workings as they could be, right along the streams and even in deep ravines cut by the streams, so that the water came down many feet deep and very swiftly.

Higher up in the Sierras, in such camps as Poker Flat, these heavy seasonal rains became equally heavy snowstorms. In fact the northern Sierra region is, by official weather-bureau measurement, the heaviest snowfall region in the world. It is not unusual to have three or four feet fall there in a day, or to have a storm continue unbroken for four or five days at a time. Usually there are high winds with the storms, too, winds which drift the snow to a depth of fifty feet and more in hollows and ravines. Hundreds of people who came to California by the overland route, especially those who took the northernmost or Lassen trail and reached the Sierras a little late, in October or November, perished in such storms. Thousands lost their wagons and animals and all their belongings. Little wonder, then, that weather became a kind of Head God, a Fate of Fates, to the forty-niners. Fortune, even life depended upon it. While a man might move on from a worked-out diggings, or quit a poker game that wasn't going well, there was nothing whatever that he could do about the weather.

There was also another side to this rugged, luck-minded life, however. Most of the men who came into it were no worse, at least when they first came, than the average of men anywhere. Excepting the frontiersmen, most of them had lived perfectly civilized lives before they came. Very few of them, at heart, liked the gold-rush life. They had to play tough with each other, after the way of men and boys alone anywhere. The harder the life was, the more they had to take it with a joke. But secretly they were often lonely, homesick and frightened. They had daydreams, and sleeping dreams too, about the life they had left behind them, the life they longed to go back to.

Thousands of them did go back after just a few weeks or months, some because they had been lucky and made their pile, but a great many more of them because they were too sick or feeble to stand the life any longer, or because they were just unbearably homesick. Many who wanted to go home stayed only because they were broke and couldn't pay the fare. (Nobody who had come out cross-country, by the grim Oregon and Humboldt trails, ever dreamed of going back that way, and the ships that took men back by Panama or around the Horn were always crowded and charged high fares.)

Others, sometimes because they had made big plans before they left, or had even boasted a bit about the fortunes they'd bring back, were too proud to return empty-handed. Still others had run away from crimes and didn't dare go back, or from grievances they still felt bitter about, so that they chose not to go back, no matter how much they disliked it where they were.

Among such men, men full of memories of a better life who nonetheless stayed on for years or for good, in that chancy, dangerous, comfortless, womanless, childless world, the personal relationships which people take for granted in most places took on very special and important meanings, meanings which begot very strong feelings. Good women, bearing with them as they did all sorts of reminders of mothers, sisters, sweethearts and, just in general, of a more decent, mannerly and homelike life, became objects of worship, not just of ordinary courtesy.

If they were also young, even very young by ordinary standards, and innocent (Piney), or even merely innocent-seeming (the Ingenue), and not downright hideous, they were beautiful to the eyes of such men, who wanted at once to protect and help them (Oakhurst and Yuba Bill), or even to court them and marry them, both for themselves and for the home life they would bring with them. Most girls in those days, especially on the frontiers, became able cooks and housekeepers long before most girls in our time even begin to think about such things.

Young children, who bore with them not only similar reminders of a better world, but also suggestions of a future, even of permanence, in a world that seemed futureless and temporary, could also rouse deep feelings.

And, most importantly, close friendship, partnership, begot a depth of feeling and took on a variety of meanings almost inconceivable to people who have never lived such a life. It meant help in trouble, care in sickness, companionship in solitude and someone to trust in a world where not much could be trusted. Often such partnerships went on through good luck and bad, for years, until the friendship became so strong and so personal that, as in the case of "Tennessee's Partner," it no longer needed reasons at all, but was its own law and reason. Partnership, in fact, was universally looked upon, all through the mining country, as the most sacred of all relationships.

Improbable as much of it may seem to us now, that is what gold-rush life was like. Nor has there been any guessing in that description of it. Thousands of early California newspapers, diaries, memoirs, official records and personal letters still offer the evidence to prove it was really like that. The shipping records in San Francisco, the chief gold-rush port, give the names of the thousands of men who went home early. Enough of the people who died in the plagues and storms (though far from all of them) are named in the vital statistics columns of the newspapers, to put the dimensions of those tragedies beyond question. And the same columns list hundreds of brides and even mothers who were fifteen or younger. Accounts of robberies, shooting and knifing affrays, lynchings and little race wars fill the columns of the old papers and abound in the diaries, memoirs and letters. Reverence for women and children and the importance of partnership were so nearly universal and so taken for granted that they were scarcely newsworthy topics or matters of record, but feelings were so much alike in all the camps that a single example of each is proof enough of their reality.

To start with the ladies, one forty-niner described at length, in his personal journal, the reception of the first woman, a storekeeper's wife, to come into the little creek camp where he was working. The storekeeper, still thinking in "civilized" terms, and seeing no other women in the neighborhood, but only tough, bearded, booted, knife- and pistol-packing men, hurried his wife into the shack he was going to use for a store, intending to keep her out of sight until he felt surer about how the men would act. The word that she was there, however, got around very quickly. The miners gathered until there were thirty or forty of them standing in front of the shack.

They ordered the storekeeper to bring his wife out, assuring him that they meant her no harm. Most of their assurances were both humorous and profane, and there were some straight-faced jokes, also, about the kind of a man who would keep a woman all to himself when nobody else had one, and the sort of thing that might happen to him. The storekeeper was frightened and begged them not to bother his wife, saying that she was sick and exhausted from the long overland journey they had just completed. The miners hooted. That was a likely story. They kept insisting. Their threatening jokes sounded less and less like jokes. Both the storekeeper and his wife were now badly frightened, but the storekeeper stood his ground, and finally his wife, more afraid of what might happen to him than she was for herself, came out of her own accord.

She wasn't exactly a raving beauty, or a young one either. She was middle-aged and—the storekeeper had been telling the truth—thin and hollow-eyed from illness, and burned to the color of leather by the long prairie and desert travel. No matter. Youth and beauty weren't the point. The profanity and the joking threats stopped the moment she appeared. They had been meant only for the storekeeper who was, after all, just another man. All the miners took off their hats, a thing many of them hadn't done for months except when they went to sleep, and stood there looking at the woman. Several of them had tears in their eyes. None of them ventured to say much more than an embarrassed, "Howdy, ma'am," and only one of them dared do more than speak. He, at last, moving as if he were in a trance, advanced a little, stopped far enough from her so that he could not possibly seem to threaten her, and bending over as far as he could, gingerly took the edge of her apron between his thumb and finger, as if to convince himself that it, and so, perhaps, the woman herself, was real. That was all. They bashfully wished her, and even the storekeeper, well, worked up a little farewell cheer, and went back to their diggings.

The storekeeper got a lot of volunteer help in setting up shop after that, and considerable help in consuming the whiskey he'd brought with him too. But nobody bothered his wife again, beyond coming to stare at some of her garments when she hung them out on the clothesline, until she was well and invited them to visit. Then they came in a body, with a few additions from farther off, all of them washed, trimmed and brushed, and some of them in new shirts, every man taking off his hat as he entered the door, and gave her a big party. They brought the makings of the party, too, food, drink and music.

Impossible? No, it happened, and the personal records tell of many other incidents of the same sort. Sentimental? Well, perhaps, at least from our comparatively casual and unemotional point of view. But if it is, the sentimentality is not in the account. It was actually there in those lonely, home-hungry miners.

Another such journal tells of a two-year-old boy (the son of a storekeeper too, as it happened—they were the men most likely to have families in those camps), whom the miners would just come and look at in much the same way, at first. When he was no longer afraid of them they would play with him whenever they came to the store, and bring him presents it had cost them much work to make or long rides or walks to buy. He became a great favorite with them, literally a kind of mascot, a lucky presence in their district. They would touch him for luck, or ask for some small token from him to carry with them when they were about to try a new digging. Needless to say, however, he was more than a little spoiled by so much attention, and he was also around them a good deal when neither their mood nor the things they talked about were meant for him, since the store was also, as it was in most of those smaller, scattered mining districts, the saloon and the *fandango* hall. Twenty years later the same journalist learned that a young man the vigilance committee had just hanged for a variety of crimes was the same little boy "grown up." He noted down his horror at the discovery, and brooded over the matter for days, wondering how much he and his fellow miners had been responsible for what had happened.

The importance of partnership can be even more directly illustrated, for Bret Harte took his idea for "Tennessee's Partner," as he did the ideas for many of his stories, from actual newspaper reports. There was one very important difference, however, between the actual trial and Bret Harte's. The real "judge" and "jury" were so moved by the partner's clumsy offer that they let the real "Tennessee" off, despite the fact that he had a good many more counts, and some worse ones, too, against him than the Tennessee of the story. Perhaps that would have made a better ending for the story than the one Bret Harte gave it. It does seem, in one way, to make even clearer how sacred the bond of partnership was, and how generally it was recognized as such, for certainly the "court" rendered its verdict for the partner's sake.

As for the "too folksy" dialogue in the stories, all these same journals, memoirs and letters, and even many of the newspaper accounts of the time, make it clear in their own language that Bret Harte was not exaggerating or inventing.

So, you see, it *was* a very special world, that gold-rush world, with ways of living, thinking, feeling and acting so particularly its own that there has never been anything quite like it anywhere, before or since. Which is what the literary histories mean when they call Bret Harte a local-color writer.

But realizing that, perhaps we can now imagine ourselves back into that world enough to read Bret Harte more nearly as the readers of his own time did. If we can, we may also notice a good many rather important things in his stories that the wholly contemporary-minded critics have missed— such things, for instance, as the fact that Tennessee's partner doesn't pine away simply because Tennessee is gone, but also because he feels that he has caused Tennessee's death; or the fact that the simultaneous vanishing of both "Lucks" from Roaring Camp might have been a truly tragic event, in the fullest sense, for men like those "real" miners who cherished the storekeeper's little son. And we will see the grim irony of the fact that it wasn't really the snowstorm, at all, which trapped the Outcasts, but the only sympathetic weakness that could have moved their thoroughly hardened hearts, a weakness for almost forgotten youth and innocence.

There are many other evidences in these stories, in every paragraph, sometimes in every sentence, of a colorful and significant era now past—its language, dress, means of travel, and its frontier humor, attitudes and philosophy, as well as actual documented incidents. Bret Harte really understood the world he wrote about.

Believe in the gold-rush world, read these stories as carefully as Bret Harte wrote them, and you will still find treasure in that old, worked-over country of the forty-niner.

Reno, Nevada
January, 1964

SELECTED SHORT STORIES

The
Outcasts
of
Poker
∾ Flat

As Mr. John Oakhurst, gambler, stepped into the main street of Poker Flat on the morning of the 23rd of November, 1850, he was conscious of a change in its moral atmosphere since the preceding night. Two or three men conversing earnestly together ceased as he approached, and exchanged significant glances. There was a Sabbath lull in the air, which in a settlement unused to Sabbath influences, looked ominous.

Mr. Oakhurst's calm handsome face betrayed small concern with these indications. Whether he was conscious of any predisposing cause was another question. I reckon they're after somebody, he reflected. Likely it's me. He returned to his pocket the handkerchief with which he had been whipping away the red dust of Poker

Flat from his neat boots, and quietly discharged his mind of any further conjecture.

In point of fact Poker Flat was "after somebody." It had lately suffered the loss of several thousand dollars, two valuable horses, and a prominent citizen. It was experiencing a spasm of virtuous reaction quite as lawless and ungovernable as any of the acts that had provoked it. A secret committee had determined to rid the town of all improper persons. This was done permanently in regard to two men who were then hanging from the boughs of a sycamore in the gulch, and temporarily in the banishment of certain other objectionable characters. I regret to say that some of these were ladies. It is but due to the sex, however, to state that their impropriety was professional, and it was only in such easily established standards of evil that Poker Flat ventured to sit in judgment.

Mr. Oakhurst was right in supposing that he was included in this category. A few of the committee had urged hanging him as a possible example and a sure method of reimbursing themselves from his pockets of the sums he had won from them. "It's agin justice," said Jim Wheeler, "to let this yer young man from Roaring Camp—an entire stranger—carry away our money." But a crude sentiment of equity residing in the breasts of those who had been fortunate enough to win from Mr. Oakhurst overruled this narrower local prejudice.

Mr. Oakhurst received his sentence with philosophic

calmness, none the less coolly because he was aware of the hesitation of his judges. He was too much of a gambler not to accept fate. With him life was at best an uncertain game, and he recognized the usual percentage in favor of the dealer.

A body of armed men accompanied the deported wickedness of Poker Flat to the outskirts of the settlement. Besides Mr. Oakhurst, who was known to be a coolly desperate man and for whose intimidation the armed escort was intended, the expatriated party consisted of a young woman familiarly known as the Duchess, another who had won the title of Mother Shipton, and Uncle Billy, a suspected sluice-robber and confirmed drunkard. The cavalcade provoked no comments from the spectators, nor was any word uttered by the escort. Only when they reached the gulch which marked the uttermost limit of Poker Flat, did the leader speak briefly and to the point. The exiles were forbidden to return at the peril of their lives.

As the escort disappeared their pent-up feelings found vent in a few hysterical tears from the Duchess, some bad language from Mother Shipton, and a Parthian volley of expletives from Uncle Billy. The philosophic Oakhurst alone remained silent. He listened calmly to Mother Shipton's desire to cut somebody's heart out, to the repeated statements of the Duchess that she would die in the road, and to the alarming oaths that seemed to be bumped out of Uncle Billy as he rode forward.

With the easy good humor characteristic of his class he insisted upon exchanging his own riding horse, Five-Spot, for the sorry mule which the Duchess rode. But even this act did not draw the party into any closer sympathy. The young woman readjusted her somewhat draggled plumes with a feeble faded coquetry; Mother Shipton eyed the possessor of Five-Spot with malevolence, and Uncle Billy included the whole party in one sweeping anathema.

The road to Sandy Bar—a camp that not having as yet experienced the regenerating influences of Poker Flat, consequently seemed to offer some invitation to the emigrants—lay over a steep mountain range. It was distant a day's severe travel. In that advanced season the party soon passed out of the moist temperate regions of the foothills into the dry cold bracing air of the Sierras. The trail was narrow and difficult. At noon the Duchess, rolling out of her saddle upon the ground, declared her intention of going no farther, and the party halted.

The spot was singularly wild and impressive. A wooded amphitheater, surrounded on three sides by precipitous cliffs of naked granite, sloped gently toward the crest of another precipice that overlooked the valley. It was undoubtedly the most suitable spot for a camp, had camping been advisable. But Mr. Oakhurst knew that scarcely half the journey to Sandy Bar was accomplished and that the party was not equipped or provisioned for delay. This fact he pointed out to his companions curtly, with a philosophic commentary on the folly of "throwing up their hand before the game was played out." But they were furnished with liquor, which in this emergency stood them in place of food, fuel, rest and prescience. In spite of his remonstrances it was not long before they were more or less under its influence. Uncle Billy passed rapidly from a bellicose state into one of stupor, the Duchess became maudlin, and Mother Shipton snored. Mr. Oakhurst alone remained erect, leaning against a rock, calmly surveying them.

Mr. Oakhurst did not drink. It interfered with a profession which required coolness, impassiveness and presence of mind, and in his own language, he "couldn't afford it." As he gazed at his recumbent fellow exiles the loneliness begotten of his pariah trade, his habits of life, his very vices, for the first time seriously oppressed him. He bestirred himself in dusting his black clothes, washing his hands and face and other acts characteristic of his studiously neat habits, and for a moment forgot his annoyance. The thought of deserting his weaker and more pitiable companions never perhaps occurred to him. Yet he could not help feeling the want of that excitement which, singularly enough, was most conducive to that calm equanimity for which he was notorious. He looked at the gloomy walls that rose a thousand feet sheer above the circling pines around him, at the sky ominously clouded, at the valley below already deepening into shadow, and suddenly heard his name called.

A horseman slowly ascended the trail. In the fresh open face of the newcomer Mr. Oakhurst recognized Tom Simson, otherwise known as the "Innocent," of Sandy Bar. He had met him some months before over a "little game," and had with perfect equanimity won the entire fortune, amounting to some forty dollars, of that guileless youth. After the game was finished, Mr. Oakhurst drew the youthful speculator behind the door and thus addressed him: "Tommy, you're a good little man but you can't gamble worth a cent. Don't try it over again." He then handed him his money back, pushed him gently from the room, and so made a devoted slave of Tom Simson.

There was a remembrance of this in his boyish and enthusiastic greeting of Mr. Oakhurst. He had started, he said, to go to Poker Flat to seek his fortune. "Alone?" No, not exactly alone. In fact (a giggle), he had run away with Piney Woods. Didn't Mr. Oakhurst remember Piney? She that used to wait on table at the Temperance House? They had been engaged a long time, but old Jake Woods had objected and so they had run away and were going to Poker Flat to be married, and here they were. And they were tired out and how lucky it was they had found a place to camp, and company. All this the Innocent delivered rapidly, while Piney, a stout comely damsel of fifteen, emerged from behind the pine tree where she had been blushing unseen, and rode to the side of her lover.

Mr. Oakhurst seldom troubled himself with sentiment, still less with propriety, but he had a vague idea
that the situation was not fortunate. He retained, however, his presence of mind sufficiently to kick Uncle
Billy, who was about to say something, and Uncle Billy
was sober enough to recognize in Mr. Oakhurst's kick a
superior power that would not bear trifling. He then
endeavored to dissuade Tom Simson from delaying further, but in vain. He even pointed out the fact that there
were no provisions or means of making a camp. But un-
luckily the Innocent met this objection by assuring the
party that he was provided with an extra mule loaded
with provisions, and by the discovery of a rude attempt
at a log house near the trail. "Piney can stay with Mrs.
Oakhurst," said the Innocent, pointing to the Duchess,
"and I can shift for myself."

Nothing but Mr. Oakhurst's admonishing foot saved
Uncle Billy from bursting into a roar of laughter. As it
was, he felt compelled to retire up the canyon until he
could recover his gravity. There he confided the joke to
the tall pine trees, with many slaps of his leg, contor-
tions of his face, and the usual profanity. But when he
returned to the party he found them seated by a fire—
for the air had grown strangely chill and the sky overcast
—in apparently amicable conversation. Piney was actually talking in an impulsive girlish fashion to the Duchess who was listening with an interest and animation she
had not shown for many days. The Innocent was hold-

ing forth apparently with equal effect, to Mr. Oakhurst and Mother Shipton, who was actually relaxing into amiability. "Is this yer a damned picnic?" said Uncle Billy with inward scorn, as he surveyed the sylvan group, the glancing firelight, and the tethered animals in the foreground. Suddenly an idea mingled with the alcoholic fumes that disturbed his brain. It was apparently of a jocular nature for he felt impelled to slap his leg again and cram his fist into his mouth.

As the shadows crept slowly up the mountain a slight breeze rocked the tops of the pine trees and moaned through their long and gloomy aisles. The ruined cabin, patched and covered with pine boughs, was set apart for the ladies. As the lovers parted they unaffectedly exchanged a kiss, so honest and sincere that it might have been heard above the swaying pines. The frail Duchess and the malevolent Mother Shipton were probably too stunned to remark upon this last evidence of simplicity, and so turned without a word to the hut. The fire was replenished; the men lay down before the door and in a few minutes were asleep.

Mr. Oakhurst was a light sleeper. Toward morning he awoke benumbed and cold. As he stirred the dying fire, the wind which was now blowing strongly brought to his cheek that which caused the blood to leave it—snow!

He started to his feet with the intention of awakening the sleepers, for there was no time to lose. But turning to where Uncle Billy had been lying, he found him gone.

A suspicion leaped to his brain and a curse to his lips. He ran to the spot where the mules had been tethered; they were no longer there. The tracks were already rapidly disappearing in the snow.

The momentary excitement brought Mr. Oakhurst back to the fire with his usual calm. He did not waken the sleepers. The Innocent slumbered peacefully with a smile on his good-humored freckled face; the virgin Piney slept beside her frailer sisters as sweetly as though attended by celestial guardians; and Mr. Oakhurst, drawing his blanket over his shoulders, stroked his mustaches and waited for the dawn. It came slowly in a whirling mist of snowflakes that dazzled and confused the eye. What could be seen of the landscape appeared magically changed. He looked over the valley and summed up the present and future in two words, "Snowed in!"

A careful inventory of the provisions which, fortunately for the party, had been stored within the hut and so escaped the felonious fingers of Uncle Billy, disclosed the fact that with care and prudence they might last ten days longer. "That is," said Mr. Oakhurst *sotto voce* to the Innocent, "if you're willing to board us. If you ain't —and perhaps you'd better not—you can wait till Uncle Billy gets back with provisions." For some occult reason Mr. Oakhurst could not bring himself to disclose Uncle Billy's rascality, and so offered the hypothesis that he had wandered from the camp and had accidentally stampeded the animals. He dropped a warning to the Duchess and Mother Shipton, who of course knew the facts of their associate's defection. "They'll find out the truth about us *all* when they find out anything," he added significantly, "and there's no good frightening them now."

Tom Simson not only put all his worldly store at the disposal of Mr. Oakhurst, but seemed to enjoy the prospect of their enforced seclusion. "We'll have a good camp for a week, and then the snow'll melt and we'll all go back together." The cheerful gaiety of the young man and Mr. Oakhurst's calm infected the others. The Innocent, with the aid of pine boughs, extemporized a thatch for the roofless cabin, and the Duchess directed Piney in the rearrangement of the interior with a taste and tact that opened the blue eyes of that provincial maiden to their fullest extent. "I reckon now you're used to fine things at Poker Flat," said Piney. The Duchess turned away sharply to conceal something that reddened her cheeks through their professional tint, and Mother Shipton requested Piney not to "chatter." But when Mr. Oakhurst returned from a weary search for the trail he heard the sound of happy laughter echoing from the rocks. He stopped in some alarm and his thoughts first naturally reverted to the whiskey, which he had prudently cached. "And yet it don't somehow sound like whiskey," said the gambler. It was not until he caught sight of the blazing fire through the still blinding storm and the group around it that he settled to the conviction that it was "square fun."

Whether Mr. Oakhurst had cached his cards with the whiskey as something debarred the free access of the community, I cannot say. It was certain that in Mother Shipton's words, he "didn't say 'cards' once" during that evening. Haply the time was beguiled by an accordion, produced somewhat ostentatiously by Tom Simson from his pack. Notwithstanding some difficulties attending the manipulation of this instrument, Piney Woods managed to pluck several reluctant melodies from its keys, to an accompaniment by the Innocent on a pair of bone castanets. But the crowning festivity of the evening was reached in a rude camp meeting hymn, which the lovers, joining hands, sang with great earnestness and vociferation. I fear that a certain defiant tone and Covenanter's swing to its chorus, rather than any devotional quality, caused it speedily to infect the others, who at last joined in the refrain:

> I'm proud to live in the service of the Lord,
> And I'm bound to die in His army.

The pines rocked, the storm eddied and whirled above the miserable group, and the flames of their altar leaped heavenward as if in token of the vow.

At midnight the storm abated, the rolling clouds parted, and the stars glittered keenly above the sleeping camp. Mr. Oakhurst's professional habits had enabled

him to live on the smallest possible amount of sleep; in
dividing the watch with Tom Simson he somehow managed to take upon himself the greater part of that duty.
He excused himself to the Innocent by saying that he
had "often been a week without sleep." "Doing what?"
asked Tom. "Poker!" replied Oakhurst sententiously.
"When a man gets a streak of luck he don't get tired.
The luck gives in first. Luck," continued the gambler
reflectively, "is a mighty queer thing. All you know
about it for certain is that it's bound to change. And it's
finding out when it's going to change that makes you.
We've had a streak of bad luck since we left Poker Flat
—you come along, and slap you get into it too. If you
can hold your cards right along you're all right. For,"
added the gambler with cheerful irrelevance:

> I'm proud to live in the service of the Lord,
> And I'm bound to die in His army.

The third day came and the sun, looking through the
white-curtained valley saw the outcasts divide their
slowly decreasing store of provisions for the morning
meal. It was one of the peculiarities of that mountain
climate that its rays diffused a kindly warmth over the
wintry landscape, as if in regretful commiseration of the
past. But it revealed drift on drift of snow piled high
around the hut—a hopeless, uncharted trackless sea of
white lying below the rocky shores to which the casta-
ways still clung. Through the marvelously clear air the

smoke of the pastoral village of Poker Flat rose miles away. Mother Shipton saw it, and from a remote pinnacle of her rocky fastness hurled in that direction a final malediction. It was her last vituperative attempt, and perhaps for that reason was invested with a certain degree of sublimity. It did her good, she privately informed the Duchess. "Just you go out there and cuss, and see." She then set herself to the task of amusing "the child," as she and the Duchess were pleased to call Piney. Piney was no chicken, but it was a soothing and original theory of the pair thus to account for the fact that she didn't swear and wasn't improper.

When night crept up again through the gorges the reedy notes of the accordion rose and fell in fitful spasms and long-drawn gasps by the flickering campfire. But music failed to fill entirely the aching void left by insufficient food, and a new diversion was proposed by Piney—storytelling. Since neither Mr. Oakhurst nor his female companions cared to relate their personal experiences this plan would have failed too, but for the Innocent. Some months before he had chanced upon a stray copy of Mr. Pope's ingenious translation of the *Iliad*. He now proposed to narrate the principal incidents of that poem—having thoroughly mastered the argument and fairly forgotten the words—in the current vernacular of Sandy Bar. And so for the rest of that night the Homeric demigods again walked the earth. Trojan bully and wily Greek wrestled in the winds, and the

great pines in the canyon seemed to bow to the wrath
of the son of Peleus. Mr. Oakhurst listened with quiet
satisfaction. Most especially was he interested in the
fate of "Ash-heels," as the Innocent persisted in denomi-
nating the "swift-footed Achilles."

So, with small food and much of Homer and the accordion, a week passed over the heads of the outcasts.
The sun again forsook them, and again from leaden skies
the snowflakes were sifted over the land. Day by day
closer around them drew the snowy circle, until at last
they looked from their prison over drifted walls of
dazzling white that towered twenty feet above their
heads. It became more and more difficult to replenish
their fires, even from the fallen trees beside them, now
half hidden in the drifts. And yet no one complained.
The lovers turned from the dreary prospect and looked
into each other's eyes, and were happy. Mr. Oakhurst
settled himself coolly to the losing game before him. The
Duchess, more cheerful than she had been, assumed the
care of Piney. Only Mother Shipton—once the strongest
of the party—seemed to sicken and fade. At midnight on
the tenth day she called Oakhurst to her side. "I'm going," she said, in a voice of querulous weakness, "but
don't say anything about it. Don't waken the kids. Take
the bundle from under my head and open it." Mr. Oakhurst did so. It contained Mother Shipton's rations for
the last week, untouched. "Give 'em to the child," she
said, pointing to the sleeping Piney. "You've starved

yourself," said the gambler. "That's what they call it," said the woman querulously as she lay down again, and turning her face to the wall, passed quietly away.

The accordion and the bones were put aside that day and Homer was forgotten. When the body of Mother Shipton had been committed to the snow, Mr. Oakhurst took the Innocent aside and showed him a pair of snow-shoes which he had fashioned from the old pack saddle. "There's one chance in a hundred to save her yet," he said, pointing to Piney, "but it's there," he added, pointing toward Poker Flat. "If you can reach there in two days she's safe." "And you?" asked Tom Simson. "I'll stay here," was the curt reply.

The lovers parted with a long embrace. "You are not going too?" said the Duchess as she saw Mr. Oakhurst apparently waiting to accompany him. "As far as the canyon," he replied. He turned suddenly and kissed the Duchess, leaving her pallid face aflame and her trembling limbs rigid with amazement.

Night came, but not Mr. Oakhurst. It brought the storm again and the whirling snow. Then the Duchess, feeding the fire, found that someone had quietly piled beside the hut enough fuel to last a few days longer. The tears rose to her eyes, but she hid them from Piney.

The women slept but little. In the morning, looking into each other's faces they read their fate. Neither spoke, but Piney accepted the position of the stronger, drew near and placed her arm around the Duchess' waist. They kept this attitude for the rest of the day. That night the storm reached its greatest fury, and rending asunder the protecting vines, invaded the very hut.

Toward morning they found themselves unable to feed the fire, which gradually died away. As the embers slowly blackened the Duchess crept closer to Piney and broke the silence of many hours. "Piney, can you pray?" "No, dear," said Piney simply. The Duchess without knowing exactly why felt relieved, and putting her head upon Piney's shoulder spoke no more. And so reclining, the younger and purer pillowing the head of her soiled sister upon her virgin breast, they fell asleep.

The wind lulled as if it feared to waken them. Feathery drifts of snow shaken from the long pine boughs flew like white-winged birds, and settled about them as they slept. The moon through the rifted clouds looked down upon what had been the camp. But all human stain, all trace of earthly travail, was hidden beneath the spotless mantle mercifully flung from above.

They slept all that day and the next, nor did they waken when voices and footsteps broke the silence of the camp. And when pitying fingers brushed the snow from their wan faces you could scarcely have told from the equal peace that dwelt upon them which was she that had sinned. Even the law of Poker Flat recognized this and turned away, leaving them still locked in each other's arms.

But at the head of the gulch, on one of the largest

pine trees they found the deuce of clubs pinned to the bark with a bowie knife. It bore the following, written in pencil in a firm hand:

✝

BENEATH THIS TREE
LIES THE BODY
OF

JOHN OAKHURST,

WHO STRUCK A STREAK OF BAD LUCK
ON THE 23RD OF NOVEMBER 1850,
AND
HANDED IN HIS CHECKS
ON THE 7TH DECEMBER, 1850.

✝

And pulseless and cold, with a derringer by his side and a bullet in his heart though still calm as in life, beneath the snow lay he who was at once the strongest and yet the weakest of the outcasts of Poker Flat.

Tennessee's
◈ Partner

I DO not think that we ever knew his real
name. Our ignorance of it certainly never gave us any
social inconvenience, for at Sandy Bar in 1854 most men
were christened anew. Sometimes these appellatives
were derived from some distinctiveness of dress, as in
the case of Dungaree Jack, or from some peculiarity of
habit, as shown in Saleratus Bill, so called from an undue proportion of that chemical in his daily bread, or
from some unlucky slip, as exhibited in The Iron Pirate,
a mild inoffensive man, who earned that baleful title
by his unfortunate mispronunciation of the term "iron
pyrites." Perhaps this may have been the beginning of
a rude heraldry, but I am constrained to think that it
was because a man's real name in that day rested solely

46

upon his own unsupported statement. "Call yourself Clifford, do you?" said Boston, addressing a timid newcomer with infinite scorn. "Hell is full of such Cliffords!" He then introduced the unfortunate man, whose name happened to be really Clifford, as "Jaybird Charley," an unhallowed inspiration of the moment that clung to him ever after.

But to return to Tennessee's Partner, whom we never knew by any other than this relative title. That he had ever existed as a separate and distinct individuality we only learned later. It seems that in 1853 he left Poker Flat to go to San Francisco, ostensibly to procure a wife. He never got any farther than Stockton. At that place he was attracted by a young person who waited upon the table at the hotel where he took his meals. One morning he said something to her which caused her to smile not unkindly, to somewhat coquettishly break a plate of toast over his upturned serious simple face and to retreat to the kitchen. He followed her, and emerged a few moments later, covered with more toast and victory. A week from that day they were married by a justice of the peace, and returned to Poker Flat. I am aware that something more might be made of this episode, but I prefer to tell it as it was current at Sandy Bar—in the gulches and barrooms where all sentiment was modified by a strong sense of humor.

Of their married felicity but little is known, perhaps for the reason that Tennessee, then living with his partner, one day took occasion to say something to the bride on his own account, at which it is said she smiled not unkindly and chastely retreated—this time as far as Marysville, where Tennessee followed her and where they went to housekeeping without the aid of a justice of the peace. Tennessee's Partner took the loss of his wife simply and seriously, as was his fashion. But to everybody's surprise, when Tennessee one day returned from Marysville without his partner's wife—she having smiled and retreated with somebody else—Tennessee's Partner was the first man to shake his hand and greet him with affection. The boys who had gathered in the canyon to see the shooting were naturally indignant. Their indignation might have found vent in sarcasm but for a certain look in Tennessee's Partner's eye that indicated a lack of humorous appreciation. In fact he was a grave man, with a steady application to practical detail which was unpleasant in a difficulty.

Meanwhile a popular feeling against Tennessee had grown up on the Bar. He was known to be a gambler; he was suspected of being a thief. In these suspicions Tennessee's Partner was equally compromised. His continued intimacy with Tennessee after the affair above quoted could only be accounted for on the hypothesis of a co-partnership of crime. At last Tennessee's guilt became flagrant. One day he overtook a stranger on his way to Red Dog. The stranger afterward related that Tennessee beguiled the time with interesting anecdote and reminiscence but illogically concluded the interview in the following words: "And now, young man, I'll trouble you for your knife, your pistols and your money. You see your weppings might get you into trouble at Red Dog, and your money's a temptation to the evilly disposed. I think you said your address was San Francisco. I shall endeavor to call." It may be stated here that Tennessee had a fine flow of humor which no business preocupation could wholly subdue.

This exploit was his last. Red Dog and Sandy Bar made common cause against the highwayman. Tennessee was hunted in very much the same fashion as his prototype, the grizzly. As the toils closed around him he made a desperate dash through Sandy Bar, emptying his revolver at the crowd before the Arcade Saloon, and so on up Grizzly Canyon. But at its farther extremity he was stopped by a small man on a gray horse. The men looked at each other a moment in silence. Both were fearless, both self-possessed and independent, and both types of a civilization that in the seventeenth century would have been called heroic, but in the nineteenth was simply reckless.

"What have you got there? I call," said Tennessee quietly.

"Two bowers and an ace," said the stranger as quietly, showing two revolvers and a bowie knife.

"That takes me," returned Tennessee, and with this gambler's epigram he threw away his useless pistol and rode back with his captor.

It was a warm night. The cool breeze which usually sprang up with the going down of the sun behind the

chaparral-crested mountain was that evening withheld
from Sandy Bar. The little canyon was stifling with
heated resinous odors, and the decaying driftwood on
the Bar sent forth faint sickening exhalations. The
feverishness of day and its fierce passions still filled the
camp. Lights moved restlessly along the bank of the
river, striking no answering reflection from its tawny
current. Against the blackness of the pines the windows
of the old loft above the express office stood out star-
ingly bright, and through their curtainless panes the
loungers below could see the forms of those who were
even then deciding the fate of Tennessee. And above all
this, etched on the dark firmament, rose the Sierra, remote and passionless, crowned with remoter passionless
stars.

The trial of Tennessee was conducted as fairly as was
consistent with a judge and jury who felt themselves to
some extent obliged to justify, in their verdict, the
previous irregularities of arrest and indictment. The
law of Sandy Bar was implacable but not vengeful. The
excitement and personal feeling of the chase were over.
With Tennessee safe in their hands they were ready to
listen patiently to any defense, which they were already
satisfied was insufficient. There being no doubt in their
own minds, they were willing to give the prisoner the
benefit of any that might exist. Secure in the hypothesis
that he ought to be hanged on general principles, they
indulged him with more latitude of defense than his

reckless hardihood seemed to ask. The judge appeared
to be more anxious than the prisoner, who otherwise
unconcerned, evidently took a grim pleasure in the responsibility he had created. "I don't take any hand in
this yer game," had been his invariable but good-humored reply to all questions. The judge, who was also
his captor, for a moment vaguely regretted that he had
not shot him on sight that morning, but presently dismissed this human weakness as unworthy of the judicial mind. Nevertheless when there was a tap at the
door and it was said that Tennessee's Partner was there
on behalf of the prisoner, he was admitted at once without question. Perhaps the younger members of the jury,
to whom the proceedings were becoming irksomely
thoughtful, hailed him as a relief.

For he was not, certainly, an imposing figure. Short
and stout, with a square face sunburned into a preternatural redness, clad in a loose duck jumper and trousers
streaked and splashed with red soil, his aspect under any
circumstances would have been quaint and was now
even ridiculous. As he stooped to deposit at his feet a
heavy carpetbag he was carrying, it became obvious
from partially developed legends and inscriptions, that
the material with which his trousers had been patched
had been originally intended for a less ambitious covering. Yet he advanced with great gravity, and after
shaking the hand of each person in the room with
labored cordiality, he wiped his serious perplexed face

on a red bandana handkerchief, a shade lighter than his complexion, laid his powerful hand upon the table to steady himself, and thus addressed the judge:

"I was passin' by," he began by way of apology, "and I thought I'd just step in and see how things was gittin' on with Tennessee thar—my pardner. It's a hot night. I disremember any sich weather before on the Bar."

He paused a moment, but nobody volunteering any other meteorological recollection, he again had recourse to his pocket handkerchief, and for some moments mopped his face diligently.

"Have you anything to say on behalf of the prisoner?" said the judge finally.

"Thet's it," said Tennessee's Partner in a tone of relief. "I come yer as Tennessee's pardner, knowin' him nigh on four year, off and on, wet and dry, in luck and out o' luck. His ways ain't aller my ways, but thar ain't any p'ints in that young man, thar ain't any liveliness as he's been up to, as I don't know. And you sez to me, sez you, confidential-like, and between man and man, sez you, 'Do you know anything in his behalf?' and I sez to you, sez I, confidential-like, as between man and man, 'What should a man know of his pardner?' "

"Is this all you have to say?" asked the judge impatiently, feeling, perhaps, that a dangerous sympathy of humor was beginning to humanize the court.

"Thet's so," continued Tennessee's Partner. "It ain't for me to say anything agin him. And now, what's the case? Here's Tennessee wants money, wants it bad, and

doesn't like to ask it of his old pardner. Well, what does
Tennessee do? He lays for a stranger and he fetches that
stranger, and you lays for *him* and you fetches *him,* and
the honors is easy. And I put it to you, bein' a fa'r-minded
man, and to you, gentlemen all, as fa'r-minded men, ef
this isn't so."

"Prisoner," said the judge, interrupting, "have you any
questions to ask this man?"

"No! no!" continued Tennessee's Partner hastily. "I
play this yer hand alone. To come down to the bedrock,
it's just this: Tennessee, thar, has played it pretty rough
and expensivelike on a stranger and on this yer camp.
And now, what's the fair thing? Some would say more,
some would say less. Here's seventeen hundred dollars
in coarse gold and a watch—it's about all my pile—and
call it square!" And before a hand could be raised to
prevent him he had emptied the contents of the carpetbag upon the table.

For a moment his life was in jeopardy. One or two
men sprang to their feet, several hands groped for hidden weapons, and a suggestion to throw him from the
window was only overridden by a gesture from the
judge. Tennessee laughed. And apparently oblivious of
the excitement, Tennessee's Partner improved the opportunity to mop his face again with his handkerchief.

When order was restored and the man was made to
understand by the use of forcible figures and rhetoric
that Tennessee's offense could not be condoned by
money, his face took a more serious and sanguinary hue,

and those who were nearest to him noticed that his rough hand trembled slightly on the table. He hesitated a moment as he slowly returned the gold to the carpetbag, as if he had not yet entirely caught the elevated sense of justice which swayed the tribunal, and was perplexed with the belief that he had not offered enough. Then he turned to the judge, and said, "This yer is a lone hand, played alone and without my pardner." He bowed to the jury and was about to withdraw when the judge called him back.

"If you have anything to say to Tennessee, you had better say it now."

For the first time that evening the eyes of the prisoner and his strange advocate met. Tennessee smiled, showed his white teeth, and saying, "Euchred, old man!" held out his hand. Tennessee's Partner took it in his own, and saying, "I just dropped in as I was passin' to see how things was gettin' on," let the hand passively fall, and adding that "it was a warm night," again mopped his face with his handkerchief and without another word withdrew.

The two men never again met each other alive. For the unparalleled insult of a bribe offered to Judge Lynch —who, whether bigoted, weak or narrow, was at least incorruptible—firmly fixed in the mind of that mythical personage any wavering determination of Tennessee's fate, and at the break of day he was marched, closely guarded, to meet it at the top of Marley's Hill.

How he met it, how cool he was, how he refused to

say anything, how perfect were the arrangements of the committee were all duly reported with the addition of a warning moral and example to all future evildoers, in the *Red Dog Clarion* by its editor, who was present and to whose vigorous English I cheerfully refer the reader. But the beauty of that midsummer morning, the blessed amity of earth and air and sky, the awakened life of the free woods and hills, the joyous renewal and promise of Nature, and above all, the infinite serenity that thrilled through each, was not reported, as not being a part of the social lesson. And yet when the weak and foolish deed was done, and a life with its possiblities and responsibilities had passed out of the misshapen thing that dangled between earth and sky, the birds sang, the flowers bloomed, the sun shone as cheerily as before; and possibly the *Red Dog Clarion* was right.

Tennessee's Partner was not in the group that surrounded the ominous tree. But as they turned to disperse, attention was drawn to the singular appearance of a motionless donkey cart halted at the side of the road. As they approached they at once recognized the venerable Jenny and the two-wheeled cart as the property of Tennessee's Partner, used by him in carrying dirt from his claim. A few paces distant the owner of the equipage himself, was sitting under a buckeye tree, wiping the perspiration from his glowing face. In answer to an inquiry, he said he had come for the body of the "diseased, if it was all the same to the commit-

tee." He didn't wish to hurry anything; he could wait.
He was not working that day, and when the gentlemen
were done with the "diseased," he would take him. "Ef
thar is any present," he added in his simple serious way,
"as would care to jine in the fun'l, they kin come." Perhaps it was from a sense of humor, which I have already
intimated was a feature of Sandy Bar; perhaps it was
from something even better than that, but two-thirds of
the loungers accepted the invitation at once.

It was noon when the body of Tennessee was delivered into the hands of his partner. As the cart drew up to
the fatal tree, we noticed that it contained a rough oblong box, apparently made from a section of sluicing,
half filled with bark and the tassels of pine. The cart
was further decorated with slips of willow and made
fragrant with buckeye blossoms. When the body was
deposited in the box, Tennessee's Partner drew over it a
piece of tarred canvas, and gravely mounting the narrow seat in front with his feet upon the shafts, urged
the little donkey forward. The equipage moved slowly
on at that decorous pace which was habitual with Jenny
even under less solemn circumstances. The men—half
curiously, half jestingly, but all good-humoredly—
strolled along beside the cart, some in advance, some
a little in the rear of the homely catafalque. But whether
from the narrowing of the road or some present sense of
decorum, as the cart passed on the company fell to the
rear in couples, keeping step and otherwise assuming
the external show of a formal procession. Jack Folinsbee,

who had at the outset played a funeral march in dumb
show upon an imaginary trombone, desisted from a lack
of sympathy and appreciation, not having, perhaps, your
true humorist's capacity to be content with the enjoyment of his own fun.

The way led through Grizzly Canyon, by this time
clothed in funereal drapery and shadows. The redwoods,
burying their moccasined feet in the red soil, stood in
Indian file along the track, trailing an uncouth benedic-
tion from their bending boughs upon the passing bier.
A hare surprised into helpless inactivity, sat upright and
pulsating in the ferns by the roadside as the cortege
went by. Squirrels hastened to gain a secure outlook
from higher boughs, and the bluejays spreading their
wings fluttered before them like outriders, until the
outskirts of Sandy Bar were reached, and the solitary
cabin of Tennessee's Partner.

Viewed under more favorable circumstances, it
would not have been a cheerful place. The unpictur-
esque site, the rude and unlovely outlines, the unsavory
details which distinguish the nest-building of the California miner, were all here with the dreariness of decay
superadded. A few paces from the cabin there was a
rough enclosure, which in the brief days of Tennessee's
Partner's matrimonial felicity, had been used as a garden but was now overgrown with fern. As we approached it we were surprised to find that what we had
taken for a recent attempt at cultivation, was the broken
soil about an open grave.

The cart was halted before the enclosure, and reject-
ing the offers of assistance with the same air of simple
self-reliance he had displayed throughout, Tennessee's
Partner lifted the rough coffin on his back and deposited
it unaided within the shallow grave. He then nailed
down the board which served as a lid, and mounting
the little mound of earth beside it, took off his hat and
slowly mopped his face with his handkerchief. This the
crowd felt was a preliminary to speech, and they disposed themselves variously on stumps and boulders and
sat expectant.

"When a man," began Tennessee's Partner slowly,
"has been runnin' free all day, what's the natural thing
for him to do? Why, to come home. And if he ain't in
a condition to go home, what can his best friend do?
Why, bring him home. And here's Tennessee has been
runnin' free, and we brings him home from his wan-
derin'." He paused and picked up a fragment of quartz,
rubbed it thoughtfully on his sleeve, and went on, "It
ain't the first time that I've packed him on my back, as
you seed me now. It ain't the first time that I brought
him to this yer cabin when he couldn't help himself. It
ain't the first time that I and Jinny have waited for him
on yon hill and picked him up and so fetched him home,
when he couldn't speak and didn't know me. And now
that it's the last time, why"—he paused and rubbed the
quartz gently on his sleeve—"you see it's sort of rough
on his pardner. And now, gentlemen," he added abruptly, picking up his long-handled shovel, "the fun'l's

over, and my thanks and Tennessee's thanks to you for your trouble."

Resisting any proffers of assistance he began to fill in the grave, turning his back upon the crowd that after a few moments' hesitation gradually withdrew. As they looked back in crossing the little ridge that hid Sandy Bar from view, some thought they could see Tennessee's Partner, his work done, sitting upon the grave with his shovel between his knees and his face buried in his red bandana handkerchief. But it was argued by others that you couldn't tell his face from his handkerchief at that distance, and the point remained undecided.

In the reaction that followed the feverish excitement of that day, Tennessee's Partner was not forgotten. A secret investigation had cleared him of any complicity in Tennessee's guilt and left only a suspicion of his general sanity. Sandy Bar made a point of calling on him and proffering various uncouth but well-meant kindnesses. But from that day his rude health and great strength seemed visibly to decline, and when the rainy season fairly set in and the tiny grass-blades were beginning to peep from the rocky mound above Tennessee's grave, he took to his bed.

One night, when the pines beside the cabin were swaying in the storm and trailing their slender fingers over the roof and the roar and rush of the swollen river were heard below, Tennessee's Partner lifted his head from the pillow, saying, "It is time to go for Tennessee. I must put Jinny in the cart." He would have risen from his bed but for the restraint of his attendant. Struggling, he still pursued his singular fancy. "There now, steady, Jinny, steady, old girl. How dark it is! Look out for the ruts—and look out for him too, old gal. Sometimes you know, when he's blind drunk, he drops down right in the trail. Keep on straight up to the pine on the top of the hill. Thar! I told you so! Thar he is—comin' this way, too—all by himself, sober, and his face a-shining. Tennessee! Pardner!"

And so they met.

An
Ingenue
of the
∾ Sierras

W<small>E ALL</small> held our breath as the coach
rushed through the semidarkness of Galloper's Ridge.
The vehicle itself was only a huge lumbering shadow;
its sidelights were carefully extinguished, and Yuba
Bill had just politely removed from the lips of an outside passenger even the cigar with which he had been
ostentatiously exhibiting his coolness. For it had been
rumored that the Ramon Martinez gang of road agents
were laying for us on the second grade, and would time
the passage of our lights across Galloper's in order to
intercept us in the brush beyond. If we could cross the
ridge without being seen and so get through the brush
before they reached it, we were safe. If they followed,
it would only be a stern chase with the odds in our
favor.

The huge vehicle swayed from side to side, rolled,
dipped, and plunged, but Bill kept the track as if, in the
whispered words of the expressman, he could feel and
smell the road he could no longer see. We knew that at

times we hung perilously over the edge of slopes that
eventually dropped a thousand feet sheer to the tops
of the sugar pines below, but we knew that Bill knew
it also. The half-visible heads of the horses, drawn
wedgewise together by the tightened reins, appeared
to cleave the darkness like a ploughshare, held between
his rigid hands. Even the hoofbeats of the six horses had
fallen into a vague monotonous distant roll. Then the
ridge was crossed and we plunged into the still blacker
obscurity of the brush. Rather we no longer seemed to
move—it was only the phantom night that rushed by us.
The horses might have been submerged in some swift
Lethean stream; nothing but the top of the coach and
the rigid bulk of Yuba Bill rose above them. Yet even in
that awful moment our speed was unslackened; it was
as if Bill cared no longer to guide but only to drive, or
as if the direction of his huge machine was determined
by other hands than his. An incautious whisperer haz-
arded the paralyzing suggestion of our meeting another
team. To our great astonishment Bill overheard it; to our
greater astonishment he replied. "It 'ud be only a neck
and neck race which would get to blazes first," he said
quietly. But we were relieved—for he had *spoken!* Almost simultaneously the wider turnpike began to glim-
mer faintly as a visible track before us; the wayside trees
fell out of line, opened up and dropped off one after another; we were on the broader tableland, out of danger
and apparently unperceived and unpursued.

Nevertheless in the conversation that broke out again

with the relighting of the lamps, and the comments, congratulations and reminiscences that were freely exchanged Yuba Bill preserved a dissatisfied and even resentful silence. The most generous praise of his skill and courage awoke no response. "I reckon the old man was just spilin' for a fight and is feelin' disappointed," said a passenger. But those who knew that Bill had the true fighter's scorn for any purely purposeless conflict were more or less concerned and watchful of him. He would drive steadily for four or five minutes with thoughtfully knitted brows, but eyes still keenly observant under his slouched hat and then, relaxing his strained attitude, would give way to a movement of impatience. "You ain't uneasy about anything, Bill, are you?" asked the expressman confidentially. Bill lifted his eyes with a slightly contemptuous surprise. "Not about anything ter *come*. It's what *hez* happened that I don't exactly *sabe*. I don't see no signs of Ramon's gang ever havin' been out at all, and ef they was out I don't see why they didn't go for us."

"The simple fact is that our ruse was successful," said an outside passenger. "They waited to see our lights on the ridge, and not seeing them missed us until we had passed. That's my opinion."

"You ain't puttin' any price on that opinion, air ye?" inquired Bill politely.

"No."

" 'Cos thar's a comic paper in Frisco pays for them things, and I've seen worse things in it."

"Come off, Bill," retorted the passenger, slightly net-
tled by the tittering of his companions. "Then what
did you put out the lights for?"

"Well," returned Bill grimly, "it mout have been because I didn't keer to hev you chaps blazin' away at the
first bush you *thought* you saw move in your skeer and
bringin' down their fire on us."

The explanation, though unsatisfactory, was by no
means an improbable one and we thought it better to
accept it with a laugh. Bill, however, resumed his abstracted manner.

"Who got in at the Summit?" he at last asked abruptly
of the expressman.

"Derrick and Simpson of Cold Spring and one of the
Excelsior[1] boys," responded the expressman.

"And that Pike County girl from Dow's Flat with her
bundles. Don't forget her," added the outside passenger
ironically.

"Does anybody here know her?" continued Bill, ignoring the irony.

"You'd better ask Judge Thompson; he was mighty
attentive to her, gettin' her a seat by the off window and
lookin' after her bundles and things."

"Gettin' her seat by the *window?*" repeated Bill.

"Yes, she wanted to see everything and wasn't afraid
of the shooting."

"Yes," broke in a third passenger, "and he was so
durned civil that when she dropped her ring in the

---

[1] *Excelsior*—the name of a mining company.

straw he struck a match agin all your rules, you know, and held it for her to find it. And it was just as we were crossin' through the brush, too. I saw the hull thing through the window, for I was hanging over the wheels with my gun ready for action. And it wasn't no fault of Judge Thompson's if his durned foolishness hadn't shown us up and got us a shot from the gang."

Bill gave a short grunt but drove steadily on without further comment or even turning his eyes to the speaker.

We were now not more than a mile from the station at the crossroads where we were to change horses. The lights already glimmered in the distance, and there was a faint suggestion of the coming dawn on the summits of the ridge to the west. We had plunged into a belt of timber, when suddenly a horseman emerged at a sharp canter from a trail that seemed to be parallel with our own. We were all slightly startled, Yuba Bill alone preserving his moody calm.

"Hullo!" he said.

The stranger wheeled to our side as Bill slackened his speed. He seemed to be a packer, or freight muleteer.

"Ye didn't get held up on the Divide?" continued Bill cheerfully.

"No," returned the packer with a laugh. "*I* don't carry treasure. But I see you're all right too. I saw you crossin' over Galloper's."

"*Saw* us?" said Bill sharply. "We had our lights out."

"Yes, but there was suthin' white, a handkerchief or woman's veil, I reckon, hangin' from the window. It was only a movin' spot agin the hillside, but ez I was lookin' out for ye I knew it was you by that. Good night!"

He cantered away. We tried to look at each other's faces and at Bill's expression in the darkness, but he neither spoke nor stirred until he threw down the reins when we stopped before the station. The passengers quickly descended from the roof; the expressman was about to follow, but Bill plucked his sleeve.

"I'm goin' to take a look over this yer stage and these yer passengers with ye afore we start."

"Why, what's up?"

"Well," said Bill, slowly disengaging himself from one of his enormous gloves, "when we waltzed down into the brush up there I saw a man ez plain ez I see you rise up from it. I thought our time had come and the band was goin' to play, when he sorter drew back, made a sign, and we just scooted past him."

"Well?"

"Well," said Bill, "it means that this yer coach was *passed through free* tonight."

"You don't object to *that*—surely? I think we were deucedly lucky."

Bill slowly drew off his other glove. "I've been riskin' my everlastin' life on this durned line three times a week," he said with mock humility, "and I'm allus thankful for small mercies. *But*," he added grimly, "when it comes down to being passed free by some pal of a hoss

thief, and thet called a speshal Providence, *I ain't in it!*
No sir, I ain't in it!"

It was with mixed emotions the passengers heard that
a delay of fifteen minutes to tighten certain screw bolts
had been ordered by the autocratic Bill. Some were anxious to get their breakfast at Sugar Pine, but others
were not averse to linger for the daylight that promised
greater safety on the road. The expressman, knowing
the real cause of Bill's delay, was nevertheless at a loss
to understand the object of it. The passengers were all
well known; any idea of complicity with the road agents
was wild and impossible, and even if there was a confederate of the gang among them he would have been
more likely to precipitate a robbery than to check it.
Again, the discovery of such a confederate—to whom
they clearly owed their safety—and his arrest would
have been quite against the Californian sense of justice,
if not actually illegal. It seemed evident that Bill's
quixotic sense of honor was leading him astray.

The station consisted of a stable, a wagon shed, and a
building containing three rooms. The first was fitted up
with bunks or sleeping berths for the employees; the
second was the kitchen; and the third and larger apartment was dining room or sitting room, and was used as
general waiting room for the passengers. It was not a
refreshment station and there was no bar. But a mysteri-

ous command from the omnipotent Bill produced a
demijohn of whiskey, with which he hospitably treated
the company. The seductive influence of the liquor
loosened the tongue of the gallant Judge Thompson. He
admitted to having struck a match to enable the fair
Pike Countian to find her ring which, however, proved
to have fallen in her lap. She was "a fine healthy young
woman—a type of the far west, sir; in fact, quite a
prairie blossom! yet simple and guileless as a child."
She was on her way to Marysville, he believed, "although she expected to meet friends, a friend, in fact,
later on." It was her first visit to a large town—in fact
to any civilized center—since she had crossed the plains
three years ago. Her girlish curiosity was quite touching, and her innocence irresistible. In fact, in a country
whose tendency was to produce "frivolity and forward-
ness in young girls" he found her "a most interesting
young person." She was even then out in the stableyard
watching the horses being harnessed, "preferring to in-
dulge a pardonable healthy young curiosity than to
listen to the empty compliments of the younger passengers."

The figure, which Bill saw thus engaged, without
being otherwise distinguished certainly seemed to justify the judge's opinion. She appeared to be a well-
matured country girl, whose frank gray eyes and large
laughing mouth expressed a wholesome and abiding
gratification in her life and surroundings. She was
watching the replacing of luggage in the boot. A little

feminine start as one of her own parcels was thrown somewhat roughly on the roof gave Bill his opportunity. "Now there," he growled to the helper, "ye ain't carting stone! Look out, will yer! Some of your things, miss?" he added with gruff courtesy, turning to her. "These yer trunks, for instance?"

She smiled a pleasant assent and Bill, pushing aside the helper, seized a large square trunk in his arms. But from excess of zeal or some other mischance, his foot slipped and he came down heavily, striking the corner of the trunk on the ground and loosening its hinges and fastenings. It was a cheap common-looking affair, but the accident discovered in its yawning lid a quantity of white lace-edged feminine apparel of an apparently superior quality. The young lady uttered another cry and came quickly forward, but Bill was profuse in his apologies, himself girded the broken box with a strap, and declared his intention of having the company "make it good" to her with a new one. Then he casually accompanied her to the door of the waiting room, entered, made a place for her before the fire by simply lifting the nearest and most youthful passenger by the coat collar from the stool that he was occupying, and installing the lady in it. He then displaced another man who was standing before the chimney and, drawing himself up to his full six feet of height in front of her, glanced down on his fair passenger as he took his waybill from his pocket.

"Your name is down here as Miss Mullins?" he said.

She looked up, became suddenly aware that she and
her questioner were the center of interest to the whole
circle of passengers, and with a slight rise of color, returned, "Yes."

"Well, Miss Mullins, I've got a question or two to ask
ye. I ask it straight out afore this crowd. It's in my
rights to take ye aside and ask it—but that ain't my style;
I'm no detective. I needn't ask it at all, but act as ef I
knowed the answer, or I might leave it to be asked by
others. Ye needn't answer it ef ye don't like; ye've got a
friend over there—Judge Thompson—who is a friend to
ye, right or wrong, jest as any other man here is—as
though ye'd packed your own jury. Well, the simple
question I've got to ask ye is *this:* Did you signal to anybody from the coach when we passed Galloper's an hour
ago?"

We all thought that Bill's courage and audacity had
reached its climax here. To openly and publicly accuse
a lady before a group of chivalrous Californians, and
that lady possessing the further attractions of youth,
good looks and innocence, was little short of desperation. There was an evident movement of adhesion toward the fair stranger, and a slight muttering broke out
on the right, but the very boldness of the act held them
in stupefied surprise. Judge Thompson, with a bland
propitiatory smile began, "Really, Bill, I must protest
on behalf of this young lady"—when the fair accused,
raising her eyes to her accuser, to the consternation of
everybody answered with the slight but convincing

hesitation of conscientious truthfulness, "I did."

"Ahem!" interposed the judge hastily, "er—that is—er—you allowed your handkerchief to flutter from the window—I noticed it myself—casually, one might say even playfully, but without any particular significance."

The girl, regarding her apologist with a singular mingling of pride and impatience, returned briefly, "I signaled."

"Who did you signal to?" asked Bill gravely.

"The young gentleman I'm going to marry."

A start, followed by a slight titter from the younger passengers, was instantly suppressed by a savage glance from Bill.

"What did you signal to him for?" he continued.

"To tell him I was here and that it was all right," returned the girl with a steadily rising pride and color.

"*Wot* was all right?" demanded Bill.

"That I wasn't followed and that he could meet me on the road beyond Cass's Ridge Station." She hesitated a moment and then with a still greater pride, in which a youthful defiance was still mingled, said, "I've run away from home to marry him. And I mean to! No one can stop me. Dad didn't like him just because he was poor, and dad's got money. Dad wanted me to marry a man I hate, and got a lot of dresses and things to bribe me."

"And you're taking them in your trunk to the other feller?" said Bill grimly.

"Yes, he's poor," returned the girl defiantly.

"Then your father's name is Mullins?" asked Bill.

"It's not Mullins. I—I—took that name," she hesitated, with her first exhibition of self-consciousness.

"Wot *is* his name?"

"Eli Hemmings."

A smile of relief and significance went around the circle. The fame of Eli or "Skinner" Hemmings as a notorious miser and usurer had passed even beyond Galloper's Ridge.

"The step that you're taking, Miss Mullins, I need not tell you, is one of great gravity," said Judge Thompson, with a certain paternal seriousness of manner in which, however, we were glad to detect a glaring affectation. "And I trust that you and your affianced have fully weighed it. Far be it from me to interfere with or question the natural affections of two young people, but may I ask you what you know of the—er—young gentlemen for whom you are sacrificing so much, and perhaps imperiling your whole future? For instance, have you known him long?"

The slightly troubled air of trying to understand, not unlike the vague wonderment of childhood, with which Miss Mullins had received the beginning of this exordium changed to a relieved smile of comprehension as she said quickly, "Oh yes, nearly a whole year."

"And," said the judge, smiling, "has he a vocation—is he in business?"

"Oh yes," she returned, "he's a collector."

"A collector?"

"Yes; he collects bills, you know—money," she went on with childish eagerness, "not for himself—*he* never has any money, poor Charley—but for his firm. It's dreadful hard work, too; keeps him out for days and nights, over bad roads and baddest weather. Sometimes when he's stole over to the ranch just to see me he's been so bad he could scarcely keep his seat in the saddle, much less stand. And he's got to take mighty big risks, too. Times the folks are cross with him and won't pay; once they shot him in the arm and he came to me and I helped do it up for him. But he don't mind. He's real brave, jest as brave as he's good." There was such a wholesome ring of truth in this pretty praise that we were touched in sympathy with the speaker.

"What firm does he collect for?" asked the judge gently.

"I don't know exactly—he won't tell me; but I think it's a Spanish firm. You see"—she took us all into her confidence with a sweeping smile of innocent yet half-mischievous artfulness—"I only know because I peeped over a letter he once got from his firm tellin' him he must hustle up and be ready for the road the next day; but I think the name was Martinez—yes, Ramon Martinez."

In the dead silence that ensued—a silence so profound that we could hear the horses in the distant stable yard rattling their harness—one of the younger Excelsior boys burst into a hysteric laugh, but the fierce eye of Yuba Bill was down upon him and seemed to instantly stiffen

him into a silent grinning mask. The young girl, however, took no note of it. Following out with loverlike
diffusiveness the reminiscences thus awakened, she
went on:

"Yes, it's mighty hard work, but he says it's all for me,
and as soon as we're married he'll quit it. He might have
quit it before but he won't take no money of me, nor
what I told him I could get out of dad! That ain't his
style. He's mighty proud—if he is poor—is Charley. Why
thar's all ma's money which she left me in the savin's
bank that I wanted to draw out, for I had the right,
and give it to him, but he wouldn't hear of it! Why he
wouldn't take one of the things I've got with me, if he
knew it. And so he goes on ridin' and ridin', here and
there and everywhere, and gettin' more and more
played out and sad and thin and pale as a spirit, and
always so uneasy about his business and startin' up at
times when we're meetin' out in the South Woods or in
the far clearin' and sayin', 'I must be goin' now, Polly,'
and yet always tryin' to be chiffle and chipper afore me.
Why, he must have rid miles and miles to have watched
for me thar in the brush at the foot of Galloper's tonight, jest to see if all was safe; and Lordy! I'd have
given him the signal and showed a light if I'd died for
it the next minit. There! That's what I know of Charley
—that's what I'm runnin' away from home for—that's
what I'm runnin' to him for, and I don't care who knows
it! And I only wish I'd done it afore—and I would—if
—if—if—he'd only *asked* me! There now!" She stopped,

panted, and choked. One of the sudden transitions of youthful emotion had overtaken the eager laughing face; it clouded up with the swift change of childhood, a lightning quiver of expression broke over it, and —then came the rain!

I think this simple act completed our utter demoralization. We smiled feebly at each other with that assumption of masculine superiority which is miserably conscious of its own helplessness at such moments. We looked out of the window, blew our noses, said, "Eh— what?" and "I say," vaguely to each other, and were greatly relieved and yet apparently astonished when Yuba Bill, who had turned his back upon the fair speaker and was kicking the logs in the fireplace, suddenly swept down upon us and bundled us all into the road, leaving Miss Mullins alone. Then he walked aside with Judge Thompson for a few moments, returned to us, autocratically demanded of the party a complete reticence toward Miss Mullins on the subject matter under discussion, reentered the station, reappeared with the young lady, suppressed a faint idiotic cheer which broke from us at the spectacle of her innocent face once more cleared and rosy, climbed the box, and in another moment we were under way.

"Then she don't know what her lover is yet?" asked the expressman eagerly.

"No."

"Are *you* certain it's one of the gang?"

"Can't say *for sure*. It mout be a young chap from

Yolo who bucked agin the tiger[1] at Sacramento, got regularly cleaned out and busted, and joined the gang for a flier. They say thar was a new hand in that job over at Keeley's, and a mighty game one, too; and ez there was some buckshot on-loaded that trip he might hev got his share, and that would tally with what the girl said about his arm. See! Ef that's the man, I've heered he was the son of some big preacher and a college sharp to boot, who ran wild in Frisco and played himself for all he was worth. They're the wust kind to kick when they once get a foot over the traces. For stiddy comf'ble kempany," added Bill reflectively, "give *me* the son of a man that was *hanged!*"

"But what are you going to do about this?"

"That depends on the feller who comes to meet her."

"But you ain't going to try to take him? That would be playing it pretty low down on them both."

"Keep your hair on, Jimmy! The Judge and me are only going to rastle with the sperrit of that gay young galoot when he drops down for his girl—and exhort him pow'ful! Ef he allows he's convicted of sin and will find the Lord, we'll marry him and the gal offhand at the next station, and the Judge will officiate himself for nothin'. We're goin' to have this yer elopement done on the square, and our waybill clean—you bet!"

"But you don't suppose he'll trust himself in your hands?"

"Polly will signal to him that it's all square."

[1] Gambled at faro.

"Ah!" said the expressman. Nevertheless in those few moments the men seemed to have exchanged dispositions. The expressman looked doubtfully, critically and even cynically before him. Bill's face had relaxed, and something like a bland smile beamed across it as he drove confidently and unhesitatingly forward.

Day, meantime, although full blown and radiant on the mountain summits around us, was yet nebulous and uncertain in the valleys into which we were plunging. Lights still glimmered in the cabins and the few ranch buildings which began to indicate the thicker settlements. The shadows were heaviest in a little copse where a note from Judge Thompson in the coach was handed up to Yuba Bill, who at once slowly began to draw up his horses. The coach stopped finally near the junction of a small crossroad. At the same moment Miss Mullins slipped down from the vehicle, and with a parting wave of her hand to the judge, who had assisted her from the steps, tripped down the crossroad and disappeared in its semiobscurity. To our surprise the stage waited, Bill holding the reins listlessly in his hands. Five minutes passed—an eternity of expectation, and as there was that in Yuba Bill's face which forbade idle questioning, an aching void of silence also! This was at last broken by a strange voice from the road:

"Go on—we'll follow."

The coach started forward. Presently we heard the sound of other wheels behind us. We all craned our necks backward to get a view of the unknown, but by

the growing light we could only see that we were followed at a distance by a buggy with two figures in it.
Evidently Polly Mullins and her lover! We hoped that
they would pass us. But the vehicle, although drawn
by a fast horse, preserved its distance always, and it
was plain that its driver had no desire to satisfy our
curiosity. The expressman had recourse to Bill.

"Is it the man you thought of?" he asked eagerly.

"I reckon," said Bill briefly.

"But," continued the expressman, returning to his former skepticism, "what's to keep them both from levant-
ing together now?"

Bill jerked his hand toward the boot with a grim
smile.

"Their baggage."

"Oh!" said the expressman.

"Yes," continued Bill. "We'll hang on to that gal's
little frills and fixin's until this yer job's settled and the
ceremony's over, jest as ef we was her own father. And
what's more, young man," he added, suddenly turning
to the expressman, "*you'll* express them trunks of hers
through to Sacramento with your kempany's labels and
hand her the receipts and checks for them, so she can
get 'em there. That'll keep *him* outer temptation and
the reach o' the gang until they get away among white
men and civilization again. When your hoary-headed
ole grandfather, or to speak plainer, that partikler old
whiskey-soaker known as Yuba Bill wot sits on this
box," he continued with a diabolical wink at the express-

man, "waltzes in to pervide for a young couple jest startin' in life, thar's nothin' mean about his style, you bet. He fills the bill every time! Speshul Providences take a back seat when he's around."

When the station hotel and straggling settlement of Sugar Pine, now distinct and clear in the growing light, at last rose within rifleshot on the plateau the buggy suddenly darted swiftly by us, so swiftly that the faces of the two occupants were barely distinguishable as they passed, and keeping the lead by a dozen lengths, reached the door of the hotel. The young girl and her companion leaped down and vanished within as we drew up. They had evidently determined to elude our curiosity, and were successful.

But the material appetites of the passengers, sharpened by the keen mountain air, were more potent than their curiosity and as the breakfast bell rang out at the moment the stage stopped, a majority of them rushed into the dining room and scrambled for places without giving much heed to the vanished couple or to the judge and Yuba Bill, who had disappeared also. The through coach to Marysville and Sacramento was likewise waiting, for Sugar Pine was the limit of Bill's ministration and the coach which we had just left went no farther. In the course of twenty minutes, however, there was a slight and somewhat ceremonious bustling in the hall and on the veranda, and Yuba Bill and the judge reappeared. The latter was leading with some elaboration of manner and detail the shapely figure of

Miss Mullins, and Yuba Bill was accompanying her companion to the buggy. We all rushed to the windows to get a good view of the mysterious stranger and probable ex-brigand whose life was now linked with our fair fellow passenger. I am afraid, however, that we all participated in a certain impression of disappointment and doubt. Handsome and even cultivated-looking he assuredly was—young and vigorous in appearance. But there was a certain half-shamed, half-defiant suggestion in his expression, yet coupled with a watchful lurking uneasiness which was not pleasant and hardly becoming in a bridegroom, and the possessor of such a bride. But the frank joyous innocent face of Polly Mullins, resplendent with a simple happy confidence, melted our hearts again and condoned the fellow's shortcomings. We waved our hands; I think we would have given three rousing cheers as they drove away if the omnipotent eye of Yuba Bill had not been upon us. It was well, for the next moment we were summoned to the presence of that softhearted autocrat.

We found him alone with the judge in a private sitting room standing before a table on which there were a decanter and glasses. As we filed expectantly into the room and the door closed behind us, he cast a glance of hesitating tolerance over the group.

"Gentlemen," he said slowly, "you was all present at the beginnin' of a little game this mornin', and the judge thar thinks that you oughter be let in at the finish. *I* don't see that it's any of *your* durned business—

so to speak; but ez the Judge here allows you're all in the secret, I've called you in to take a partin' drink to the health of Mr. and Mrs. Charley Byng—ez is now comf'ably off on their bridal tower. What *you* know or what *you* suspects of the young galoot that's married the gal ain't worth shucks to anybody and I wouldn't give it to a yaller pup to play with, but the judge thinks you ought all to promise right here that you'll keep it dark. That's his opinion. Ez far as my opinion goes, gen'l'men," continued Bill with greater blandness and apparent cordiality, "I wanter simply remark in a keerless offhand gin'ral way, that ef I ketch any God-forsaken lop-eared chuckleheaded blatherin' idjet airin' *his* opinion——"

"One moment, Bill," interposed Judge Thompson with a grave smile. "Let me explain. You understand, gentlemen," he said turning to us, "the singular and I may say affecting situation which our goodhearted friend here has done so much to bring to what we hope will be a happy termination. I want to give here as my professional opinion, that there is nothing in his request which in your capacity as good citizens and law-abiding men you may not grant. I want to tell you also that you are condoning no offense against the statutes. There is not a particle of legal evidence before us of the criminal antecedents of Mr. Charles Byng except that which has been told you by the innocent lips of his betrothed, which the law of the land has now sealed forever in the mouth of his wife; and our own actual experience of his acts has been in the main exculpatory of any previous irregularity—if not incompatible with it. Briefly, no judge would charge, no jury convict on such evidence. When I add that the young girl is of legal age, that there is no evidence of any previous undue influence, but rather of the reverse on the part of the bridegroom, and that I was content as a magistrate to perform the ceremony, I think you will be satisfied to give your promise for the sake of the bride, and drink a happy life to them both."

I need not say that we did this cheerfully, and even extorted from Bill a grunt of satisfaction. The majority of the company, however, who were going with the through coach to Sacramento, then took their leave and as we accompanied them to the veranda we could see that Miss Polly Mullins's trunks were already transferred to the other vehicle under the protecting seals and labels of the all-potent express company. Then the whip cracked, the coach rolled away, and the last traces of the adventurous young couple disappeared in the hanging red dust of its wheels.

But Yuba Bill's grim satisfaction at the happy issue of the episode seemed to suffer no abatement. He even exceeded his usual deliberately regulated potations, and standing comfortably with his back to the center of the now deserted barroom, was more than usually loquacious with the expressman. "You see," he said, in bland reminiscence, "when your old Uncle Bill takes hold of a job like this he puts it straight through without changin' hosses. Yet thar was a moment, young feller, when I thought I was stompt! It was when we'd made up our mind to make that chap tell the gal fust all what he was! Ef she'd rared or kicked in the traces, or hung back only ez much ez that, we'd hev given him jest five minits' law to get up and get and leave her, and we'd hev toted that gal and her fixin's back to her dad again! But she jest gave a little scream and start and then went off inter hysterics, right on his buzzum, laughin' and cryin' and sayin' that nothin' should part 'em. Gosh! if I didn't think *he* was more cut up than she about it; a minit it looked as ef *he* didn't allow to marry her arter all, but that passed and they was married hard and fast—you bet! I reckon he's had enough of stayin' out o' nights to last him, and ef the valley settlements hevn't got hold of a very shinin' member at least the foothills hev got shut of one more of the Ramon Martinez gang."

"What's that about the Ramon Martinez gang?" said a quiet yet powerful voice.

Bill turned quickly. It was the voice of the divisional superintendent of the express company, a man of eccentric determination of character and one of the few whom the autocratic Bill recognized as an equal, who had just entered the barroom. His dusty pongee cloak and soft hat indicated that he had that morning arrived on a round of inspection.

"Don't care if I do, Bill," he continued in response to Bill's invitatory gesture, walking to the bar. "It's a little raw out on the road. Well, what were you saying about Ramon Martinez gang? You haven't come across one of 'em, have you?"

"No," said Bill with a slight blinking of his eye as he ostentatiously lifted his glass to the light.

"And you *won't*," added the superintendent, leisurely sipping his liquor. "For the fact is, the gang is about played out. Not from want of a job now and then, but from the difficulty of disposing of the results of their work. Since the new instructions to the agents to identify and trace all dust and bullion offered to them went into force, you see, they can't get rid of their swag. All the gang are spotted at the offices and it costs too much for them to pay a fence or a middleman of any standing. Why, all that flaky river gold they took from the Excelsior Company can be identified as easy as if it was stamped with the company's mark. They can't melt it down themselves; they can't get others to do it for them; they can't ship it to the mint or assay offices in Marysville and Frisco, for they won't take it without our certificate and seals; and *we* don't take any undeclared freight within the lines that we've drawn around their beat, except from people and agents known. Why, *you* know that well enough, Jim," he said, suddenly appealing to the expressman, "don't you?"

Possibly the suddenness of the appeal caused the expressman to swallow his liquor the wrong way, for he was overtaken with a fit of coughing and stammered hastily as he laid down his glass, "Yes, er—certainly."

"No sir," resumed the superintendent cheerfully,

"they're pretty well played out. And the best proof of it is that they've lately been robbing ordinary passengers' trunks. There was a freight wagon held up near Dow's Flat the other day and a lot of baggage gone through. I had to go down there to look into it. Darned if they hadn't lifted a lot o' woman's wedding things from that rich couple who got married the other day out at Marysville. Looks as if they were playing it rather low down, don't it? Coming down to hardpan and the bedrock —eh?"

The expressman's face was turned anxiously toward Bill, who after a hurried gulp of his remaining liquor still stood staring at the window. Then he slowly drew on one of his large gloves. "Ye didn't," he said, with a slow drawling but perfectly distinct articulation, "happen to know old Skinner Hemmings when you were over there?"

"Yes."

"And his daughter?"

"He hasn't got any."

"A sort o' mild innocent guileless child of nature?" persisted Bill with a yellow face, a deadly calm and Satanic deliberation.

"No. I tell you he *hasn't* any daughter. Old man Hemmings is a confirmed old bachelor. He's too mean to support more than one."

"And you didn't happen to know any o' that gang, did ye?" continued Bill with infinite protraction.

"Yes. Knew 'em all. There was French Pete, Cherokee

Bob, Kanaka Joe, One-eyed Stillson, Softy Brown, Spanish Jack and two or three Mexicans."

"And ye didn't know a man by the name of Charley Byng?"

"No," returned the superintendent, with a slight suggestion of weariness and a distraught glance toward the door.

"A dark stylish chap with shifty black eyes and a curled-up merstache?" continued Bill, with dry colorless persistence.

"No. Look here, Bill, I'm in a little bit of a hurry—but I suppose you must have your little joke before we part. Now, what *is* your little game?"

"Wot you mean?" demanded Bill with sudden brusqueness.

"Mean? Well, old man, you know as well as I do. You're giving me the very description of Ramon Martinez himself, ha! ha! No, Bill! You didn't play me this time. You're mighty spry and clever but you didn't catch on just then."

He nodded and moved away with a light laugh. Bill turned a stony face to the expressman. Suddenly a gleam of mirth came into his gloomy eyes. He bent over the young man and said in a hoarse chuckling whisper:

"But I got even after all!"

"How?"

"He's tied up to that lying little she-devil, hard and fast!"

The
Luck
of
Roaring
∾ Camp

THERE was commotion in Roaring Camp. It could not have been a fight, for in 1850 that was not novel enough to have called together the entire settlement. The ditches and claims were not only deserted, but Tuttle's grocery had contributed its gamblers who, it will be remembered, calmly continued their game the day that French Pete and Kanaka Joe shot each other to death over the bar in the front room. The whole camp was collected before a rude cabin on the outer edge of the clearing. Conversation was carried on in a low tone, but the name of a woman was frequently repeated. It was a name familiar enough in the camp—"Cherokee Sal."

Perhaps the less said of her the better. She was a coarse and, it is to be feared, a very sinful woman. But at that time she was the only woman in Roaring Camp, and was just then lying in sore extremity when she most needed the ministration of her own sex. Dissolute, abandoned and irreclaimable, she was yet suffering a martyrdom hard enough to bear even when veiled by sympathizing womanhood, but now terrible in her loneliness. The primal curse had come to her in that original isolation which must have made the punishment of the first transgression so dreadful. It was, perhaps, part of the expiation of her sin that at a moment when she most lacked her sex's intuitive tenderness and care, she met only the half-contemptuous faces of her masculine associates. Yet a few of the spectators were, I think, touched by her sufferings. Sandy Tipton thought it was "rough on Sal," and in the contemplation of her condition for a moment rose superior to the fact that he had an ace and two bowers in his sleeve.

It will be seen also that the situation was novel. Deaths were by no means uncommon in Roaring Camp, but a birth was a new thing. People had been dismissed from the camp effectively, finally, and with no possibility of return; but this was the first time that anybody had been introduced *ab initio*. Hence the excitement.

"You go in there, Stumpy," said a prominent citizen known as Kentuck, addressing one of the loungers. "Go in there and see what you kin do. You've had experience in them things."

Perhaps there was a fitness in the selection. Stumpy in other climes had been the putative head of two families.

In fact, it was owing to some legal informality in these proceedings that Roaring Camp, a city of refuge, was indebted to his company. The crowd approved the choice and Stumpy was wise enough to bow to the majority. The door closed on the extempore surgeon and midwife, and Roaring Camp sat down outside, smoked its pipe and awaited the issue.

The assemblage numbered about a hundred men. One or two of these were actual fugitives from justice, some were criminal and all were reckless. Physically they exhibited no indication of their past lives and character. The greatest scamp had a Raphael face with a profusion of blond hair. Oakhurst, a gambler, had the melancholy air and intellectual abstraction of a Hamlet. The coolest and most courageous man was scarcely over five feet in height, with a soft voice and an embarrassed timid manner. The term "roughs" applied to them was a distinction rather than a definition. Perhaps in the minor details of fingers, toes, ears, etc. the camp may have been deficient, but these slight omissions did not detract from their aggregate force. The strongest man had but three fingers on his right hand; the best shot had but one eye.

Such was the physical aspect of the men that were dispersed around the cabin. The camp lay in a triangular valley between two hills and a river. The only outlet was a steep trail over the summit of a hill that faced the cabin, now illuminated by the rising moon. The suffering woman might have seen it from the rude bunk whereon she lay, seen it winding like a silver thread until it was lost in the stars above.

A fire of withered pine boughs added sociability to the gathering. By degrees the natural levity of Roaring Camp returned. Bets were freely offered and taken regarding the result. Three to five that "Sal would get through with it," even that the child would survive; side bets as to the sex and complexion of the coming stranger. In the midst of an excited discussion an exclamation came from those nearest the door, and the camp stopped to listen. Above the swaying and moaning of the pines, the swift rush of the river, and the crackling of the fire rose a sharp querulous cry—a cry unlike anything heard before in the camp. The pines stopped moaning, the river ceased to rush, and the fire to crackle. It seemed as if Nature had stopped to listen too.

The camp rose to its feet as one man. It was proposed to explode a barrel of gunpowder, but in consideration of the situation of the mother better counsels prevailed, and only a few revolvers were discharged. For whether owing to the rude surgery of the camp or for some other reason, Cherokee Sal was sinking fast. Within an hour she had climbed, as it were, that rugged road that led to the stars and so passed out of Roaring Camp, its sin and shame, forever. I do not think that the announcement disturbed them much, except in speculation as to the fate of the child. "Can he live now?" was asked of Stumpy. The answer was doubtful. The only other being of Cherokee Sal's sex and maternal condition in the set-

tlement was an ass. There was some conjecture as to
fitness, but the experiment was tried. It was less prob-
lematical than the ancient treatment of Romulus and
Remus, and apparently as successful.

When these details were completed, which exhausted
another hour, the door was opened, and the anxious
crowd of men who had already formed themselves into
a queue entered in single file. Beside the low bunk or
shelf on which the figure of the mother was starkly outlined below the blankets stood a pine table. On this a
candle-box was placed, and within it, swathed in staring
red flannel, lay the last arrival at Roaring Camp. Beside
the candle-box was placed a hat. Its use was soon indicated. "Gentlemen," said Stumpy, with a singular mixture of authority and *ex officio* complacency, "gentlemen
will please pass in at the front door, around the table,
and out at the back door. Then as wishes to contribute
anything toward the orphan will find a hat handy." The
first man entered with his hat on; he uncovered, however, as he looked about him, and so unconsciously set
an example to the next. In such communities good and
bad actions are catching.

As the procession filed in, comments were audible—
criticisms addressed perhaps rather to Stumpy in the
character of showman: "Is that him?" "Mighty small
specimen." "Hasn't more'n got the color." "Ain't bigger
nor a derringer." The contributions were as characteristic: a silver tobacco box, a doubloon, a silver-mounted
navy revolver, a gold specimen, a very beautiful em-

broidered lady's handkerchief (from Oakhurst the gambler), a diamond breastpin, a diamond ring (suggested
by the pin, with the remark from the giver that he "saw
that pin and went two diamonds better"), a slingshot, a
Bible (contributor not detected), a golden spur, a silver
teaspoon (the initials, I regret to say, were not the
giver's), a pair of surgeon's shears, a lancet, a Bank of
England note for £5, and about $200 in loose gold and
silver coin. During these proceedings Stumpy maintained a silence as impassive as the dead on his left, a
gravity as inscrutable as that of the newly born on his
right.

Only one incident occurred to break the monotony of
the curious procession. As Kentuck bent over the candle-
box half curiously, the child turned, and in a spasm of
pain caught at his groping finger and held it fast for a
moment. Kentuck looked foolish and embarrassed.
Something like a blush tried to assert itself in his
weather-beaten cheek. "The durned little cuss!" he said,
as he extricated his finger with perhaps more tenderness
and care than he might have been deemed capable of
showing. He held that finger a little apart from its fellows as he went out, and examined it curiously. The
examination provoked the same original remark in regard to the child. In fact, he seemed to enjoy repeating
it. "He wrastled with my finger," he remarked to Tipton,
holding up the member, "the durned little cuss!"

It was four o'clock before the camp sought repose. A
light burnt in the cabin where the watchers sat, for

Stumpy did not go to bed that night. Nor did Kentuck. He drank quite freely and related with great gusto his experience, invariably ending with his characteristic condemnation of the newcomer. It seemed to relieve him of any unjust implication of sentiment, and Kentuck had the weaknesses of the nobler sex. When everybody else had gone to bed he walked down to the river and whistled reflectingly. Then he walked up the gulch past the cabin, still whistling with demonstrative unconcern. At a large redwood tree he paused and retraced his steps and again passed the cabin. Halfway down to the river's bank he again paused, and then returned and knocked at the door. It was opened by Stumpy. "How goes it?" said Kentuck, looking past Stumpy toward the candle-box. "All serene!" replied Stumpy. "Anything up?" "Nothing." There was a pause—an embarrassing one—Stumpy still holding the door. Then Kentuck had recourse to his finger, which he held up to Stumpy. "Wrastled with it, the durned little cuss," he said, and retired.

The next day Cherokee Sal had such rude sepulture as Roaring Camp afforded. After her body had been committed to the hillside, there was a formal meeting of the camp to discuss what should be done with her infant. A resolution to adopt it was unanimous and enthusiastic. But an animated discussion in regard to the manner and feasibility of providing for its wants at once sprang up. It was remarkable that the argument partook of none of those fierce personalities with which discussions were usually conducted at Roaring Camp. Tipton proposed that they should send the child to Red Dog, a distance of forty miles, where female attention could be procured. But the unlucky suggestion met with fierce and unanimous opposition. It was evident that no plan which entailed parting from their new acquisition would for a moment be entertained. "Besides," said Tom Ryder, "them fellows at Red Dog would swap it and ring in somebody else on us." A disbelief in the honesty of other camps prevailed at Roaring Camp as in other places.

The introduction of a female nurse in the camp also met with objection. It was argued that no decent woman could be prevailed to accept Roaring Camp as her home, and the speaker urged that "they didn't want any more of the other kind." This unkind allusion to the defunct mother, harsh as it may seem, was the first spasm of propriety, the first symptom of the camp's regeneration. Stumpy advanced nothing. Perhaps he felt a certain delicacy in interfering with the selection of a possible succesor in office. But when questioned, he averred stoutly that he and Jinny—the mammal before alluded to—could manage to rear the child. There was something original, independent and heroic about the plan that pleased the camp. Stumpy was retained. Certain articles were sent for to Sacramento. "Mind," said the treasurer as he pressed a bag of gold dust into the expressman's hand, "the best that can be got—lace, you know, and filigree-work and frills—damn the cost!"

Strange to say, the child thrived. Perhaps the invigorating climate of the mountain camp was compensation for material deficiencies. Nature took the foundling to her broader breast. In that rare atmosphere of the Sierra foothills, that air pungent with balsamic odor, that ethereal cordial at once bracing and exhilarating, he may have found food and nourishment, or a subtle chemistry that transmuted ass's milk to lime and phosphorus. Stumpy inclined to the belief that it was the latter and good nursing. "Me and that ass," he would say, "has been father and mother to him! Don't you," he would add, apostrophizing the helpless bundle before him, "never go back on us."

By the time he was a month old the necessity of giving him a name became apparent. He had generally been known as The Kid, Stumpy's Boy, The Coyote (an allusion to his vocal powers), and even by Kentuck's endearing, "the durned little cuss." But these were felt to be vague and unsatisfactory, and were at last dismissed under another influence. Gamblers and adventurers are generally superstitious, and Oakhurst one day declared that the baby had brought "the luck" to Roaring Camp. It was certain that of late they had been successful. Luck was the name agreed upon, with the prefix of Tommy for greater convenience. No allusion was made to the mother, and the father was unknown. "It's better," said the philosophical Oakhurst, "to take a fresh deal all

around. Call him Luck and start him fair." A day was
accordingly set apart for the christening. What was
meant by this ceremony the reader, who has already
gathered some idea of the reckless irreverence of Roaring Camp, may imagine. The master of ceremonies was
one Boston, a noted wag, and the occasion seemed to
promise the greatest facetiousness. This ingenious satirist had spent two days in preparing a burlesque of the
church service, with pointed local allusions. The choir
was properly trained, and Sandy Tipton was to stand
godfather. But after the procession had marched to the
grove with music and banners and the child had been
deposited before a mock altar, Stumpy stepped before
the expectant crowd. "It ain't my style to spoil fun,
boys," said the little man, stoutly eying the faces around
him, "but it strikes me that this thing ain't exactly on
the squar. It's playin' it pretty low down on this yer baby
to ring in fun on him that he ain't goin' to understand.
And ef there's goin' to be any godfathers round, I'd like
to see who's got any better rights than me." A silence
followed Stumpy's speech. To the credit of all humorists
be it said that the first man to acknowledge its justice
was the satirist thus stopped of his fun. "But," said
Stumpy, quickly following up his advantage, "we're here
for a christening, and we'll have it. I proclaim you
Thomas Luck, according to the laws of the United States
and the State of California, so help me God." It was the
first time that the name of the Deity had been other-

wise uttered than profanely in the camp. The form of
christening was perhaps even more ludicrous than the
satirist had conceived; but strangely enough, nobody
saw it and nobody laughed. Tommy was christened as
seriously as he would have been under a Christian roof,
and cried and was comforted in as orthodox fashion.

And so the work of regeneration began in Roaring
Camp. Almost imperceptibly a change came over the
settlement. The cabin assigned to Tommy Luck, or The
Luck, as he was more frequently called, first showed
signs of improvement. It was kept scrupulously clean
and whitewashed. Then it was boarded, clothed and
papered. The rosewood cradle, packed eighty miles by
mule had, in Stumpy's way of putting it, "sorter killed
the rest of the furniture." So the rehabilitation of the
cabin became a necessity. The men who were in the
habit of lounging in at Stumpy's to see "how The Luck
got on" seemed to appreciate the change, and in self
defense the rival establishment of Tuttle's Grocery bestirred itself and imported a carpet and mirrors. The
reflections of the latter on the appearance of Roaring
Camp tended to produce stricter habits of personal
cleanliness. Again Stumpy imposed a kind of quarantine
upon those who aspired to the honor and privilege of
holding The Luck. It was a cruel mortification to Kentuck—who in the carelessness of a large nature and the
habits of frontier life, had begun to regard all garments
as a second cuticle which, like a snake's, only sloughed

off through decay—to be debarred this privilege from
certain prudential reasons. Yet such was the subtle influence of innovation that he thereafter appeared regularly every afternoon in a clean shirt and face still
shining from his ablutions. Nor were moral and social
sanitary laws neglected. Tommy, who was supposed to
spend his whole existence in a persistent attempt to
repose, must not be disturbed by noise. The shouting
and yelling which had gained the camp its infelicitous
title were not permitted within hearing distance of
Stumpy's. The men conversed in whispers or smoked
with Indian gravity. Profanity was tacitly given up in
these sacred precincts, and throughout the camp the
popular forms of expletives known as "Damn the luck!"
and "Curse the luck!" were abandoned as having a new
personal bearing. Vocal music was not interdicted, being
supposed to have a soothing, tranquilizing quality; and
one song, sung by Man-o'-War Jack, an English sailor
from Her Majesty's Australian colonies, was quite popular as a lullaby. It was a lugubrious recital of the
exploits of "The *Arethusa*, Seventy-four," in a muffled
minor, ending with a prolonged dying fall at the burden
of each verse, "On b-oo-o-ard of the *Arethusa*." It was a
fine sight to see Jack holding The Luck, rocking from
side to side as if with the motion of a ship, and crooning
forth this naval ditty. Either through the peculiar rocking of Jack or the length of his song—it contained ninety
stanzas, and was continued with conscientious deliberation to the bitter end—the lullaby generally had the

desired effect. At such times the men would lie at full length under the trees in the soft summer twilight, smoking their pipes and drinking in the melodious utterances. An indistinct idea that this was pastoral happiness pervaded the camp. "This 'ere kind o' think," said the Cockney Simmons, meditatively reclining on his elbow, "is 'evingly." It reminded him of Greenwich.

On the long summer days The Luck was usually carried to the gulch from whence the golden store of Roaring Camp was taken. There, on a blanket spread over pine boughs, he would lie while the men were working in the ditches below. Latterly there was a rude attempt to decorate this bower with flowers and sweet-smelling shrubs, and generally someone would bring him a cluster of wild honeysuckles, azaleas or the painted blossoms of las mariposas. The men had suddenly awakened to the fact that there were beauty and significance in these trifles which they had so long trodden carelessly beneath their feet. A flake of glittering mica, a fragment of variegated quartz, a bright pebble from the bed of the creek, became beautiful to eyes thus cleared and strengthened, and were invariably put aside for The Luck. It was wonderful how many treasures the woods and hillsides yielded that "would do for Tommy." Surrounded by playthings such as never child out of fairyland had before, it is to be hoped that Tommy was content. He appeared to be serenely happy, albeit there was an infantine gravity about him, a contemplative light in his round gray eyes, that sometimes worried Stumpy. He was always tractable and quiet, and it is recorded that once, having crept beyond his "corral"—a hedge of tessellated pine boughs which surrounded his bed—he dropped over the bank on his head in the soft earth, and remained with his mottled legs in the air in that position for at least five minutes with unflinching gravity. He was extricated without a murmur. I hesitate to record the many other instances of his sagacity which rest, unfortunately, upon the statements of prejudiced friends. Some of them were not without a tinge of superstition. "I crep' up the bank just now," said Kentuck one day in a breathless state of excitement, "and durn my skin if he wasn't a-talkin' to a jaybird as was a-sittin' on his lap. There they was, just as free and sociable as anything you please, a-jawin' at each other just like two cherrybums." Howbeit, whether creeping over the pine boughs or lying lazily on his back blinking at the leaves above him, to him the birds sang, the squirrels chattered, and the flowers bloomed. Nature was his nurse and playfellow. For him she would let slip between the leaves golden shafts of sunlight that fell just within his grasp; she would send wandering breezes to visit him with the balm of bay and resinous gum; to him the tall redwoods nodded familiarly and sleepily, the bumblebees buzzed, and the rooks cawed a slumbrous accompaniment.

Such was the golden summer of Roaring Camp. They were flush times, and the luck was with them. The claims had yielded enormously. The camp was jealous of its privileges and looked suspiciously on strangers. No encouragement was given to immigration, and to make their seclusion more perfect, the land on either side of the mountain wall that surrounded the camp they duly pre-empted. This and a reputation for singular proficiency with the revolver kept the reserve of Roaring Camp inviolate. The expressman—their only connecting link with the surrounding world—sometimes told wonderful stories of the camp. He would say, "They've a street up there in Roaring that would lay over any street in Red Dog. They've got vines and flowers around their houses and they wash themselves twice a day. But they're mighty rough on strangers and they worship an Ingin baby."

With the prosperity of the camp came a desire for further improvement. It was proposed to build a hotel in the following spring and to invite one or two decent families to reside there for the sake of The Luck, who might perhaps profit by female companionship. The sacrifice that this concession to the sex cost these men, who were fiercely skeptical in regard to its general virtue and usefulness, can only be accounted for by their affection for Tommy. A few still held out. But the resolve could not be carried into effect for three months, and the minority meekly yielded in the hope that something might turn up to prevent it. And it did.

The winter of 1851 will long be remembered in the foothills. The snow lay deep on the Sierras, and every mountain creek became a river and every river a lake.

Each gorge and gulch was transformed into a tumultuous watercourse that descended the hillsides, tearing
down giant trees and scattering its drift and debris along
the plain. Red Dog had been twice under water, and
Roaring Camp had been forewarned. "Water put the
gold into them gulches," said Stumpy. "It's been here
once and will be here again!" And that night the North
Fork suddenly leaped over its banks and swept up the
triangular valley of Roaring Camp.

In the confusion of rushing water, crashing trees and
crackling timber, and the darkness which seemed to
flow with the water and blot out the fair valley, little
could be done to collect the scattered camp. When the
morning broke, the cabin of Stumpy, nearest the riverbank, was gone. Higher up the gulch they found the
body of its unlucky owner; but the pride, the hope, the
joy, The Luck of Roaring Camp had disappeared. They
were returning with sad hearts when a shout from the
bank recalled them.

It was a relief boat from down the river. They had
picked up, they said, a man and an infant, nearly
exhausted, about two miles below. Did anybody know
them, and did they belong here?

It needed but a glance to show them Kentuck lying
there, cruelly crushed and bruised, but still holding
The Luck of Roaring Camp in his arms. As they bent
over the strangely assorted pair, they saw that the child
was cold and pulseless. "He is dead," said one. Kentuck

opened his eyes. "Dead?" he repeated feebly. "Yes, my man, and you are dying too." A smile lit the eyes of the expiring Kentuck. "Dying!" he repeated; "he's a-takin' me with him. Tell the boys I've got The Luck with me now." And the strong man, clinging to the frail babe as a drowning man is said to cling to a straw, drifted away into the shadowy river that flows forever to the un-known sea.

Lanty
Foster's
❧ Mistake

LANTY FOSTER was crouching on a low stool before the dying kitchen fire, the better to get its fading radiance on the book she was reading. Beyond, through the open window and door, the fire was also slowly fading from the sky and the mountain ridge whence the sun had dropped half an hour before. The view was uphill, and the skyline of the hill was marked by two or three gibbetlike poles from which, on a now invisible line between them, depended certain objects— mere black silhouettes against the sky—which bore weird likeness to human figures. Absorbed as she was in her book, she nevertheless occasionally cast an impatient glance in that direction, as the sunlight faded more quickly than her fire. For the fluttering objects were the week's wash which had to be brought in before night fell and the mountain wind rose. It was strong at that

altitude, and before this had ravished the clothes from
the line and scattered them along the highroad leading
over the ridge, once even lashing the shy schoolmaster
with a pair of Lanty's own stockings and blinding the
parson with a really tempestuous petticoat.

A whiff of wind down the big-throated chimney
stirred the long embers on the hearth. The girl jumped
to her feet, closing the book with an impatient snap. She
knew her mother's voice would follow. It was hard to
leave her heroine at the crucial moment of receiving an
explanation from a presumed faithless lover, just to
climb a hill and take in a lot of soulless washing, but
such are the infelicities of stolen romance reading. She
threw the clothes basket over her head like a hood, the
handle resting across her bosom and shoulders, and with
both her hands free started out of the cabin. But the
darkness had come up from the valley in one stride after
its mountain fashion, had outstripped her and she was
instantly plunged in it. High above her, the outline of
the ridge was still clearly visible, but now overhead
shone the white steadfast stars that were not there a
moment ago, and by that sign she knew she was late.
She had to battle against the rushing wind now, which
sang through the inverted basket over her head and
held her back. With bent shoulders she at last reached
the top of the ridge and the level. Yet here, owing to the
shifting of the lighter background above her, she now
found herself again encompassed with the darkness. The
outlines of the poles had disappeared, the white flutter-

ing garments were distinct apparitions waving in the
wind, like dancing ghosts. But there certainly was a
queer misshapen bulk moving beyond which she did not
recognize, and as she at last reached one of the poles, a
shock was communicated to it through the clothesline
and the bulk beyond. Then she heard a voice say impatiently:

"What the devil am I running into now?"

It was a man's voice, and from its elevation the voice
of a man on horseback. She answered without fear and
with slow deliberation:

"Inter our clothesline, I reckon."

"Oh!" said the man in a half-apologetic tone. Then
in brisker accents, "The very thing I want! I say, can
you give me a bit of it? The ring of my saddle girth has
fetched loose. I can fasten it with that."

"I reckon," replied Lanty with the same unconcern,
moving nearer the bulk which now separated into two
parts as the man dismounted. "How much do you
want?"

"A foot or two will do."

They were now in front of each other, although their
faces were not distinguishable to either. Lanty, who
had been following the lines with her hand, here came
upon the end knotted around the last pole. This she
began to untie.

"What a place to hang clothes," he said curiously.

"Mighty dryin', though," returned Lanty laconically.

"And your house? Is it nearby?" he continued.

"Just down the ridge—ye kin see from the edge. Got a knife?" She had untied the knot.

"No—yes—wait." He had hesitated a moment and then produced something from his breast pocket, which he however kept in his hand. As he did not offer it to her she simply held out a section of the rope between her hands, which he divided with a single cut. She saw only that the instrument was long and keen. Then she lifted the flap of the saddle for him as he attempted to fasten the loose ring with the rope, but the darkness made it impossible. With an ejaculation he fumbled in his pockets. "My last match!" he said, striking it as he crouched over to protect it from the wind. Lanty leaned over also with her apron raised between it and the blast. The flame for an instant lit up the ring, and the man's dark face and mustache, and his white teeth and set jaw as he tugged at the girth. It also revealed Lanty's brown velvet eyes and soft round cheek framed by the basket. Then the flame went out, but the ring was secured.

"Thank you," said the man with a short laugh. "I thought you were a humpbacked witch in the dark there."

"And I couldn't make out whether you was a cow or a b'ar," returned the young girl simply.

Here, however, he quickly mounted his horse, but in the action something slipped from his clothes, struck a stone, and bounded away into the darkness.

"My knife," he said hurriedly. "Please hand it to me." But although the girl dropped on her knees and searched

the ground diligently, it could not be found. The man
with a restrained ejaculation again dismounted and
joined in the search.

"Haven't you got another match?" suggested Lanty.

"No—it was my last!" he said impatiently.

"Just you hol' on here," she said suddenly, "and I'll
run down to the kitchen and fetch you a light. I won't
be long."

"No! no!" said the man quickly. "Don't! I couldn't
wait. I've been here too long now. Look here. You come
in daylight and find it, and—just keep it for me, will
you?" He laughed. "I'll come for it. And now if you'll
only help to set me on that road again, for it's so infernal
black I can't see the mare's ears ahead of me, I won't
bother you any more. Thank you."

Lanty had quietly moved to his horse's head and
taken the bridle in her hand, and at once seemed to be
lost in the gloom. But in a few moments he felt the
muffled thud of his horse's hoof on the thick dust of the
highway and its still hot impalpable powder rising to
his nostrils.

"Thank you," he said again, "I'm all right now." In
the pause that followed it seemed to Lanty that he had
extended a parting hand to her in the darkness. She put
up her own to meet it but missed his, which had
blundered onto her shoulder. Before she could grasp it,
she felt him stooping over her, the light brush of his soft
mustache on her cheek, and then the starting forward of
his horse. But the retaliating box on the ear she had

promptly aimed at him spent itself in the black space which seemed suddenly to have swallowed up the man and even his light laugh.

For an instant she stood still and then, swinging the basket indignantly from her shoulder, took up her suspended task. It was no light one in the increasing wind, and the unfastened clothesline had precipitated a part of its burden to the ground through the loosening of the rope. But on picking up the trailing garments her hand struck an unfamiliar object. The stranger's lost knife! She thrust it hastily into the bottom of the basket and completed her work. As she began to descend with her burden she saw that the light of the kitchen fire, seen through the windows, was augmented by a candle. Her mother was evidently awaiting her.

"Pretty time to be fetchin' in the wash," said Mrs. Foster querulously. "But what can you expect when folks stand gossipin' and philanderin' on the ridge instead o' tendin' to their work?"

Now Lanty knew that she had *not* been "gossipin'" nor "philanderin'," yet as the parting salute might have been open to that imputation and as she surmised that her mother might have overheard their voices, she briefly said, to prevent further questioning, that she had shown a stranger the road. But for her mother's unjust accusation she would have been more communicative. As Mrs. Foster went back grumblingly into the sitting room Lanty resolved to keep the knife at present a secret from her mother, and to that purpose removed it from the basket. But in the light of the candle she saw it for the first time plainly—and started.

For it was really a dagger!—jeweled-handled and richly wrought—such as Lanty had never looked upon before. The hilt was studded with gems, and the blade, which had a cutting edge, was damascened in blue and gold. Her soft eyes reflected the brilliant setting, her lips parted breathlessly. Then as her mother's voice arose in the other room she thrust it back into its velvet sheath and clapped it into her pocket. Its rare beauty had confirmed her resolution of absolute secrecy. To have shown it now would have made "no end of talk." And she was not sure but that her parents would have demanded its custody! And it was given to *her* by *him* to keep. This settled the question of moral ethics. She took the first opportunity to run up to her bedroom and hide it under the mattress.

Yet the thought of it filled the rest of her evening. When her household duties were done she took up her novel again, partly from force of habit and partly as an attitude in which she could think of *It* undisturbed. For what was fiction to her now? True, it possessed a certain reminiscent value. A dagger had appeared in several romances she had devoured, but she never had a clear idea of one before. "The Count sprang back, and drawing from his belt a richly jeweled dagger, hissed between his teeth." Or more to the purpose: " 'Take this,' said Orlando, handing her the ruby-hilted poniard which had gleamed upon his thigh, 'and should the caitiff attempt thy unguarded innocence—' "

"Did ye hear what your father was sayin'?" Lanty started. It was her mother's voice in the doorway, and she had been vaguely conscious of another voice pitched in the same querulous key, which indeed was the dominant expression of the small ranchers of that fertile neighborhood. Possibly a too complaisant and unaggressive Nature had spoiled them.

"Yes!—no!" said Lanty abstractedly, "what'd he say?"

"If you wasn't taken up with that fool book," said Mrs. Foster, glancing at her daughter's slightly conscious color, "ye'd know! He allowed ye'd better not leave yer filly in the far pasture nights. That gang o' Mexican horse thieves is out again and raided McKinnon's stock last night."

This touched Lanty closely. The filly was her own property, and she was breaking it for her own riding. But her distrust of her parents' interference was greater than any fear of horse stealers. "She's mighty uneasy in the barn. And," she added, with a proud consciousness of that beautiful yet carnal weapon upstairs, "I reckon I ken protect her and myself agin any Mexican horse thieves."

"My! but we're gettin' high and mighty," responded Mrs. Foster with deep irony. "Did you git all that outer your fool book?"

"Mebbe," said Lanty curtly.

Nevertheless, her thoughts that night were not entirely based on written romance. She wondered if the
stranger knew that she had really tried to box his ears
in the darkness, also if he had been able to see her face.
His she remembered, at least the flash of his white teeth
against his dark face and darker mustache, which was
quite as soft as her own hair. But if he thought "for a
minit" that she was "goin' to allow an entire stranger to
kiss her—he was mighty mistaken." She should let him
know it "pretty quick"! She should hand him back the
dagger "quite careless-like," and never let on that she'd
thought anything of it. Perhaps that was the reason
why before she went to bed she took a good look at it,
and after taking off her straight beltless calico gown she
even tried the effect of it, thrust in the stiff waistband
of her petticoat with the jeweled hilt displayed, and
thought it looked charming—as indeed it did. And then,
having said her prayers like a good girl and supplicated
that she should be less "tetchy" with her parents, she
went to sleep and dreamed that she had gone out to take
in the wash again, but that the clothes had all changed
to the queerest lot of folks who were all fighting and
struggling with each other until she, Lanty, drawing
her dagger, rushed up single-handed among them crying, "Disperse, ye craven curs—disperse, I say!" And
they dispersed.

Yet even Lanty was obliged to admit the next morning that all this was somewhat incongruous with the
baking of corn dodgers, the frying of fish, the making

of beds, and her other household duties, and dismissed
the stranger from her mind until he should happen
along. In her freer and more acceptable outdoor duties
she even tolerated the advances of neighboring swains
who made a point of passing by Foster's Ranch and who
were quite aware that Atalanta Foster, *alias* "Lanty,"
was one of the prettiest girls in the county. But Lanty's
toleration consisted in that singular performance known
to herself as "giving them as good as they sent," being
a lazy traversing, qualified with scorn, of all that they
advanced. How long they would have put up with this
from a plain girl I do not know, but Lanty's short upper
lip seemed framed for indolent and fascinating scorn,
and her dreamy eyes usually looked beyond the questioner or blunted his bolder glances in their velvety sur-
faces. The libretto of these scenes was not exhaustive,
e.g.:

The Swain (with bold bad gaiety): "Saw that shy
schoolmaster hangin' round your ridge yesterday! Orter
know by this time that shyness with a gal don't pay."

Lanty (decisively): "Mebbe he allows it don't get left
as often as impudence."

The Swain (ignoring the reply and his previous attitude and becoming more direct): "I was calkilatin' to
say that with these yer hoss thieves about, yer filly ain't
safe in the pasture. I took a turn round there two or
three times last evening to see if she was all right."

Lanty (with a flattering show of interest): "No! *did*
ye, now? I was jest wonderin'—"

The Swain (eagerly): "I did—quite late, too! Why, that's nothin', Miss Atalanty, to what I'd do for you."

Lanty (musing, with far-off eyes): "Then that's why she was so awful skeerd and frightened! Just jumpin' outer her skin with horror. I reckoned it was a b'ar or panther or a spook! You ought to have waited till she got accustomed to your looks."

Nevertheless, despite this elegant raillery, Lanty was enough concerned in the safety of her horse to visit it the next day with a view of bringing it nearer home. She had just stepped into the alder fringe of a dry run when she came suddenly upon the figure of a horseman in the run, who had been hidden by the alders from the plain beyond and who seemed to be engaged in examining the hoof marks in the dust of the old ford. Something about his figure struck her recollection. As he looked up quickly she saw it was the owner of the dagger. But he appeared to be lighter of hair and complexion, and was dressed differently and more like a vaquero. Yet there was the same flash of his teeth as he recognized her, and she knew it was the same man.

Alas for her preparation! Without the knife she could not make that haughty return of it which she had contemplated. And more than that, she was conscious she was blushing! Nevertheless she managed to level her pretty brown eyebrows at him, and said sharply that if he followed her to her home she would return his property at once.

"But I'm in no hurry for it," he said with a laugh—the same light laugh and pleasant voice she remembered— "and I'd rather not come to the house just now. The knife is in good hands I know, and I'll call for it when I want it! Until then, if it's all the same to you, keep it to yourself—keep it dark, as dark as the night I lost it!"

"I don't go about blabbing my affairs," said Lanty indignantly. "And if it hadn't been dark that night you'd have had your ears boxed—you know why!"

The stranger laughed again, waved his hand to Lanty and galloped away.

Lanty was a little disappointed. The daylight had taken away some of her illusions. He was certainly very good-looking but not quite as picturesque, mysterious and thrilling as in the dark! And it was very queer—he certainly did look darker that night! Who was he? And why was he lingering near her? He was different from her neighbors, her admirers. He might be one of those locaters from the big towns who prospect the lands with a view of settling government warrants on them. They were always so secret until they had found what they wanted. She did not dare to seek information from her friends for the same reason that she had concealed his existence from her mother—it would provoke awkward questions. And it was evident that he was trusting to her secrecy, too. The thought thrilled her with a new pride and was some compensation for the loss of her more intangible romance. It would be mighty fine, when

he did call openly for his beautiful knife and declared
himself, to have them all know that *she* knew about it
all along.

When she reached home, to guard against another
such surprise she determined to keep the weapon with
her. Distrusting her pocket, she confided it to the cheap
little country-made corset which only for the last year
had confined her budding figure and which now, perhaps, heaved with an additional pride. She was quite
abstracted during the rest of the day and paid but little
attention to the gossip of the farm lads, who were full
of a daring raid two nights before by the Mexican gang
on the large stock farm of a neighbor. The vigilance
committee had been baffled. It was even alleged that
some of the smaller ranchmen and herders were in
league with the gang. It was also believed to be a wide-
spread conspiracy, to have a political complexion in its
combination of an alien race with southwestern filibus-
ters. The legal authorities had been reinforced by special
detectives from San Francisco. Lanty seldom troubled
herself with these matters. She knew the exaggeration
and she suspected the ignorance of her rural neighbors.
She roughly referred to it, in her own vocabulary, as
"jaw," a peculiarly masculine quality. But later in the
evening when the domestic circle in the sitting room had
been augmented by a neighbor and Lanty had taken
refuge behind her novel as an excuse for silence, Zob
Hopper, the enamored swain of the previous evening,
burst in with more astounding news. A posse of the

sheriff had just passed along the ridge. They had corraled part of the gang and rescued some of the stock. The leader of the gang had escaped but his capture was inevitable, as the roads were stopped. "All the same, I'm glad to see ye took my advice, Miss Atalanty, and brought in your filly," he concluded with an insinuating glance at the young girl.

But Miss Atalanty, curling a quarter of an inch of scarlet lip above the edge of her novel, here "allowed" that if his advice or the filly had to be "took," she didn't know which was worse.

"I wonder ye kin talk to sech peartness, Mr. Hopper," said Mrs. Foster severely. "She ain't got eyes nor sense for anythin' but that book."

"Talkin' o' what's to be 'took,'" put in the diplomatic neighbor, "you bet it ain't that Mexican leader! No sir! He's been stopped before this—and then got clean away all the same! One o' them detectives got him once and disarmed him, but he managed to give them the slip after all. Why he's that full o' shifts and disguises thar ain't no spottin' him. He walked right under the constable's nose oncet and took a drink with the sheriff that was arter him—and the blamed fool never knew it. He kin change even the color of his hair quick as winkin'."

"Is he a real Mexican?" asked the paternal Foster.

"No! They say he comes o' old Spanish stock, a bad egg they threw outer the nest I reckon," put in Hopper eagerly, seeing a strange animated interest dilating

Lanty's eyes and hoping to share in it. "But he's reg'lar high-toned, you bet! Why, I knew a man who seed him in his own camp—prinked out in a velvet jacket and silk sash with gold chains and buttons down his wide pants and a dagger stuck in his sash, with a handle just blazin' with jew'ls. Yes! Miss Atalanty, they say that one stone at the top—a green stone, what they call an em'ral'—was worth the price o' a Frisco house lot. True ez you live! Eh—what's up now?"

Lanty's book had fallen on the floor as she was rising to her feet with a white face, still more strange and distorted in an affected yawn behind her little hand. "Yer makin' me that sick and nervous with yer fool yarns," she said hysterically, "that I'm goin' to get a little fresh air. It's just stifling here with lies and terbacker!" With another high laugh she brushed past him into the kitchen, opened the door, and then paused, and turning ran rapidly up to her bedroom. Here she locked herself in, tore open the bosom of her dress, plucked out the dagger and threw it on the bed, where the green stone gleamed for an instant in the candlelight. Then she dropped on her knees beside the bed, her whirling head buried in her cold hands.

It had all come to her in a flash, like a blaze of lightning—the black haunting figure on the ridge, the broken saddle girth, the abandonment of the dagger in the exigencies of flight and concealment; and then the second meeting—the skulking in the dry alder-hidden run, the changed dress, the lighter-colored hair, but always the same voice and laugh. He was the leader, the fugitive, the Mexican horse thief! And she, the God-forsaken, chuckle-headed fool, with not half the sense of her own filly or that sop-headed Hopper, had never seen it! She —*she* who would be the laughing-stock of them all—she had thought him a "locater," a "towny" from Frisco! And she had consented to keep his knife until he would call for it. Yes, call for it with fire and flame perhaps, the trampling of hoofs, pistol shots—and—yet—

Yet—he had *trusted* her. Yes! Trusted her when he knew a word from her lips would have brought the whole district down on him! When the mere exposure of that dagger would have identified and damned him! Trusted her a second time, when she was within cry of her house! When he might have taken her filly without her knowing it! And now she remembered vaguely that the neighbors had said how strange it was that her father's stock had not suffered as theirs had. *He* had protected them—he who was now a fugitive—and their men pursuing him! She rose suddenly with a single stamp of her narrow foot, and as suddenly became cool and sane. And then, quite her old self again, she lazily picked up the dagger and restored it to its place in her bosom. That done, with her color back and her eyes a little brighter, she deliberately went downstairs again, stuck her little brown head into the sitting room, said cheerfully, "Still yawpin', you folks?" and quietly passed out into the darkness.

She ran swiftly up to the ridge, impelled by the blind

memory of having met him there at night and the one vague thought to give him warning. But it was dark and empty, with no sound but the rushing wind. And then an idea seized her. If he were haunting the vicinity still, he might see the fluttering of the clothes upon the line and believe she was there. She stooped quickly, and in the merciful and exonerating darkness stripped off her only white petticoat and pinned it on the line. It flapped, fluttered and streamed in the mountain wind. She lingered and listened. But there came a sound she had not counted on—the clattering hoofs of not *one* but many horses on the lower road. She ran back to the house to find its inmates already hastening toward the road for news. She took that chance to slip in quietly and go to her room. Her window commanded a view of the ridge, and crouching low behind it, she listened. She could hear the sound of voices and the dull trampling of heavy boots on the dusty path toward the barnyard on the other side of the house—a pause, and then the return of the trampling boots and the final clattering of hoofs on the road again. Then there was a tap on her door and her mother's querulous voice.

"Oh! yer there, are ye? Well, it's the best place fer a girl, with all these man's doin's goin' on! They've got that Mexican horse thief and have tied him up in your filly's stall in the barn—till the Frisco deputy gets back from rounding up the others. So ye jest stay where ye are till they've come and gone, and we're shut o' all that cattle. Are ye mindin'?"

"All right, maw; 'tain't no call o' mine anyhow," returned Lanty through the half-open door.

At another time her mother might have been startled at her passive obedience. Still more would she have been startled had she seen her daughter's face now, behind the closed door, with her little mouth set over her clinched teeth. And yet it was her own child, and Lanty was her mother's real daughter; the same pioneer blood filled their veins, the blood that had never nourished cravens or degenerates but had given itself to sprinkle and fertilize desert solitudes where man might follow. Small wonder then that this frontier-born Lanty, whose first infant cry had been answered by the yelp of wolf and scream of panther, whose father's rifle had been leveled across her cradle to cover the stealthy Indian who prowled outside—small wonder that she should feel herself equal to these "man's doin's" and be prompt to take a part. For even in the first shock of the news of the capture she recalled the fact that the barn was old and rotten, that only that day the filly had kicked a board loose from behind her stall which she, Lanty, had lightly returned to avoid "making a fuss." If his captors had not noticed it, or trusted only to their guards, she might make the opening wide enough to free him!

Two hours later the guard nearest the now sleeping house, a farm hand of the Fosters, saw his employer's daughter slip out and cautiously approach him. A devoted slave of Lanty's and familiar with her impulses, he guessed her curiosity and was not averse to satisfying it and the sense of his own importance. To her whispers of affected half-terrified interest, he responded in whispers that the captive was really in the filly's stall, securely bound by his wrists behind his back, and his feet hobbled to a post. Lanty couldn't see him, for it was dark inside and he was sitting with his back to the wall, as he couldn't "sleep comf'ble lyin' down." Lanty's eyes glowed but her face was turned aside.

"And ye ain't reckonin' his friends will come and rescue him?" said Lanty, gazing with affected fearfulness in the darkness.

"Not much! There's two other guards down in the corral, and I'd fire my gun and bring 'em up."

But Lanty was gazing open-mouthed toward the ridge. "What's that wavin' on the ridge?" she said in awe-stricken tones.

She was pointing to the petticoat—a vague distant moving object against the horizon.

"Why, that's some o' the wash on the line, ain't it?"

"Wash—*two days in the week!*" said Lanty sharply. "Wot's gone of you?"

"Thet's so," muttered the man, "and it wa'nt there at sundown, I'll swear! P'r'aps I'd better call the guard," and he raised his rifle.

"Don't," said Lanty, catching his arm. "Suppose it's nothin'; they'll laugh at ye. Creep up softly and see; ye ain't afraid, are ye? If ye are, give me yer gun, and *I'll* go."

This settled the question, as Lanty expected. The man

cocked his piece, and bending low began cautiously to mount the acclivity. Lanty waited until his figure began to fade and then ran like fire to the barn.

She had arranged every detail of her plan beforehand. Crouching beside the wall of the stall she hissed through a crack in thrilling whispers, "Don't move! Don't speak for your life's sake! Wait till I hand you back your knife, then do the best you can." Then slipping aside the loosened board she saw dimly the black outline of curling hair, back, shoulders and tied wrists of the captive. Drawing the knife from her pocket, with two strokes of its keen cutting edge she severed the cords, threw the knife into the opening, and darted away. Yet in that moment she knew that the man was instinctively turning toward her. But it was one thing to free a horse thief, and another to stop and "philander" with him.

She ran halfway up the ridge and met the farm hand returning. It was only a bit of washing after all, and he was glad he hadn't fired his gun. On the other hand, Lanty confessed she had got "so skeert" being alone that she came to seek him. She had the shivers. Wasn't her hand cold? It was, but thrilling even in its coldness to the bashfully admiring man. And she was that weak and dizzy, he must let her lean on his arm going down, and they must go *slow*. She was sure he was cold too, and if he would wait at the back door she would give him a drink of whiskey. Thus Lanty, with her brain afire, her eyes and ears straining into the darkness, and the vague outline of the barn beyond! Another moment was pro-

tracted over the drink of whiskey and then Lanty, with
a faint archness, made him promise not to tell her mother
of her escapade, and she promised on her part not to say
anything about his "stalkin' a petticoat on the clothesline," and then shyly closed the door and regained her
room. *He* must have got away by this time or have been
discovered; she believed they would not open the barn
door until the return of the posse.

She was right. It was near daybreak when they returned, and again crouching low beside her window she
heard with a fierce joy, the sudden outcry, the oaths, the
wrangling voices, the summoning of her father to the
front door, and then the tumultuous sweeping away
again of the whole posse, and a blessed silence falling
over the rancho. And then Lanty went quietly to bed
and slept like a three-year child!

Perhaps that was the reason why she was able at
breakfast to listen with lazy and even rosy indifference
to the startling events of the night, to the sneers of the
farm hands at the posse who had overlooked the knife
when they searched their prisoner, as well as the stu-
pidity of the corral guard who had never heard him
make a hole "the size of a house" in the barn side! Once
she glanced demurely at Silas Briggs, the farm hand,
and the poor fellow felt consoled in his shame at the
remembrance of their confidences.

But Lanty's tranquility was not destined to last long.
There was again the irruption of exciting news from the
highroad. The Mexican leader had been recaptured and

was now safely lodged in Brownsville jail! Those who
were previously loud in their praises of the successful
horse thief who had baffled the vigilance of his pursuers
were now equally keen in their admiration of the new
San Francisco deputy who, in turn, had outwitted the
whole gang. It was *he* who was fertile in expedients; *he*
who had studied the whole country and even risked his
life among the gang, and *he* who had again closed the
meshes of the net around the escaped outlaw. He was
already returning by way of the rancho and might stop
there a moment. So they could all see the hero. Such
was the power of success on the countryside! Outwardly
indifferent, inwardly bitter, Lanty turned away. She
would not grace his triumph, if she kept in her room all
day! And when there was a clatter of hoofs on the road
again, Lanty slipped upstairs.

But in a few moments she was summoned. Captain
Lance Wetherby, Assistant Chief of Police of San
Francisco, Deputy Sheriff and ex-United States scout,
had requested to see Miss Foster a few moments alone.
Lanty knew what it meant—her secret had been discovered! But she was not the girl to shirk the responsibility. She lifted her little brown head proudly, and with
the same resolute step with which she had left the house
the night before, descended the stairs and entered the sitting room. At first she saw nothing. Then a remembered
voice struck her ear; she started, looked up, and gasping,
fell back against the door. It was the stranger who had
given her the dagger, the stranger she had met in the

run—the horse thief himself! No! no! She saw it all now—
she had cut loose the wrong man!

He looked at her with a smile of sadness, as he drew
from his breast pocket that dreadful dagger, the very
sight of which Lanty now loathed! "This is the *second*
time, Miss Foster," he said gently, "that I have taken
this knife from Murietta, the Mexican bandit: once
when I disarmed him three weeks ago and he escaped,
and last night when he had again escaped and I recaptured him. After I lost it that night I understood from
you that you had found it and were keeping it for me."
He paused a moment and went on, "I don't ask you
what happened last night. I don't condemn you for it. I
can believe what a girl of your courage and sympathy
might rightly do if her pity were excited. I only ask—
why did you give *him* back that knife *I* trusted you
with?"

"Why? Why did I?" burst out Lanty in a daring gush
of truth, scorn and temper. "*Because I thought you were
that horse thief.* There!"

He drew back astonished, and then suddenly came
that laugh that Lanty remembered and now hailed with
joy. "I believe you, by Jove!" he gasped. "That first night
I wore the disguise in which I have tracked him and
mingled with his gang. Yes! I see it all now—and more.
I see that to *you* I owe his recapture!"

"To me!" echoed the bewildered girl. "How?"

"Why, instead of making for his cave he lingered here
in the confines of the ranch! He thought you were in

love with him because you freed him and gave him his knife, and he stayed to see you!"

But Lanty had her apron to her eyes, whose first tears were filling their velvet depths. And her voice was broken as she said:

"Then he—cared—a good deal more for me—than some people!"

But there is every reason to believe that Lanty was wrong. At least later events that are part of the history of Foster's Ranch and of the Foster family pointed distinctly to the contrary.

How
Santa Claus
Came to
Simpson's
∾ Bar

IT HAD been raining in the valley of the Sacramento. The North Fork had overflowed its banks, and Rattlesnake Creek was impassable. The few boulders that had marked the summer ford at Simpson's Crossing were obliterated by a vast sheet of water stretching to the foothills. The up-stage was stopped at Granger's. The last mail had been abandoned in the tules,[1] the rider swimming for his life. "An area," remarked the *Sierra Avalanche* with pensive local pride, "as large as the State of Massachusetts is now under water."

Nor was the weather any better in the foothills. The mud lay deep on the mountain road. Wagons that neither physical force nor moral objurgation could move from the evil ways into which they had fallen encum-

---

[1] *Tules:* bulrushes which grow abundantly in California and Mexico on overflowed lands.

bered the track; and the way to Simpson's Bar was indicated by broken-down teams and hard swearing. And further on, cut off and inaccessible, rained upon and bedraggled, smitten by high winds and threatened by high water, Simpson's Bar, on the eve of Christmas Day, 1862, clung like a swallow's nest to the rocky entablature and splintered capitals of Table Mountain and shook in the blast.

As night shut down on the settlement a few lights gleamed through the mist from the windows of cabins on either side of the highway, now crossed and gullied by lawless streams and swept by marauding winds. Happily most of the population were gathered at Thompson's store, clustered around a red-hot stove at which they silently spat in some accepted sense of social communion that perhaps rendered conversation unnecessary. Indeed most methods of diversion had long since been exhausted on Simpson's Bar. High water had suspended the regular occupations on gulch and on river, and a consequent lack of money and whiskey had taken the zest from most illegitimate recreation. Even Mr. Hamlin was fain to leave the Bar with fifty dollars in his pocket—the only amount actually realized of the large sums won by him in the successful exercise of his arduous profession.

"Ef I was asked," he remarked somewhat later, "ef I was asked to pint out a purty little village where a retired sport as didn't care for money could exercise hisself frequent and lively, I'd say Simpson's Bar; but for a young man with a large family depending on his exertions, it don't pay." As Mr. Hamlin's family consisted mainly of female adults, this remark is quoted rather to show the breadth of his humor than the exact extent of his responsibilities.

Howbeit, the unconscious objects of this satire sat that evening in the listless apathy begotten of idleness and lack of excitement. Even the sudden splashing of hoofs before the door did not arouse them. Dick Bullen alone paused in the act of scraping out his pipe and lifted his head but no other one of the group indicated any interest in, or recognition of, the man who entered.

It was a figure familiar enough to the company and known in Simpson's Bar as the Old Man. He was a man of perhaps fifty years, grizzled and scant of hair but still fresh and youthful of complexion, his face full of ready but not very powerful sympathy, with a chameleonlike aptitude for taking on the shade and color of contiguous moods and feelings. He had evidently just left some hilarious companions and did not at first notice the gravity of the group, but clapped the shoulder of the nearest man jocularly and threw himself into a vacant chair.

"Jest heard the best thing out, boys! Ye know Smiley over yar—Jim Smiley—funniest man in the Bar? Well, Jim was jest telling the richest yarn about—"

"Smiley's a durned fool," interrupted a gloomy voice.

"A particular low down skunk," added another in sepulchral accents.

A silence followed these positive statements. The Old Man glanced quickly around the group. Then his face slowly changed. "That's so," he said reflectively, after a pause, "certainly a sort of a skunk and suthin' of a fool. In course." He was silent for a moment, as if in painful contemplation of the unsavoriness and folly of the unpopular Smiley. "Dismal weather, ain't it?" he added, now fully embarked on the current of prevailing sentiment. "Mighty rough papers on the boys, and no show for money this season. And tomorrow's Christmas."

There was a movement among the men at this announcement but whether of satisfaction or disgust was not plain. "Yes," continued the Old Man in the lugubrious tone he had within the last few moments unconsciously adopted, "yes, Christmas, and tonight's Christmas Eve. Ye see, boys, I kinder thought—that is, I sorter had an idee, jest passin' like, you know—that maybe ye'd all like to come over to my house tonight and have a sort of tear around. But I suppose, now, you wouldn't? Don't feel like it, maybe?" he added with anxious sympathy, peering into the faces of his companions.

"Well, I don't know," responded Tom Flynn with some cheerfulness. "P'r'aps we may. But how about your wife, Old Man? What does *she* say to it?"

The Old Man hesitated. His conjugal experience had not been a happy one and the fact was known to Simpson's Bar. His first wife, a delicate pretty little woman, had suffered keenly and secretly from the jealous suspi-

cions of her husband, until one day he invited the whole
bar to his house to expose her infidelity. On arriving the
party found the shy petite creature quietly engaged in
her household duties, and retired abashed and discom-
fited. But the sensitive woman did not easily recover
from the shock of this extraordinary outrage. It was with
difficulty she regained her equanimity sufficiently to
release her lover from the closet in which he was concealed, and escape with him. She left a boy of three
years to comfort her bereaved husband. The Old Man's
present wife had been his cook. She was large, loyal and
aggressive.

Before he could reply, Joe Dimmick suggested with
great directness that it was the Old Man's house and
that, invoking the Divine Power, if the case were his
own he would invite whom he pleased, even if in so
doing he imperiled his salvation. The Powers of Evil, he
further remarked, should contend against him vainly.
All this delivered with a terseness and vigor lost in this
necessary translation.

"In course. Certainly. Thet's it," said the Old Man
with a sympathetic frown. "Thar's no trouble about thet.
It's my own house, built every stick on it myself. Don't
you be afeard o' her, boys. She *may* cut up a trifle rough
—ez wimmen do—but she'll come round." Secretly the
Old Man trusted to the exaltation of liquor and the
power of courageous example to sustain him in such an
emergency.

As yet Dick Bullen, the oracle and leader of Simpson's Bar, had not spoken. He now took his pipe from his lips. "Old Man, how's that yer Johnny gettin' on? Seems to me he didn't look so peart last time I seed him on the bluff heavin' rocks at a work gang up the river. Didn't seem to take much interest in it. Maybe now, we'd be in the way ef he wus sick?"

The father, evidently touched by the considerable delicacy of the speaker, hastened to assure him that Johnny was better and that "a little fun might liven him up." Whereupon Dick rose, shook himself, and saying, "I'm ready. Lead the way, Old Man; here goes," himself led the way with a leap and a characteristic howl, and darted out into the night. As he passed through the outer room he caught up a blazing brand from the hearth. The action was repeated by the rest of the party, closely following and elbowing each other, and before the astonished proprietor of Thompson's grocery was aware of the intention of his guests, the room was deserted.

The night was pitch dark. In the first gust of wind their temporary torches were extinguished, and only the red brands dancing and flitting in the gloom like drunken will-o'-the-wisps indicated their whereabouts. Their way led up Pine Tree Canyon, at the head of which a broad, low bark-thatched cabin burrowed in the mountainside. It was the home of the Old Man, and the entrance to the tunnel in which he worked when he worked at all. Here the crowd paused for a moment out

of delicate deference to their host, who came up panting
in the rear.

"P'r'aps ye'd better hold on a second out yer, whilst I
go in and see that things is all right," said the Old Man
with an indifference he was far from feeling. The suggestion was graciously accepted, the door opened and
closed on the host, and the crowd, leaning their backs
against the wall and cowering under the eaves, waited
and listened.

For a few moments there was no sound but the dripping of water from the eaves and the stir and rustle of
the boughs above them. Then the men became uneasy,
and whispered suggestions and suspicions passed from
one to the other. "Reckon she's caved in his head the
first lick!" "Decoyed him inter the tunnel and barred
him up, likely." "Got him down and sittin' on him."
"Prob'ly biling suthin' to heave on us. Stand clear the
door, boys!" For just then the latch clicked, the door
slowly opened, and a voice said, "Come in out o' the
wet."

The voice was neither that of the Old Man nor of his
wife. It was the voice of a small boy, its weak treble
broken by that preternatural hoarseness which only
vagabondage and the habit of premature self-assertion
can give. It was the face of a small boy that looked up
at theirs—a face that might have been pretty and even
refined, but that it was darkened by evil knowledge
from within, and dirt and hard experience from without.

He had a blanket around his shoulders and had evidently just risen from his bed. "Come in," he repeated, "and don't make no noise. The Old Man's in there talking to maw," he continued, pointing to an adjacent room which seemed to be a kitchen, from which the Old Man's voice came in deprecating accents. "Let me be," he added querulously to Dick Bullen, who had caught him up, blanket and all, and was affecting to toss him into the fire. "Let go o' me, you durned old fool, d' ye hear?"

Thus adjured, Dick Bullen lowered Johnny to the ground with a smothered laugh while the men, entering quietly, ranged themselves around a long table of rough boards which occupied the center of the room. Johnny then gravely proceeded to a cupboard and brought out several articles, which he deposited on the table. "Thar's whiskey. And crackers. And red herons. And cheese." He took a bite of the latter on his way to the table. "And sugar." He scooped up a mouthful en route with a small and very dirty hand. "And terbacker. Thar's dried appils too on the shelf, but I don't admire 'em. Appils is swellin'. Thar," he concluded, "now wade in and don't be afeard. *I* don't mind the old woman. She don't b'long to *me*. S'long."

He had stepped to the threshold of a small room scarcely larger than a closet, partitioned off from the main apartment and holding in its dim recess a small bed. He stood there a moment looking at the company, with his bare feet peeping from the blanket, and nodded.

"Hello, Johnny! You ain't goin' to turn in agin, are ye?" said Dick.

"Yes I are," responded Johnny decidedly.

"Why, wot's up, old fellow?"

"I'm sick."

"How sick?"

"I've got a fevier. And childblains. And rheumatiz," returned Johnny, and vanished within. After a moment's pause he added in the dark, apparently from under the bedclothes, "and biles!"

There was an embarrassing silence. The men looked at each other and at the fire. Even with the appetizing banquet before them, it seemed as if they might again fall into the despondency of Thompson's grocery when the voice of the Old Man, incautiously lifted, came deprecatingly from the kitchen.

"Certainly! Thet's so. In course they is. A gang o' lazy drunken loafers, and that ar Dick Bullen's the ornariest of all. Didn't hev no more *sabe* than to come round yer with sickness in the house and no provision. Thet's what I said. 'Bullen,' sez I, 'it's crazy drunk you are, or a fool,' sez I, 'to think o' such a thing.' 'Staples,' I sez, 'be you a man, Staples, and 'spect to raise hell under my roof and invalids lyin' around?' But they would come, they would. Thet's wot you must 'spect o' such trash as lays around the Bar."

A burst of laughter from the men followed this unfortunate exposure. Whether it was overheard in the kitchen or whether the Old Man's irate companion had just then exhausted all other modes of expressing her contemptuous indignation I cannot say, but a back door was suddenly slammed with great violence. A moment later the Old Man reappeared, haply unconscious of the cause of the late hilarious outburst, and smiled blandly.

"The old woman thought she'd jest run over to Mrs. MacFadden's for a sociable call," he explained with jaunty indifference as he took a seat at the board.

Oddly enough it needed this untoward incident to relieve the embarrassment that was beginning to be felt by the party, and their natural audacity returned with their host. I do not propose to record the convivialities of that evening. The inquisitive reader will accept the statement that the conversation was characterized by the same intellectual exaltation, the same cautious reverence, the same fastidious delicacy, the same rhetorical precision, and the same logical and coherent discourse somewhat later in the evening, which distinguish similar gatherings of the masculine sex in more civilized localities and under more favorable auspices. No glasses were broken in the absence of any. No liquor was uselessly spilt on the floor or table in the scarcity of that article.

It was nearly midnight when the festivities were interrupted. "Hush," said Dick Bullen, holding up his hand. It was the querulous voice of Johnny from his adjacent closet, "Oh dad!"

The Old Man arose hurriedly and disappeared in the closet. Presently he reappeared. "His rheumatiz is comin' on agin bad," he explained, "and he wants rubbin'." He lifted the demijohn of whiskey from the table and shook it. It was empty. Dick Bullen put down his tin cup with an embarrassed laugh. So did the others. The Old Man examined their contents and said hopefully, "I reckon that's enough; he don't need much. You hold on all o' you for a spell, and I'll be back." He vanished into the closet with an old flannel shirt and the whiskey. The door closed but imperfectly, and the following dialogue was distinctly audible:

"Now, sonny, whar does she ache worst?"

"Sometimes over yer and sometimes under yer, but it's most powerful from yer to yer. Rub yer, dad."

A silence seemed to indicate a brisk rubbing. Then Johnny:

"Hevin' a good time out yer, dad?"

"Yes, sonny."

"Tomorrer's Chrismiss, ain't it?"

"Yes, sonny. How does she feel now?"

"Better. Rub a little furder down. Wot's Chrismiss, anyway? Wot's it all about?"

"Oh, it's a day."

This exhaustive definition was apparently satisfactory, for there was a silent interval of rubbing. Presently Johnny again:

"Maw sez that everywhere else but yer everybody gives things to everybody Chrismiss, and then she jist waded inter you. She sez thar's a man they call Sandy Claws, not a white man, you know, but a kind o' Chinemin, comes down the chimbley night afore Chrismiss and gives things to chillern, boys like me. Puts 'em in their boots! Thet's what she tried to play on me. Easy, now, pop, whar are you rubbin' to—thet's a mile from the place. She jest made that up, didn't she, jest to aggrewate me and you? Don't rub thar. . . . Why, dad!"

In the great quiet that seemed to have fallen upon the house the sigh of the near pines and the drip of leaves without were very distinct. Johnny's voice, too, was lowered as he went on, "Don't you take on now, for I'm gettin' all right fast. Wot's the boys doin' out thar?"

The Old Man partly opened the door and peered through. His guests were sitting there sociably enough, and there were a few silver coins and a lean buckskin purse on the table. "Bettin' on suthin'—some little game or 'nother. They're all right," he replied to Johnny and recommenced his rubbing.

"I'd like to take a hand and win some money," said Johnny reflectively after a pause.

The Old Man glibly repeated what was evidently a familiar formula, that if Johnny would wait until he struck it rich in the tunnel he'd have lots of money, etc., etc.

"Yes," said Johnny, "but you don't. And whether you strike it or I win it, it's about the same. It's all luck. But it's mighty cur'o's about Chrismiss—ain't it? Why do they call it Chrismiss?"

Perhaps from some instinctive deference to the over-hearing of his guests, or from some vague sense of incon-gruity, the Old Man's reply was so low as to be inaudi-ble beyond the room.

"Yes," said Johnny with some slight abatement of in-terest, "I've heerd o' *him* before. Thar, that'll do, dad. I don't ache near so bad as I did. Now wrap me tight in this yer blanket. So. Now," he added in a muffled whisper, "sit down yer by me till I go asleep." To as-sure himself of obedience, he disengaged one hand from the blanket, and grasping his father's sleeve, again com-posed himself to rest.

For some moments the Old Man waited patiently. Then the unwonted stillness of the house excited his curiosity, and without moving from the bed he cau-tiously opened the door with his disengaged hand and looked into the main room. To his infinite surprise it was dark and deserted. But even then a smoldering log on the hearth broke, and by the upspringing blaze he saw the figure of Dick Bullen sitting by the dying embers.

"Hello!"

Dick started, rose and came somewhat unsteadily to-ward him.

"Whar's the boys?" said the Old Man.

"Gone up the canyon on a little *pasear*. They're comin' back for me in a minit. I'm waitin' around for 'em. What are you starin' at, Old Man?" he added with a forced laugh. "Do you think I'm drunk?"

The Old Man might have been pardoned the supposition, for Dick's eyes were humid and his face flushed. He loitered and lounged back to the chimney, yawned, shook himself, buttoned up his coat and laughed. "Liquor ain't so plenty as that, Old Man. Now don't you git up," he continued, as the Old Man made a movement to release his sleeve from Johnny's hand. "Don't you mind manners. Sit jest whar you be. I'm goin' in a jiffy. Thar, that's them now."

There was a low tap at the door. Dick Bullen opened it quickly, nodded "Good-night" to his host, and disappeared. The Old Man would have followed him but for the hand that still unconsciously grasped his sleeve. He could have easily disengaged it; it was small, weak and emaciated. But perhaps because it *was* small, weak and emaciated he changed his mind, and drawing his chair closer to the bed, rested his head upon it. In this defenseless attitude the potency of his earlier potations surprised him. The room flickered and faded before his eyes, reappeared, faded again, went out, and left him —asleep.

Meantime Dick Bullen, closing the door, confronted his companions. "Are you ready?" said Staples.

"Ready," said Dick. "What's the time?"

"Past twelve," was the reply. "Can you make it? It's nigh on fifty miles, the round trip hither and yon."

"I reckon," returned Dick shortly. "Whar's the mare?"

"Bill and Jack's holdin' her at the crossin'."

"Let 'em hold on a minit longer," said Dick.

He turned and re-entered the house softly. By the light

of the guttering candle and dying fire he saw that the door of the little room was open. He stepped toward it on tiptoe and looked in. The Old Man had fallen back in his chair, snoring, his helpless feet thrust out in a line with his collapsed shoulders, his hat pulled over his eyes. Beside him on a narrow wooden bedstead lay Johnny, muffled tightly in a blanket that hid all save a strip of forehead and a few curls damp with perspiration. Dick Bullen made a step forward, hesitated and glanced over his shoulder into the deserted room. Everything was quiet. With a sudden resolution he parted his huge mustaches with both hands and stooped over the sleeping boy. But even as he did so a mischievous blast lying in wait swooped down the chimney, rekindled the hearth, and lit up the room with a shameless glow from which Dick fled in bashful terror.

His companions were already waiting for him at the crossing. Two of them were struggling in the darkness with some strange misshapen bulk, which as Dick came nearer took the semblance of a great yellow horse.

It was the mare. She was not a pretty picture. From her Roman nose to her rising haunches, from her arched spine hidden by the stiff *machillas* of a Mexican saddle to her thick straight bony legs, there was not a line of equine grace. In her half-blind but wholly vicious white eyes, in her protruding underlip, in her monstrous color, there was nothing but ugliness and vice.

"Now then," said Staples, "stand cl'ar of her heels, boys, and up with you. Don't miss your first holt of her mane, and mind ye get your off stirrup *quick*. Ready!"

There was a leap, a scrambling struggle, a bound, a wild retreat of the crowd, a circle of flying hoofs, two springless leaps that jarred the earth, a rapid play and jingle of spurs, a plunge, and then the voice of Dick somewhere in the darkness. "All right!"

"Don't take the lower road back onless you're hard pushed for time! Don't hold her in down hill. We'll be at the ford at five. G'lang! Hoopa! Mula! GO!"

A splash, a spark struck from the ledge in the road, a clatter in the rocky cut beyond, and Dick was gone.

Sing, O Muse, of the ride of Richard Bullen! Sing, O Muse, of chivalrous men! The sacred quest, the doughty deeds, the battery of low churls, the fearsome ride and gruesome perils of the Flower of Simpson's Bar! Alack! She is dainty, this Muse! She will have none of this bucking brute and swaggering ragged rider, and I must fain follow him in prose, afoot!

It was one o'clock and yet he had only gained Rattle-snake Hill. For in that time Jovita had rehearsed to him all her imperfections and practiced all her vices. Thrice had she stumbled. Twice had she thrown up her Roman nose in a straight line with the reins, and resisting bit and spur, struck out madly across country. Twice had she reared, and rearing, fallen backward; and twice had the agile Dick, unharmed, regained his seat before she found her vicious legs again. And a mile beyond them, at the foot of a long hill, was Rattlesnake Creek. Dick knew that here was the crucial test of his ability to perform his enterprise. He set his teeth grimly, put his knees well into her flanks, and changed his defensive tactics to brisk aggression. Bullied and maddened, Jovita began the descent of the hill. Here the artful Richard pretended to hold her in with ostentatious objurgation and well-feigned cries of alarm. It is unnecessary to add that Jovita instantly ran away. Nor need I state the time made in the descent. It is written in the chronicles of Simpson's Bar. Enough that in another moment, as it seemed to Dick, she was splashing on the overflowed banks of Rattlesnake Creek. As Dick expected, the momentum she had acquired carried her beyond the point of balking, and holding her well together for a mighty leap, they plunged into the middle of the swiftly flowing current. A few moments of kicking, wading and swimming and Dick pulled up on the opposite bank.

The road from Rattlesnake Creek to Red Mountain was tolerably level. Either the plunge in Rattlesnake Creek had dampened her baleful fire or the art which led to it had shown her the superior wickedness of her rider, for Jovita no longer wasted her surplus energy in wanton conceits. Once she bucked, but it was from force of habit; once she shied, but it was from a new freshly painted meetinghouse at the crossing of the county road. Hollows, ditches, gravelly deposits, patches of freshly springing grasses flew from beneath her rattling hoofs. She began to smell unpleasantly, once or twice she coughed slightly, but there was no abatement of her strength or speed. By two o'clock he had passed Red Mountain and begun the descent to the plain. Ten minutes later the driver of the fast Pioneer coach was overtaken and passed by a "man on a Pinto hoss"—an event sufficiently notable for remark. At half past two Dick rose in his stirrups with a great shout. Stars were glittering through the rifted clouds, and beyond him out of the plain rose two spires, a flagstaff and a straggling line of black objects. Dick jingled his spurs and swung his riata. Jovita bounded forward and in another moment they swept into Tuttleville and drew up before the wooden piazza of The Hotel of All Nations.

What transpired that night at Tuttleville is not strictly a part of this record. Briefly I may state, however, that after Jovita had been handed over to a sleepy ostler whom she at once kicked into unpleasant consciousness, Dick sallied out with the barkeeper for a tour of the sleeping town. Lights still gleamed from a few saloons and gambling houses. But avoiding these they stopped before several closed shops, and by persistent tapping and judicious outcry roused the proprietors from their beds and made them unbar the doors of their magazines and expose their wares. Sometimes they were met by curses but oftener by interest and some concern in their needs, and the interview was invariably concluded by a drink. It was three o'clock before this pleasantry was abandoned, and with a small waterproof bag of India rubber strapped on his shoulders, Dick returned to the hotel. But here he was waylaid by Beauty—Beauty opulent in charms, affluent in dress, persuasive in speech, and Spanish in accent! In vain she repeated the invitation in "Excelsior," happily scorned by all Alpine-climbing youth and rejected by this child of the Sierras —a rejection softened in this instance by a laugh and his last gold coin. And then he sprang to the saddle and dashed down the lonely street and out into the lonelier plain, where presently the lights, the black line of houses, the spires and the flagstaff sank into the earth behind him again and were lost in the distance.

The storm had cleared away, the air was brisk and cold, the outlines of adjacent landmarks were distinct, but it was half-past four before Dick reached the meeting-house and the crossing of the county road. To avoid the rising grade he had taken a longer and more circuitous road, in whose viscid mud Jovita sank fetlock-deep at every bound. It was a poor preparation for a steady ascent of five more miles. But Jovita, gathering her legs under her, took it with her usual blind unreasoning fury, and a half hour later reached the long level that led to Rattlesnake Creek. Another half hour would bring him to the creek. He threw the reins lightly upon the mare's neck, chirruped to her, and began to sing.

Suddenly Jovita shied with a bound that would have unseated a less practiced rider. Hanging to her rein was a figure that had leaped from the bank, and at the same time from the road before her arose a shadowy horse and rider.

"Throw up your hands," commanded the second apparition with an oath.

Dick felt the mare tremble, quiver and apparently sink under him. He knew what it meant and was prepared.

"Stand aside, Jack Simpson. I know you, you damned thief! Let me pass, or—"

He did not finish the sentence. Jovita rose straight in the air with a terrific bound, throwing the figure from her bit with a single shake of her vicious head, and charged with deadly malevolence down on the impediment before her. An oath, a pistol shot, and horse and highwayman rolled over in the road; the next moment Jovita was a hundred yards away. But the good right arm of her rider, shattered by a bullet, dropped helplessly at his side.

Without slacking his speed he shifted the reins to his left hand. But a few moments later he was obliged to halt and tighten the saddle girths that had slipped in the onset. This in his crippled condition took some time. He had no fear of pursuit, but looking up he saw that the eastern stars were already paling, and that the distant peaks had lost their ghostly whiteness and now stood out blackly against a lighter sky. Day was upon him. Then completely absorbed in a single idea he forgot the pain of his wound, and mounting again dashed on toward Rattlesnake Creek. But now Jovita's breath came broken by gasps, Dick reeled in his saddle and brighter and brighter grew the sky.

Ride, Richard; run, Jovita; linger, O day!

For the last few rods there was a roaring in his ears.
Was it exhaustion from loss of blood, or what? He was
dazed and giddy as he swept down the hill, and did
not recognize his surroundings. Had he taken the wrong
road, or was this Rattlesnake Creek?

It was. But the brawling creek he had swam a few
hours before had risen more than double its volume,
and now rolled a swift and resistless river between him
and Rattlesnake Hill. For the first time that night
Richard's heart sank within him. The river, the mountain, the quickening east swam before his eyes. He shut
them to recover his self-control. In that brief interval,
by some fantastic mental process the little room at
Simpson's Bar and the figures of the sleeping father and
son rose upon him. He opened his eyes wildly, cast off
his coat, pistol, boots and saddle, bound his precious
pack tightly to his shoulders, grasped the bare flanks of
Jovita with his bared knees, and with a shout dashed
into the yellow water. A cry rose from the opposite
bank as the head of a man and horse struggled for a few
moments against the battling current and then were
swept away amidst uprooted trees and whirling driftwood.

The Old Man started and woke. The fire on the hearth
was dead, the candle in the outer room flickering in its
socket, and somebody was rapping at the door. He

opened it but fell back with a cry before the dripping half-naked figure that reeled against the doorpost.

"Dick?"

"Hush! Is he awake yet?"

"No, but Dick—"

"Dry up, you old fool! Get me some whiskey, *quick!*" The Old Man flew and returned with—an empty bottle! Dick would have sworn, but his strength was not equal to the occasion. He staggered, caught at the handle of the door and motioned to the Old Man.

"Thar's suthin' in my pack yer for Johnny. Take it off. I can't."

The Old Man unstrapped the pack and laid it before the exhausted man.

"Open it, quick."

He did so with trembling fingers. It contained only a few poor toys—cheap and barbaric enough, goodness knows, but bright with paint and tinsel. One of them was broken. Another, I fear, was irretrievably ruined by water and on the third—ah me! there was a cruel spot.

"It don't look like much, that's a fact," said Dick ruefully. "But it's the best we could do. Take 'em, Old Man, and put 'em in his stocking, and tell him—tell him, you know—hold me, Old Man." The Old Man caught at his sinking figure. "Tell him," said Dick with a weak little laugh—"tell him Sandy Claws has come."

And even so, bedraggled, ragged, unshaven and unshorn, with one arm hanging helplessly at his side,

Santa Claus came to Simpson's Bar and fell fainting on the first threshold. The Christmas dawn came slowly after, touching the remoter peaks with the rosy warmth of ineffable love. And it looked so tenderly on Simpson's Bar that the whole mountain, as if caught in a generous action, blushed to the skies.

The
Youngest
Miss
~ Piper

I DO NOT think that any of us who enjoyed
the acquaintance of the Piper girls or the hospitality of
Judge Piper, their father, ever cared for the youngest
sister. Not on account of her extreme youth, for the
eldest Miss Piper confessed to twenty-six, and the youth
of the youngest sister was established solely, I think,
by one big braid down her back. Neither was it because
she was the plainest, for the beauty of the Piper girls
was a recognized general distinction and the youngest
Miss Piper was not entirely devoid of the family charms.
Nor was it from any lack of intelligence, nor from any
defective social quality, for her precocity was astounding, and her good-humored frankness alarming. Neither
do I think it could be said that a slight deafness, which
might impart an embarrassing publicity to any statement

—the reverse of our general feeling—that might be confided by anyone to her private ear, was a sufficient reason, for it was pointed out that she always understood everything that Tom Sparrell told her in his ordinary tone of voice. Briefly, it was very possible that Delaware, the youngest Miss Piper, did not like us.

Yet it was fondly believed by us that the other sisters failed to show that indifference to our existence shown by Miss Delaware, although the heartburnings, misunderstandings, jealousies, hopes and fears, and finally the chivalrous resignation with which we at last accepted the long foregone conclusion that they were not for us and far beyond our reach, is not a part of this veracious chronicle. Enough that none of the flirtations of her elder sisters affected or were shared by the youngest Miss Piper. She moved in this heartbreaking atmosphere with sublime indifference, treating her sisters' affairs with what we considered rank simplicity or appalling frankness. Their few admirers who were weak enough to attempt to gain her mediation or confidence had reason to regret it.

"It's no kind o' use givin' me goodies," she said to a helpless suitor of Louisiana Piper's who had offered to bring her some sweets, "for I ain't got no influence with Lu, and if I don't give 'em up to her when she hears of it, she'll nag me and hate you like pizen. Unless," she added thoughtfully, "it was wintergreen lozenges; Lu can't stand them, or anybody who eats them within a mile." It is needless to add that the miserable man, thus put upon his gallantry, was obliged in honor to provide Del with the wintergreen lozenges that kept him in disfavor and at a distance. Unfortunately, too, any predilection or pity for any particular suitor of her sister's was attended by even more disastrous consequences. It was reported that while acting as "gooseberry"—a role usually assigned to her—between Virginia Piper and an exceptionally timid young surveyor during a ramble, she conceived a rare sentiment of humanity toward the unhappy man. After once or twice lingering behind in the ostentatious picking of a wayside flower or "running on ahead" to look at a mountain view without any apparent effect on the shy and speechless youth, she decoyed him aside while her elder sister rambled indifferently and somewhat scornfully on. The youngest Miss Piper leaped upon the rail of a fence and with the stalk of a thimbleberry in her mouth swung her small feet to and fro and surveyed him dispassionately.

"Ye don't seem to be ketchin' on?" she said tentatively.

The young man smiled feebly and interrogatively.

"Don't seem to be either follering suit nor trumpin'," continued Del bluntly.

"I suppose so—that is, I fear that Miss Virginia"—he stammered.

"Speak up! I'm a little deaf. Say it again!" said Del, screwing up her eyes and eyebrows.

The young man was obliged to admit in stentorian tones that his progress had been scarcely satisfactory.

"You're goin' on too slow—that's it," said Del criti-

cally. "Why, when Captain Savage meandered along
here with Jinny last week, afore we got as far as this
he'd reeled off a heap of Byron and Jamieson [Tenny-
son] and sich. And only yesterday Jinny and Doctor
Beveridge was blowin' thistletops to know which was
a flirt all along the trail past the crossroads. Why, ye
ain't picked ez much as a single berry for Jinny, let alone
lad's love or Johnny-jump-ups and kiss-me's, and ye
keep talkin' across me, you two, till I'm tired. Now look
here," she burst out with sudden decision, "Jinny's
gone on ahead in a kind o' huff; but I reckon she's done
that afore too, and you'll find her, jest as Spinner did,
on the rise of the hill sittin' on a pine stump and lookin'
like this." (Here the youngest Miss Piper locked her fingers over her left knee and drew it slightly up—with a
sublime indifference to the exposure of considerable
small-ankled red stocking—and with a far-off, plaintive
stare achieved a colorable imitation of her elder sister's
probable attitude.) "Then you jest go up softly, like as
you was a bear, and clap your hands on her eyes and say
in a disguised voice like this" (here Del turned on a
high falsetto beyond any masculine compass), " 'Who's
who?' Jest like in forfeits."

"But she'll be sure to know me," said the surveyor
timidly.

"She won't," said Del in scornful skepticism.

"I hardly think," stammered the young man with an
awkward smile, "that I—in fact—she'll discover me—before I can get beside her."

"Not if you go softly, for she'll be sittin' back to the road, so—gazin' away, so"—the youngest Miss Piper again stared dreamily in the distance—"and you'll creep up just behind, like this."

"But won't she be angry? I haven't known her long—that is—don't you see?" He stopped embarrassedly.

"Can't hear a word you say," said Del, shaking her head decisively. "You've got my deaf ear. Speak louder or come closer."

But here the instruction suddenly ended, once and for all time! For whether the young man was seriously anxious to perfect himself, whether he was truly grateful to the young girl and tried to show it, whether he was emboldened by the childish appeal of the long brown distinguishing braid down her back, or whether he suddenly found something peculiarly provocative in the reddish-brown eyes between their thickset hedge of lashes, and the trim figure and piquant pose, or whether he was seized with that hysteric desperation which sometimes attacks timidly itself, I cannot say! Enough that he suddenly put his arm around her waist and his lips to her soft satin cheek, peppered and salted as it was by sun-freckles and mountain air, and received a sound box on the ear for his pains. The incident was closed. He did not repeat the experiment on either sister. The disclosure of his rebuff seemed, however, to give a singular satisfaction to Red Gulch.

While it may be gathered from this that the youngest Miss Piper was impervious to general masculine ad-

vances, it was not until later that Red Gulch was thrown
into skeptical astonishment by the rumors that all this
time she really had a lover! Allusion has been made to
the charge that her deafness did not prevent her from
perfectly understanding the ordinary tone of voice of a
certain Mr. Thomas Sparrell.

No undue significance was attached to this fact
through the very insignificance and impossibility of that
individual, a lanky, red-haired youth incapacitated for
manual labor through lameness, a clerk in a general
store at the crossroads! He had never been the recipient
of Judge Piper's hospitality; he had never visited the
house even with parcels; apparently his only interviews
with her or any of the family had been over the counter.
To do him justice he certainly had never seemed to seek
any nearer acquaintance. He was not at the church
door when her sisters, beautiful in their Sunday gowns,
filed into the aisle with little Delaware bringing up the
rear. He was not at the Democratic barbecue that we
attended without reference to our personal politics and
solely for the sake of Judge Piper and the girls, nor did
he go to the Agricultural Fair Ball—open to all. His ab-
stention we believed to be owing to his lameness, to a
wholesome consciousness of his own social defects, or
an inordinate passion for reading cheap scientific text-
books which did not, however, add fluency or conviction to his speech. Neither had he the abstraction of a
student, for his accounts were kept with an accuracy
which struck us, who dealt at the store, as ignobly prac-

tical and even malignant. Possibly we might have expressed this opinion more strongly but for a certain rude vigor of repartee which he possessed, and a suggestion that he might have a temper on occasion. "Them red-haired chaps is like to be tetchy and to kinder see blood through their eyelashes," had been suggested by an observing customer.

In short, little as we knew of the youngest Miss Piper, Thomas Sparrell was the last man we would have expected her to select as an admirer. What we did know of their public relations, purely commercial ones, implied the reverse of any cordial understanding. The provisioning of the Piper household was entrusted to Del along with other practical, not ornamental, odds and ends of housekeeping, and the following is said to be a truthful record of one of their overheard interviews at the store:

The youngest Miss Piper, entering, displacing a quantity of goods in the center to make a sideways seat for herself, and looking around loftily as she takes a memorandum book and pencil from her pocket.

"Ahem! If I ain't taking you away from your studies, Mr. Sparrell, maybe you'll be good enough to look here a minit. But" (in affected politeness) "if I'm disturbing you I can come another time."

Sparrell, placing the book he had been reading carefully under the counter and advancing to Miss Delaware, completely ignoring her irony: "What can we do for you today, Miss Piper?"

Miss Delaware with great suavity of manner examining her memorandum book: "I suppose it wouldn't be shocking your delicate feelings too much to inform you that the canned lobster and oysters you sent us yesterday wasn't fit for hogs?"

Sparrell (blandly): "They weren't intended for them, Miss Piper. If we had known you were having company over from Red Gulch to dinner we might have provided something more suitable for them. We have a fair quality of oil cake and corncobs in stock at reduced figures. But the canned provisions were for your own family."

Miss Delaware (secretly pleased at this sarcastic allusion to her sister's friends, but concealing her delight): "I admire to hear you talk that way, Mr. Sparrell; it's better than minstrels or a circus. I suppose you get it outer that book," indicating the concealed volume. "What do you call it?"

Sparrell (politely): *The First Principles of Geology.*

Miss Delaware, leaning sideways and curling her little finger around her pink ear: "Did you say the first principles of 'geology' or 'grocery'? You know I am so deaf; but of course it couldn't be that."

Sparrell (easily): "Oh, no, you seem to have that in your hand"—pointing to Miss Delaware's memorandum book. "You were quoting from it when you came in."

Miss Delaware, after an affected silence of deep resignation: "Well! it's too bad folks can't just spend their lives listenin' to such elegant talk. I'd admire to do nothing else! But there's my family up at Cottonwood—

and they must eat. They're that low that they expect me to waste my time getting food for 'em here, instead of drinking in the *First Principles of the Grocery.*"

"Geology," suggested Sparrell blandly. "The history of rock formation."

"Geology," accepted Miss Delaware apologetically, "the history of rocks, which is so necessary for knowing just how much sand you can put in the sugar. So I reckon I'll leave my list here and you can have the things toted to Cottonwood when you've got through with your *First Principles.*"

She tore out a list of her commissions from a page of her memorandum book, leaped lightly from the counter, threw her brown braid from her left shoulder to its proper place down her back, shook out her skirts deliberately, and saying, "Thank you for a most improvin' afternoon, Mr. Sparrell," sailed demurely out of the store.

A few auditors of this narrative thought it inconsistent that a daughter of Judge Piper and a sister of the angelic host should put up with a mere clerk's familiarity, but it was pointed out that "she gave him as good as he sent," and the story was generally credited. But certainly no one ever dreamed that it pointed to any more precious confidences between them.

I think the secret burst upon the family, with other things, at the big picnic at Reservoir Canyon. This festivity had been arranged for weeks previously and was undertaken chiefly by the Red Gulch contingent,

as we were called, as a slight return to the Piper family
for their frequent hospitality. The Piper sisters were expected to bring nothing but their own personal graces
and attend to the ministration of such viands and deli-
cacies as the boys had profusely supplied.

The site selected was Reservoir Canyon, a beautiful
triangular valley with very steep sides, one of which
was crowned by the immense reservoir of the Pioneer
Ditch Company. The sheer flanks of the canyon descended in furrowed lines of vines and clinging bushes,
like folds of falling skirts, until they broke again into
flounces of spangled shrubbery over a broad level carpet
of monkshood, mariposas, lupines, poppies and daisies.
Tempered and secluded from the sun's rays by its lofty
shadows, the delicious obscurity of the canyon was in
sharp contrast to the fiery mountain trail that in the
full glare of the noonday sky made its tortuous way
down the hillside like a stream of lava, to plunge suddenly into the valley and extinguish itself in its coolness
as in a lake. The heavy odors of wild honeysuckle,
syringa and ceanothus that hung over it were lightened
and freshened by the sharp spicing of pine and bay. The
mountain breeze which sometimes shook the serrated
tops of the large redwoods above with a chill from the
remote snow peaks even in the heart of summer, never
reached the little valley.

It seemed an ideal place for a picnic. Everybody was
therefore astonished to hear that an objection was sud-

denly raised to this perfect site. They were still more
astonished to know that the objector was the youngest
Miss Piper! Pressed to give her reasons she had replied
that the locality was dangerous; that the reservoir
placed upon the mountain, notoriously old and worn
out, had been rendered more unsafe by false economy
in unskillful and hasty repairs to satisfy speculating
stockbrokers, and that it had lately shown signs of leak-
age and sapping of its outer walls; that in the event of
an outbreak, the little triangular valley from which
there was no outlet would be instantly flooded. Asked
still more pressingly to give her authority for these details, she at first hesitated, and then gave the name of
Tom Sparrell.

The derision with which this statement was received
by us all, as the opinion of a sedentary clerk, was quite
natural and obvious, but not the anger which it excited
in the breast of Judge Piper. It was not generally known
that the judge was the holder of a considerable number
of shares in the Pioneer Ditch Company, and that large
dividends had been lately kept up by a false economy of
expenditure to expedite a sharp deal in the stock, by
which the judge and others could sell out of a failing
company. Rather, it was believed that the judge's anger
was due only to the discovery of Sparrell's influence over
his daughter and his interference with the social affairs
of Cottonwood. It was said that there was a sharp scene
between the youngest Miss Piper and the combined

forces of the judge and the elder sisters, which ended in the former's resolute refusal to attend the picnic at all if that site was selected.

As Delaware was known to be fearless even to the point of recklessness, and fond of gaiety, her refusal only intensified the belief that she was merely "stickin' up for Sparrell's judgment" without any reference to her own personal safety or that of her sisters. The warning was laughed away, the opinion of Sparrell treated with ridicule as the dyspeptic and envious expression of an impractical man. It was pointed out that the reservoir had lasted a long time even in its alleged ruinous state. Only a miracle of coincidence could make it break down that particular afternoon of the picnic. Even if it did happen, there was no direct proof that it would seriously flood the valley, or add more than a spice of excitement to the affair. The Red Gulch contingent, who *would* be there, was quite as capable of taking care of the ladies in case of any accident as any lame crank who wouldn't, but could only croak a warning to them from a distance. A few even wished something might happen that they might have an opportunity of showing their superior devotion. Indeed, the prospect of carrying the half-submerged sisters, in a condition of helpless loveliness, in their arms to a place of safety was a fascinating possibility. The warning was conspicuously ineffective. Everybody looked eagerly forward to the day and the unchanged locality. To the greatest hopefulness and anticipation was added the stirring of defiance, and when at last the appointed hour had arrived, the picnic party passed down the twisting mountain trail through the heat and glare in a fever of enthusiasm.

It was a pretty sight to view this sparkling procession —the girls cool and radiant in their white, blue and yellow muslins and flying ribbons, the contingent in its cleanest ducks and blue and red flannel shirts, the judge white-waistcoated and Panama-hatted, with a new dignity borrowed from the previous circumstances, and three or four impressive Chinese bringing up the rear with hampers—as it at last debouched into Reservoir Canyon.

Here they dispersed themselves over the limited area, scarcely half an acre, with the freedom of escaped school children. They were secure in their woodland privacy. They were overlooked by no high road and its passing teams; they were safe from accidental intrusion from the settlement; indeed, they went so far as to effect the exclusiveness of cliques. At first they amused themselves by casting humorously defiant eyes at the long low Ditch Reservoir, which peeped over the green wall of the ridge, six hundred feet above them; at times they even simulated an exaggerated terror of it, and one recognized humorist declaimed a grotesque appeal to its forbearance, with delightful local allusions. Others pretended to discover near a woodman's hut, among the belt of pines at the top of the descending trail, the peeping figure of the ridiculous and envious Sparrell. But all this was presently forgotten in the actual fes-

tivity. Small as was the range of the valley, it still allowed retreats during the dances for waiting couples
among the convenient laurel and manzanita bushes
which flounced the mountainside. After the dancing,
old-fashioned children's games were revived with great
laughter and halfhearted and coy protests from the
ladies; notably one pastime known as "I'm a-pinin'," in
which ingenious performance the victim was obliged
to stand in the center of a circle and publicly "pine"
for a member of the opposite sex. Some hilarity was occasioned by the mischievous Miss Georgy Piper declar-
ing when it came to her turn, that she was "pinin'" for
a look at the face of Tom Sparrell just now!

In this local trifling two hours passed, until the
party sat down to the long-looked-for repast. It was
here that the health of Judge Piper was neatly proposed
by the editor of the *Argus*. The judge responded with
great dignity and some emotion. He reminded them that
it had been his humble endeavor to promote harmony
—that harmony so characteristic of American principles
—in social as he had in political circles, and particularly
among the strangely constituted yet purely American
elements of frontier life. He accepted the present festivity with its overflowing hospitalities, not in recognition of himself—("yes! yes!")—nor of his family—(enthusiastic protests)—but of that American principle! If
at one time it seemed probable that these festivities
might be marred by the machinations of envy—(groans)
—or that harmony interrupted by the importation of

low-toned material interests—(groans)—he could say that, looking around him, he had never before felt—er—that— Here the judge stopped short, reeled slightly forward, caught at a campstool, recovered himself with an apologetic smile, and turned inquiringly to his neighbor.

A light laugh, instantly suppressed, at what was at first supposed to be the effect of the "overflowing hospitality" upon the speaker himself, went around the male circle until it suddenly appeared that half a dozen others had started to their feet at the same time with white faces, and that one of the ladies had screamed.

"What is it?" everybody was asking with interrogatory smiles.

It was Judge Piper who replied.

"A little shock of earthquake," he said blandly, "a mere thrill! I think," he added with a faint smile, "we may say that Nature herself has applauded our efforts in good old Californian fashion and signified her assent. What are you saying, Fludder?"

"I was thinking, sir," said Fludder deferentially, in a lower voice, "that if anything was wrong in the reservoir, this shock, you know, might"—

He was interrupted by a faint crashing and crackling sound, and looking up beheld a good-sized boulder, evidently detached from some greater height, strike the upland plateau at the left of the trail and bound into the fringe of forest beside it. A slight cloud of dust marked its course and then lazily floated away in mid-air. But it had been watched agitatedly, and it was evident that

that singular loss of nervous balance which is apt to affect all those who go through the slightest earthquake experience was felt by all. But some sense of humor however, remained.

"Looks as if the water risks we took ain't goin' to cover earthquakes," drawled Dick Frisney. "Still that wasn't a bad shot if we only knew what they were aimin' at."

"Do be quiet," said Virginia Piper, her cheeks pink with excitement. "Listen, can't you? What's that funny murmuring you hear now and then up there?"

"It's only the snow wind playin' with the pines on the summit. You girls won't allow anybody any fun but yourselves."

But here a scream from Georgy who, assisted by Captain Fairfax, had mounted a campstool at the mouth of the valley, attracted everybody's attention. She was standing upright with dilated eyes, staring a the top of the trail. "Look!" she said excitedly, "if the trail isn't moving!"

Everybody faced in that direction. At the first glance it seemed indeed as if the trail was actually moving, wriggling and undulating its tortuous way down the mountain like a huge snake swollen to twice its usual size. But the second glance showed it to be no longer a trail but a channel of water whose stream, lifted in a borelike wall four or five feet high, was plunging down into the valley.

For an instant they were unable to comprehend even the nature of the catastrophe. The reservoir was directly over their heads. The bursting of its wall they had imagined would naturally bring down the water in a dozen trickling streams or falls over the cliff above them and along the flanks of the mountain. But that its suddenly liberated volume should overflow the upland beyond and then descend in a pent-up flood by their own trail and their only avenue of escape had been beyond their wildest fancy.

They met this smiting truth with that characteristic short laugh with which the American usually receives the blow of Fate or the unexpected—as if he recognized only the absurdity of the situation. Then they ran to the women, collected them together, and dragged them to vantages of fancied security among the bushes which flounced the long skirts of the mountain walls. But I leave this part of the description to the characteristic language of one of the party:

"When the flood struck us, it didn't seem to take any stock of us in particular, but laid itself out to go for that picnic for all it was worth! It wiped it off the face of the earth in about twenty-five seconds! It first made a clean break from stem to stern, carryin' everything along with it. The first thing I saw was old Jedge Piper, puttin' on his best licks to get away from a big can of strawberry ice cream that was trundlin' after him and tryin' to empty itself on his collar whenever a bigger wave lifted it. He was followed by what was left of the brass band, the big drum just humpin' itself to keep abreast o' the ice cream and mixed up with campstools, music stands, a few Chinese, and then what they call in them big San Francisco processions 'citizens generally.' The hull thing swept up the canyon inside o' thirty seconds. Then what Captain Fairfax called 'the reflex action in the laws o' motion' happened, and durned if the hull blamed procession didn't sweep back again—this time all the heavy artillery, such as camp kettles, lager beer kegs, bottles, glasses and crockery that was left behind takin' the lead now, and Jedge Piper and that ice cream can bringin' up the rear. As the jedge passed us the second time we noticed that that ice cream can— hevin' swallowed water—was kinder losin' its wind, and we encouraged the old man by shoutin' out, 'Five to one on him!' And then, you wouldn't believe what followed. Why durn my skin, when that 'reflex' met the current at the other end, it just swirled around again in what Captain Fairfax called the 'centrifugal curve,' and just went round and round the canyon like ez when yer washin' the dirt out o' a prospectin' pan—every now and then washin' some one of the boys that was in it, like scum, up agin the banks.

"We managed in this way to snake out the jedge jest ez he was sailin' round on the home stretch, passin' the quarter post two lengths ahead o' the can. A good deal o' the ice cream had washed away, but it took us ten minutes to shake the cracked ice and powdered salt out o' the old man's clothes and warm him up again in the laurel bush where he was clingin'. This sort o' 'here we go round the mulberry bush' kep' on until most o' the humans was got out and only the furniture o' the picnic was left in the race. Then it got kinder mixed up and went sloshin' round here and there, ez the water kep' comin' down by the trail. Then Lulu Piper, what I was holdin' up all the time in a laurel bush, gets an idea for all she was wet and draggled, and ez the things went bobbin' round she calls out the figures o' a cotillon to 'em. 'Two campstools forward.' 'Sashay and back to your places.' 'Change partners.' 'Hands all round.'

"She was clear grit, you bet! And the joke caught on and the other girls jined in and it kinder cheered 'em, for they was wantin' it. Then Fludder allowed to pacify 'em by sayin' he just figured up the size o' the reservoir and the size o' the canyon, and he kalkilated that the cube was about ekal and the canyon couldn't flood any more. And then Lulu—who was peart as a jay and couldn't be fooled—speaks up and says, 'What's the matter with the ditch, Dick?'

"Lord! Then we knew that she knew the worst, for of course all the water in the ditch itself—fifty miles of it!—was drainin' now into that reservoir and was bound to come down to the canyon."

It was at this point that the situation became really desperate, for they had now crawled up the steep sides as far as the bushes afforded foothold, and the water was still rising. The chatter of the girls ceased, there were long silences in which the men discussed the wildest plans and proposed to tear their shirts into strips to make ropes to support the girls by sticks driven into the

mountainside. It was in one of those intervals that the
distinct strokes of a woodman's ax were heard high on
the upland at the point where the trail descended to
the canyon. Every ear was alert, but only those on one
side of the canyon could get a fair view of the spot.
This was the good fortune of Captain Fairfax and
Georgy Piper, who had climbed to the highest bush on
that side and were now standing up, gazing excitedly
in that direction.

"Someone is cutting down a tree at the head of the
trail," shouted Fairfax. The response and joyful explanation, "for a dam across the trail," was on everybody's lips at the same time.

But the strokes of the ax were slow and painfully intermittent. Impatience burst out.

"Yell to him to hurry up! Why haven't they brought
two men?"

"It's only one man," shouted the captain, "and he
seems to be a cripple. By Jiminy!—it is—yes!—it's Tom
Sparrell!"

There was a dead silence. Then, I grieve to say,
shame and its twin brother rage took possession of their
weak humanity. Oh, yes! It was all of a piece! Why in
the name of Folly hadn't he sent for an able-bodied
man? Were they to be drowned through his cranky ob-
stinacy?

The blows still went on slowly. Presently, however,
they seemed to alternate with other blows—but alas!
they were slower and if possible feebler!

"Have they got another cripple to work?" roared the contingent in one furious voice.

"No—it's a woman—a little one—yes! a girl. Hello! Why, sure as you live, it's Delaware!"

A spontaneous cheer burst from the contingent, partly as a rebuke to Sparrell, I think, partly from some shame over their previous rage. He could take it as he liked.

Still the blows went on distressingly slow. The girls were hoisted on the men's shoulders; the men were half submerged. There was a painful pause, then a crumbling crash. Another cheer went up from the canyon.

"It's down! straight across the trail," shouted Fairfax, "and a part of the bank on the top of it."

There was another moment of suspense. Would it hold or be carried away by the momentum of the flood? It held! In a few moments Fairfax again gave voice to the cheering news that the flow had stopped and the submerged trail was reappearing. In twenty minutes it was clear—a muddy river bed, but possible of ascent! Of course there was no diminution of the water in the canyon, which had no outlet, but it now was possible for the party to swing from bush to bush along the mountainside until the foot of the trail—no longer an opposing one—was reached. There were some missteps and mishaps, flounderings in the water, and some dangerous rescues, but in half an hour the whole concourse stood upon the trail and commenced the ascent. It was a slow, difficult and lugubrious procession—I fear not the best-tempered one, now that the stimulus of danger

and chivalry was past. When they reached the dam
made by the fallen tree, although they were obliged to
make a long detour to avoid its steep sides, they could
see how successfully it had diverted the current to a
declivity on the other side.

But strangely enough they were greeted by nothing
else! Sparrell and the youngest Miss Piper were gone,
and when they at last reached the high road they were
astounded to hear from a passing teamster that no one
in the settlement knew anything of the disaster!

This was the last drop in their cup of bitterness! They
who had expected that the settlement was waiting
breathlessly for their rescue, who anticipated that they
would be welcomed as heroes, were obliged to meet the
ill-concealed amusement of passengers and friends at
their disheveled and bedraggled appearance, which
suggested only the blundering mishaps of an ordinary
summer outing! "Boatin' in the reservoir and fell in?"
"Playing at canal boat in the ditch?" were some of the
cheerful hypotheses. The fleeting sense of gratitude
they had felt for their deliverers was dissipated by the
time they had reached their homes, and their rancor increased with the information that when the earthquake occurred Mr. Tom Sparrell and Miss Delaware
were enjoying a *pasear* in the forest—he having a half
holiday by virtue of the festival—and that the earthquake had revived his fears of a catastrophe. The two
had procured axes in the woodman's hut and did what

they thought was necessary to relieve the situation of
the picnickers. But the very modesty of this account of
their own performance had the effect of belittling the
catastrophe itself, and the picnickers' report of their exceeding peril was received with incredulous laughter.

For the first time in the history of Red Gulch there
was a serious division between the Piper family, supported by the contingent and the rest of the settlement.
Tom Sparrell's warning was remembered by the latter
and the ingratitude of the picknickers to their rescuers
commented upon. The actual calamity to the reservoir
was more or less attributed to the imprudent and reckless contiguity of the revelers on that day, and there
were not wanting those who referred the accident itself
to the machinations of the scheming Ditch Director
Piper!

It was said that there was a stormy scene in the
Piper household that evening. The judge had demanded
that Delaware should break off her acquaintance with
Sparrell and she had refused; the judge had demanded
of Sparrell's employer that he should discharge him and
had been met with the astounding information that
Sparrell was already a silent partner in the concern. At
this revelation Judge Piper was alarmed. While he
might object to a clerk who could not support a wife, as
a consistent Democrat he could not oppose a fairly
prosperous tradesman. A final appeal was made to Delaware. She was implored to consider the situation of her

sisters who had all made more ambitious marriages or were about to make them. Why should she now degrade the family by marrying a country storekeeper?

It was said that here the youngest Miss Piper made a memorable reply, and a revelation the truth of which was never gainsaid:

"You all wanter know why I'm going to marry Tom Sparrell?" she queried, standing up and facing the whole family circle.

"Yes."

"Why I prefer him to the hull caboodle that you girls have married or are going to marry?" she continued, meditatively biting the end of her braid.

"Yes."

"Well, he's the only man of the whole lot that hasn't proposed to me first."

It is presumed that Sparrell made good the omission, or that the family were glad to get rid of her, for they were married that autumn. And really a later comparison of the family records shows that while Captain Fairfax remained "Captain Fairfax," and the other sons-in-law did not advance proportionately in standing or riches, the lame storekeeper of Red Gulch became the Honorable Senator Tom Sparrell.

A
Yellow
❧ Dog

I NEVER knew why in the Western states of America a yellow dog should be proverbially considered the acme of canine degradation and incompetency, nor why the possession of one should seriously affect the social standing of its possessor. But the fact being established, I think we accepted it at Rattlers Ridge without question. The matter of ownership was more difficult to settle, and although the dog I have in my mind at the present writing attached himself impartially and equally to every one in camp, no one ventured to exclusively claim him; while after the perpetration of any canine atrocity, everybody repudiated him with indecent haste.

"Well, I can swear he hasn't been near our shanty for weeks," or the retort, "He was last seen comin' out of *your* cabin," expressed the eagerness with which Rattlers Ridge washed its hands of any responsibility. Yet he was by no means a common dog or even an unhandsome dog, and it was a singular fact that his severest critics vied with each other in narrating instances of his sagacity, insight and agility which they themselves had witnessed.

He had been seen crossing the flume that spanned Grizzly Canyon, at a height of nine hundred feet, on a plank six inches wide. He had tumbled down the shoot to the South Fork a thousand feet below, and was found sitting on the riverbank "without a scratch, 'cept th' one he was lazily givin' himself with his off hind paw." He had been forgotten in a snowdrift on a Sierran shelf and had come home in the early spring with the conceited complacency of an Alpine traveler and a plumpness alleged to have been the result of an exclusive diet of buried mail bags and their contents. He was generally believed to read the advance election posters and disappear a day or two before the candidates and the brass band, which he hated, came to the Ridge. He was suspected of having overlooked Colonel Johnson's hand at poker and of having conveyed to the Colonel's adversary, by a succession of barks, the danger of betting against four kings.

While these statements were supplied by wholly unsupported witnesses it was a very human weakness of Rattlers Ridge that the responsibility of corroboration was passed to the dog *himself*, and *he* was looked upon as a consummate liar.

"Snoopin' round yer and callin' yourself a poker

sharp, are ye! Scoot, you yaller pizin!" was a common ad-
juration whenever the unfortunate animal intruded
upon a card party. "Ef thar was a spark, an *atom* of
truth in *that dog,* I'd believe my own eyes that I saw
him sittin' up and tryin' to magnetize a jaybird off a
tree. But wot are ye goin' to do with a yaller equivo-
cator like that?"

I have said that he was yellow—or to use the ordinary
expression, "yaller." Indeed I am inclined to believe
that much of the ignominy attached to the epithet lay
in this favorite pronunciation. Men who habitually spoke
of a *"yellow* bird," a *"yellow* hammer," a *"yellow* leaf"
always alluded to him as a *"yaller* dog."

He certainly *was* yellow. After a bath—usually compulsory—he presented a decided gamboge streak down
his back from the top of his forehead to the stump of his
tail, fading in his sides and flank to a delicate straw
color. His breast, legs and feet—when not reddened by
slumgullion, in which he was fond of wading—were
white. A few attempts at ornamental decoration from
the India inkpot of the storekeeper failed, partly through
the yellow dog's excessive agility which would never
give the paint time to dry on him, and partly through
his success in transferring his markings to the trousers
and blankets of the camp.

The size and shape of his tail that had been cut off
before his introduction to Rattlers Ridge, were favorite
sources of speculation to the miners, both as deter-
mining his breed and his moral responsibility in com-

ing into camp in that defective condition. There was a general opinion that he couldn't have looked worse with a tail, and its removal was therefore a gratuitous effrontery.

His best feature was his eyes, which were a lustrous Vandyke brown, and sparkling with intelligence. But here again he suffered from evolution through environment, and their original trustful openness was marred by the experience of watching for flying stones, sods and passing kicks from the rear, so that the pupils were continually reverting to the outer angle of the eyelid.

Nevertheless none of these characteristics decided the vexed question of his *breed*. His speed and scent pointed to a hound, and it is related that on one occasion he was laid on the trail of a wildcat with such success that he followed it apparently out of the state, returning at the end of two weeks, footsore but blandly contented.

Attaching himself to a prospecting party, he was sent under the same belief into the brush to drive off a bear who was supposed to be haunting the campfire. He returned in a few minutes *with* the bear, driving it into the unarmed circle and scattering the whole party. After this the theory of his being a hunting dog was abandoned. Yet it was said—on the usual uncorroborated evidence—that he had put up a quail, and his qualities as a retriever were for a long time accepted until, during a shooting expedition for wild ducks, it was discovered that the one he had brought back had never been *shot*, and the party was obliged to compound damages with an adjacent settler.

His fondness for paddling in the ditches and slumgullion at one time suggested a water spaniel. He could swim, and would occasionally bring out of the river sticks and pieces of bark that had been thrown in, but as *he* always had to be thrown in with them, and he was a good-sized dog, his aquatic reputation faded also. He remained simply "a yaller dog." What more could be said? His actual name was Bones—given to him, no doubt, through the provincial custom of confounding the occupation of the individual with his quality, for which it was pointed out precedent could be found in some old English family names.

But if Bones generally exhibited no preference for any particular individual in camp, he always made an exception in favor of drunkards. Even an ordinary roistering bacchanalian party brought him out from under a tree or a shed in the keenest satisfaction. He would accompany them through the long straggling street of the settlement, barking his delight at every step or misstep of the revelers, and exhibiting none of that mistrust of eye which marked his attendance upon the sane and the respectable. He accepted even their uncouth play without a snarl or a yelp, hypocritically pretending even to like it, and I conscientiously believe would have allowed a tin can to be attached to his tail if the hand that tied it on were only unsteady, and the voice that bade him "lie still" were husky with liquor. He would

see the party cheerfully into a saloon, wait outside
the door—his tongue fairly lolling from his mouth in enjoyment—until they reappeared, permit them even to
tumble over him with pleasure and then gambol away
before them, heedless of awkwardly projected stones
and epithets. He would afterward accompany them
separately home, or lie with them at crossroads until
they were assisted to their cabins. Then he would trot
rakishly to his own haunt by the saloon stove with the
slightly conscious air of having been a bad dog, yet of
having had a good time.

We never could satisfy ourselves whether his enjoyment arose from some merely selfish conviction that he
was more secure with the physically and mentally in-
competent, from some active sympathy with active
wickedness, or from a grim sense of his own mental
superiority at such moments. But the general belief
leaned toward his kindred sympathy as a "yaller dog"
with all that was disreputable. And this was supported
by another very singular canine manifestation—the "sincere flattery" of simulation or imitation.

Uncle Billy Riley for a short time enjoyed the position of being the camp drunkard, and at once became
an object of Bones' greatest solicitude. He not only accompanied him everywhere, curled at his feet or head
according to Uncle Billy's attitude at the moment but,
it was noticed, began presently to undergo a singular
alteration in his own habits and appearance. From being

an active tireless scout and forager, a bold and unovertakable marauder, he became lazy and apathetic, allowed gophers to burrow under him without endeavoring to undermine the settlement in his frantic endeavors to dig them out, permitted squirrels to flash their tails at him a hundred yards away, forgot his usual caches, and left his favorite bones unburied and bleaching in the sun. His eyes grew dull, his coat lusterless in proportion as his companion became blear-eyed and ragged; in running, his usual arrowlike directness began to deviate, and it was not unusual to meet the pair together, zigzagging up the hill. Indeed Uncle Billy's condition could be predetermined by Bones' appearance at times when his temporary master was invisible. "The old man must have an awful jag on today," was casually remarked when an extra fluffiness and imbecility was noticeable in the passing Bones. At first it was believed that he drank also, but when careful investigation proved this hypothesis untenable, he was freely called a "durned time-servin', yaller hypocrite." Not a few advanced the opinion that if Bones did not actually lead Uncle Billy astray he at least slavered over him and coddled him until the old man got conceited in his wickedness. This undoubtedly led to a compulsory divorce between them, and Uncle Billy was happily dispatched to a neighboring town and a doctor.

Bones seemed to miss him greatly, ran away for two days, and was supposed to have visited him, to have been shocked at his convalescence, and to have been "cut" by Uncle Billy in his reformed character. He returned to his old active life again and buried his past with his forgotten bones. It was said that he was afterward detected trying to lead an intoxicated tramp into camp, after the methods employed by a blind man's dog, but was discovered in time by the—of course—uncorroborated narrator.

I should be tempted to leave him thus in his original and picturesque sin, but the same veracity which compelled me to transcribe his faults and iniquities obliges me to describe his ultimate and somewhat monotonous reformation, which came from no fault of his own.

It was a joyous day at Rattlers Ridge that was equally the advent of his change of heart, and of the first stagecoach that had been induced to diverge from the high road and stop regularly at our settlement. Flags were flying from the post office and Polka Saloon—and Bones was flying before the brass band that he detested, when the sweetest girl in the county, Pinkey Preston, daughter of the county judge and hopelessly beloved by all Rattlers Ridge, stepped from the coach which she had glorified by occupying as an invited guest.

"What makes him run away?" she asked quickly, opening her lovely eyes in a possible innocent wonder that anything could be found to run away from her.

"He don't like the brass band," we explained eagerly.

"How funny," murmured the girl. "Is it as out of tune as all that?"

This irresistible witticism alone would have been enough to satisfy us—we did nothing but repeat it to each other all the next day—but we were positively transported when we saw her suddenly gather her dainty skirts in one hand and trip off through the red dust toward Bones, who with his eyes over his yellow shoulder, had halted in the road and half turned in mingled disgust and rage at the spectacle of the descending trombone. We held our breath as she approached him. Would Bones evade her as he did us at such moments, or would he save our reputation and consent, for the moment, to accept her as a new kind of inebriate? She came nearer; he saw her; he began to slowly quiver with excitement, his stump of a tail vibrating with such rapidity that the loss of the missing portion was scarcely noticeable. Suddenly she stopped before him, took his yellow head between her little hands, lifted it and looked down in his handsome brown eyes with her two lovely blue ones. What passed between them in that magnetic glance no one ever knew. She returned with him, said to him casually, "We're not afraid of brass bands, are we?" to which he apparently acquiesced, at least stifling his disgust of them while he was near her—which was nearly all the time.

During the speechmaking her gloved hand and his yellow head were always near together, and at the crowning ceremony—her public checking of Yuba Bill's waybill on behalf of the township with a gold pencil presented to her by the stage company—Bones' joy, far from knowing no bounds, seemed to know nothing but them, and he witnessed it apparently in the air. No one dared to interfere. For the first time a local pride in Bones sprang up in our hearts, and we lied to each other in his praises openly and shamelessly.

Then the time came for parting. We were standing by the door of the coach, hats in hand, as Miss Pinkey was about to step into it. Bones was waiting by her side, confidently looking into the interior and apparently selecting his own seat on the lap of Judge Preston in the corner, when Miss Pinkey held up the sweetest of admonitory fingers. Then taking his head between her two hands she again looked into his brimming eyes and said simply, "*Good* dog," with the gentlest of emphasis on the adjective, and popped into the coach.

The six bay horses started as one, the gorgeous green and gold vehicle bounded forward, the red dust rose behind and the yellow dog danced in and out of it to the very outskirts of the settlement. And then he soberly returned.

A day or two later he was missed—but the fact was afterward known that he was at Spring Valley, the county town where Miss Preston lived—and he was forgiven. A week afterward he was missed again, but this time for a longer period, and then a pathetic letter arrived from Sacramento for the storekeeper's wife.

"Would you mind," wrote Miss Pinkey Preston, "asking some of your boys to come over here to Sacramento and bring back Bones? I don't mind having the dear dog walk out with me at Spring Valley, where everyone knows me, but here he *does* make one so noticeable on account of his *color*. I've got scarcely a frock that he agrees with. He don't go with my pink muslin, and that lovely buff tint he makes three shades lighter. You know yellow is *so* trying."

A consultation was quickly held by the whole settlement and a deputation sent to Sacramento to relieve the unfortunate girl. We were all quite indignant with Bones but, oddly enough, I think it was greatly tempered with our new pride in him. While he was with us alone his peculiarities had been scarcely appreciated, but the recurrent phrase, "that yellow dog that they keep at the Rattlers," gave us a mysterious importance along the countryside, as if we had secured a mascot or some zoological curiosity.

This was further indicated by a singular occurrence. A new church had been built at the crossroads, and an eminent divine had come from San Francisco to preach the opening sermon. After a careful examination of the camp's wardrobe and some felicitous exchange of apparel, a few of us were deputed to represent Rattlers at the Sunday service. In our white ducks, straw hats and flannel blouses we were sufficiently picturesque and distinctive as "honest miners" to be shown off in one of the front pews.

Seated near the prettiest girls, who offered us their hymnbooks—in the cleanly odor of fresh pine shavings and ironed muslin, and blown over by the spices of our own woods through the open windows, a deep sense of the abiding peace of Christian communion settled upon us. At this supreme moment someone murmured in an awe-stricken whisper:

"*Will* you look at Bones?"

We looked. Bones had entered the church and gone up in the gallery through a pardonable ignorance and modesty; but perceiving his mistake, he was now calmly walking along the gallery rail before the astounded worshipers. Reaching the end he paused for a moment, and carelessly looked down. It was about fifteen feet to the floor below—the simplest jump in the world for the mountainbred Bones. Daintily, gingerly, lazily and yet with a conceited airiness of manner as if, humanly speaking, he had one leg in his pocket and were doing it on three, he cleared the distance, dropping just in front of the chancel without a sound, turned himself around three times, and lay comfortably down.

Three deacons were instantly in the aisle coming up before the eminent divine who, we fancied, wore a restrained smile. We heard the hurried whispers—"Belongs to them," "Quite a local institution here, you know"; "Don't like to offend sensibilities"—and the minister's prompt "By no means," as he went on with his service.

A short month ago we would have repudiated Bones; today we sat there in slightly supercilious attitudes, as if to indicate that any affront offered to Bones would be an insult to ourselves and followed by our instantaneous withdrawal in a body.

All went well, however, until the minister, lifting the large Bible from the communion table and holding it in both hands before him, walked toward a reading stand by the altar rails. Bones uttered a distinct growl. The minister stopped.

We and we alone comprehended in a flash the whole situation. The Bible was nearly the size and shape of one of those soft clods of sod which we were in the playful habit of launching at Bones when he lay half asleep in the sun, in order to see him cleverly evade it.

We held our breath. What was to be done? But the opportunity belonged to our leader, Jeff Briggs, a confoundedly good-looking fellow with the golden mustache of a northern Viking and the curls of an Apollo. Secure in his beauty and bland in his self-conceit, he rose from the pew and stepped before the chancel rails.

"I would wait a moment if I were you, sir," he said respectfully, "and you will see that he will go out quietly."

"What is wrong?" whispered the minister with some concern.

"He thinks you are going to heave that book at him, sir, without giving him a fair show, as we do."

The minister looked perplexed but remained motionless, with the book in his hands. Bones arose, walked halfway down the aisle, and vanished like a yellow flash!

With this justification of his reputation, Bones disappeared for a week. At the end of that time we received a polite note from Judge Preston saying that the dog had become quite domiciled in their house and begging that the camp, without yielding up their valuable *property* in him, would allow him to remain at Spring Valley for an indefinite time; that both the judge and his daughter, with whom Bones was already an old friend, would be glad if the members of the camp would visit their old favorite whenever they desired, to assure themselves that he was well cared for.

I am afraid that the bait thus ingenuously thrown out had a good deal to do with our ultimate yielding. However, the reports of those who visited Bones were wonderful and marvelous. He was residing there in state, lying on rugs in the drawing room, coiled up under the judicial desk in the judge's study, sleeping regularly on the mat outside Miss Pinkey's bedroom door, or lazily snapping at flies on the judge's lawn.

"He's as yaller as ever," said one of our informants, "but it don't somehow seem to be the same back that we used to break clods over in the old time just to see him scoot out of the dust."

And now I must record a fact which I am aware all lovers of dogs will indignantly deny, and which will be furiously bayed at by every faithful hound since the days of Ulysses. Bones not only *forgot*, but absolutely *cut* us! Those who called upon the judge in "store clothes" he would perhaps casually notice, but he would sniff at them as if detecting and resenting them under their superficial exterior. The rest he simply paid no attention to. The more familiar term of Bonesy, formerly applied to him in our rare moments of endearment, produced no response. This pained, I think, some of the more youthful of us, but through some strange human weakness it also increased the camp's respect for him. Nevertheless we spoke of him familiarly to strangers at the very moment he ignored us. I am afraid that we also took some pains to point out that he was getting fat and unwieldy and losing his elasticity, implying covertly that his choice was a mistake and his life a failure.

A year afterward, he died in the odor of sanctity and respectability, being found one morning coiled up and stiff on the mat outside Miss Pinkey's door. When the news was conveyed to us we asked permission, the camp being in a prosperous condition, to erect a stone over his grave. But when it came to the inscription we could only think of the two words murmured to him by Miss Pinkey, which we always believe effected his conversion:

"*Good* Dog!"

The
Right
Eye
of the
～ Commander

THE YEAR of grace 1797 passed away on the coast of California in a southwesterly gale. The little bay of San Carlos, albeit sheltered by the headlands of the Blessed Trinity, was rough and turbulent; its foam clung quivering to the seaward wall of the mission garden; the air was filled with flying sand and spume, and as the Señor Comandante, Hermenegildo Salvatierra looked from the deep embrasured window of the presidio guardroom, he felt the salt breath of the distant sea buffet the color into his smoke-dried cheeks.

The commander, I have said, was gazing thoughtfully from the window of the guardroom. He may have been reviewing the events of the year now about to pass away. But, like the garrison at the presidio, there was little to review. The year, like its predecessors, had been uneventful—the days had slipped by in a delicious

190

monotony of simple duties, unbroken by incident or interruption. The regularly recurring feasts and saints'
days, the half-yearly courier from San Diego, the rare
transport ship and rarer foreign vessel were the mere
details of his patriarchal life. If there was no achieve-
ment, there was certainly no failure. Abundant harvests
and patient industry amply supplied the wants of presidio and mission. Isolated from the family of nations,
the wars which shook the world concerned them not so
much as the last earthquake; the struggle that emanci-
pated their sister colonies on the other side of the con-
tinent to them had no suggestiveness. In short, it was
that glorious Indian summer of Californian history
around which so much poetical haze still lingers—that
bland indolent autumn of Spanish rule, so soon to be
followed by the wintry storms of Mexican independence
and the reviving spring of American conquest.

The commander turned from the window and walked
toward the fire that burned brightly on the deep oven-
like hearth. A pile of copybooks, the work of the presidio school, lay on the table. As he turned over the leaves
with a paternal interest and surveyed the fair round
Scripture text, the first pious pothooks of the pupils of
San Carlos, an audible commentary fell from his lips:
" 'Abimelech took her from Abraham'—ah, little one, excellent! 'Jacob sent to see his brother'—body of Christ!
That upstroke of thine, Paquita, is marvelous; the governor shall see it!" A film of honest pride dimmed the
commander's left eye. The right, alas! twenty years be-

fore had been sealed by an Indian arrow. He rubbed it softly with the sleeve of his leather jacket and continued, " 'The Ishmaelites having arrived—' "

He stopped, for there was a step in the courtyard, a foot upon the threshold, and a stranger entered. With the instinct of an old soldier the commander, after one glance at the intruder, turned quickly toward the wall where his trusty Toledo hung, or should have been hanging. But it was not there, and as he recalled that the last time he had seen that weapon it was being ridden up and down the gallery by Pepito, the infant son of Bautista the tortilla-maker, he blushed and then contented himself with frowning upon the intruder.

But the stranger's air though irreverent was decidedly peaceful. He was unarmed and wore the ordinary cape of tarpaulin and sea boots of a mariner. Except for a villainous smell of codfish there was little about him that was peculiar.

His name, as he informed the commander in Spanish that was more fluent than elegant or precise—his name was Peleg Scudder. He was master of the schooner *General Court*, of the port of Salem in Massachusetts, on a trading voyage to the south seas but now driven by stress of weather into the bay of San Carlos. He begged permission to ride out the gale under the headlands of the Blessed Trinity, and no more. Water he did not need, having taken in a supply at Bodega. He knew the strict surveillance of the Spanish port regulations in regard to foreign vessels and would do nothing against the severe discipline and good order of the settlement. There was a slight tingle of sarcasm in his tone as he glanced toward the desolate parade ground of the presidio and the open unguarded gate. The fact was that the sentry, Felipe Gomez, had discreetly retired to shelter at the beginning of the storm, and was then sound asleep in the corridor.

The commander hesitated. The port regulations were severe, but he was accustomed to exercise individual authority, and beyond an old order issued ten years before regarding the American ship *Columbia* there was no precedent to guide him. The storm was severe and a sentiment of humanity urged him to grant the stranger's request. It is but just to the commander to say that his inability to enforce a refusal did not weigh with his decision. He would have denied with equal disregard of consequences that right to a seventy-four-gun ship which he now yielded so gracefully to this Yankee trading schooner. He stipulated only that there should be no communication between the ship and shore. "For yourself, Señor Captain," he continued, "accept my hospitality. The fort is yours as long as you shall grace it with your distinguished presence." And with old-fashioned courtesy he made the semblance of withdrawing from the guardroom.

Master Peleg Scudder smiled as he thought of the half-dismantled fort, the two moldy brass cannon cast in Manila a century previous, and the shiftless garrison. A wild thought of accepting the commander's offer literally, conceived in the reckless spirit of a man who never let slip an offer for trade, for a moment filled his brain but a timely reflection of the commercial unimportance of the transaction checked him. He only took a capacious quid of tobacco as the commander gravely drew a settle before the fire and in honor of his guest untied the black silk handkerchief that bound his grizzled brows.

What passed between Salvatierra and his guest that night it becomes me not, as a grave chronicler of the salient points of history, to relate. I have said that Master Peleg Scudder was a fluent talker, and under the influence of divers strong waters furnished by his host he became still more loquacious. And think of a man with a twenty years' budget of gossip! The commander learned for the first time how Great Britain lost her colonies, of the French Revolution, of the great Napoleon whose achievements, perhaps, Peleg colored more highly than the commander's superiors would have liked. And when Peleg turned questioner the commander was at his mercy. He gradually made himself master of the gossip of the mission and presidio, the "small beer" chronicles of that pastoral age, the conversion of the heathen, the presidio schools, and even asked the commander how he had lost his eye. It is said that at this point of the conversation Master Peleg produced from about his person divers small trinkets, kickshaws and newfangled trifles, and even forced some of them upon his host. It is further alleged that under the malign influence of Peleg and several glasses of *aguardiente* the commander lost somewhat of his decorum and behaved in a manner unseemly for one in his position, reciting high-flown Spanish poetry and even piping in a thin high voice divers madrigals and heathen *canzonets* of an amorous complexion, chiefly in regard to a "little one" who was his, the commander's, "soul." These allegations, perhaps unworthy of notice of a serious chronicler, should be received with great caution and are introduced here as simple hearsay. That the commander, however, took a handkerchief and attempted to show his guest the mysteries of the *semi-cuacua*, capering in an agile but indecorous manner about the apartment, has been denied. Enough for the purposes of this narrative that at midnight Peleg assisted his host to bed with many protestations of undying friendship and then, as the gale had abated, took his leave of the presidio and hurried aboard the *General Court*. When the day broke the ship was gone.

I know not if Peleg kept his word with his host. It is said that the holy Fathers at the mission that night heard a loud chanting in the plaza as of the heathens singing psalms through their noses; that for many days after an odor of salt codfish prevailed in the settlement; that a dozen hard nutmegs which were unfit for spice or seed were found in the possession of the wife of the baker; and that several bushels of shoe pegs which bore a pleasing resemblance to oats but were quite inadequate to the purposes of provender, were discovered

in the stable of the blacksmith. But when the reader re-
flects upon the sacredness of a Yankee trader's word, the
stringent discipline of the Spanish port regulations, and
the proverbial indisposition of my countrymen to im-
pose upon the confidence of a simple people, he will at
once reject this part of the story.

A roll of drums ushering in the year 1798 awoke
the commander. The sun was shining brightly, and the
storm had ceased. He sat up in bed and through the
force of habit rubbed his left eye. As the remembrance
of the previous night came back to him, he jumped from
his couch and ran to the window. There was no ship
in the bay. A sudden thought seemed to strike him, and
he rubbed both of his eyes. Not content with this, he
consulted the metallic mirror which hung beside his
crucifix. There was no mistake; the commander had a
visible second eye—a right one—as good, save for the
purposes of vision, as the left.

Whatever might have been the true secret of this
transformation, but one opinion prevailed at San Carlos.
It was one of those rare miracles vouchsafed a pious
Catholic community as an evidence to the heathen,
through the intercession of the blessed San Carlos himself. That their beloved commander, the temporal de-
fender of the Faith, should be the recipient of this
miraculous manifestation was most fit and seemly. The
commander himself was reticent; he could not tell a
falsehood—he dared not tell the truth. After all, if the
good folk of San Carlos believed that the powers of his

right eye were actually restored, was it wise and discreet for him to undeceive them? For the first time in his life the commander thought of policy—for the first time he quoted that text which has been the lure of so many well-meaning but easy Christians, of being "all things to all men." *Infeliz* Hermenegildo Salvatierra!

For by degrees an ominous whisper crept through the little settlement. The right eye of the commander, although miraculous, seemed to exercise a baleful effect upon the beholder. No one could look at it without blinking. It was cold, hard, relentless and unflinching. More than that, it seemed to be endowed with a dreadful prescience—a faculty of seeing through and into the inarticulate thoughts of those it looked upon. The soldiers of the garrison obeyed the eye rather than the voice of their commander, and answered his glance rather than his lips in questioning. The servants could not evade the ever-watchful but cold attention that seemed to pursue them. The children of the presidio school smirched their copybooks under the awful supervision, and poor Paquita, the prize pupil, failed utterly in that marvelous upstroke when her patron stood beside her. Gradually distrust, suspicion, self-accusation and timidity took the place of trust, confidence and security throughout San Carlos. Wherever the right eye of the commander fell, a shadow fell with it.

Nor was Salvatierra entirely free from the baleful influence of his miraculous acquisition. Unconscious of its effect upon others, he only saw in their actions evidence of certain things that the crafty Peleg had hinted on that eventful New Year's Eve. His most trusty retainers stammered, blushed and faltered before him. Self-accusations, confessions of minor faults and delinquencies, or extravagant excuses and apologies met his mildest inquiries. The very children that he loved—his pet pupil, Paquita—seemed to be conscious of some hidden sin. The result of this constant irritation showed itself more plainly. For the first half-year the commander's voice and eye were at variance. He was still kind, tender and thoughtful in speech. Gradually, however, his voice took upon itself the hardness of his glance and its skeptical impassive quality, and as the year again neared its close it was plain that the commander had fitted himself to the eye, and not the eye to the commander.

It may be surmised that these changes did not escape the watchful solicitude of the Fathers. Indeed the few who were first to ascribe the right eye of Salvatierra to miraculous origin and the special grace of the blessed San Carlos now talked openly of witchcraft and the agency of *Luzbel* the evil one. It would have fared ill with Hermenegildo Salvatierra had he been aught but commander or amenable to local authority. But the reverend Father, Friar Manuel de Cortes, had no power over the political executive, and all attempts at spiritual advice failed signally. He retired baffled and confused from his first interview with the commander, who seemed now to take a grim satisfaction in the fateful power of his glance. The holy Father contradicted himself, exposed the fallacies of his own arguments and even, it is asserted, committed himself to several undoubted heresies. When the commander stood up at mass, if the officiating priest caught that skeptical and searching eye, the service was inevitably ruined. Even the power of the Holy Church seemed to be lost, and the last hold upon the affections of the people and the good order of the settlement departed from San Carlos.

As the long dry summer passed, the low hills that surrounded the white walls of the presidio grew more and more to resemble in hue the leathern jacket of the commander, and Nature herself seemed to have borrowed his dry hard glare. The earth was cracked and seamed with drought; a blight had fallen upon the orchards and vineyards, and the rain, long delayed and ardently prayed for, came not. The sky was as tearless as the right eye of the commander. Murmurs of discontent, insubordination and plotting among the Indians reached his ear; he only set his teeth the more firmly, tightened the knot of his black silk handkerchief, and looked up at his Toledo.

The last day of the year 1798 found the commander sitting at the hour of evening prayers alone in the guard-room. He no longer attended the services of the Holy Church, but crept away at such times to some solitary spot where he spent the interval in silent meditation. The firelight played upon the low beams and rafters but left the bowed figure of Salvatierra in darkness. Sitting thus, he felt a small hand touch his arm, and looking

down saw the figure of Paquita, his little Indian pupil,
at his knee. "Ah! littlest of all," said the commander
with something of his old tenderness, lingering over
the endearing diminutives of his native speech—"sweet
one, what doest thou here? Art thou not afraid of him
whom everyone shuns and fears?"

"No," said the little Indian readily, "not in the dark.
I hear your voice—the old voice; I feel your touch—the
old touch; but I see not your eye, Señor Comandante.
That only I fear—and that, O señor, O my father," said
the child, lifting her little arms toward his, "that I know
is not thine own!"

The commander shuddered and turned away. Then
recovering himself, he kissed Paquita gravely on the
forehead and bade her retire. A few hours later, when
silence had fallen upon the presidio, he sought his own
couch and slept peacefully.

At about the middle watch of the night a dusky figure
crept through the low embrasure of the commander's
apartment. Other figures were flitting through the
parade ground, which the commander might have seen
had he not slept so deeply. The intruder stepped noiselessly to the couch and listened to the sleeper's deep-
drawn respiration. Something glittered in the firelight
as the savage lifted his arm; another moment and the
sore perplexities of Hermenegildo Salvatierra would
have been over, when suddenly the savage started and
fell back in a paroxysm of terror. The commander slept
peacefully, but his right eye, widely opened, fixed and

unaltered, glared coldly on the would-be assassin. The man fell to the earth in a fit, and the noise awoke the sleeper.

To rise to his feet, grasp his sword, and deal blows thick and fast upon the mutinous savages who now thronged the room was the work of a moment. Help opportunely arrived, and the undisciplined Indians were speedily driven beyond the walls; but in the scuffle the commander received a blow upon his right eye, and lifted his hand to that mysterious organ; it was gone. Never again was it found and never again, for bale or bliss, did it adorn the right orbit of the commander.

With it passed away the spell that had fallen upon San Carlos. The rain returned to invigorate the languid soil; harmony was restored between priest and soldier; the green grass presently waved over the sere hillsides; the children flocked again to the side of their martial preceptor, a *Te Deum* was sung in the mission church; and pastoral content once more smiled upon the gentle valleys of San Carlos. And far southward crept the *General Court* with its master, Peleg Scudder, trafficking in beads and peltries with the Indians, and offering glass eyes, wooden legs and other Boston notions to the chiefs.

Salomy Jane's ∾ Kiss

ONLY one shot had been fired. It had gone wide of its mark—the ringleader of the vigilantes—and had left Red Pete, who had fired it, covered by their rifles and at their mercy. For his hand had been cramped by hard riding and his eye distracted by their sudden onset, and so the inevitable end had come. He submitted sullenly to his captors; his companion fugitive and horse thief gave up the protracted struggle with a feeling not unlike relief. Even the hot and revengeful victors were content. They had taken their men alive. At any time during the long chase they could have brought them down by a rifle shot, but it would have been unsportsmanlike and have ended in a free fight instead of an example. Besides, their doom was already sealed. Their end, by a rope and a tree, although not sanctified by law, would have at least the deliberation of justice. It was the tribute paid by the vigilantes to that order

202

which they had themselves disregarded in the pursuit
and capture. Yet this strange logic of the frontier sufficed
them and gave a certain dignity to the climax.

"Ef you've got anythin' to say to your folks, say it *now*
and say it quick," said the ringleader.

Red Pete glanced around him. He had been run to
earth at his own cabin in the clearing, whence a few
relations and friends, mostly women and children, non-
combatants, had outflowed, gazing vacantly at the
twenty vigilantes who surrounded them. All were accustomed to scenes of violence, blood feud, chase and
hardship; it was only the suddenness of the onset and its
quick result that had surprised them. They looked on
with dazed curiosity and some disappointment; there
had been no fight to speak of—no spectacle! A boy,
nephew of Red Pete, got upon the rain barrel to view
the proceedings more comfortably; a tall handsome lazy
Kentucky girl, a visiting neighbor, leaned against the
doorpost, chewing gum. Only a yellow hound was ac-
tively perplexed. He could not make out if a hunt was
just over or beginning, and ran eagerly backward and
forward, leaping alternately upon the captives and the
captors.

The ringleader repeated his challenge. Red Pete gave
a reckless laugh and looked at his wife.

At which Mrs. Red Pete came forward. It seemed that
she had much to say incoherently, furiously, vindic-
tively to the ringleader. His soul would roast in hell for
that day's work! He called himself a man, skunkin' in the

open and afraid to show himself except with a crowd of other "Kiyi's" around a house of women and children. Heaping insult upon insult, inveighing against his low blood, his ancestors, his dubious origin she at last flung out a wild taunt of his invalid wife, the insult of a woman to a woman, until his white face grew rigid and only that western American fetish of the sanctity of sex kept his twitching fingers from the lock of his rifle. Even her husband noticed it and with a half-authoritative "Let up on that, old gal," and a pat of his freed left hand on her back, took his last parting. The ringleader, still white under the lash of the woman's tongue, turned abruptly to the second captive. "And if *you've* got anybody to say good-by to, now's your chance."

The man looked up. Nobody stirred or spoke. He was a stranger there, being a chance confederate picked up by Red Pete and known to no one. Still young, but an outlaw from his abandoned boyhood of which father and mother were only a forgotten dream, he loved horses and stole them, fully accepting the frontier penalty of life for the interference with that animal on which a man's life so often depended. But he understood the good points of a horse as was shown by the one he bestrode, until a few days before the property of Judge Boompointer. This was his sole distinction.

The unexpected question stirred him for a moment out of the attitude of reckless indifference, for attitude it was, and a part of his profession. But it may have touched him that at that moment he was less than his

companion and his virago wife. However he only shook
his head. As he did so his eye casually fell on the handsome girl by the doorpost, who was looking at him. The
ringleader too may have been touched by his complete
loneliness, for *he* hesitated. At the same moment he saw
that the girl was looking at his friendless captive.

A grotesque idea struck him.

"Salomy Jane, ye might do worse than come yer and
say good-by to a dyin' man, and him a stranger," he said.

There seemed to be a subtle stroke of poetry and
irony in this that equally struck the apathetic crowd. It
was well known that Salomy Jane Clay thought no small
potatoes of herself and always held off the local swains
with a lazy nymphlike scorn. Nevertheless she slowly
disengaged herself from the doorpost, and to everybody's
astonishment lounged with languid grace and outstretched hand toward the prisoner. The color came into
the gray reckless mask which the doomed man wore as
her right hand grasped his left, just loosed by his captors. Then she paused; her shy fawnlike eyes grew bold
and fixed themselves upon him. She took the chewing
gum from her mouth, wiped her red lips with the back
of her hand, by a sudden lithe spring placed her foot on
his stirrup, and bounding to the saddle, threw her arms
about his neck and pressed a kiss upon his lips.

They remained thus for a hushed moment—the man
on the threshold of death, the young woman in the full-
ness of youth and beauty—linked together. Then the
crowd laughed; in the audacious effrontery of the girl's

act the ultimate fate of the two men was forgotten. She slipped languidly to the ground; *she* was the focus of all eyes, she only! The ringleader saw it and his opportunity. He shouted: "Time's up! Forward!"—and urged his horse beside his captives. The next moment the whole cavalcade was sweeping over the clearing into the darkening woods.

Their destination was Sawyer's Crossing, the headquarters of the committee, where the council was still sitting and where both culprits were to expiate the offense of which that council had already found them guilty. They rode in great and breathless haste, a haste in which, strangely enough, even the captives seemed to join. That haste possibly prevented them from noticing the singular change which had taken place in the second captive since the episode of the kiss. His high color remained as if it had burned through his mask of indifference; his eyes were quick, alert and keen, his mouth half open as if the girl's kiss still lingered there. And that haste had made them careless, for the horse of the man who led him slipped in a gopher hole, rolled over, unseated his rider, and even dragged the bound and helpless second captive from Judge Boompointer's favorite mare. In an instant they were all on their feet again, but in that supreme moment the second captive felt the cords which bound his arms had slipped to his wrists. By keeping his elbows to his sides and obliging the others to help him mount it escaped their notice. By riding close to his captors and keeping in the crush of the throng he further concealed the accident, slowly working his hands downward out of his bonds.

Their way lay through a sylvan wilderness, mid-leg deep in ferns, whose tall fronds brushed their horses' sides in their furious gallop and concealed the flapping of the captive's loosened cords. The peaceful vista, more suggestive of the offerings of nymph and shepherd than of human sacrifice, was in a strange contrast to this whirlwind rush of stern armed men. The westering sun pierced the subdued light and the tremor of leaves with yellow lances; birds started into song on blue and dove-like wings, and on either side of the trail of this vengeful storm could be heard the murmur of hidden and tranquil waters. In a few moments they would be on the open ridge whence sloped the common turnpike to Sawyer's, a mile away. It was the custom of returning cavalcades to take this hill at headlong speed with shouts and cries that heralded their coming. They withheld the latter that day as inconsistent with their dignity; but emerging from the wood, swept silently like an avalanche down the slope. They were well under way, looking only to their horses, when the second captive slipped his right arm from the bonds and succeeded in grasping the reins that lay trailing on the horse's neck. A sudden vaquero jerk which the well-trained animal understood threw him on his haunches with his forelegs firmly planted on the slope. The rest of the cavalcade swept on; the man who was leading the captive's horse by the riata, thinking only of another accident, dropped the line to save himself from being dragged backward from his horse. The captive wheeled and the next moment was galloping furiously up the slope.

It was the work of a moment, a trained horse and an experienced hand. The cavalcade had covered nearly fifty yards before they could pull up; the freed captive had covered half that distance uphill. The road was so narrow that only two shots could be fired, and these broke dust two yards ahead of the fugitive. They had not dared to fire low; the horse was the more valuable animal. The fugitive knew this in his extremity also, and would have gladly taken a shot in his own leg to spare that of his horse. Five men were detached to recapture or kill him. The latter seemed inevitable. But he had calculated his chances; before they could reload he had reached the woods again; winding in and out between the pillared tree trunks, he offered no mark. They knew his horse was superior to their own; at the end of two hours they returned, for he had disappeared without track or trail. The end was briefly told in the *Sierra Record:*

> Red Pete, the notorious horse thief who had so long eluded justice, was captured and hung by the Sawyer's Crossing Vigilantes last week; his confederate unfortunately escaped on a valuable horse belonging to Judge Boompointer. The judge had refused one thousand dollars for the horse only a week before. As the thief who is still at large would find it difficult to dispose of so valuable an animal without detection the chances are against either of them turning up again.

Salomy Jane watched the cavalcade until it had disappeared. Then she became aware that her brief popularity had passed. Mrs. Red Pete in stormy hysterics had included her in a sweeping denunciation of the whole universe, possibly for simulating an emotion in which she herself was deficient. The other women hated her for her momentary exaltation above them; only the children still admired her as one who had undoubtedly "canoodled" with a man "a-goin' to be hung"—a daring flight beyond their wildest ambition. Salomy Jane accepted the charge with charming unconcern. She put on her yellow nankeen sunbonnet—a hideous affair that would have ruined any other woman but which only enhanced the piquancy of her fresh brunette skin—tied the strings letting her blue-black braids escape below its frilled curtain behind, jumped on her mustang with a casual display of agile ankles in shapely white stockings, whistled to the hound, and waving her hand with a "So long, sonny!" to the lately bereft but admiring nephew, flapped and fluttered away in her short brown holland gown.

Her father's house was four miles distant. Contrasted with the cabin she had just left it was a superior dwelling with a long lean-to at the rear, which brought the eaves almost to the ground and made it look like a low triangle. It had a long barn and cattlesheds, for Madison Clay was a great stock raiser and the owner of a quarter section. It had a sitting room and a parlor organ whose transportation thither had been a marvel of packing.

These things were supposed to give Salomy Jane an undue importance, but the girl's reserve and inaccessibility to local advances were rather the result of a cool lazy temperament and the preoccupation of a large protecting admiration for her father, for some years a widower. For Mr. Madison Clay's life had been threatened in one or two feuds, not without cause, it was said, and it is possible that the pathetic spectacle of her father doing his visiting with a shotgun may have touched her closely and somewhat prejudiced her against the neighboring masculinity. The thought that cattle, horses and quarter section would one day be hers did not disturb her calm. As for Mr. Clay, he accepted her as housewifely though somewhat interfering, and being one of his own womankind, not without some degree of merit.

"Wot's this yer I'm hearin' of your doin's over at Red Pete's? Honeyfoglin' with a horse thief, eh?" said Mr. Clay two days later at breakfast.

"I reckon you heard about the straight thing, then," said Salomy Jane unconcernedly, without looking around.

"What do you calkilate Rube will say to it? What are you goin' to tell *him?*" said Mr. Clay sarcastically.

Rube, or Reuben Waters was a swain supposed to be favored particularly by Mr. Clay. Salomy Jane looked up.

"I'll tell him that when *he's* on his way to be hung, I'll kiss him—not till then," said the young lady brightly.

This delightful witticism suited the paternal humor,

and Mr. Clay smiled; nevertheless he frowned a moment afterward.

"But this yer hoss thief got away arter all, and that's a hoss of a different color," he said grimly.

Salomy Jane put down her knife and fork. This was certainly a new and different phase of the situation. She had never thought of it before, and strangely enough, for the first time she became interested in the man. "Got away?" she repeated. "Did they let him off?"

"Not much," said her father briefly. "Slipped his cords and goin' down the grade pulled up short, just like a vaquero agin a lassoed bull, almost draggin' the man leadin' him off his hoss, and then skyuted up the grade. For that matter, on that hoss o' Judge Boompointer's he mout have dragged the whole posse of 'em down on their knees ef he liked! Sarved 'em right, too. Instead of stringin' him up afore the door or shootin' him on sight they must allow to take him down afore the hull committee 'for an example.' Example be blowed! Ther' 's example enough when some stranger comes unbeknownst slap onter a man hanged to a tree and plugged full of holes. *That's* an example, and *he* knows what it means. Wot more do ye want? But then those vigilantes is allus clingin' and hangin' onter some mere scrap o' the law they're pretendin' to despise. It makes me sick! Why, when Jake Myers shot your ole Aunt Viney's second husband, and I laid in wait for Jake afterwards in the Butternut Hollow, did *I* tie him to his hoss and fetch

him down to your Aunt Viney's cabin 'for an example'
before I plugged him? No!" in deep disgust. "No! Why,
I just meandered through the woods, careless-like, till
he comes out, and I just rode up to him, and I said—"

But Salomy Jane had heard her father's story before.
Even one's dearest relatives are apt to become tiresome
in narration. "I know, dad," she interrupted; "but this
yer man—this hoss thief—did *he* get clean away without
gettin' hurt at all?"

"He did, and unless he's fool enough to sell the hoss,
he kin keep away, too. So ye see ye can't ladle out
purp stuff about a dyin' stranger to Rube. He won't
swaller it."

"All the same, dad," returned the girl cheerfully, "I
reckon to say it, and say more; I'll tell him that ef *he*
manages to get away too, I'll marry him—there! But ye
don't ketch Rube takin' any such risks in gettin' ketched,
or in gettin' away arter!"

Madison Clay smiled grimly, pushed back his chair,
rose, dropped a perfunctory kiss on his daughter's hair,
and taking his shotgun from the corner, departed on a
peaceful Samaritan mission to a cow who had dropped
a calf in the far pasture. Inclined as he was to Reuben's
wooing from his eligibility as to property, he was conscious that he was sadly deficient in certain qualities
inherent in the Clay family. It certainly would be a
kind of *mésalliance*.

Left to herself Salomy Jane stared a long while at the
coffee pot, and then called the two squaws who assisted

her in her household duties to clear away the things while
she went up to her own room to make her bed. Here she
was confronted with a possible prospect of that proverbial bed she might be making in her willfulness, and on
which she must lie, in the photograph of a somewhat
serious young man of refined features—Reuben Waters—
stuck in her window frame. Salomy Jane smiled over her
last witticism regarding him and enjoyed it like your
true humorist, and then, catching sight of her own handsome face in the little mirror, smiled again. But wasn't
it funny about that horse thief getting off after all? Good
Lordy! Fancy Reuben hearing he was alive and going
around with that kiss of hers set on his lips! She laughed
again, a little more abstractedly. And he had returned it
like a man, holding her tight and almost breathless, and
he going to be hung the next minute! Salomy Jane had
been kissed at other times by force, chance or stratagem.
In a certain ingenuous forfeit game of the locality known
as "I'm a-pinin'," many had "pined" for a "sweet kiss"
from Salomy Jane, which she had yielded in a sense of
honor and fair play. She had never been kissed like this
before—she would never again—and yet the man was
alive! And behold, she could see in the mirror that she
was blushing!

She should hardly know him again. A young man with
very bright eyes, a flushed and sunburnt cheek, a kind
of fixed look in the face and no beard; no, none that she
could feel. Yet he was not at all like Reuben, not a bit.
She took Reuben's picture from the window and laid it

on her workbox. And to think she did not even know
this young man's name! That was queer. To be kissed by
a man whom she might never know! Of course he knew
hers. She wondered if he remembered it and her. But of
course he was so glad to get off with his life that he
never thought of anything else. Yet she did not give
more than four or five minutes to these speculations, but
like a sensible girl thought of something else. Once
again, however, in opening the closet she found the
brown holland gown she had worn on the day before;
she thought it very unbecoming and regretted that she
had not worn her best gown on her visit to Red Pete's
cottage. On such an occasion she really might have been
more impressive.

When her father came home that night she asked him
the news. No, they had *not* captured the second horse
thief, who was still at large. Judge Boompointer talked
of invoking the aid of the despised law. It remained,
then, to see whether the horse thief was fool enough to
try to get rid of the animal. Red Pete's body had been
delivered to his widow. Perhaps it would only be neigh-
borly for Salomy Jane to ride over to the funeral. But
Salomy Jane did not take to the suggestion kindly, nor
yet did she explain to her father that as the other man
was still living, she did not care to undergo a second
disciplining at the widow's hands. Nevertheless she contrasted her situation with that of the widow with a new
and singular satisfaction. It might have been Red Pete

who had escaped. But he had not the grit of the name-
less one. She had already settled his heroic quality.

"Ye ain't harkenin' to me, Salomy."

Salomy Jane started.

"Here I'm askin' ye if ye've see that hound Phil Larrabee sneakin' by yer today?"

Salomy Jane had not. But she became interested and
self-reproachful, for she knew that Phil Larrabee was
one of her father's enemies. "He wouldn't dare to go by
here unless he knew you were out," she said quickly.

"That's what gets me," he said, scratching his grizzled
head. "I've been kind o' thinkin' o' him all day, and one
of them Chinese said he saw him at Sawyer's Crossing.
He was a kind of friend o' Pete's wife. That's why I
thought yer might find out ef he'd been there." Salomy
Jane grew more self-reproachful at her father's self-in-
terest in her neighborliness. "But that ain't all," continued Mr. Clay. "Thar was tracks over the far pasture
that warn't mine. I followed 'em, and they went round
and round the house two or three times, ez ef they mout
hev bin prowlin', and then I lost 'em in the woods again.
It's just like that sneakin' hound Larrabee to hev bin
lyin' in wait for me and afraid to meet a man fair and
square in the open."

"You just lie low, dad, for a day or two more and let
me do a little prowlin'," said the girl with sympathetic
indignation in her dark eyes. "Ef it's that skunk, I'll spot
him soon enough and let you know whar he's hidin'."

"You'll just stay where ye are, Salomy," said her father decisively. "This ain't no woman's work—though I ain't sayin' you haven't got more head for it than some men I know."

Nevertheless, that night after her father had gone to bed, Salomy Jane sat by the open window of the sitting room in an apparent attitude of languid contemplation, but alert and intent of eye and ear. It was a fine moonlit night. Two pines near the door, solitary pickets of the serried ranks of distant forest, cast long shadows like paths to the cottage and sighed their spiced breath in the windows. For there was no frivolity of vine or flower around Salomy Jane's bower. The clearing was too recent, the life too practical for vanities like these. But the moon added a vague elusiveness to everything, softened the rigid outlines of the sheds, gave shadows to the lidless windows, and touched with merciful indirectness the hideous debris of refuse gravel and the gaunt scars of burnt vegetation before the door. Even Salomy Jane was affected by it and exhaled something between a sigh and a yawn with the breath of the pines. Then she suddenly sat upright.

Her quick ear had caught a faint "click, click" in the direction of the wood; her quicker instinct and rustic training enabled her to determine that it was the ring of a horse's shoe on flinty ground; her knowledge of the locality told her it came from the spot where the trail passed over an outcrop of flint, scarcely a quarter of a mile from where she sat, and within the clearing. It was no errant stock, for the foot was shod with iron; it was a mounted trespasser by night and boded no good to a man like Clay.

She rose, threw her shawl over her head more for disguise than shelter, and passed out of the door. A sudden impulse made her seize her father's shotgun from the corner where it stood—not that she feared any danger to herself but it gave her an excuse. She made directly for the wood, keeping in the shadow of the pines as long as she could. At the fringe she halted; whoever was there must pass her before reaching the house.

Then there seemed to be a suspense of all nature. Everything was deadly still; even the moonbeams appeared no longer tremulous. Soon there was a rustle as of some stealthy animal among the ferns, and then a dismounted man stepped into the moonlight. It was the horse thief—the man she had kissed!

For a wild moment a strange fancy seized her usually sane intellect and stirred her temperate blood. The news they had told her was *not* true; he had been hung and this was his ghost! He looked as white and spiritlike in the moonlight, and was dressed in the same clothes as when she saw him last. He had evidently seen her approaching and moved quickly to meet her. But in his haste he stumbled slightly; she reflected suddenly that ghosts did not stumble, and a feeling of relief came over her. It was no assassin of her father that had been prowling around—only this unhappy fugitive. A momentary color came into her cheek; her coolness and hardihood returned; it was with a tinge of sauciness in her voice that she said:

"I reckoned you were a ghost."

"I mout have been," he said, looking at her fixedly. "But I reckon I'd have come back here all the same."

"It's a little riskier comin' back alive," she said with a levity that died on her lips, for a singular nervousness, half fear and half expectation, was beginning to take the place of her relief of a moment ago. "Then it was *you* who was prowlin' round and makin' tracks in the far pasture?"

"Yes; I came straight here when I got away."

She felt his eyes were burning her but did not dare to raise her own. "Why," she began, hesitated, and ended vaguely. "*How* did you get here?"

"You helped me!"

"I?"

"Yes. That kiss you gave me put life into me, gave me strength to get away. I swore to myself I'd come back and thank you, alive or dead."

Every word he said she could have anticipated, so plain the situation seemed to her now. And every word he said she knew was the truth. Yet her cool common sense struggled against it.

"What's the use of your escapin' ef you're comin' back here to be ketched again?" she said pertly.

He drew a little nearer to her, but seemed to her the more awkward as she resumed her self-possession. His voice, too, was broken as if by exhaustion as he said, catching his breath at intervals:

"I'll tell you. You did more for me than you think. You made another man o' me. I never had a man, woman or child do to me what you did. I never had a friend— only a pal like Red Pete who picked me up on shares. I want to quit this yer—what I'm doin'. I want to begin by doin' the square thing to you." He stopped, breathed hard and then said brokenly, "My hoss is over thar, staked out. I want to give him to you. Judge Boom-pointer will give you a thousand dollars for him. I ain't lyin'; it's God's truth! I saw it on the handbill agin a tree. Take him and I'll get away afoot. Take him. It's the only thing I can do for you, and I know it don't half pay for what you did. Take it; your father can get the reward for you if you can't."

Such were the ethics of this strange locality that neither the man who made the offer nor the girl to whom it was made was struck by anything that seemed illogical or indelicate, or at all inconsistent with justice or the horse thief's real conversion. Salomy Jane nevertheless dissented, from another and weaker reason.

"I don't want your hoss, though I reckon dad might; but you're just starvin'. I'll get suthin'." She turned toward the house.

"Say you'll take the hoss first," he said, grasping her hand. At the touch she felt herself coloring and struggled, expecting perhaps another kiss. But he dropped

her hand. She turned again with a saucy gesture, said,
"Hol' on; I'll come right back," and slipped away, the
mere shadow of a coy and flying nymph in the moonlight, until she reached the house.

Here she not only procured food and whiskey but
added a long dust coat and hat of her father's to her
burden. They would serve as a disguise for him and hide
that heroic figure, which she thought everybody must
now know as she did. Then she rejoined him breathlessly. But he put the food and whiskey aside.

"Listen," he said. "I've turned the hoss into your
corral. You'll find him there in the morning, and no one
will know but that he got lost and joined the other
horses."

Then she burst out. "But you—*you*—what will become
of you? You'll be ketched!"

"I'll manage to get away," he said in a low voice, "ef
—ef—"

"Ef what?" she said tremblingly.

"Ef you'll put the heart in me agin, as you did!" he
gasped.

She tried to laugh, to move away. She could do
neither. Suddenly he caught her in his arms with a long
kiss, which she returned again and again. Then they
stood embraced as they had embraced two days before,
but no longer the same. For the cool, lazy Salomy Jane
had been transformed into another woman—a passionate
clinging savage. Perhaps something of her father's blood

had surged within her at that supreme moment. The man stood erect and determined.

"Wot's your name?" she whispered quickly. It was a woman's quickest way of defining her feelings.

"Dart."

"Yer first name?"

"Jack."

"Let me go now, Jack. Lie low in the woods till to-morrow sunup. I'll come again."

He released her. Yet she lingered a moment. "Put on those things," she said, with a sudden happy flash of eyes and teeth, "and lie close till I come." And then she sped away home.

But midway up the distance she felt her feet going slower, and something at her heartstrings seemed to be pulling her back. She stopped, turned and glanced to where he had been standing. Had she seen him then she might have returned. But he had disappeared. She gave her first sigh, and then ran quickly again. It must be nearly one o'clock! It was not very long to morning!

She was within a few steps of her own door when the sleeping woods and silent air appeared to suddenly awake with a sharp "crack!"

She stopped, paralyzed. Another "crack!" followed, that echoed over the far corral. She recalled herself instantly and dashed off wildly to the woods again.

As she ran she thought of one thing only. He had been dogged by one of his old pursuers and attacked. But there were two shots and he was unarmed. Suddenly she remembered that she had left her father's gun standing against the tree where they were talking. Thank God! She might again have saved him. She ran to the tree; the gun was gone. She ran hither and thither, dreading at every step to fall upon his lifeless body. A new thought struck her; she ran to the corral. The horse was not there! He must have been able to regain it and escape *after* the shots had been fired. She drew a long breath of relief, but it was caught up in an apprehension of alarm. Her father, awakened from his sleep by the shots, was hurriedly approaching her.

"What's up now, Salomy Jane?" he demanded excitedly.

"Nothin'," said the girl, with an effort. "Nothin', at least, that *I* can find." She was usually truthful because fearless, and a lie stuck in her throat; but she was no longer fearless, thinking of *him*. "I wasn't abed; so I ran out as soon as I heard the shots fired," she answered in return to his curious gaze.

"And you've hid my gun somewhere where it can't be found," he said reproachfully. "Ef it was that sneak Larrabee and he fired them shots to lure me out, he might have potted me without a show a dozen times in the last five minutes."

She had not thought since of her father's enemy! It might indeed have been he who had attacked Jack. But she made a quick point of the suggestion. "Run in, dad, run in and find the gun; you've got no show out here without it." She seized him by the shoulders from behind, shielding him from the woods and hurried him, half expostulating, half struggling, to the house.

But there no gun was to be found. It was strange; it must have been mislaid in some corner! Was he sure he had not left it in the barn? But no matter now. The danger was over; the Larrabee trick had failed. He must go to bed now and in the morning they would make a search together. At the same time she had inwardly resolved to rise before him and make another search of the wood, and perhaps—fearful joy as she recalled her promise!—find Jack alive and well, awaiting her!

Salomy Jane slept little that night, nor did her father. But toward morning he fell into a tired man's slumber until the sun was well up the horizon. Far different was it with his daughter; she lay with her face to the window, her head half lifted to catch every sound, from the creaking of the sun-warped shingles above her head to the far-off moan of the rising wind in the pine trees. Sometimes she fell into a breathless half-ecstatic trance, living over every moment of the stolen interview, feeling the fugitive's arm still around her, hearing his whispered voice in her ears—the birth of her new life! This was followed again by a period of agonizing dread—that he might even then be lying in the woods, his life ebbing away, with her name on his lips and she resting here inactive, until she half started from her bed to go to his succor. And this went on until a pale opal glow came into the sky, followed by a still paler pink on the summit of the white Sierras. Then she rose and hurriedly began to dress. Still so sanguine was her hope of meeting him that she lingered yet a moment to select the brown holland skirt and yellow sunbonnet she had worn when she first saw him. And she had only seen him twice! Only *twice!* It would be cruel, too cruel, not to see him again!

She crept softly down the stairs, listening to the long-drawn breathing of her father in his bedroom, and then by the light of a guttering candle scrawled a note to him, begging him not to trust himself out of the house until she returned from her search. Then leaving the note open on the table she swiftly ran out into the growing day.

Three hours afterward Mr. Madison Clay awoke to the sound of loud knocking. At first this forced itself upon his consciousness as his daughter's regular morning summons, and was responded to by a grunt of recognition and a nestling closer in the blankets. Then he awoke with a start and a muttered oath, remembered the events of last night and his intention to get up early, and rolled out of bed. Becoming aware by this time that the knocking was at the outer door and hearing the shout of a familiar voice he hastily pulled on his boots and his jean trousers, and fastened a single suspender over his shoulder as he clattered downstairs. The outside door was open, and waiting on the threshold was his kinsman, an old ally in many a blood feud—Breckenridge Clay!

"You *are* a cool one, Mad!" said the latter in half-admiring indignation.

"What's up?" said the bewildered Madison.

"*You* ought to be, and scootin' out o' this," said Breckenridge grimly. "It's all very well to know nothin', but here Phil Larrabee's friends hev just picked him up drilled through with slugs and deader nor a crow, and now they're lettin' loose Larrabee's two half-brothers on you. And you must go like a durned fool and leave these yer things behind you in the bresh," he went on querulously, lifting Madison Clay's dust coat, hat and shotgun from his horse, which stood saddled at the door. "Luckily I picked them up in the woods comin' here. Ye ain't got more than time to get over the state line and among your folks thar afore they'll be down on you. Hustle, old man! What are you gawkin' and starin' at?"

Madison Clay had stared amazed and bewildered—horrorstricken. The incidents of the past night for the first time flashed upon him clearly—hopelessly! The shots, his finding Salomy Jane alone in the woods, her confusion and anxiety to rid herself of him, the disappearance of the shotgun, and now this new discovery of the taking of his hat and coat for a disguise! *She* had killed Phil Larrabee in that disguise after provoking his first harmless shot! She, his own child, Salomy Jane, had disgraced herself by a man's crime, had disgraced him by usurping his right and taking a mean advantage, by deceit, of a foe!

"Gimme that gun," he said hoarsely.

Breckenridge handed him the gun in wonder and slowly gathering suspicion. Madison examined nipple and muzzle; one barrel had been discharged. It was true! The gun dropped from his hand.

"Look here, old man," said Breckenridge, with a darkening face, "there's bin no foul play here. Thar's bin no hiring of men, no deputy to do this job. *You* did it fair and square—yourself?"

"Yes, by God!" burst out Madison Clay in a hoarse voice. "Who says I didn't?"

Reassured, yet believing that Madison Clay had nerved himself for the act by an overdraught of whiskey which had affected his memory, Breckenridge said curtly, "Then wake up and lite out ef ye want me to stand by you."

"Go to the corral and pick me out a hoss," said Madison slowly yet not without a certain dignity of manner. "I've suthin' to say to Salomy Jane afore I go." He was holding her scribbled note, which he had just discovered, in his shaking hand.

Struck by his kinsman's manner and knowing the dependent relations of father and daughter, Breckenridge nodded and hurried away. Left to himself, Madison Clay ran his fingers through his hair and straightened out the paper on which Salomy Jane had scrawled her note, turned it over, and wrote on the back:

You might have told me you did it, and not leave your ole father to find it out how you disgraced yourself with him, too, by a lowdown, underhanded woman's trick!

I've said I done it and took the blame myself, and all the
sneakiness of it that folks suspect. If I get away alive,
and I don't care much which, you needn't foller. The
house and stock are yours; but you ain't any longer the
daughter of your disgraced father.

MADISON CLAY.

He had scarcely finished the note, when with a clatter
of hoofs and a led horse, Breckenridge reappeared at
the door, elated and triumphant. "You're in luck, Mad!
I found that stole hoss of Judge Boompointer's had got
away and strayed among your stock in the corral. Take
him and you're safe; he can't be outrun this side of the
state line."

"I ain't no hoss thief," said Madison grimly.

"Nobody sez ye are, but you'd be wuss—a fool—ef you
didn't take him. I'm testimony that you found him
among your hosses; I'll tell Judge Boompointer you've
got him, and ye kin send him back when you're safe.
The judge will be mighty glad to get him back and call
it quits. So ef you've writ to Salomy Jane, come."

Madison Clay no longer hesitated. Salomy Jane might
return at any moment—it would be part of her "fool
womanishness"—and he was in no mood to see her before a third party. He laid the note on the table, gave a
hurried glance around the house which he grimly believed he was leaving forever, and striding to the door,
leaped on the stolen horse and swept away with his
kinsman.

But that note lay for a week undisturbed on the table
in full view of the open door. The house was invaded by

leaves, pine cones, birds and squirrels during the hot, silent, empty days, and at night by shy, stealthy creatures, but never again, day or night, by any of the Clay family. It was known in the district that Clay had flown across the state line; his daughter was believed to have joined him the next day; and the house was supposed to be locked up. It lay off the main road and few passed that way. The starving cattle in the corral at last broke bounds and spread over the woods. And one night a stronger blast than usual swept through the house and carried the note from the table to the floor where, whirled into a crack in the flooring, it slowly rotted.

But though the sting of her father's reproach was spared her, Salomy Jane had no need of the letter to know what had happened. For as she entered the woods in the dim light of that morning she saw the figure of Dart gliding from the shadow of a pine toward her. The unaffected cry of joy that rose from her lips died there as she caught sight of his face in the open light.

"You are hurt," she said, clutching his arm passionately.

"No," he said. "But I wouldn't mind that if—"

"You're thinkin' I was afeard to come back last night when I heard the shootin', but I *did* come," she went on feverishly. "I ran back here when I heard the two shots, but you was gone. I went to the corral but your hoss wasn't there, and I thought you'd got away."

"I *did* get away," said Dart gloomily. "I killed the

man, thinkin' he was huntin' *me* and forgettin' I was disguised. He thought I was your father."

"Yes," said the girl joyfully, "he was after dad and you —*you* killed him." She again caught his hand admiringly.

But he did not respond. Possibly there were points of honor which this horse thief felt vaguely with her father. "Listen," he said grimly. "Others think it was your father killed him. When *I* did it—for he fired at me first—I ran to the corral agin and took my hoss, thinkin' I might be follered. I made a clear circuit of the house, and when I found he was the only one and no one was follerin', I come back here and took off my disguise. Then I heard his friends find him in the woods and I know they suspected your father. And then another man come through the woods while I was hidin' and found the clothes and took 'em away." He stopped and stared at her gloomily.

But all this was unintelligible to the girl. "Dad would have got the better of him ef you hadn't," she said eagerly, "so what's the difference?"

"All the same," he said, "I must take his place."

She did not understand, but turned her head to her master. "Then you'll go back with me and tell him *all?*" she said obediently.

"Yes," he said.

She put her hand in his and they crept out of the wood together. She foresaw a thousand difficulties, but chiefest of all, that he did not love as she did. *She* would not have taken these risks against their happiness.

But alas for ethics and heroism. As they were issuing

from the wood they heard the sound of galloping hoofs and had barely time to hide themselves before Madison Clay, on the stolen horse of Judge Boompointer, swept past them with his kinsman.

Salomy Jane turned to her lover.

And here I might, as a moral romancer, pause, leaving the guilty, passionate girl eloped with her disreputable lover, destined to lifelong shame and misery, misunderstood to the last by a criminal fastidious parent. But I am confronted by certain facts, on which this romance is based. A month later a handbill was posted on one of the sentinel pines announcing that the property would be sold by auction to the highest bidder by Mrs. John Dart, daughter of Madison Clay, Esq., and it was sold accordingly. Still later, by ten years, the chronicler of these pages visited a certain stock or breeding farm in the Blue Grass Country, famous for the popular racers it has produced. He was told that the owner was the "best judge of horseflesh in the country." "Small wonder," added his informant, "for they say as a young man out in California he was a horse thief, and only saved himself by eloping with some rich farmer's daughter. But he's a straight-out and respectable man now, whose word about horses can't be bought; and as for his wife, *she's* a beauty! To see her at the Springs, rigged out in the latest fashion, you'd never think she had ever lived out of New York or wasn't the wife of a millionaire."

An
Esmeralda
of
Rocky
∼ Canyon

 IT IS to be feared the hero of this chronicle
began life as an impostor. For he was offered to the
credulous and sympathetic family of a San Francisco
citizen as a lamb who, unless bought as a playmate for
the children, would inevitably pass into the butcher's
hands. A combination of refined sensibility and urban
ignorance of nature prevented them from discerning
certain glaring facts that betrayed his caprid origin. So
a ribbon was duly tied around his neck, and in pleasing
emulation of the legendary Mary he was taken to school
by the confiding children. Here, alas! the fraud was discovered and history was reversed by his being turned
out by the teacher because he was *not* a lamb at school.
Nevertheless the kindhearted mother of the family persisted in retaining him on the plea that he might yet
become useful. To her husband's feeble suggestion of

"gloves," she returned a scornful negative, and spoke of the weakly infant of a neighbor who might later receive nourishment from this providential animal. But even this hope was destroyed by the eventual discovery of his sex. Nothing remained now but to accept him as an ordinary kid and to find amusement in his accomplishments—eating, climbing and butting. It must be confessed that these were of a superior quality: a capacity to eat everything from a cambric handkerchief to an election poster, an agility which brought him even to the roofs of houses, and a power of overturning by a single push the chubbiest child who opposed him, made him a fearful joy to the nursery. This last quality was incautiously developed in him by a servant boy, who later was hurriedly propelled down a flight of stairs by his too proficient scholar. Having once tasted victory, Billy the goat needed no further incitement to his performances. The small wagon he sometimes consented to draw for the benefit of the children never hindered his attempts to butt the passer-by. On the contrary, on well-known scientific principles he added the impact of the bodies of the children projected over his head in his charge, and the infelicitous pedestrian found himself not only knocked off his legs by Billy, but bombarded by the whole nursery.

Delightful as was this recreation to juvenile limbs, it was felt to be dangerous to the adult public. Indignant protestations were made, and as Billy could not be kept in the house, he may be said to have at last butted him-

self out of that sympathetic family and into a hard and
unfeeling world. One morning he broke his tether in
the small backyard. For several days thereafter he displayed himself in guilty freedom on the tops of adjacent
walls and outhouses. The San Francisco suburb where
his credulous protectors lived was still in a volcanic
state of disruption, caused by the grading of new streets
through rocks and sandhills. In consequence the roofs of
some houses were on the level of the doorsteps of others,
and were especially adapted to Billy's performances.
One afternoon, to the admiring and perplexed eyes of
the nursery, he was discovered standing on the apex of
a neighbor's new Elizabethan chimney on a space
scarcely larger than the crown of a hat, calmly surveying
the world beneath him. High infantile voices appealed
to him in vain; baby arms were outstretched to him in
hopeless invitation; he remained exalted and obdurate
like Milton's hero, probably by his own merit "raised to
that bad eminence." Indeed, there was already something Satanic in his budding horns and pointed mask as
the smoke curled softly around him. Then he appropriately vanished and San Francisco knew him no more.
At the same time, however, one Owen M'Ginnis, a
neighboring sandhill squatter, also disappeared, leaving
San Francisco for the southern mines. He was said to
have taken Billy with him—for no conceivable reason
except for companionship. Howbeit, it was the turning
point of Billy's career. Such restraint as kindness, civilization or even policemen had exercised upon his nature

was gone. He retained, I fear, a certain wicked intelligence picked up in San Francisco with the newspapers and theatrical and election posters he had consumed. He reappeared at Rocky Canyon among the miners as an exceedingly agile chamois with the low cunning of a satyr. That was all that civilization had done for him!

If Mr. M'Ginnis had fondly conceived that he would make Billy useful as well as companionable, he was singularly mistaken. Horses and mules were scarce in Rocky Canyon, and he attempted to utilize Billy by making him draw a small cart laden with auriferous earth from his claim to the river. Billy, rapidly gaining strength, was quite equal to the task but alas! not his inborn propensity. An incautious gesture from the first passing miner Billy chose to construe into the usual challenge. Lowering his head, from which his budding horns had been already pruned by his master, he instantly went for his challenger, cart and all. Again the scientific law already pointed out prevailed. With the shock of the onset the entire contents of the cart rose and poured over the astonished miner, burying him from sight. In any other but a Californian mining camp such a propensity in a draught animal would have been condemned on account of the damage and suffering it entailed, but in Rocky Canyon it proved unprofitable to the owner from the very amusement and interest it excited. Miners lay in wait for Billy with a "greenhorn," or newcomer, whom they would put up to challenge the animal by some indiscreet gesture. In this way hardly a cartload of pay-gravel ever arrived safely at its destination, and the unfortunate M'Ginnis was compelled to withdraw Billy as a beast of burden. It was whispered that so great had his propensity become under repeated provocation, that M'Ginnis himself was no longer safe. Going ahead of his cart one day to remove a fallen bough from the trail, Billy construed the act of stooping into a playful challenge from his master—with the inevitable result.

The next day M'Ginnis appeared with a wheelbarrow but without Billy. From that day he was relegated to the rocky crags above the camp, from whence he was only lured occasionally by the mischievous miners who wished to exhibit his peculiar performances. For although Billy had ample food and sustenance among the crags he still had a civilized longing for posters. And whenever a circus, a concert or a political meeting was billed in the settlement, he was on hand while the paste was yet fresh and succulent. In this way it was averred that he once removed a gigantic theater bill setting forth the charms of the Sacramento Pet, and being caught in the act by the advance agent, was pursued through the main street carrying the damp bill on his horns, eventually affixing it, after his own peculiar fashion, on the back of Judge Boompointer, who was standing in front of his own courthouse.

In connection with the visits of this young lady, another story concerning Billy survives in the legends of Rocky Canyon. Colonel Starbottle was at that time

passing through the settlement on election business, and
it was part of his chivalrous admiration for the sex to
pay a visit to the pretty actress. The single waiting room
of the little hotel gave upon the veranda, which was also
level with the street. After a brief yet gallant interview
in which he oratorically expressed the gratitude of the
settlement with old-fashioned southern courtesy, Colonel Starbottle lifted the chubby little hand of the Pet
to his lips, and with a low bow backed out upon the
veranda. But the Pet was astounded by his instant
reappearance and by his apparently casting himself passionately and hurriedly at her feet! It is needless to say
that he was followed closely by Billy, who from the
street had casually noticed him and construed his novel
exit into an ungentlemanly challenge.

Billy's visits, however, became less frequent, and as
Rocky Canyon underwent the changes incidental to
mining settlements he was presently forgotten in the
invasion of a few southwestern families and the adop-
tion of amusements less practical and turbulent than he
had afforded. It was alleged that he was still seen in the
more secluded fastnesses of the mountains, having reverted to a wild state, and it was suggested by one or
two of the more adventurous that he might yet become
edible and a fair object of chase. A traveler through the
upper pass of the canyon related how he had seen a
savage-looking hairy animal like a small elk perched
upon inaccessible rocks, but always out of gunshot. But

these and other legends were set at naught and overthrown by an unexpected incident.

The Pioneer coach was toiling up the long grade toward Skinners Pass when Yuba Bill suddenly pulled up
with his feet on the brake.

"Jiminy!" he ejaculated, drawing a deep breath.

The startled passenger beside him on the box followed the direction of his eyes. Through an opening in
the wayside pines he could see, a few hundred yards
away, a cuplike hollow in the hillside, of the vividest
green. In the center a young girl of fifteen or sixteen was
dancing and keeping step to the castanet click of a pair
of bones held in her hands above her head. But more
singular still, a few paces before her a large goat with its
neck roughly wreathed with flowers and vines was taking ungainly bounds and leaps in imitation of its companion. The wild background of the Sierras, the pastoral
hollow, the incongruousness of the figures, and the vivid
color of the girl's red flannel petticoat showing beneath
her calico skirt that had been pinned around her waist,
made a striking picture which by this time had attracted
all eyes. Perhaps the dancing of the girl suggested a
shuffle rather than any known sylvan measure; but all
this and even the clatter of the bones was made gracious by the distance.

"Esmeralda! by the living Harry!" shouted the excited
passenger on the box.

Yuba Bill took his feet off the brake and turned a look

of deep scorn upon his companion as he gathered the reins again.

"It's that blanked goat, outer Rocky Canyon beyond, and Polly Harkness! How did she ever come to take up with *him?*"

Nevertheless as soon as the coach reached Rocky Canyon, the story was quickly told by the passengers, corroborated by Yuba Bill, and highly colored by the observer on the box seat. Harkness was known to be a newcomer who lived with his wife and only daughter on the other side of Skinners Pass. He was a logger and charcoal burner who had eaten his way into the serried ranks of pines below the pass, and established in these efforts an almost insurmountable cordon of fallen trees, stripped bark and charcoal pits around the clearing where his rude log hut stood—which kept his seclusion unbroken. He was said to be a half-savage mountaineer from Georgia, in whose rude fastnesses he had distilled unlawful whiskey, and that his tastes and habits unfitted him for civilization. His wife chewed and smoked, and he was believed to make a fiery brew of his own from acorns and pine nuts. He seldom came to Rocky Canyon except for provisions. His logs were slipped down a shoot or slide to the river, where they voyaged once a month to a distant mill, but *he* did not accompany them. The daughter, seldom seen at Rocky Canyon, was a half grown girl, brown as autumn fern, wild-eyed, disheveled, in a homespun skirt, sunbonnet and boy's brogans. Such were the plain facts which skeptical

Rocky Canyon opposed to the passengers' legends. Nevertheless some of the younger miners found it not out of their way to go over Skinners Pass on the journey to the river, but with what success was not told. It was said, however, that a celebrated New York artist making a tour of California was on the coach one day going through the pass, and preserved the memory of what he saw there in a well-known picture entitled *Dancing Nymph and Satyr*, said by competent critics to be "replete with the study of Greek life." This did not affect Rocky Canyon, where the study of mythology was presumably displaced by an experience of more wonderful flesh-and-blood people, but later it was remembered with some significance.

Among the improvements already noted, a zinc and wooden chapel had been erected in the main street, where a certain popular revivalist preacher of a peculiar southwestern sect regularly held exhortatory services. His rude emotional power over his ignorant fellow sectarians was well known, while curiosity drew others. His effect upon the females of his flock was hysterical and sensational. Women prematurely aged by frontier drudgery and childbearing, girls who had known only the rigors and pains of a half-equipped, ill-nourished youth in their battling with the hard realities of nature around them, all found a strange fascination in the extravagant glories and privileges of the unseen world he pictured to them, which they might have found in the fairy tales and nursery legends of civilized children had

they known them. Personally he was not attractive. His
thin pointed face and bushy hair rising on either side of
his square forehead in two rounded knots, his long
straggling wiry beard and strong neck and shoulders
were indeed of a common southwestern type; yet in him
they suggested something more. This was voiced by a
miner who attended his first service, and as the Reverend Mr. Withholder rose in the pulpit the former was
heard to audibly ejaculate, "Dod blasted!—if it ain't
Billy!" But when on the following Sunday, to everybody's astonishment, Polly Harkness in a new white
muslin frock and broad-brimmed Leghorn hat appeared
before the church door with the real Billy and exchanged conversation with the preacher, the likeness
was appalling.

I grieve to say that the goat was at once christened by
Rocky Canyon as the Reverend Billy, and the minister
himself was Billy's "brother." More than that, when an
attempt was made by outsiders during the service to
inveigle the tethered goat into his old butting performances, and he took not the least notice of their insults
and challenges, the epithet "blanked hypocrite" was
added to his title.

Had he really reformed? Had his pastoral life with
his nymphlike mistress completely cured him of his
pugnacious propensity, or had he simply found it was
inconsistent with his dancing, and seriously interfered
with his fancy steps? Had he found tracts and hymn
books were as edible as theater posters? These were

questions that Rocky Canyon discussed lightly, although
there was always the more serious mystery of the relations of the Reverend Mr. Withholder, Polly Harkness
and the goat toward each other. The appearance of Polly
at church was no doubt due to the minister's active
canvass of the districts. But had he ever heard of Polly's
dancing with the goat? And where in this plain, angular,
badly dressed Polly was hidden that beautiful vision of
the dancing nymph which had enthralled so many? And
when had Billy ever given any suggestion of his terpsi-
chorean abilities—before or since? Were there any points
of the kind to be discerned in him now? None! Was it
not more probable that the Reverend Mr. Withholder
had himself been dancing with Polly and been mistaken
for the goat? Passengers who could have been so deceived with regard to Polly's beauty might have as easily
mistaken the minister for Billy. About this time another
incident occurred which increased the mystery.

The only male in the settlement who apparently dissented from the popular opinion regarding Polly was a
newcomer, Jack Filgee. While discrediting her performance with the goat, which he had never seen, he was
evidently greatly prepossessed with the girl herself. Unfortunately he was equally addicted to drinking, and as
he was exceedingly shy and timid when sober and quite
unpresentable at other times, his wooing, if it could be
so called, progressed but slowly. Yet when he found that
Polly went to church, he listened so far to the exhorta-
tions of the Reverend Mr. Withholder as to promise to

come to Bible class immediately after the Sunday service. It was a hot afternoon and Jack, who had kept sober
for two days, incautiously fortified himself for the ordeal
by taking a drink before arriving. He was nervously
early and immediately took a seat in the empty church
near the open door. The quiet of the building, the
drowsy buzzing of flies, and perhaps the soporific effect
of the liquor caused his eyes to close and his head to fall
forward on his breast repeatedly. He was recovering
himself for the fourth time when he suddenly received
a violent cuff on the ear and was knocked backward off
the bench on which he was sitting. That was all he
knew.

He picked himself up with a certain dignity, partly
new to him, and partly the result of his condition and
staggered, somewhat bruised and disheveled, to the
nearest saloon. Here a few frequenters who had seen
him pass, who knew his errand and the devotion to
Polly which had induced it, exhibited a natural concern.

"How's things down at the gospel shop?" said one.
"Look as ef you'd been wrastlin' with the Sperit, Jack!"

"Old man must hev exhorted pow'ful," said another,
glancing at his disordered Sunday attire.

"Ain't be'n hevin' a row with Polly? I'm told she slings
an awful left."

Jack, instead of replying, poured out a dram of whiskey, drank it, and putting down his glass, leaned heavily
against the counter as he surveyed his questioners with
a sorrow chastened by reproachful dignity.

"I'm a stranger here, gentlemen," he said slowly. "Ye've known me only a little, but ez ye've seen me both blind drunk and sober I reckon ye've caught on to my gin'ral gait! Now I wanter put it to you, ez fair-minded men, ef you ever saw me strike a parson?"

"No," said a chorus of sympathetic voices. The bar-keeper, however, with a swift recollection of Polly and the Reverend Withholder and some possible contingent jealousy in Jack, added prudently, "Not yet."

The chorus instantly added reflectively, "Well, no—not yet."

"Did ye ever," continued Jack solemnly, "know me to cuss, sass, bully-rag or say anything agin parsons or the church?"

"No," said the crowd, overthrowing prudence in curiosity, "ye never did—we swear it! And now, what's up?"

"I ain't what you call a member in good standin'," he went on, artistically protracting his climax. "I ain't be'n convicted o' sin; I ain't a meek an' lowly follower; I ain't be'n exactly what I orter be'n; I hevn't lived anywhere up to my lights; but is thet a reason why a parson should strike me?"

"Why? What? When did he? Who did?" asked the eager crowd with one voice.

Jack then painfully related how he had been invited by the Reverend Mr. Withholder to attend the Bible class. How he had arrived early and found the church empty. How he had taken a seat near the door to be handy when the parson came. How he just felt "kinder

kam and good, listenin' to the flies buzzin', and must
have fallen asleep—only he pulled himself up every
time—though, after all, it warn't no crime to fall asleep
in an empty church!" How "all of a suddent" the parson
came in, "give him a clip side o' the head," and knocked
him off the bench and left him there!

"But what did he *say?*" queried the crowd.

"Nuthin'. Afore I could get up, he got away."

"Are you sure it was him?" they asked. "You know
you *say* you was asleep."

"Am I sure?" repeated Jack scornfully. "Don't I know
thet face and beard? Didn't I feel it hangin' over me?"

"What are you going to do about it?" continued the
crowd eagerly.

"Wait till he comes out—and you'll see," said Jack
with dignity.

This was enough for the crowd. They gathered excitedly at the door where Jack was already standing,
looking toward the church. The moments dragged
slowly; it might be a long meeting. Suddenly the church
door opened and a figure appeared, looking up and
down the street. Jack colored—he recognized Polly—and
stepped out into the road. The crowd delicately but
somewhat disappointedly drew back in the saloon. They
did not care to interfere in *that* sort of thing.

Polly saw him and came hurriedly toward him. She
was holding something in her hand.

"I picked this up on the church floor," she said shyly,

"so I reckoned you *had* be'n there—though the parson said you hadn't—and I just excused myself and ran out to give it ye. It's yourn, ain't it?" She held up a gold specimen pin, which he had put on in honor of the occasion. "I had a harder time though, to git this yer—it's yourn too—for Billy was layin' down in the yard back o' the church and just comf'bly swallerin' it."

"Who?" said Jack quickly.

"Billy, my goat."

Jack drew a long breath and glanced back at the saloon. "Ye ain't goin' back to class now, are ye?" he said hurriedly. "Ef you ain't, I'll—I'll see ye home."

"I don't mind," said Polly demurely, "if it ain't takin' ye outer y'ur way."

Jack offered his arm, and hurrying past the saloon, the happy pair were soon on the road to Skinners Pass.

Jack did not, I regret to say, confess his blunder, but left the Reverend Mr. Withholder to remain under suspicion of having committed an unprovoked assault and battery. It was characteristic of Rocky Canyon, however, that this suspicion, far from injuring his clerical reputation, incited a respect that had been hitherto denied him. A man who could hit out straight from the shoulder had, in the language of the critics, "suthin' in him." Oddly enough the crowd that had at first sympathized with Jack now began to admit provocations.

His subsequent silence, a disposition when questioned on the subject to smile inanely, and later, when insidiously asked if he had ever seen Polly dancing with the goat, his bursting into uproarious laughter completely turned the current of opinion against him. The public mind, however, soon became engrossed by a more interesting incident.

The Reverend Mr. Withholder had organized a series of Biblical tableaux at Skinnerstown for the benefit of his church. Illustrations were to be given of *Rebecca at the Well, The Finding of Moses,* and *Joseph and his Brethren.* But Rocky Canyon was more particularly excited by the announcement that Polly Harkness would impersonate *Jephthah's Daughter.* On the evening of the performance, however, it was found that this tableau had been withdrawn and another substituted, for reasons not given. Rocky Canyon, naturally indignant at this omission to represent native talent, indulged in a hundred wild surmises. But it was generally believed that Jack Filgee's revengeful animosity to the Reverend Mr. Withholder was at the bottom of it. Jack, as usual, smiled inanely, but nothing was to be got from him. It was not until a few days later, when another incident crowned the climax of these mysteries, that a full disclosure came from his lips.

One morning a flaming poster was displayed at Rocky Canyon, with a charming picture of the Sacramento Pet in the briefest of skirts, disporting with a tambourine before a goat garlanded with flowers who bore, however, an undoubted likeness to Billy. The text in enormous letters and bristling with points of admiration stated that the Pet would appear as *Esmeralda*, assisted by a performing goat especially trained by the gifted actress. The goat would dance, play cards and perform those tricks of magic familiar to the readers of Victor Hugo's beautiful story of *The Hunchback of Notre Dame*, and finally knock down and overthrow the designing seducer, Captain Phœbus. The marvelous spectacle would be produced under the patronage of the Hon. Colonel Starbottle and the Mayor of Skinnerstown.

As all Rocky Canyon gathered open-mouthed around the poster, Jack demurely joined the group. Every eye was turned upon him.

"It don't look as if yer Polly was in *this* show, any more that she was in the tablows," said one, trying to conceal his curiosity under a slight sneer. "She don't seem to be doin' any dancin'!"

"She never *did* any dancin'," said Jack with a smile.

"Never *did!* Then what was all these yarns about her dancin' up at the pass?"

"It was the Sacramento Pet who did all the dancin'; Polly only *lent* the goat. Ye see, the Pet kinder took a shine to Billy arter he bowled Starbottle over thet day at the hotel, and she thought she might teach him tricks. So she *did*, doin' all her teachin' and stage-rehearsin' up there at the pass, so's to be outer sight and keep this thing dark. She bribed Polly to lend her the goat and keep her secret, and Polly never let on a word to anybody but me."

"Then it was the Pet that Yuba Bill saw dancin' from the coach?"

"Yes."

"And that yer artist from New York painted as an *Imp and Satire?*"

"Yes."

"Then that's how Polly didn't show up in them tablows at Skinnerstown? It was Withholder who kinder smelt a rat, eh? And found out it was only a theayter gal all along that did the dancin'?"

"Well, you see," said Jack with affected hesitation, "thet's another yarn. I don't know mebbe ez I oughter tell it. Et ain't got anything to do with this advertisement o' the Pet, and might be rough on old man Withholder! Ye mustn't ask me, boys."

But there was that in his eye, and above all in this lazy procrastination of the true humorist when he is approaching his climax, which rendered the crowd clamorous and unappeasable. They *would* have the story!

Seeing which, Jack leaned back against a rock with great gravity, put his hands in his pockets, looked discontentedly at the ground and began: "You see, boys, old Parson Withholder had heard all these yarns about Polly and thet trick goat, and he kinder reckoned that she might do for some one of his tablows. So he axed

her if she'd mind standin' with the goat and a tambourine for *Jephthah's Daughter* at about the time when
old Jeph comes home, sailin' in and vowin' he'll kill the
first thing he sees—jest as it is in the Bible story. Well,
Polly didn't like to say it wasn't *her* that performed with
the goat but the Pet, for thet would give the Pet dead
away. So Polly agrees to come thar with the goat and
rehearse the tablow. Well Polly's thar, a little shy, and
Billy—you bet *he's* all thar and ready for the fun. But
the darned fool who plays Jephthah ain't worth shucks,
and when *he* comes in he does nothin' but grin at Polly
and seem skeert at the goat. This makes old Withholder
jest wild, and at last he goes on the platform hisself to
show them how the thing oughter be done. So he comes
bustlin' and prancin' in, and ketches sight o' Polly
dancin' in with the goat to welcome him; and then he
clasps his hands—so, and drops on his knees and hangs
down his head—so, and sez, 'Me chyld! Me vow! Oh,
heavens!' But jest then Billy, who's gettin' rather tired o'
all this foolishness, kinder slues round on his hind legs
and ketches sight o' the parson!" Jack paused a moment,
and thrusting his hands still deeper in his pockets said
lazily, "I don't know if you fellers have noticed how
much old Withholder looks like Billy?"

There was a rapid and impatient chorus of "Yes! yes!"
and "Go on!"

"Well," continued Jack, "when Billy sees Withholder
kneelin' thar with his head down, he gives a kind o'
joyous leap and claps his hoofs together, ez much ez to

say, 'I'm on in this scene,' drops his own head, and jest lights out for the parson!"

"And butts him clean through the side scenes into the street," interrupted a delighted auditor.

But Jack's face never changed. "Ye think so?" he said gravely. "But thet's jest whar ye slip up, and thet's jest whar Billy slipped up!" he added slowly. "Mebbe ye've noticed, too, thet the parson's built kinder solid about the head and shoulders. It mout hev be'n thet, or thet Billy didn't get a fair start. But thet goat went down on his forelegs like a shot, and the parson gave one heave and jest scooted him off the platform! Then the parson reckoned thet this yer 'tablow' had better be left out, as thar didn't seem to be any other man who could play Jephthah and it wasn't dignified for *him* to take the part. But the parson allowed thet it might be a great moral lesson to Billy!"

And it *was*, for from that moment Billy never attempted to butt again. He performed with great docility later on in the Pet's engagement at Skinnerstown; he played a distinguished role throughout the provinces. He had had the advantages of Art from the Pet, and of Simplicity from Polly, but only Rocky Canyon knew that his real education had come with his first rehearsal with the Reverend Mr. Withholder.

Wan Lee,
the
❧ Pagan

As I opened Hop Sing's letter there fluttered to the ground a square strip of yellow paper covered with hieroglyphics, which at first glance I innocently took to be the label from a pack of Chinese firecrackers. But the same envelope also contained a smaller strip of rice paper, with two Chinese characters traced in India ink, that I at once knew to be Hop Sing's visiting card. The whole, as afterward literally translated, ran as follows:

> To the stranger the gates of my house are not closed; the rice jar is on the left, and the sweetmeats on the right, as you enter.
> Two sayings of the Master:
>> Hospitality is the virtue of the son and the wisdom of the ancestor.
>> The superior man is lighthearted after the crop-gathering; he makes a festival.

When the stranger is in your melon patch observe him
not too closely; inattention is often the highest form
of civility.
Happiness, Peace, and Prosperity.

Hop Sing

Admirable, certainly, as was this morality and proverbial wisdom, and although this last axiom was very
characteristic of my friend Hop Sing, who was that
most somber of all humorists, a Chinese philosopher, I
must confess that even after a very free translation I was
at a loss to make any immediate application of the message. Luckily I discovered a third enclosure in the shape
of a little note in English and Hop Sing's own commercial hand. It ran thus:

The pleasure of your company is requested at No.—
Sacramento Street, on Friday evening at eight o'clock.
A cup of tea at nine—sharp.

Hop Sing

This explained all. It meant a visit to Hop Sing's warehouse, the opening and exhibition of some rare Chinese
novelties and curios, a chat in the back office, a cup of
tea of a perfection unknown beyond these sacred precincts, cigars, and a visit to the Chinese Theater or
Temple. This was in fact the favorite program of Hop
Sing when he exercised his functions of hospitality as
the chief factor or superintendent of the Ning Foo
Company.

At eight o'clock on Friday evening I entered the warehouse of Hop Sing. There was that deliciously commingled mysterious foreign odor that I had so often noticed; there was the old array of uncouth-looking objects, the long procession of jars and crockery, the same singular blending of the grotesque and the mathematically neat and exact, the same endless suggestions of frivolity and fragility, the same want of harmony in colors that were each, in themselves, beautiful and rare. Kites in the shape of enormous dragons and gigantic butterflies; kites so ingeniously arranged as to utter at intervals, when facing the wind, the cry of a hawk; kites so large as to be beyond any boy's power of restraint—so large that you understood why kite-flying in China was an amusement for adults; gods of china and bronze so gratuitously ugly as to be beyond any human interest or sympathy from their very impossibility; jars of sweetmeats covered all over with moral sentiments from Confucius; hats that looked like baskets, and baskets that looked like hats; silk so light that I hesitate to record the incredible number of square yards that you might pass through the ring on your little finger—these and a great many other indescribable objects were all familiar to me. I pushed my way through the dimly lighted warehouse until I reached the back office or parlor, where I found Hop Sing waiting to receive me.

He was, on the whole, a rather grave, decorous, handsome gentleman. His complexion, which extended all over his head except where his long pigtail grew, was like a fine glazed brown paper muslin. His eyes were black and bright and his eyelids set at an angle of 15°, his nose straight and delicately formed, his mouth small, and his teeth white and clean. He wore a dark blue silk blouse, and in the streets on cold days a short jacket of astrakhan fur. He wore also a pair of drawers of blue brocade gathered tightly over his calves and ankles, offering a general sort of suggestion that he had forgotten his trousers that morning, but that so gentlemanly were his manners, his friends had forborne to mention the fact to him. His manner was urbane, although quite serious. He spoke French and English fluently. In brief, I doubt if you could have found the equal of this pagan shopkeeper among the Christian traders of San Francisco.

There were a few others present: a judge of the federal court, an editor, a high government official, and a prominent merchant. After we had drunk our tea and tasted a few sweetmeats from a mysterious jar, Hop Sing arose, and gravely beckoning us to follow him, began to descend to the basement. When we got there, we were amazed at finding it brilliantly lighted, and that a number of chairs were arranged in a half circle on the asphalt pavement. When he had courteously seated us, he said—

"I have invited you to witness a performance which I can at least promise you no other foreigners but yourselves have ever seen. Wang, the court juggler, arrived here yesterday morning. He has never given a performance outside of the palace before. I have asked him to entertain my friends this evening. He requires no theater or stage accessories, or any confederate—nothing more than you see here. Will you be pleased to examine the ground yourselves, gentlemen."

Of course we examined the premises. It was the ordinary basement or cellar of the San Francisco storehouse, cemented to keep out the damp. We poked our sticks into the pavement and rapped on the walls to satisfy our polite host, but for no other purpose. We were quite content to be the victims of any clever deception. For myself, I knew I was ready to be deluded to any extent, and if I had been offered an explanation of what followed, I should have probably declined it.

Although I am satisfied that Wang's general performance was the first of that kind ever given on American soil, it has probably since become so familiar to many of my readers that I shall not bore them with it here. He began by setting to flight, with the aid of his fan, the usual number of butterflies made before our eyes of little bits of tissue paper, and kept them in the air during the remainder of the performance. I have a vivid recollection of the judge trying to catch one that had lit on his knee, and of its evading him with the pertinacity of a living insect. And even at this time Wang, still plying his fan, was taking chickens out of hats, making oranges disappear, pulling endless yards of silk from his sleeve, apparently filling the whole area of the basement with goods that appeared mysteriously from the ground, from his own sleeves, from nowhere! He swallowed knives to the ruin of his digestion for years to come; he dislocated every limb of his body; he reclined in the air, apparently upon nothing. But his crowning performance, which I have never yet seen repeated, was the most weird, mysterious, and astounding. It is my apology for this long introduction, my sole excuse for writing this article, the genesis of this veracious history.

He cleared the ground of its encumbering articles for a space of about fifteen feet square, and then invited us all to walk forward and again examine it. We did so gravely; there was nothing but the cemented pavement below to be seen or felt. He then asked for the loan of a handkerchief, and as I chanced to be nearest him I offered mine. He took it and spread it open upon the floor. Over this he spread a large square of silk, and over this again a large shawl nearly covering the space he had cleared. He then took a position at one of the points of this rectangle and began a monotonous chant, rocking his body to and fro in time with the somewhat lugubrious air.

We sat still and waited. Above the chant we could hear the striking of the city clocks and the occasional rattle of a cart in the street overhead. The absolute watchfulness and expectation, the dim mysterious half-light of the cellar, falling in a gruesome way upon the misshapen bulk of a Chinese deity in the background, a faint smell of opium smoke mingling with spice, and the dreadful uncertainty of what we were really waiting for, sent an uncomfortable thrill down our backs, and made us look at each other with a forced and unnatural smile. This feeling was heightened when Hop Sing slowly rose, and without a word, pointed with his finger to the center of the shawl.

There was something beneath the shawl! Surely—and something that was not there before. At first a mere suggestion in relief, a faint outline, but growing more and more distinct and visible every moment. The chant still continued, the perspiration began to roll from the singer's face, gradually the hidden object took upon itself a shape and bulk that raised the shawl in its center some five or six inches. It was now unmistakably the outline of a small but perfect human figure, with extended arms and legs. One or two of us turned pale; there was a feeling of general uneasiness until the editor broke the silence by a gibe that, poor as it was, was received with spontaneous enthusiasm. Then the chant suddenly ceased. Wang arose, and with a quick dexterous movement stripped both shawl and silk away, and discovered, sleeping peacefully upon my handkerchief, a tiny Chinese baby!

The applause and uproar which followed this revelation ought to have satisfied Wang, even if his audience was a small one; it was loud enough to awaken the baby —a pretty little boy about a year old, looking like a Cupid cut out of sandalwood. He was whisked away almost as mysteriously as he appeared. When Hop Sing

returned my handkerchief to me with a bow, I asked if
the juggler was the father of the baby. "No sabe!" said
the imperturbable Hop Sing, taking refuge in that Spanish form of noncommittalism so common in California.

"But does he have a new baby for every performance?" I asked.

"Perhaps. Who knows?"

"But what will become of this one?"

"Whatever you choose, gentlemen," replied Hop Sing,
with a courteous inclination. "It was born here—you are
its godfathers."

There were two characteristic peculiarities of any
Californian assemblage in 1856: it was quick to take a
hint, and generous to the point of prodigality in its
response to any charitable appeal. No matter how sordid
or avaricious the individual, he could not resist the in-
fection of sympathy. I doubled the points of my handkerchief into a bag, dropped a coin into it, and without
a word, passed it to the judge. He quietly added a
twenty-dollar gold piece and passed it to the next; when
it was returned to me it contained over a hundred
dollars. I knotted the money in the handkerchief and
gave it to Hop Sing.

"For the baby, from its godfathers."

"But what name?" said the judge. There was a running fire of "Erebus," "Nox," "Plutus," "Terra Cotta,"
"Antæus," etc., etc. Finally the question was referred to
our host.

"Why not his own name," he said quietly, "Wan Lee?"
And thus was Wan Lee, on the night of Friday the 5th
of March, 1856, born into this veracious chronicle.

The last form of the *Northern Star* for the 19th of
July, 1865—the only daily paper published in Klamath
County—had just gone to press, and at 3 A.M. I was
putting aside my proofs and manuscripts preparatory to
going home, when I discovered a letter lying under
some sheets of paper which I must have overlooked.
The envelope was considerably soiled. It had no post-
mark, but I had no difficulty in recognizing the hand
of my friend Hop Sing. I opened it hurriedly, and read
as follows:

MY DEAR SIR,—I do not know whether the bearer will
suit you, but unless the office of "devil" in your newspaper is a purely technical one, I think he has all the
qualities required. He is very quick, active and intelligent. He understands English better than he speaks it,
and makes up for any defect by his habits of observation and initiation. You have only to show him how to
do a thing once and he will repeat it, whether it is an
offense or a virtue. But you certainly know him already;
you are one of his godfathers. For is he not Wan Lee,
the reputed son of Wang the conjurer, to whose performance I had the honor to introduce you? But perhaps you have forgotten it.

I shall send him with a gang of coolies to Stockton,
thence by express to your town. If you can use him
there you will do me a favor and probably save his life,
which is at present in great peril from the hands of the

younger members of your Christian and highly civilized
race who attend the enlightened schools in San Francisco.

He has acquired some singular habits and customs
from his experience of Wang's profession, which he
followed for some years until he became too large to go
in a hat, or be produced from his father's sleeve. The
money you left with me has been expended on his education; he has gone through the triliteral classics, but, I
think, without much benefit. He knows but little of
Confucius and absolutely nothing of Mencius. Owing to
the negligence of his father he associated, perhaps too
much, with American children.

I should have answered your letter before, by post,
but I thought that Wan Lee himself would be a better
messenger for this.

Yours respectfully,

HOP SING

And this was the long-delayed answer to my letter to
Hop Sing. But where was "the bearer?" How was the
letter delivered? I summoned hastily the foreman,
printers and office boy, but without eliciting anything.
No one had seen the letter delivered or knew anything
of the bearer. A few days later I had a visit from my
laundryman, Ah Ri.

"You wantee debbil? All lightee; me catchee him."

He returned in a few moments with a bright-looking
Chinese boy, about ten years old, with whose appearance and general intelligence I was so greatly impressed
that I engaged him on the spot. When the business was
concluded, I asked his name.

"Wan Lee," said the boy.

"What! Are you the boy sent out by Hop Sing? What the devil do you mean by not coming here before, and how did you deliver that letter?"

Wan Lee looked at me and laughed. "Me pitchee in top side window."

I did not understand. He looked for a moment perplexed, and then, snatching the letter out of my hand, ran down the stairs. After a moment's pause, to my great astonishment, the letter came flying in at the window, circled twice around the room, and then dropped gently like a bird upon my table. Before I had recovered from my surprise Wan Lee reappeared, smiled, looked at the letter and then at me, said, "So, John," and then remained gravely silent. I said nothing further, but it was understood that this was his first official act.

His next performance, I grieve to say, was not attended with equal success. One of our regular paper carriers fell sick and at a pinch, Wan Lee was ordered to fill his place. To prevent mistakes he was shown over the route the previous evening, and supplied at about daylight with the usual number of subscribers' copies. He returned after an hour, in good spirits and without the papers. He had delivered them all, he said.

Unfortunately for Wan Lee, at about eight o'clock indignant subscribers began to arrive at the office. They had received their copies, but how? In the form of hard-pressed cannon balls, delivered by a single shot and a mere tour de force through the glass of bedroom windows. They had received them full in the face, like a

baseball, if they happened to be up and stirring; they
had received them in quarter sheets, tucked in at separate windows; they had found them in the chimney,
pinned against the door, shot through attic windows,
delivered in long slips through convenient keyholes,
stuffed into ventilators, and left inside the can of morning milk. One subscriber, who waited for some time at
the office door to have a personal interview with Wan
Lee (then comfortably locked in my bedroom), told me
with tears of rage in his eyes that he had been awakened
at five o'clock by a most hideous yelling below his windows. Arising in great agitation he was startled by the
sudden appearance of the *Northern Star*, rolled hard
and bent into the form of a boomerang or East Indian
club that sailed into the window, described a number
of fiendish circles in the room, knocked over the light,
slapped the baby's face, "took" him (the subscriber) "in
the jaw," and then returned out of the window, and
dropped helplessly in the area. During the rest of the
day wads and strips of soiled paper, purporting to be
copies of the *Northern Star* of that morning's issue, were
brought indignantly to the office. An admirable editorial
on "The Resources of Humboldt County," which I had
constructed the evening before, and which, I have reason to believe, might have changed the whole balance of
trade during the ensuing year and left San Francisco
bankrupt at her wharves, was lost to the public.

It was deemed advisable for the next three weeks to
keep Wan Lee closely confined to the printing office

and the purely mechanical part of the business. Here he developed a surprising quickness and adaptability, winning even the favor and good will of the printers and foreman, who at first looked upon his introduction into the secrets of their trade as fraught with the gravest political significance. He learned to set type readily and neatly, his wonderful skill in manipulation aiding him in the mere mechanical act, and his ignorance of the language confining him simply to the mechanical effort —confirming the printer's axiom that the printer who considers or follows the ideas of his copy makes a poor compositor. He would set up deliberately long diatribes against himself, composed by his fellow printers and hung on his hook as copy, and even such short sentences as "Wan Lee is the devil's own imp," "Wan Lee is a Mongolian rascal," and bring the proof to me with happiness beaming from every tooth and satisfaction shining in his black eyes.

It was not long, however, before he learned to retaliate on his mischievous persecutors. I remember one instance in which his reprisal came very near involving me in a serious misunderstanding. Our foreman's name was Webster, and Wan Lee presently learned to know and recognize the individual and combined letters of his name. It was during a political campaign, and the eloquent and fiery Colonel Starbottle of Siskiyou had delivered an effective speech, which was reported especially for the *Northern Star*. In a very sublime peroration Colonel Starbottle had said, "In the language of the godlike Webster, I repeat—" and here followed the quotation which I have forgotten. Now, it chanced that Wan Lee, looking over the galley after it had been revised, saw the name of his chief persecutor, and of course imagined the quotation to be his. After the form was locked up, Wan Lee took advantage of Webster's absence to remove the quotation and substitute a thin piece of lead of the same size as the type, engraved with Chinese characters, making a sentence which, I had reason to believe, was an utter and abject confession of the incapacity and offensiveness of the Webster family generally, and exceedingly eulogistic of Wan Lee himself personally.

The next morning's paper contained Colonel Starbottle's speech in full, in which it appeared that the "godlike" Webster had on one occasion uttered his thoughts in excellent but perfectly enigmatical Chinese. The rage of Colonel Starbottle knew no bounds. I have a vivid recollection of that admirable man walking into my office and demanding a retraction of the statement.

"But, my dear sir," I asked, "are you willing to deny, over your own signature, that Webster ever uttered such a sentence? Dare you deny that with Mr. Webster's well-known attainments, a knowledge of Chinese might not have been among the number? Are you willing to submit a translation suitable to the capacity of our readers, and deny, upon your honor as a gentleman, that the late Mr. Webster ever uttered such a sentiment? If you are, sir, I am willing to publish your denial."

The Colonel was not, and left highly indignant.

Webster, the foreman, took it more coolly. Happily he was unaware that for two days afterward Chinese from the laundries, from the gulches, from the kitchens, looked in the front office door with faces beaming with sardonic delight, and that three hundred extra copies of the *Star* were ordered for the wash-houses on the river. He only knew that during the day Wan Lee occasionally went off into convulsive spasms and that he was obliged to kick him into consciousness again. A week after the occurrence I called Wan Lee into my office.

"Wan," I said gravely, "I should like you to give me, for my own personal satisfaction, a translation of that Chinese sentence which my gifted countryman, the late godlike Webster, uttered upon a public occasion." Wan Lee looked at me intently, and then the slightest possible twinkle crept into his black eyes. Then he replied, with equal gravity—

"Mishtel Webstel—he say: 'China boy makee me belly much foolee. China boy makee me heap sick.'" Which I have reason to think was true.

But I fear I am giving but one side, and not the best, of Wan Lee's character. As he imparted it to me, his had been a hard life. He had known scarcely any childhood—he had no recollection of a father or mother. The conjurer Wang had brought him up. He had spent the first seven years of his life in appearing from baskets, in dropping out of hats, in climbing ladders, in putting his little limbs out of joint in posturing. He had lived in an

atmosphere of trickery and deception; he had learned
to look upon mankind as dupes of their senses; in fine,
if he had thought at all, he would have been a skeptic;
if he had been a little older, he would have been a
cynic; if he had been older still, he would have been a
philosopher. As it was, he was a little imp! A good-
natured imp it was, too—an imp whose moral nature had
never been awakened, an imp up for a holiday, and willing to try virtue as a diversion. I don't know that he had
any spiritual nature. He was very superstitious, and
carried about with him a hideous little porcelain god
which he was in the habit of alternately reviling and
propitiating. He was too intelligent for the common
vices of stealing or gratuitous lying. Whatever discipline
he practiced was taught by his intellect.

I am inclined to think that his feelings were not altogether unimpressible—although it was almost impossible
to extract an expression from him—and I conscientiously
believe he became attached to those that were good to
him. What he might have become under more favorable
conditions than the bondsman of an overworked, under-
paid literary man, I don't know. I only know that the
scant, irregular, impulsive kindnesses that I showed him
were gratefully received. He was very loyal and patient
—two qualities rare in the average American servant. He
was like Malvolio, "sad and civil" with me; only once,
and then under great provocation, do I remember his
exhibiting any impatience. It was my habit after leaving
the office at night to take him with me to my rooms, as

the bearer of any supplemental or happy afterthought
in the editorial way that might occur to me before the
paper went to press. One night I had been scribbling
away past the usual hour of dismissing Wan Lee, and
had become quite oblivious of his presence in a chair
near my door, when suddenly I became aware of a voice
saying, in plaintive accents, something that sounded
like "Chy Lee."

I faced around sternly.

"What did you say?"

"Me say, 'Chy Lee.'"

"Well?" I said impatiently.

"You sabe, 'How do, John'?"

"Yes."

"You sabe, 'So long, John'?"

"Yes."

"Well, 'Chy Lee' allee same!"

I understood him quite plainly. It appeared that "Chy
Lee" was a form of "good night," and that Wan Lee was
anxious to go home. But an instinct of mischief which I
fear I possessed in common with him impelled me to
act as if oblivious of the hint. I muttered something
about not understanding him, and again bent over my
work. In a few minutes I heard his wooden shoes patter-
ing pathetically over the floor. I looked up. He was
standing near the door.

"You no sabe, 'Chy Lee'?"

"No," I said sternly.

"You sabe muchee big foolee!—allee same!"

And with this audacity upon his lips he fled. The next morning, however, he was as meek and patient as before, and I did not recall his offense. As a probable peace-offering, he blacked all my boots—a duty never required of him—including a pair of buff deerskin slippers and an immense pair of horseman's jack boots, on which he indulged his remorse for two hours.

I have spoken of his honesty as being a quality of his intellect rather than his principle, but I recall about this time two exceptions to the rule. I was anxious to get some fresh eggs as a change to the heavy diet of a mining town, and knowing that Wan Lee's countrymen were great poultry-raisers, I applied to him. He furnished me with them regularly every morning, but refused to take any pay, saying that the man did not sell them—a remarkable instance of self-abnegation, as eggs were then worth half a dollar apiece. One morning, my neighbor, Foster, dropped in upon me at breakfast, and took occasion to bewail his own ill fortune, as his hens had lately stopped laying, or wandered off in the bush. Wan Lee, who was present during our colloquy, preserved his characteristic sad taciturnity. When my neighbor had gone, he turned to me with a slight chuckle—"Flostel's hens—Wan Lee's hens—allee same!" His other offense was more serious and ambitious. It was a season of great irregularities in the mails, and Wan Lee had heard me deplore the delay in the delivery of my letters and newspapers. On arriving at my office one day, I was amazed to find my table covered with letters, evidently just from the post office, but unfortunately not one addressed to me. I turned to Wan Lee, who was surveying them with a calm satisfaction, and demanded an explanation. To my horror he pointed to an empty mailbag in the corner, and said, "Postman he say, 'No lettee, John—no lettee, John.' Postman plentee lie! Postman no good. Me catchee lettee last night—allee same!" Luckily it was still early; the mails had not been distributed; I had a hurried interview with the postmaster, and Wan Lee's bold attempt at robbing the U. S. mail was finally condoned, by the purchase of a new mailbag, and the whole affair thus kept a secret.

If my liking for my little pagan page had not been sufficient, my duty to Hop Sing was enough to cause me to take Wan Lee with me when I returned to San Francisco, after my two years' experience with the *Northern Star*. I do not think he contemplated the change with pleasure. I attributed his feelings to a nervous dread of crowded public streets—when he had to go across town for me on an errand, he always made a long circuit of the outskirts—to his dislike for the discipline of the Chinese and English school to which I proposed to send him, and to his fondness for the free vagrant life of the mines, to sheer willfulness! That it might have been a superstitious premonition did not occur to me until long afterward.

Nevertheless it really seemed as if the opportunity I had long looked for and confidently expected had come —the opportunity of placing Wan Lee under gently re-

straining influences, of subjecting him to a life and experience that would draw out of him what good my superficial care and ill-regulated kindness could not reach.
Wan Lee was placed at the school of a Chinese missionary—an intelligent and kind-hearted clergyman who
had shown great interest in the boy, and who, better
than all, had a wonderful faith in him. A home was
found for him in the family of a widow, who had a bright
and interesting daughter about two years younger than
Wan Lee. It was this bright, cheery, innocent and art-
less child that touched and reached a depth in the
boy's nature that hitherto had been unsuspected—that
awakened a moral susceptibility which had lain for
years insensible alike to the teachings of society or the
ethics of the theologian.

These few brief months, bright with a promise that
we never saw fulfilled, must have been happy ones to
Wan Lee. He worshiped his little friend with something
of the same superstition, but without any of the caprice,
that he bestowed upon his porcelain pagan god. It was
his delight to walk behind her to school, carrying her
books—a service always fraught with danger to him from
the little hands of his Caucasian Christian brothers. He
made her the most marvelous toys; he would cut out of
carrots and turnips the most astonishing roses and
tulips; he made lifelike chickens out of melon seeds; he
constructed fans and kites, and was singularly proficient
in the making of dolls' paper dresses. On the other hand
she played and sang to him, and taught him a thousand

little prettinesses and refinements only known to girls.
She read to him and showed him wherein he was original and valuable. And she took him to Sunday school
with her, against the precedents of the school, and
small-womanlike, triumphed. I wish I could add here
that she effected his conversion and made him give up
his porcelain idol, but I am telling a true story, and this
little girl was quite content to fill him with her own
Christian goodness without letting him know that he
was changed. So they got along very well together—this
little Christian girl with her shining cross hanging
around her plump white little neck, and this dark little
pagan with his hideous porcelain god hidden away in
his blouse.

There were two days of that eventful year which will
long be remembered in San Francisco—two days when a
mob of her citizens set upon and killed unarmed defenseless foreigners, because they were foreigners and
of another race, religion and color, and worked for what
wages they could get. There were some public men so
timid that, seeing this, they thought the end of the world
had come. There were some eminent statesmen, whose
names I am ashamed to write here, who began to think
that the passage in the Constitution which guarantees
civil and religious liberty to every citizen or foreigner
was a mistake. But there were also some men who were
not so easily frightened, and in twenty-four hours we
had things so arranged that the timid men could wring
their hands in safety, and the eminent statesmen utter

their doubts without hurting anybody or anything. And in the midst of this I got a note from Hop Sing, asking me to come to him immediately.

I found his warehouse closed and strongly guarded by the police against any possible attack of the rioters. Hop Sing admitted me through a barred grating with his usual imperturbable calm, but as it seemed to me, with more than his usual seriousness. Without a word he took my hand and led me to the rear of the room, and thence downstairs into the basement. It was dimly lighted, but there was something lying on the floor covered by a shawl. As I approached, he drew the shawl away with a sudden gesture, and revealed Wan Lee the pagan, lying there dead!

Dead, my reverend friends, dead! Stoned to death in the streets of San Francisco in the year of grace, eighteen hundred and sixty-nine, by a mob of half-grown boys and Christian school children!

As I put my hand reverently upon his breast, I felt something crumbling beneath his blouse. I looked inquiringly at Hop Sing. He put his hand between the folds of silk and drew out something with the first bitter smile I had ever seen on the face of that pagan gentleman.

It was Wan Lee's porcelain god, crushed by a stone from the hands of those Christian iconoclasts!

Dick
Spindler's
Family
∾ Christmas

THERE was surprise and sometimes disappointment in Rough and Ready when it was known that Dick Spindler intended to give a "family" Christmas party at his own house. That he should take an early opportunity to celebrate his good fortune and show hospitality was only expected from the man who had just made a handsome strike on his claim; but that it should assume so conservative, old-fashioned and respectable a form was quite unlooked for by Rough and Ready, and was thought by some a trifle pretentious. There were not half a dozen families in Rough and Ready; nobody ever knew before that Spindler had any relations, and this ringing in of strangers to the settlement seemed to indicate at least a lack of public spirit.

"He might," urged one of his critics, "hev given the boys that had worked alongside o' him in the ditches by day and slung lies with him around the campfire by

night—he might hev given them a square blowout and
kep' the leavin's for his old Spindler crew, just as other
families do. Why when old man Scudder had his house-
raisin' last year, his family lived for a week on what was
left over arter the boys had waltzed through the house
that night—and the Scudders warn't strangers, either."

It was also evident there was an uneasy feeling that
Spindler's action indicated an unhallowed leaning toward the minority of respectability and exclusiveness,
and a desertion—without the excuse of matrimony—of
the convivial and independent bachelor majority of
Rough and Ready.

"Ef he was stuck after some gal and was kinder
lookin' ahead, I'd hev understood it," argued another
critic.

"Don't ye be too sure he ain't," said Uncle Jim Starbuck gloomily. "Ye'll find that some blamed woman is
at the bottom of this yer family gatherin'. That and
trouble is almost all they're made for!"

There happened to be some truth in this dark proph-
ecy, but none of the kind that the misogynist supposed.
In fact Spindler had called a few evenings before at the
house of the Reverend Mr. Saltover; Mrs. Saltover, having one of her "saleratus headaches," had turned him
over to her widowed sister, Mrs. Huldy Price, who
obediently bestowed upon him that practical and critical
attention which she divided with the stocking she was
darning. A woman of thirty-five, of singular nerve and
practical wisdom, she had once smuggled her wounded

husband home from a border affray, calmly made coffee
for his deceived pursuers while he lay hidden in the loft,
walked four miles for that medical assistance which arrived too late to save him, and buried him secretly in
his own quarter section[1] with only one other witness
and mourner. And so she saved her position and property in that wild community, who believed he had fled.
There was very little of this experience to be traced in
her round, fresh-colored brunette cheek, her calm black
eyes set in a prickly hedge of stiff lashes, her plump
figure, or her frank courageous laugh. The latter appeared as a smile when she welcomed Mr. Spindler. She
hadn't seen him for a "coon's age," but "reckoned" he
was "busy fixin' up" his new house.

"Well yes," said Spindler with a slight hesitation. "Ye
see, I'm reckonin' to hev a kinder Christmas gatherin' of
my"—he was about to say "folks" but finally settled upon
"relatives" as being more correct in a preacher's house.

Mrs. Price thought it a very good idea. Christmas was
the natural season for the family to gather to "see who's
here and who's there, who's gettin' on and who isn't,
and who's dead and buried. It was lucky for them who
were so placed that they could do so and be joyful." Her
invincible philosophy probably carried her past any
dangerous recollections of the lonely grave in Kansas,
and holding up the stocking to the light she glanced
cheerfully along its level to Mr. Spindler's embarrassed
face by the fire.

[1] Tract of land, usually half a mile square.

"Well, I can't say much ez to that," responded Spindler, awkwardly, "for you see I don't know much about it anyway."

"How long since you've seen 'em?" asked Mrs. Price, apparently addressing herself to the stocking.

Spindler gave a weak laugh. "Well, you see, ef it comes to that, I've never seen 'em!"

Mrs. Price put the stocking in her lap and opened her direct eyes on Spindler. "Never seen 'em?" she repeated. "Then, they're not near relations?"

"There are three cousins," said Spindler, checking them off on his fingers, "a half-uncle, a kind of brother-in-law that is, the brother of my sister-in-law's second husband, and a niece. That's six."

"But if you've not seen them, I suppose they've corresponded with you?" said Mrs. Price.

"They've nearly all of 'em written to me for money, seein' my name in the paper ez hevin' made a strike," returned Spindler simply, "and hevin' sent it, I jest know their addresses."

"Oh!" said Mrs. Price, returning to the stocking.

Something in the tone of her ejaculation increased Spindler's embarrassment, but it also made him desperate. "You see, Mrs. Price," he blurted out, "I oughter tell ye that I reckon they are the folks that hevn't got on, don't you see, and so it seemed only the square thing for me, ez had got on, to give them a sort o' Christmas festival. Suthin', don't ye know, like what your brother-

in-law was sayin' last Sunday in the pulpit about this yer
peace and goodwill 'twixt man and man."

Mrs. Price looked again at the man before her. His
sallow perplexed face exhibited some doubt, and yet a
certain determination regarding the prospect the quotation had opened to him. "A very good idea, Mr. Spindler,
and one that does you great credit," she said gravely.

"I'm mighty glad to hear you say so, Mrs. Price," he
said with an accent of great relief, "for I reckoned to ask
you a great favor! You see," he fell into his former hesitation, "that is—the fact is—that this sort o' thing is
rather suddent to me—a little outer my line, don't you
see, and I was goin' to ask ye ef you'd mind takin' the
hull thing in hand and runnin' it for me."

"Runnin' it for you?" said Mrs. Price with a quick
glance from under the edge of her lashes. "Man alive!
What are you thinking of?"

"Bossin' the whole job for me," hurried on Spindler
with nervous desperation. "Gettin' together all the
things and makin' ready for 'em, orderin' in everythin'
that's wanted and fixin' up the rooms—I kin step out
while you're doin' it—and then helpin' me receive 'em,
and sittin' at the head o' the table, you know—like ez ef
you was the mistress."

"But," said Mrs. Price with her frank laugh, "that's
the duty of one of your relations—your niece, for instance—or cousin, if one of them is a woman."

"But," persisted Spindler, "you see they're strangers to

me. I don't know 'em and I do you. You'd make it easy
for them and for me, don't you see? Kinder introduce
'em, don't you know? A woman of your gin'ral experience would smooth down all them little difficulties,"
continued Spindler with a vague recollection of the
Kansas story, "and put everybody on velvet. Don't say
no, Mrs. Price! I'm just calkilatin' on you."

Sincerity and persistency in a man go a great way
with even the best of women. Mrs. Price who had at first
received Spindler's request as an amusing originality
now began to incline secretly toward it. And, of course,
began to suggest objections.

"I'm afraid it won't do," she said thoughtfully, awakening to the fact that it would do and could be done.
"You see, I've promised to spend Christmas at Sacramento with my nieces from Baltimore. And then there's
Mr. Saltover and my sister to consult."

But here Spindler's simple face showed such signs of
distress that the widow declared she would think it over
—a process which the sanguine Spindler seemed to consider so nearly akin to talking it over that Mrs. Price began to believe it herself as he hopefully departed.

She thought it over sufficiently to go to Sacramento
and excuse herself to her nieces. But here she permitted
herself to talk it over, to the infinite delight of those
Baltimore girls who thought this extravaganza of
Spindler's "so Californian and eccentric!" So it was
not strange that presently the news came back to Rough
and Ready, and his old associates learned for the first

time that he had never seen his relatives and that they
would be doubly strangers. This did not increase his
popularity; neither, I grieve to say, did the intelligence
that his relatives were probably poor, and that the Reverend Mr. Saltover had approved of his course, and had
likened it to the rich man's feast to which the halt and
blind were invited. Indeed the allusion was supposed to
add hypocrisy and a bid for popularity to Spindler's defection, for it was argued that he might have feasted
Wall-eyed Joe or Tanglefoot Billy, who had once been
"chawed" by a bear while prospecting, if he had been
sincere. Howbeit, Spindler's faith was oblivious to these
criticisms in his joy at Mr. Saltover's adhesion to his
plans and the loan of Mrs. Price as a hostess. In fact he
proposed to her that the invitations should also convey
that information in the expression "by the kind permission of the Reverend Mr. Saltover" as a guarantee of
good faith, but the widow would have none of it. The
invitations were duly written and dispatched.

"Suppose," suggested Spindler, with a sudden lugubrious apprehension, "suppose they shouldn't come?"

"Have no fear of that," said Mrs. Price with a frank
laugh.

"Or ef they was dead," continued Spindler.

"They couldn't all be dead," said the widow cheerfully.

"I've written to another cousin by marriage," said
Spindler dubiously, "in case of accident. I didn't think
of him before because he was rich."

"And have you ever seen him either, Mr. Spindler?" asked the widow with a slight mischievousness.

"Lordy! No!" he responded with unaffected concern.

Only one mistake was made by Mrs. Price in her arrangements for the party. She had noticed what the simple-minded Spindler could never have conceived— the feeling toward him held by his old associates—and had tactfully suggested that a general invitation should be extended to them in the evening.

"You can have refreshments, you know, after the dinner, and games and music, too."

"But," said the unsophisticated host, "won't the boys think I'm playin' it rather low down on them, so to speak, givin' 'em a kind o' second table, as ef it was the tailin's after a strike?"

"Nonsense," said Mrs. Price with decision. "It's quite fashionable in San Francisco and just the thing to do."

To this decision Spindler, in his blind faith in the widow's management, weakly yielded. An announcement in the *Weekly Banner* that:

> On Christmas evening Richard Spindler, Esq., proposed to entertain his friends and fellow citizens at an "at home," in his own residence,

not only widened the breach between him and the boys, but awakened an active resentment that only waited for an outlet. It was understood that they were all coming, but that they should have some fun out of it which might not coincide with Spindler's or his relatives' sense of humor seemed a foregone conclusion.

Unfortunately, too, subsequent events lent themselves to the irony of the situation. A few mornings after the invitations were dispatched, Spindler at one of his daily conferences with Mrs. Price took a newspaper from his pocket. "It seems," he said, looking at her with an embarrassed gravity, "that we will have to take one o' them names off that list—the name o' Sam Spindler—and calkilate upon only six relations comin'."

"Ah," said Mrs. Price interestedly, "then you have had an answer, and he has declined?"

"Not that exactly," said Spindler slowly, "but from remarks in this yer paper, he was hung last week by the vigilance committee of Yolo."

Mrs. Price opened her eyes on Spindler's face as she took the paper from his hand. "But," she said quickly, "this may be all a mistake, some other Spindler! You know, you say you've never seen them!"

"I reckon it's no mistake," said Spindler with patient gravity, "for the committee sent me back my invitation with the kinder disparagin' remark that they've 'sent him where it ain't bin the habit to keep Christmas!'"

Mrs. Price gasped, but a glance at Spindler's patient wistful, inquiring eyes brought back her old courage. "Well," she said cheerfully, "perhaps it's just as well he didn't come."

"Are ye sure o' that, Mrs. Price?" said Spindler with a slightly troubled expression. "Seems to me, now, that he was the sort as might hev bin gathered in at the feast and kinder snatched like a brand from the burnin', accordin' to Scripter. But ye know best."

"Mr. Spindler," said Mrs. Price suddenly with a slight snap in her black eyes; "are your—are the others like this? Or"—here her eyes softened again and her laugh returned, albeit slightly hysterical—"is this kind of thing likely to happen again?"

"I think we're pretty sartin o' hevin' six to dinner," returned Spindler simply. Then as if noticing some other significance in her speech he added wistfully, "But you won't go back on me, Mrs. Price, ef things ain't pannin' out exackly as I reckoned? You see, I never really knew these yer relations."

He was so obviously sincere in his intent, and above all seemed to place such a pathetic reliance on her judgment that she hesitated to let him know the shock his revelation had given her. And what might his other relations prove to be? Good Lord! Yet oddly enough she was so prepossessed by him and so fascinated by his very quixotism, that it was perhaps for these complex reasons she said a little stiffly:

"One of these cousins, I see, is a lady, and then there is your niece. Do you know anything about them, Mr. Spindler?"

His face grew serious. "No more than I know of the others," he said apologetically. After a moment's hesita-

tion he went on, "Now you speak of it, it seems to me
I've heard that my niece was di-vorced. But," he added,
brightening up, "I've heard that she was popular."

Mrs. Price gave a short laugh and was silent for a few
minutes. Then this sublime little woman looked up at
him. What he might have seen in her eyes was more
than he expected or, I fear, deserved. "Cheer up, Mr.
Spindler," she said determinedly. "I'll see you through
this thing, don't you mind! But don't you say anything
about—about—this vigilance committee business to anybody. Nor about your niece—it was your niece, wasn't
it?—being divorced. Charley, the late Mr. Price, had a
queer sort of sister who—but that's neither here nor
there! And your niece mayn't come, you know, or if she
does you ain't bound to bring her out to the general
company."

At parting Spindler, in sheer gratefulness, pressed her
hand and lingered so long over it that a little color
sprang into the widow's brown cheek. Perhaps a fresh
courage sprang into her heart, too, for she went to Sacramento the next day, previously enjoining Spindler on no
account to show any answers he might receive. At
Sacramento her nieces flew to her with confidences.

"We so wanted to see you, Aunt Huldy, for we've
heard something so delightful about your funny Christmas party!" Mrs. Price's heart sank but her eyes snapped.
"Only think of it! One of Mr. Spindler's long-lost relatives, a Mr. Wragg, lives in this hotel and papa knows
him. He's a sort of half-uncle, I believe, and he's just

furious that Spindler should have invited him. He showed papa the letter, said it was the greatest piece of insolence in the world, that Spindler was an ostentatious fool who had made a little money and wanted to use him to get into society! And the fun of the thing is that this half-uncle and whole brute is himself a parvenu, a vulgar ostentatious creature who was only a——"

"Never mind what he was, Kate," interrupted Mrs. Price hastily. "I call his conduct a shame."

"So do we," said both girls eagerly. After a pause Kate clasped her knees with her locked fingers, and rocking backward and forward said, "Milly and I have got an idea and don't you say no to it. We've had it ever since that brute talked in that way. Now, through him we know more about this Mr. Spindler's family connections than you do, and we know all the trouble you and he'll have in getting up this party. You understand? Now we first want to know what Spindler's like. Is he a savage bearded creature, like the miners we saw on the boat?"

Mrs. Price said that on the contrary he was very gentle, soft-spoken, and rather good-looking.

"Young or old?"

"Young, in fact a mere boy, as you may judge from his actions," returned Mrs. Price with a suggestive matronly air.

Kate here put up a long-handled eyeglass to her fine gray eyes, fitted it ostentatiously over her aquiline nose, and then said in a voice of simulated horror, "Aunt Huldy, this revelation is shocking!"

Mrs. Price laughed her usual frank laugh, albeit her brown cheek took upon it a faint tint of Indian red. "If that's the wonderful idea you girls have got, I don't see how it's going to help matters," she said dryly.

"No, that's not it! We really have an idea. Now look here."

Mrs. Price "looked here." This process seemed to the superficial observer to be merely submitting her waist and shoulders to the arms of her nieces and her ears to their confidential and coaxing voices.

Twice she said "it couldn't be thought of" and "it was impossible," once addressed Kate as "you limb,"[1] and finally said that she "wouldn't promise, but might write!"

It was two days before Christmas. There was nothing in the air, sky or landscape of that Sierran slope to suggest the season to the eastern stranger. A soft rain had been dropping for a week on laurel, pine and buckeye, and the blades of springing grasses and shyly opening flowers. Sedate and silent hillsides that had grown dumb and parched toward the end of the dry season became gently articulate again. There were murmurs in hushed and forgotten canyons, the leap and laughter of water among the dry bones of dusty creeks, and the full

[1] Scamp.

song of the larger forks and rivers. Southwest winds
brought the warm odor of the pine sap swelling in
the forest or the faint far-off spice of wild mustard
springing in the lower valleys. But, as if by some irony
of Nature, this gentle invasion of spring in the wild
wood brought only disturbance and discomfort to the
haunts and works of man. The ditches were overflowing,
the fords of the Fork impassable, the sluicing adrift, and
the trails and wagon roads to Rough and Ready knee-
deep in mud. The stagecoach from Sacramento entering the settlement by the mountain highway, its wheels
and panels clogged and crusted with an unctuous pig-
ment like mud and blood, passed out of it through the
overflowed and dangerous ford, and emerged in spotless purity, leaving its stains behind with Rough and
Ready. A week of enforced idleness on the river's bank,
or bar, had driven the miners to the more comfortable
recreation of the saloon bar, its mirrors, its florid paint-
ings, its armchairs and its stove. The steam of their wet
boots and the smoke of their pipes hung over the latter
like the sacrificial incense from an altar. But the attitude
of the men was more critical and censorious than contented, and showed little of the gentleness of the
weather or season.

"Did you hear if the stage brought down any more relations of Spindler's?"

The barkeeper, to whom this question was addressed
shifted his lounging position against the bar and said, "I
reckon not, ez far ez I know."

"And that old bloat of a second cousin, that crimson beak what kem down yesterday, he ain't bin hangin' round here today for his reg'lar pizin?"

"No," said the barkeeper thoughtfully, "I reckon Spindler's got him locked up and is settin' on him to keep him sober till after Christmas, and prevent you boys gettin' at him."

"He'll have the jimjams before that," returned the first speaker. "And how about that dead beat of a half-nephew who borrowed twenty dollars of Yuba Bill on the way down and then wanted to get off at Shooters-ville, but Bill wouldn't let him and scooted him down to Spindler's and collected the money from Spindler him-self afore he'd give him up?"

"He's up thar with the rest of the menagerie," said the barkeeper, "but I reckon that Mrs. Price hez bin feedin' him up. And ye know the old woman, that fifty-fifty cousin by marriage who Joe Chandler swears he remembers ez an old cook for a Chinese restaurant in Stockton, durn my skin ef that Mrs. Price hasn't rigged her out in some fancy duds of her own and made her look quite decent."

A deep groan here broke from Uncle Jim Starbuck.

"Didn't I tell ye?" he said, turning appealingly to the others. "It's that darned widow that's at the bottom of it all! She first put Spindler up to givin' the party and now, durn my skin, ef she ain't goin' to fix up these ragamuffins and drill 'em so we can't get any fun outer 'em after all! And it bein' a woman that's bossin' the job and not Spindler, we've got to draw things mighty fine and not cut up too rough, or some of the boys will kick."

"You bet," said a surly but decided voice in the crowd.

"And," said another voice, "Mrs. Price didn't live in Bleedin' Kansas for nothing."

"Wot's the program you've settled on, Uncle Jim?" said the barkeeper lightly, to check what seemed to promise a dangerous discussion.

"Well," said Starbuck, "we calkilate to gather early Christmas night in Hooper's Hollow and rig ourselves up Injun fashion, and then start for Spindler's with pitch pine torches and have a torchlight dance around the house. Them ez does the dancin' and yellin' outside 'll take their turn at goin' in and hevin' refreshment. Jake Cooledge of Boston sez if anybody objects to it we've only got to say we're 'mummers of the olden times,' sabe? Then later we'll have *Them Sabbath Evening Bells* performed on prospectin' pans by the band. Then at the finish, Jake Cooledge is goin' to give one of his surkastic speeches kinder welcomin' Spindler's family to the free openin' of Spindler's Almshouse and Reformatory."

He paused, possibly for that approbation, which, however, did not seem to come spontaneously. "It ain't much," he added apologetically, "for we're hampered by women, but we'll add to the program ez we see how things pan out. Ye see, from what we can hear, all of Spindler's relations ain't on hand yet! We've got to wait, like at election time, for returns from the back counties. Hello! What's that?"

It was the swish and splutter of hoofs on the road before the door. The Sacramento coach! In an instant every man was expectant, and Starbuck darted outside on the platform. Then there was the usual greeting and bustle, the hurried ingress of thirsty passengers into the saloon, and a pause. Uncle Jim returned, excited and panting. "Look yer, boys! Ef this ain't the richest thing out! They say there's two more relations o' Spindler's on the coach, come down as express freight, consigned— d' ye hear?—consigned to Spindler!"

"Stiffs in coffins?" suggested an eager voice.

"I didn't get to hear more. But here they are."

There was the sudden irruption of a laughing curious crowd into the barroom, led by Yuba Bill the driver. Then the crowd parted and out of their midst stepped two children, a boy and a girl, the oldest apparently not more than six years, holding each other's hands. They were coarsely yet cleanly dressed with a certain uniform precision that suggested formal charity. But more remarkable than all, around the neck of each was a little steel chain from which depended the regular check and label of the powerful express company, Wells, Fargo & Co., and the words:

> *To Richard Spindler* — FRAGILE
> WITH GREAT CARE — COLLECT ON DELIVERY

Occasionally their little hands went up automatically
and touched their labels as if to show them. They surveyed the crowd, the floor, the gilded bar and Yuba Bill
without fear and without wonder. There was a pathetic
suggestion that they were accustomed to this scrutiny.

"Now Bobby," said Yuba Bill, leaning back against
the bar with an air half paternal, half managerial, "tell
these gents how you came here."

"By Wellth, Fargoth Expreth," lisped Bobby.

"Whar from?"

"Wed Hill, Owegon."

"Red Hill, Oregon? Why, it's a thousand miles from
here," said a bystander.

"I reckon," said Yuba Bill coolly. "They kem by stage
to Portland, by steamer to Frisco, steamer again to
Stockton, and then by stage over the whole line. Allers
by Wells, Fargo & Co.'s express, from agent to agent
and from messenger to messenger. Fact! They ain't bin
tetched or handled by anyone but the kempany's agents;
they ain't had a line or direction except them checks
around their necks! And they've wanted for nothin'.
Why I've carried heaps o' treasure before, gentlemen,
and once a hundred thousand dollars in greenbacks but
I never carried anythin' that was watched and guarded
as them kids! Why, the division inspector at Stockton
wanted to go with 'em over the line. But Jim Bracy,
the messenger, said he'd call it a reflection on himself
and resign ef they didn't give 'em to him with the other

packages! Ye had a pretty good time, Bobby, didn't ye? Plenty to eat and drink, eh?"

The two children laughed a little weak laugh, turned each other bashfully around, and then looked up shyly at Yuba Bill and said, "Yeth."

"Do you know where you are goin'?" asked Starbuck in a constrained voice.

It was the little girl who answered quickly and eagerly:

"Yes, to Krissmass and Sandy Claus."

"To what?" asked Starbuck.

Here the boy interposed with a superior air:

"Thee meanth Couthin Dick. He 'th got Krithmath."

"Where's your mother?"

"Dead."

"And your father?"

"In orthpittal."

There was a laugh somewhere on the outskirts of the crowd. Everyone faced angrily in that direction but the laugher had disappeared. Yuba Bill, however, sent his voice after him. "Yes, in the hospital! Funny, ain't it?—amoosin' place! Try it. Step over here, and in five minutes, by the livin' Hoky, I'll qualify you for admission and not charge you a cent!" He stopped, gave a sweeping glance of dissatisfaction around him and then leaning back against the bar, beckoned to someone near the door and said in a disgusted tone, "You tell these galoots how it happened, Bracy. They make me sick!"

Thus appealed to, Bracy the express messenger stepped forward in Yuba Bill's place.

"It's nothing particular, gentlemen," he said with a laugh, "only it seems that some man called Spindler, who lives about here, sent an invitation to the father of these children to bring his family to a Christmas party. It wasn't a bad sort of thing for Spindler to do, considering that they were his poor relations, though they didn't know him from Adam—was it?" He paused. Several of the bystanders cleared their throats but said nothing. "At least," resumed Bracy, "that's what the boys up at Red Hill, Oregon, thought when they heard of it. Well, as the father was in the hospital with a broken leg and the mother only a few weeks dead, the boys thought it mighty rough on these poor kids if they were done out of their fun because they had no one to bring them. The boys couldn't afford to go themselves but they got a little money together and then got the idea of sendin' 'em by express. Our agent at Red Hill tumbled to the idea at once, but he wouldn't take any money in advance and said he would send 'em c.o.d. like any other package. And he did, and here they are! That's all! And now, gentlemen, as I've got to deliver them personally to this Spindler and get his receipt and take off their checks, I reckon we must toddle. Come, Bill, help take 'em up!"

"Hold on!" said a dozen voices. A dozen hands were thrust into a dozen pockets. I grieve to say some were regretfully withdrawn empty, for it was a hard season

in Rough and Ready. But the expressman stepped before them with warning uplifted hand.

"Not a cent, boys, not a cent! Wells Fargo's Express
company don't undertake to carry bullion with those
kids, at least on the same contract!" He laughed and
then looking around him, said confidentially in a lower
voice which, however, was quite audible to the children, "There's as much as three bags of silver in quarter
and half dollars in my treasure box in the coach that has
been poured, yes, just showered upon them ever since
they started, and has been passed over from agent to
agent and messenger to messenger. Why there's enough
to pay their passage from here to China! It's time to say
quits now. But bet your life, they're not going to that
Christmas party poor!"

He caught up the boy as Yuba Bill lifted the little
girl to his shoulder, and both passed out the door. Then
one by one the loungers in the barroom silently and awkwardly followed. When the barkeeper turned back from
putting away his decanters and glasses, to his astonishment the room was empty.

Spindler's house, or Spindler's Splurge, as Rough and
Ready chose to call it, stood above the settlement on
a deforested hillside which, however, revenged itself by
producing not enough vegetation to cover even the few
stumps that were ineradicable. A large wooden structure
in the pseudo-classic style affected by westerners, with an
incongruous cupola, it was oddly enough relieved by a
still more incongruous veranda extending around its

four sides, upheld by wooden Doric columns which were already picturesquely covered with flowering vines and sun-loving roses. Mr. Spindler had trusted the furnishing of its interior to the same contractor who had upholstered the gilded barroom of the Eureka Saloon, and who had apparently bestowed the same design and material impartially on each. There were gilded mirrors all over the house and chilly marble-topped tables, gilt plaster cupids in the corners and stuccoed lions "in the way" everywhere. The tactful hands of Mrs. Price had screened some of these with seasonable laurels, fir boughs and berries and had imparted a slight Christmas flavor to the house. But the greater part of her time had been employed in trying to subdue the eccentricities of Spindler's amazing relations—in tranquilizing Mrs. "Aunt" Martha Spindler, the elderly cook before alluded to, who was inclined to regard the gilded splendors of the house as indicative of dangerous immorality; in restraining Cousin Morley Hewlett from considering the dining room buffet as a bar for intermittent refreshment; and in keeping the weak-minded nephew Phinney Spindler from shooting at bottles from the veranda or wearing his uncle's clothes or running up an account in his uncle's name for various articles at the general stores. Yet the unlooked-for arrival of the two children had been the one great compensation and diversion for her. She wrote at once to her nieces a brief account of her miraculous deliverance. "I think these poor children dropped from the skies here to make our Christmas party possible, to say nothing of the sympathy they have created in Rough and Ready for Spindler. He is going to keep them as long as he can and is writing to the father. Think of the poor little tots traveling a thousand miles to 'Krissmass,' as they call it!—though they were so well cared for by the messengers that their little bodies were positively stuffed like quails. So you see, dear, we will be able to get along without airing your famous idea. I'm sorry, for I know you're just dying to see it all."

Whatever Kate's idea might have been, there certainly seemed now no need of any extraneous aid to Mrs. Price's management. Christmas came at last, and the dinner passed off without serious disaster. But the ordeal of the reception of Rough and Ready was still to come. For Mrs. Price well knew that although "the boys" were more subdued, and indeed inclined to sympathize with their host's uncouth endeavor, there was still much in the aspect of Spindler's relations to excite their sense of the ludicrous.

But here Fortune again favored the house of Spindler with a dramatic surprise even greater than the advent of the children had been. In the change that had come over Rough and Ready, the boys had decided out of deference to the women and children to omit the first part of their program, and had approached and entered the house as soberly and quietly as ordinary guests. But before they had shaken hands with the host and hostess and seen the relations, the clatter of wheels was heard

before the open door and its lights flashed upon a carriage and pair—an actual private carriage—the like of
which had not been seen since the governor of the state
had come down to open the new ditch! Then there was
a pause, the flash of the carriage lamps upon white silk,
the light tread of a satin foot on the veranda and in the
hall, and the entrance of a vision of loveliness! Middle-
aged men and old dwellers of cities remembered their
youth; younger men bethought themselves of Cinderella
and the prince! There was a thrill and a hush as this last
guest—a beautiful girl radiant with youth and adornment—put a dainty glass to her sparkling eye, and advanced familiarly with outstretched hand to Dick
Spindler. Mrs. Price gave a single gasp and drew back
speechless.

"Uncle Dick," said a laughing contralto voice which
indeed somewhat recalled Mrs. Price's own in its
courageous frankness, "I am so delighted to come, even
if a little late, and so sorry that Mr. M'Kenna could not
come on account of business."

Everybody listened eagerly, but none more eagerly
and surprisingly than the host himself. M'Kenna! The
rich cousin who had never answered the invitation! And
"Uncle Dick!" This, then, was his divorced niece. Yet
even in his astonishment he remembered that of course
no one but himself and Mrs. Price knew it, and that lady
had glanced discreetly away.

"Yes," continued the half-niece brightly. "I came
from Sacramento with some friends to Shootersville,

and from thence I drove here. And though I must return tonight I could not forego the pleasure of coming, if it was only for an hour or two, to answer the invitation of the uncle I have not seen for years." She paused, and raising her glasses turned a politely questioning eye toward Mrs. Price. "One of our relations?" she said smilingly to Spindler.

"No," said Spindler with some embarrassment. "A—a friend!"

The half-niece extended her hand. Mrs. Price took it.

But the fair stranger—what she did and said were the only things remembered in Rough and Ready on that festive occasion. No one thought of the other relations; no one recalled them or their eccentricities; Spindler himself was forgotten. People only recollected how Spindler's lovely niece lavished her smiles and courtesies on everyone and brought to her feet particularly, the misogynist Starbuck and the sarcastic Cooledge, oblivious of his previously scheduled speech. She sat at the piano and sang like an angel, hushing the most hilarious and excited into sentimental and even maudlin silence. Graceful as a nymph she led with "Uncle Dick" a Virginia reel until the whole assembly joined, eager for a passing touch of her dainty hand in its changes. And when two hours had passed, all too swiftly for the guests, they stood with bared heads and glistening eyes on the veranda to see the fairy coach whirl the fairy princess away! How—but this incident was never known to Rough and Ready.

It happened in the sacred dressing room, where Mrs. Price was cloaking with her own hands the departing half-niece of Mr. Spindler. Taking that opportunity to seize the lovely relative by the shoulders and shake her violently, she said: "Oh yes, and it's all very well for you, Kate, you limb! For you're going away and will never see Rough and Ready and poor Spindler again. But what am I to do, miss? How am I to face it out? For you know I've got to tell *him* at least that you're no half-niece of his!"

"Have you?" said the young lady.

"Have I?" repeated the widow impatiently. "Have I? Of course I have! What are you thinking of?"

"I was thinking, aunty," said the girl audaciously, "that from what I've seen and heard tonight, if I'm not his half-niece now, it's only a question of time! So you'd better wait. Good night, dear."

And really, it turned out that she was right!

Chu

ༀ Chu

I DO NOT believe that the most enthusiastic lover of that useful and noble animal, the horse, will claim for him the charm of geniality, humor or expansive confidence. Any creature who will not look you squarely in the eye—whose only oblique glances are inspired by fear, distrust or a view to attack, who has no way of returning caresses, and whose favorite expression is one of head-lifting disdain may be noble or useful, but can be hardly said to add to the gaiety of nations. Indeed it may be broadly stated that with the single exception of goldfish, of all animals kept for the recreation of mankind the horse is alone capable of exciting a passion that shall be absolutely hopeless. I deem these general remarks necessary to prove that my unreciprocated affection for Chu Chu was not purely individual or singular. And I may add that to these general characteristics she brought the waywardness of her capricious sex.

She came to me out of the rolling dust of an emigrant wagon, behind whose tailboard she was gravely trotting. She was a half-broken colt—in which character she had at different times unseated everybody in the train—and although covered with dust, she had a beautiful coat and the most lambent gazellelike eyes I had ever seen. I think she kept these latter organs purely for ornament —apparently looking at things with her nose, her sensitive ears, and sometimes even a slight lifting of her slim near foreleg. On our first interview I thought she favored me with a coy glance, but as it was accompanied by an irrelevant "Look out!" from her owner, the teamster, I was not certain. I only know that after some conversation, a good deal of mental reservation, and the disbursement of considerable coin I found myself standing in the dust of the departing emigrant wagon with one end of a forty-foot riata in my hand and Chu Chu at the other.

I pulled invitingly at my own end and even advanced a step or two toward her. She then broke into a long disdainful pace and began to circle around me at the extreme limit of her tether. I stood admiring her free action for some moments—not always turning with her, which was tiring—until I found that she was gradually winding herself up *on me!* Her frantic astonishment when she suddenly found herself thus brought up against me was one of the most remarkable things I ever saw, and nearly took me off my legs. Then, when she had pulled against the riata until her narrow head and prettily arched neck were on a perfectly straight line with it, she as suddenly slackened the tension and condescended to follow me at an angle of her own choosing. Sometimes it was on one side of me, sometimes on the other. Even then the sense of my dreadful contiguity apparently would come upon her like a fresh discovery, and she would become hysterical. But I do not think that she really *saw* me. She looked at the riata and sniffed it disparagingly; she pawed some pebbles that were near me tentatively with her small hoof; she started back with a Robinson Crusoe-like horror of my footprints in the wet gully, but my actual personal presence she ignored. She would sometimes pause with her head thoughtfully between her forelegs and apparently say, "There is some extraordinary presence here: animal, vegetable or mineral—I can't make out which—but it's not good to eat, and I loathe and detest it."

When I reached my house in the suburbs, before entering the fifty vara[1] lot enclosure, I deemed it prudent to leave her outside while I informed the household of my purchase, and with this object I tethered her by the long riata to a solitary sycamore which stood in the center of the road, the crossing of two frequented thoroughfares. It was not long, however, before I was interrupted by shouts and screams from that vicinity, and

[1] Spanish unit of length, equal to about 34 inches.

on returning thither I found that Chu Chu, with the assistance of her riata, had securely wound up two of my neighbors to the tree, where they presented the appearance of early Christian martyrs. When I released them it appeared that they had been attracted by Chu Chu's graces and had offered her overtures of affection, to which she had characteristically rotated with this miserable result. I led her with some difficulty, warily keeping clear of the riata, to the enclosure from whose fence I had previously removed several bars. Although the space was wide enough to have admitted a troop of cavalry she affected not to notice it and managed to kick away part of another section on entering. She resisted the stable for some time, but after carefully examining it with her hoofs, and an affectedly meek outstretching of her nose, she consented to recognize some oats in the feed box—without looking at them—and was formally installed. All this while she had resolutely ignored my presence. As I stood watching her she suddenly stopped eating; the same reflective look came over her. "Surely I am not mistaken; that same obnoxious creature is somewhere about here!" she seemed to say, and shivered at the possibility.

It was probably this which made me confide my unreciprocated affection to one of my neighbors—a man supposed to be an authority on horses, particularly of that wild species to which Chu Chu belonged. It was he who, leaning over the edge of the stall where she was complacently and as usual, obliviously munching, absolutely dared to toy with a pet lock of hair which she wore over the pretty star on her forehead.

"Ye see, captain," he said with jaunty easiness, "hosses is like wimmen; ye don't want ter use any standoffishness or shyness with *them;* a stiddy but keerless sort o' familiarity, a kind o' free but firm handlin', jess like this, to let her see who's master—"

We never clearly knew *how* it happened, but when I picked up my neighbor from the doorway amid the broken splinters of the stall rail and a quantity of oats that mysteriously filled his hair and pockets, Chu Chu was found to have faced around the other way and was contemplating her forelegs, with her hind ones in the other stall. My neighbor spoke of damages while he was in the stall and of physical coercion when he was out of it again. But here Chu Chu in some marvelous way righted herself, and my neighbor departed hurriedly with a brimless hat and an unfinished sentence.

My next intermediary was Enriquez Saltello, a youth of my own age and the brother of Consuelo Saltello, whom I adored. As a Spanish Californian he was presumed, on account of Chu Chu's half-Spanish origin, to have superior knowledge of her character, and I even vaguely believed that his language and accent would fall familiarly on her ear. There was the drawback, however, that he always preferred to talk in a marvelous English, combining Castilian precision with what he fondly believed to be Californian slang.

"To confer then as to thees horse, which is not—ob-

serve me—a Mexican plug! Ah, no! you can your boots
bet on that. She is of Castilian stock—believe me and
strike me dead! I will myself at different times over-
look and affront her in the stable, examine her as to the
assault, and why she should do thees thing. When she is
of the exercise I will also accost and restrain her. Remain tranquil, my friend! When a few days shall pass
much shall be changed, and she will be as another.
Trust your oncle to do thees thing! Comprehend me?
Everything shall be lovely and the goose hang high!"

Conformably with this he "overlooked" her the next
day, with a cigarette between his yellow-stained finger-
tips, which made her sneeze in a silent pantomimic way,
and certain Spanish blandishments of speech which she
received with more complacency. But I don't think
she ever even looked at him. In vain he protested that
she was the dearest and littlest of his "little loves"—in
vain he asserted that she was his patron saint and that
it was his soul's delight to pray to her; she accepted the
compliment with her eyes fixed upon the manger. When
he had exhausted his whole stock of endearing diminutives, adding a few playful and more audacious sallies,
she remained with her head down as if inclined to medi-
tate upon them. This he declared was at least an improvement on her former performances. It may have
been my own jealousy, but I fancied she was only
saying to herself, "Gracious! can there be *two* of them?"

"Courage and patience, my friend," he said as we
were slowly quitting the stable. "Thees horse is yonge

and has not yet the habitude of the person. Tomorrow, at another season, I shall give to her a foundling" (fondling, I have reason to believe, was the word intended by Enriquez)—"and we shall see. It shall be as easy as to fall away from a log. A leetle more of this chin music which your friend Enriquez possesses, and some tapping of the head and neck, and you are there. You are ever the right side up. Houp la! But let us not precipitate this thing. The more haste, we do not so much accelerate ourselves."

He appeared to be suiting the action to the word as he lingered in the doorway of the stable. "Come on," I said.

"Pardon," he returned, with a bow that was both elaborate and evasive, "but you shall yourself precede me—the stable is *yours*."

"Oh, come along!" I continued impatiently. To my surprise he seemed to dodge back into the stable again. After an instant he reappeared.

"Pardon! but I am re-strain! Of a truth, in this instant I am grasp by the mouth of thees horse in the coattail of my dress! She will that I should remain. It would seem"—he disappeared again—"that"—he was out once more—"the experiment is a sooccess! She reciprocate! She is, of a truth, gone on me. It is lofe!"—a stronger pull from Chu Chu here sent him in again—"but"—he was out now triumphantly with half his garment torn away—"I shall coquet."

Nothing daunted, however, the gallant fellow was

back next day with a Mexican saddle and attired in the complete outfit of a vaquero. Overcome though *he* was by heavy deerskin trousers open at the side from the knees down and fringed with bullion buttons, an enormous flat sombrero, and a stiff short embroidered velvet jacket, I was more concerned at the ponderous saddle and equipments intended for the slim Chu Chu. That these would hide and conceal her beautiful curves and contour as well as overweight her, seemed certain; that she would resist them all to the last seemed equally clear. Nevertheless to my surprise, when she was led out and the saddle thrown deftly across her back, she was passive. Was it possible that some drop of her old Spanish blood responded to its clinging embrace? She did not either look at it or smell it. But when Enriquez began to tighten the cinch or girth a more singular thing occurred. Chu Chu visibly distended her slender barrel to twice its dimensions; the more he pulled the more she swelled, until I was actually ashamed of her. Not so Enriquez. He smiled at us and complacently stroked his thin mustache.

"Eet is ever so! She is the child of her grandmother! Even when you shall make saddle thees old Castilian stock, it will make large—it will become a balloon! Eet is a trick—eet is a leetle game—believe me. For why?"

I had not listened as I was at that moment astonished to see the saddle slowly slide under Chu Chu's belly and her figure resume, as if by magic, its former slim proportions. Enriquez followed my eyes, lifted his shoulders, shrugged them and said smilingly, "Ah, you see!"

When the girths were drawn in again with an extra pull or two from the indefatigable Enriquez, I fancied that Chu Chu nevertheless secretly enjoyed it, as her sex is said to appreciate tight lacing. She drew a deep sigh, possibly of satisfaction, turned her neck, and apparently tried to glance at her own figure—Enriquez promptly withdrawing to enable her to do so easily. Then the dread moment arrived. Enriquez, with his hand on her mane, suddenly paused and with exaggerated courtesy lifted his hat and made an inviting gesture.

"You will honor me to precede."

I shook my head laughingly.

"I see," responded Enriquez gravely. "You have to attend the obsequies of your aunt who is dead, at two of the clock. You have to meet your broker who has bought you feefty share of the Comstock lode—at thees moment —or you are loss! You are excuse! Attend! Gentlemen, make your bets! The band has arrived to play! 'Ere we are!"

With a quick movement the alert young fellow had vaulted into the saddle. But to the astonishment of both of us, the mare remained perfectly still. There was Enriquez bolt upright in the stirrups, completely overshadowing by his saddle flaps, leggings and gigantic spurs the fine proportions of Chu Chu, until she might have been a placid Rosinante, bestridden by some

youthful Quixote. She closed her eyes, she was going to
sleep! We were dreadfully disappointed. This clearly
would not do. Enriquez lifted the reins cautiously! Chu
Chu moved forward slowly—then stopped, apparently
lost in reflection.

"Affront her on thees side."

I approached her gently. She shot suddenly into the
air, coming down again on perfectly stiff legs with a
springless jolt. This she instantly followed by a succession of other rocketlike propulsions, utterly unlike a
leap, all over the enclosure. The movements of the unfortunate Enriquez were equally unlike any equitation
I ever saw. He appeared occasionally over Chu Chu's
head, astride of her neck and tail, or in the free air, but
never *in* the saddle. His rigid legs, however, never lost
the stirrups, but came down regularly, accentuating her
springless hops. More than that, the disproportionate
excess of rider, saddle and accoutrements was so great
that he had at times the appearance of lifting Chu Chu
forcibly from the ground by superior strength, and of
actually contributing to her exercise! As they came toward me, a wild tossing and flying mass of hoofs and
spurs, it was not only difficult to tell them apart, but to
ascertain how much of the jumping was done by Enriquez separately. At last Chu Chu brought matters to a
close by making for the low-stretching branches of an
oak tree which stood at the corner of the lot. In a few
moments she emerged from it—but without Enriquez.

I found the gallant fellow disengaging himself from

the fork of a branch in which he had been firmly wedged, but still smiling and confident, his cigarette between his teeth. Then for the first time he removed it, and seating himself easily on the branch with his legs dangling down, he blandly waved aside my anxious queries with a gentle reassuring gesture.

"Remain tranquil, my friend. Thees does not count! I have conquer—you observe—for why? I have *never* for once *arrive at the ground!* Consequent she is disappoint! She will ever that I *should!* But I have got her when the hair is not long! Your oncle Henry"—with an angelic wink—"is fly! He is ever a bully boy, with the eye of glass! Believe me. Behold! I am here! Big Injun! Whoop!"

He leaped lightly to the ground. Chu Chu, standing watchfully at a little distance, was evidently astonished at his appearance. She threw out her hind hoofs violently, shot up into the air until the stirrups crossed each other high above the saddle, and made for the stable in a succession of rabbitlike bounds—taking the precaution to remove the saddle on entering by striking it against the lintel of the door.

"You observe," said Enriquez blandly, "she would make that thing of *me*. Not having the good occasion, she ees dissatisfied. Where are you now?"

Two or three days afterward he rode her again with the same result—accepted by him with the same heroic complacency. As we did not for certain reasons care to use the open road for this exercise, and as it was impossible to remove the tree, we were obliged to submit to the inevitable. On the following day I mounted her—undergoing the same experience as Enriquez, with the individual sensation of falling from a third-story window on top of a countinghouse stool, and the variation of being projected over the fence. When I found that Chu Chu had not accompanied me, I saw Enriquez at my side.

"More than ever it is become necessary that we should do thees things again," he said gravely as he assisted me to my feet. "Courage, my noble General! God and Liberty! Once more on to the breach! Charge, Chestare, charge! Come on, Don Stanley! 'Ere we are!"

He helped me none too quickly to catch my seat again, for it apparently had the effect of the turned peg on the enchanted horse in the Arabian Nights, and Chu Chu instantly rose into the air. But she came down this time before the open window of the kitchen, and I alighted easily on the dresser. The indefatigable Enriquez followed me.

"Won't this do?" I asked meekly.

"It ees *better*—for you arrive *not* on the ground," he said cheerfully; "but you should not once but a thousand times make trial! Ha! Go and win! Nevare die and say so! 'Eave ahead! 'Eave! There you are!"

Luckily this time I managed to lock the rowels of my long spurs under her girth, and she could not unseat me. She seemed to recognize the fact after one or two plunges, when to my great surprise, she suddenly sank to the ground and quietly rolled over me. The action disengaged my spurs, but righting herself without getting up, she turned her beautiful head and absolutely *looked* at me!—still in the saddle. I felt myself blushing! But the voice of Enriquez was at my side.

"Errise, my friend; you have conquer! It is *she* who has arrive at the ground! *You* are all right. It is done; believe me, it is feenish! No more shall she make thees thing. From thees instant you shall ride her as the cow —as the rail of thees fence—and remain tranquil. For she is a-broke! Ta-ta! Regain your hats, gentlemen! Pass in your checks! It is ovar! How are you now?" He lit a fresh cigarette, put his hands in his pockets, and smiled at me blandly.

For all that, I ventured to point out that the habit of alighting in the fork of a tree, or the disengaging of one's self from the saddle on the ground, was attended with inconvenience and even ostentatious display. But Enriquez swept the objections away with a single gesture. "It is the *preencipal*—the bottom fact—at which you arrive. The next come of himself! Many horse have achieve to mount the rider by the knees, and relinquish after thees same fashion. My grandfather had a barb of thees kind—but she has gone dead, and so have my grandfather. Which is sad and strange! Otherwise I shall make of them both an instant example!"

I ought to have said that although these performances were never actually witnessed by Enriquez's sister—for reasons which he and I thought sufficient—the dear girl displayed the greatest interest in them, and perhaps aided by our mutually complimentary accounts of each other, looked upon us both as invincible heroes. It is possible also that she overestimated our success, for she suddenly demanded that I should *ride* Chu Chu to her house that she might see her. It was not far; by going through a back lane I could avoid the trees which exercised such a fatal fascination for Chu Chu. There was a pleading childlike entreaty in Consuelo's voice that I could not resist, with a slight flash from her lustrous dark eyes that I did not care to encourage. So I resolved to try it at all hazards.

My equipment for the performance was modeled after Enriquez's previous costume with the addition of a few fripperies of silver and stamped leather out of compliment to Consuelo, and even with a faint hope that it might appease Chu Chu. *She* certainly looked beautiful in her glittering accoutrements, set off by her jet black shining coat. With an air of demure abstraction she permitted me to mount her, and even for a hundred yards or so indulged in a mincing maidenly amble that was not without a touch of coquetry. Encouraged by this, I addressed a few terms of endearment to her, and in the exuberance of my youthful enthusiasm I even confided to her my love for Consuelo, and begged her to be good and not disgrace herself and me before my Dulcinea. In my foolish trustfulness I was rash enough to add a caress, and to pat her soft neck. She stopped instantly with an hysteric shudder. I knew what was passing through her mind: she had suddenly become aware of my baleful existence.

The saddle and bridle Chu Chu was becoming accustomed to, but who was this living breathing object that had actually touched her? Presently her oblique vision was attracted by the fluttering movement of a fallen oak leaf in the road before her. She had probably seen many oak leaves many times before; her ancestors had no doubt been familiar with them on the trackless hills and in field and paddock, but this did not alter her profound conviction that I and the leaf were identical, that our baleful touch was something indissolubly connected. She reared before that innocent leaf, she revolved around it and then fled from it at top speed.

The lane passed before the rear wall of Saltellos' garden. Unfortunately, at the angle of the fence stood a beautiful madrona tree, brilliant with scarlet berries and endeared to me as Consuelo's favorite haunt, under whose protecting shade I had more than once avowed my youthful passion. By the irony of fate Chu Chu caught sight of it and with a succession of spirited bounds instantly made for it. In another moment I was beneath it, and Chu Chu shot like a rocket into the air. I had barely time to withdraw my feet from the stirrups, to throw up one arm to protect my glazed sombrero and grasp an overhanging branch with the other, before Chu Chu darted off. But to my consternation, as I gained a secure perch on the tree and looked about me, I saw her

—instead of running away—quietly trot through the open gate into the Saltellos' garden.

Need I say that it was to the beneficent Enriquez that I again owed my salvation? Scarcely a moment elapsed before his bland voice rose in a concentrated whisper from the corner of the garden below me. He had divined the dreadful truth!

"For the love of God, collect to yourself many kinds of thees berry! All you can! Your full arms round! Rest tranquil. Leave to your ole oncle to make for you a delicate exposure. At the instant!"

He was gone again. I gathered, wonderingly, a few of the larger clusters of parti-colored fruit, and patiently waited. Presently he reappeared, and with him the lovely Consuelo—her dear eyes filled with an adorable anxiety.

"Yes," continued Enriquez to his sister, with a confidential lowering of tone but great distinctness of utterance, "it is ever so with the American! He will ever make *first* the salutation of the flower or the fruit, picked to himself by his own hand, to the lady where he call. It is the custom of the American hidalgo! My God—what will you? *I* make it not—it is so! Without doubt he is in this instant doing thees thing. That is why he have let go his horse to precede him here; it is always the etiquette to offer these things on the feet. Ah! behold! it is he!—Don Francisco! Even now he will descend from thees tree! Ah! You make the blush, little sister (archly)! I will retire! I am discreet; two is not company for the one! I make tracks! I am gone!"

How far Consuelo entirely believed and trusted her ingenious brother I do not know, nor even then cared to inquire. For there was a pretty mantling of her olive cheek as I came forward with my offering, and a certain significant shyness in her manner that were enough to throw me into a state of hopeless imbecility. And I was always miserably conscious that Consuelo possessed an exalted sentimentality and a predilection for the highest medieval romance, in which I knew I was lamentably deficient. Even in our most confidential moments I was always aware that I weakly lagged behind this daughter of a gloomily distinguished ancestry, in her frequent incursions into a vague but poetic past. There was something of the dignity of the Spanish châtelaine in the sweetly grave little figure that advanced to accept my specious offering. I think I should have fallen on my knees to present it, but for the presence of the all-seeing Enriquez. But why did I even at that moment remember that he had early bestowed upon her the nickname of Pomposa? This, as Enriquez himself might have observed, was sad and strange.

I managed to stammer out something about the madrona berries being at her "disposicion" (the tree was in her own garden!), and she took the branches in her little brown hand with a soft response to my unutterable glances.

But here Chu Chu, momentarily forgotten, executed

a happy diversion. To our astonishment she gravely walked up to Consuelo and stretching out her long slim neck not only sniffed curiously at the berries, but even protruded a black underlip toward the young girl herself. In another instant Consuelo's dignity melted. Throwing her arms around Chu Chu's neck she embraced and kissed her. Young as I was, I understood the divine significance of a girl's vicarious effusiveness at such a moment and felt delighted. But I was the more astonished that the usually sensitive horse not only submitted to these caresses but actually responded to the extent of affecting to nip my mistress's little right ear.

This was enough for the impulsive Consuelo. She ran hastily into the house, and in a few moments reappeared in a bewitching riding skirt gathered round her jimp waist. In vain Enriquez and myself joined in earnest entreaty: the horse was hardly broken for even a man's riding yet; the saints alone could tell what the nervous creature might do with a woman's skirt flapping at her side! We begged for delay, for reflection, for at least time to change the saddle—but with no avail! Consuelo was determined, indignant, distressingly reproachful! Ah, well! if Don Pancho (an ingenious diminutive of my Christian name) valued his horse so highly—if he were jealous of the evident devotion of the animal to herself, he would— But here I succumbed! And then I had the felicity of holding that little foot for one brief moment in the hollow of my hand, of readjusting the skirt as she threw her knee over the saddle horn, of clasping her tightly—only half in fear—as I surrendered the reins to her grasp. And to tell the truth, as Enriquez and I fell back, although I had insisted upon still keeping hold of the end of the riata, it was a picture to admire. The petite figure of the young girl and the graceful folds of her skirt admirably harmonized with Chu Chu's lithe contour, and as the mare arched her slim neck and raised her slender head under the pressure of the reins it was so like the lifted velvet-capped toreador crest of Consuelo herself that they seemed of one race.

"I would not that you should hold the riata," said Consuelo petulantly.

I hesitated—Chu Chu looked certainly very amiable— I let go. She began to amble toward the gate, not mincingly as before but with a freer and fuller stride. In spite of the incongruous saddle the young girl's seat was admirable. As they neared the gate she cast a single mischievous glance at me, jerked at the rein, and Chu Chu sprang into the road at a rapid canter. I watched them fearfully and breathlessly until at the end of the lane I saw Consuelo rein in slightly, wheel easily and come flying back. There was no doubt about it; the horse was under perfect control. Her second subjugation was complete and final!

Overjoyed and bewildered I overwhelmed them with congratulations, Enriquez alone retaining the usual brotherly attitude of criticism and a superior toleration of a lover's enthusiasm. I ventured to hint to Consuelo (in what I believed was a safe whisper) that Chu Chu only showed my own feelings toward her.

"Without doubt," responded Enriquez gravely. "She have of herself assist you to climb to the tree to pull to yourself the berry for my sister."

But I felt Consuelo's little hand return my pressure and I forgave and even pitied him.

From that day forward, Chu Chu and Consuelo were not only firm friends but daily companions. In my devotion I would have presented the horse to the young girl, but with flattering delicacy she preferred to call it mine.

"I shall erride it for you, Pancho," she said. "I shall feel," she continued, with exalted although somewhat vague poetry, "that it is of *you!* You lofe the beast—it is therefore of a necessity *you*, my Pancho! It is *your* soul I shall erride like the wings of the wind—your lofe in this beast shall be my only cavalier forever."

I would have preferred something whose vicarious qualities were less uncertain than I still felt Chu Chu's to be, but I kissed the girl's hand submissively. It was only when I attempted to accompany her in the flesh, on another horse, that I felt the full truth of my instinctive fears. Chu Chu would not permit any one to approach her mistress' side. My mounted presence revived in her all her old blind astonishment and disbelief in my existence; she would start suddenly, face about, and back away from me in utter amazement as if I had been only recently created, or with an affected modesty as if I had been just guilty of some grave indecorum toward her sex which she really could not stand. The frequency of these exhibitions in the public highway were not only distressing to me as a simple escort, but as it had the effect on the casual spectators of making Consuelo seem to participate in Chu Chu's objections, I felt that as a lover it could not be borne. Any attempt to coerce Chu Chu ended in her running away. And my frantic pursuit of her was open to equal misconstruction.

"Go it, miss, the little dude is gainin' on you!" shouted by a drunken teamster to the frightened Consuelo, once checked me in mid-career.

Even the dear girl herself saw the uselessness of my real presence and after a while was content to ride with my "soul."

Notwithstanding this, I am not ashamed to say that it was my custom whenever she rode out, to keep a slinking and distant surveillance of Chu Chu on another horse until she had fairly settled down to her pace. A little nod of Consuelo's round black and red toreador hat or a kiss tossed from her riding whip was reward enough!

I remember a pleasant afternoon when I was thus awaiting her in the outskirts of the village. The eternal smile of the Californian summer had begun to waver and grow less fixed; dust lay thick on leaf and blade; the dry hills were clothed in russet leather; the trade winds were shifting to the south with an ominous warm humidity; a few days longer and the rains would be here. It so chanced that this afternoon my seclusion on the roadside was accidentally invaded by a village belle—a western young lady somewhat older than myself and of flirtatious reputation. As she persistently and—as I now have reason to believe—mischievously lingered, I had only a passing glimpse of Consuelo riding past at an unaccustomed speed which surprised me at the moment. But as I reasoned later that she was only trying to avoid a merely formal meeting, I thought no more about it. It was not until I called at the house to fetch Chu Chu at the usual hour and found that Consuelo had not yet returned, that a recollection of Chu Chu's furious pace again troubled me. An hour passed—it was getting toward sunset but there were no signs of Chu Chu or her mistress. I became seriously alarmed. I did not care to reveal my fears to the family, for I felt myself responsible for Chu Chu. At last I desperately saddled my horse and galloped off in the direction she had taken. It was the road to Rosario and the hacienda of one of her relations, where she sometimes halted.

The road was a very unfrequented one, twisting like a mountain river; indeed, it was the bed of an old water-course, between brown hills of wild oats, debouching at last into a broad blue lakelike expanse of alfalfa meadows. In vain I strained my eyes over the monotonous level; nothing appeared to rise above or move across it. In the faint hope that she might have lingered at the hacienda, I was spurring on again when I heard a slight splashing on my left. I looked around. A broad patch of fresher-colored herbage and a cluster of dwarfed alders

indicated a hidden spring. I cautiously approached its
quaggy edges, when I was shocked by what appeared
to be a sudden vision! Mid-leg deep in the center of a
greenish pool stood Chu Chu! But without a strap or
buckle of harness upon her—as naked as when she was
foaled!

For a moment I could only stare at her in bewildered
terror. Far from recognizing me, she seemed to be
absorbed in a nymphlike contemplation of her own
graces in the pool. Then I called, "Consuelo!" and galloped frantically around the spring. But there was no
response, nor was there anything to be seen but the all-
unconscious Chu Chu. The pool, thank Heaven! was not
deep enough to have drowned anyone; there were no
signs of a struggle on its quaggy edges. The horse might
have come from a distance! I galloped on, still calling.
A few hundred yards further I detected the vivid glow
of Chu Chu's scarlet saddle blanket in the brush near
the trail. My heart leaped—I was on the track. I called
again. This time a faint reply in accents I knew too well
came from the field beside me!

Consuelo was there, reclining beside a manzanita
bush which screened her from the road, in what struck
me even at that supreme moment as a judicious and picturesquely selected couch of scented Indian grass and
dry tussocks. The velvet hat with its balls of scarlet
plush was laid carefully aside; her lovely blue-black
hair retained its tight coils undisheveled; her eyes were
luminous and tender. Shocked as I was at her apparent

helplessness I remember being impressed with the fact that it gave so little indication of violent usage or disaster.

I threw myself frantically on the ground beside her.

"You are hurt, Consita! For Heaven's sake, what has happened?"

She pushed my hat back with her little hand and tumbled my hair gently.

"Nothing. *You* are here, Pancho—eet is enofe! What shall come after thees—when I am perhaps gone among the grave—make nothing! *You* are here—I am happy. For a little, perhaps—not mooch."

"But," I went on desperately, "was it an accident? Were you thrown? Was it Chu Chu?" For somehow in spite of her languid posture and voice I could not, even in my fears, believe her seriously hurt.

"Beat not the poor beast, Pancho. It is not from *her* comes thees thing. She have make nothing—believe me! I have come upon your assignation with Miss Essmith! I make but to pass you—to fly—to never come back! I have say to Chu Chu, 'Fly!' We fly many miles. Sometimes together, sometimes not so mooch! Sometimes in the saddle, sometimes on the neck! Many things remain in the road; at the end, I myself remain! I have say, 'Courage, Pancho will come!' Then I say, 'No, he is talk with Miss Essmith!' I remember not more. I have creep here on the hands. Eet is feenish!"

I looked at her distractedly. She smiled tenderly, and

slightly smoothed down and rearranged a fold of her dress to cover her delicate little boot.

"But," I protested, "you are not much hurt, dearest. You have broken no bones. Perhaps," I added, looking at the boot, "only a slight sprain. Let me carry you to my horse; I will walk beside you, home. Do, dearest Consita!"

She turned her lovely eyes toward me sadly.

"You comprehend not, my poor Pancho! It is not of the foot, the ankle, the arm or the head that I can say, 'She is broke!' I would it were even so. But"—she lifted her sweet lashes slowly—"I have derrange my inside. It is an affair of my family. My grandfather have once toomble over the bull at a rodeo. He speak no more; he is dead. For why? He has derrange his inside. Believe me, it is of the family. You comprehend? The Saltellos are not as the other peoples for this. When I am gone you will bring to me the berry to grow upon my tomb, Pancho, the berry you have picked for me. The little flower will come too, the little star will arrive, but Consuelo who lofe you, she will come not more! When you are happy and talk in the road to the Essmith you will not think of me. You will not see my eyes, Pancho; thees little grass"—she ran her plump little fingers through a tussock—"will hide them; and the small animals in the black coats that lif here will have much sorrow—but you will not. It ees better so! My father will not that I, a Catholique, should marry into a camp meeting, and lif

in a tent, and make howl like the coyote." (It was one of
Consuelo's bewildering beliefs that there was only one
form of dissent—Methodism!) "He will not that I should
marry a man who possess not the many horses, ox and
cow, like him. But *I* care not. *You* are my only religion,
Pancho! I have enofe of the horse and ox and cow when
you are with me! Kiss me, Pancho. Perhaps it is for the
last time—the feenish! Who knows?"

There were tears in her lovely eyes; I felt that my own
were growing dim. The sun was sinking over the dreary
plain to the slow rising of the wind; an infinite loneliness
had fallen upon us, and yet I was miserably conscious
of some dreadful unreality in it all. A desire to laugh,
which I felt must be hysterical, was creeping over me;
I dared not speak. But her dear head was on my shoulder and the situation was not unpleasant.

Nevertheless something must be done! This was the
more difficult as it was by no means clear what had already been done. Even while I supported her drooping
figure I was straining my eyes across her shoulder for
succor of some kind. Suddenly the figure of a rapid rider
appeared upon the road. It seemed familiar. I looked
again—it was the blessed Enriquez! A sense of deep
relief came over me. I loved Consuelo; but never before
had lover ever hailed the irruption of one of his beloved's family with such complacency.

"You are safe, dearest; it is Enriquez!"

I thought she received the information coldly. Suddenly she turned upon me her eyes, now bright and glittering.

"Swear to me at the instant, Pancho, that you will not again look upon Miss Essmith, even for once."

I was simple and literal. Miss Smith was my nearest neighbor, and unless I was stricken with blindness, compliance was impossible. I hesitated—but swore.

"Enofe—you have hesitate—I will no more."

She rose to her feet with grave deliberation. For an instant, with the recollection of the delicate internal organization of the Saltellos on my mind, I was in agony lest she should totter and fall even then, yielding up her gentle spirit on the spot. But when I looked again she had a hairpin between her white teeth and was carefully adjusting her toreador hat. And beside us was Enriquez —cheerful, alert, voluble and undaunted.

"Eureka! I have found! We are all here! Eet is a leetle public—eh? a leetle too much of a front seat for a tête-à-tête, my yonge friends," he said, glancing at the remains of Consuelo's bower, "but for the accounting of taste there is none. What will you? The meat of the one man shall envenom the meat of the other. But" (in a whisper to me) "as to thees horse—thees Chu Chu, which I have just pass—why is she undress? Surely you would not make an exposition of her to the traveler to suspect! And if not, why so?"

I tried to explain, looking at Consuelo, that Chu Chu had run away, that Consuelo had met with a terrible accident, had been thrown, and I feared had suffered serious internal injury. But to my embarrassment Consuelo maintained a half-scornful silence, and an inconsistent freshness of healthful indifference as Enriquez approached her with an engaging smile.

"Ah yes, she have the headache and the molligrubs. She will sit on the damp stone when the gentle dew is falling. I comprehend. Meet me in the lane when the clock strike nine! But," in a lower voice, "of thees undress horse I comprehend nothing! Look you—it is sad and strange."

He went off to fetch Chu Chu, leaving me and Consuelo alone. I do not think I ever felt so utterly abject and bewildered before in my life. Without knowing why, I was miserably conscious of having in some way offended the girl for whom I believed I would have given my life, and I had made her and myself ridiculous in the eyes of her brother. I had again failed in my slower western nature to understand her high romantic Spanish soul! Meantime she was smoothing out her riding habit, and looking as fresh and pretty as when she first left her house.

"Consita," I said hesitatingly, "you are not angry with me?"

"Angry?" she repeated haughtily, without looking at me. "Oh, no! Of a possibility eet is Mees Essmith who is angry that I have interroopt her tête-à-tête with you, and have send here my brother to make the same with me."

"But," I said eagerly, "Miss Smith does not even know Enriquez!"

Consuelo turned on me a glance of unutterable significance.

"Ah!" she said darkly, "you *tink!*"

Indeed I *knew*. But here I believed I understood Consuelo, and was relieved. I even ventured to say gently, "And you are better?"

She drew herself up to her full height, which was not much.

"Of my health, what is it? A nothing. Yes! Of my soul let us not speak."

Nevertheless when Enriquez appeared with Chu Chu she ran toward her with outstretched arms. Chu Chu protruded about six inches of upper lip in response—apparently under the impression, which I could quite understand, that her mistress was edible. And I may have been mistaken, but their beautiful eyes met in an absolute and distinct glance of intelligence!

During the home journey Consuelo recovered her spirits and parted from me with a magnanimous and forgiving pressure of the hand. I do not know what explanation of Chu Chu's original escapade was given to Enriquez and the rest of the family; the inscrutable forgiveness extended to me by Consuelo precluded any further inquiry on my part. I was willing to leave it a secret between her and Chu Chu. But strange to say, it seemed to complete our own understanding, and precipitated not only our love-making but the final catastrophe which culminated that romance. For we had resolved to elope. I do not know that this heroic remedy was absolutely necessary from the attitude of either Consuelo's family or my own; I am inclined to think we preferred it because it involved no previous explanation or advice. Need I say that our confidant and firm ally was Consuelo's brother—the alert, the linguistic, the ever happy, ever ready Enriquez! It was understood that his presence would give a certain mature respectability to our performance—and I do not think we would have contemplated this step without it. During one of our riding excursions we were to secure the services of a Methodist minister in the adjoining county, and later that of the mission padre—when the secret was out.

"I will gif her away," said Enriquez confidently. "It will on the instant propitiate the old shadbelly who shall perform the affair, and withhold his jaw. A little chin music from your oncle 'Arry shall finish it! Remain tranquil and forget not a ring! One does not always, in the agony and dissatisfaction of the moment, a ring remember. I shall bring two in the pocket of my jacket."

If I did not entirely participate in this roseate view it may have been because Enriquez, although a few years my senior, was much younger looking, and with his demure deviltry of eye and his upper lip close shaven for this occasion, he suggested a depraved acolyte rather than a responsible member of a family. Consuelo had also confided to me that her father—possibly owing to some rumors of our previous escapade—had forbidden any further excursions with me alone. The innocent man did not know that Chu Chu had forbidden it also, and that even on this momentous occasion both Enriquez and myself were obliged to ride in opposite fields like out flankers. But we nevertheless felt the full guilt of disobedience added to our desperate enterprise. Meanwhile, although pressed for time and subject to discovery at any moment, I managed at certain points of the road to dismount and walk beside Chu Chu (who did not seem to recognize me on foot), holding Consuelo's hand in my own, with the discreet Enriquez leading my horse in the distant field. I retain a very vivid picture of that walk—the ascent of a gentle slope toward a prospect as yet unknown but full of glorious possibilities; the tender dropping light of an autumn sky slightly filmed with the promise of the future rains, like foreshadowed tears, and the half-frightened, half-serious talk into which Consuelo and I had insensibly fallen. And then I don't know how it happened, but as we reached the summit Chu Chu suddenly reared, wheeled, and the next moment was flying back along the road we had just traveled, at top speed! It might have been that after her abstracted fashion she only at that moment detected my presence. But so sudden and complete was her evolution that before I could regain my horse from the astonished Enriquez she was already a quarter of a mile on the homeward stretch with the frantic Consuelo pulling hopelessly at the bridle. We started in pursuit. But a horrible despair seized us. To attempt to overtake her, to even follow at the same rate of speed, would only excite Chu Chu and endanger Consuelo's life. There was absolutely no help for it, nothing could be done; the mare had taken her determined long continuous stride; the road was straight steady descent all the way back to the village; Chu Chu had the bit between her teeth, and there was no prospect of swerving her. We could only follow hopelessly, idiotically, furiously, until Chu Chu dashed triumphantly into the Saltellos' courtyard, carrying the half-fainting Consuelo back to the arms of her assembled and astonished family.

It was our last ride together. It was the last I ever saw of Consuelo before her transfer to the safe seclusion of a convent in Southern California. It was the last I ever saw of Chu Chu, who in the confusion of that encounter was overlooked in her half-loosed harness and allowed to escape through the back gate to the fields. Months afterward it was said that she had been identified among a band of wild horses in the Coast Range, as a strange and beautiful creature who had escaped the brand of the rodeo and become a myth. There was another legend that she had been seen sleek, fat and gorgeously caparisoned, issuing from the gateway of the Rosario patio before a lumbering Spanish cabriolet in which a short stout matron was seated—but I will have none of it. For there are days when she still lives, and I can see her plainly still climbing the gentle slope toward the summit with Consuelo on her back and myself at her side, pressing eagerly forward toward the illimitable prospect that opens in the distance.

The
Iliad
of
Sandy
ᴥ Bar

Before nine o'clock it was pretty well known all along the river that the two parties of the Amity Claim had quarreled and separated at daybreak. At that time the attention of their nearest neighbor had been attracted by the sounds of altercations and two consecutive pistol shots. Running out, he had seen dimly in the gray mist that rose from the river the tall form of Scott, one of the partners, descending the hill toward the canyon. A moment later York, the other partner, had appeared from the cabin and walked in an opposite direction toward the river, passing within a few feet of the curious watcher. Later it was discovered that John, a serious-faced Chinese cutting wood before the cabin, had witnessed part of the quarrel. But John was stolid, indifferent and reticent. "Me choppee wood, me no fightee," was his serene response to all anxious queries.

"But what did they *say*, John?" John did not "sabe." Colonel Starbottle deftly ran over the various popular epithets which a generous public sentiment might accept as reasonable provocation for an assault. But John did not recognize them. "And this yer," said the Colonel with some severity, " 'swhat some thinks oughter be allowed to testify in court! Git—you heathen!"

Still the quarrel remained inexplicable. That two men whose amiability and grave tact had earned for them the title of the Peacemakers in a community not greatly given to the passive virtues—that these men, singularly devoted to each other, should suddenly and violently quarrel, might well excite the curiosity of the camp. A few of the more inquisitive visited the late scene of conflict, now deserted by its former occupants. There was no trace of disorder or confusion in the neat cabin. The rude table was arranged as if for breakfast; the pan of yellow biscuit still sat upon that hearth whose dead embers might have typified the evil passions that had raged there but an hour before. But Colonel Starbottle's eye, albeit somewhat bloodshot and rheumy, was more intent on practical details. On examination, a bullet hole was found in the doorpost, and another nearly opposite in the casing of the window. The Colonel called attention to the fact that the one agreed with the bore of Scott's revolver, and the other with that of York's derringer. "They must hev stood about yer," said the Colonel, taking position. "Not more'n three feet apart, and —missed!" There was a fine touch of pathos in the falling inflection of the Colonel's voice, which was not without effect. A delicate perception of wasted opportunity thrilled his auditors.

But the Bar was destined to experience a greater disappointment. The two antagonists had not met since the quarrel and it was vaguely rumored that on the occasion of a second meeting, each had determined to kill the other on sight. There was, consequently, some excitement—and it is to be feared no little gratification—when at ten o'clock York stepped from the Magnolia Saloon into the one long straggling street of the camp, at the same moment that Scott left the blacksmith's shop at the forks of the road. It was evident at a glance that a meeting could only be avoided by the actual retreat of one or the other.

In an instant the doors and windows of the adjacent saloons were filled with faces. Heads unaccountably appeared above the riverbanks and from behind boulders. An empty wagon at the crossroad was suddenly crowded with people, who seemed to have sprung from the earth. There was much running and confusion on the hillside. On the mountain road Mr. Jack Hamlin had reined up his horse and was standing upright on the seat of his buggy. And the two objects of this absorbing attention approached each other.

"York's got the sun," "Scott'll line him on that tree," "He's waiting to draw his fire," came from the cart, and then it was silent. But above this human breathlessness the river rushed and sang, and the wind rustled the treetops with an indifference that seemed obtrusive. Colonel Starbottle felt it, and in a moment of sublime preoccupation, without looking around, waved his cane behind him warningly to all Nature and said, "Shu!"

The men were now within a few feet of each other. A hen ran across the road before one of them. A feathery seed vessel wafted from a wayside tree fell at the feet of the other. And unheeding this irony of Nature the two opponents came nearer, erect and rigid, looked in each other's eyes—and passed!

Colonel Starbottle had to be lifted from the cart. "This yer camp is played out," he said gloomily, as he effected to be supported into the Magnolia. With what further expression he might have indicated his feelings it was impossible to say, for at that moment Scott joined the group. "Did you speak to me?" he asked of the colonel, dropping his hand, as if with accidental familiarity, on that gentleman's shoulder. The colonel, recognizing some occult quality in the touch and some unknown quantity in the glance of his questioner, contented himself by replying, "No, sir," with dignity. A few rods away York's conduct was as characteristic and peculiar. "You had a mighty fine chance; why didn't you plump him?" said Jack Hamlin as York drew near the buggy. "Because I hate him," was the reply heard only by Jack. Contrary to popular belief this reply was not hissed between the lips of the speaker, but was said in an ordinary tone. But Jack Hamlin, who was an observer of mankind, noticed that the speaker's hands were cold and his lips dry as he helped him into the buggy and accepted the seeming paradox with a smile.

When Sandy Bar became convinced that the quarrel between York and Scott could not be settled after the usual local methods it gave no further concern thereto. But presently it was rumored that the Amity Claim was in litigation and that its possession would be expensively disputed by each of the partners. As it was well known that the claim in question was worked out and worthless and that the partners whom it had already enriched had talked of abandoning it but a day or two before the quarrel, this proceeding could only be accounted for as gratuitous spite. Later, two San Francisco lawyers made their appearance in this guileless Arcadia and were eventually taken into the saloons, and —what was pretty much the same thing—the confidences of the inhabitants. The results of this unhallowed intimacy were many subpœnas; and, indeed, when the "Amity Claim" came to trial, all of Sandy Bar that was not in compulsory attendance at the county seat came there from curiosity. The gulches and ditches for miles around were deserted. I do not propose to describe that already famous trial. Enough that in the language of the plaintiff's counsel "it was one of no ordinary significance, involving the inherent rights of that untiring industry which had developed the Pactolian resources of this golden land." In the homelier phrase of Colonel Starbottle it was "a fuss that gentlemen might hev settled in ten minutes over a social glass, ef they meant business,

or in ten seconds with a revolver, ef they meant fun."
Scott got a verdict, from which York instantly appealed.
It was said that he had sworn to spend his last dollar in
the struggle.

In this way Sandy Bar began to accept the enmity of
the former partners as a lifelong feud and the fact that
they had ever been friends was forgotten. The few who
expected to learn from the trial the origin of the quarrel
were disappointed. Among the various conjectures, that
which ascribed some occult feminine influence as the
cause was naturally popular in a camp given to dubious
compliment of the sex. "My word for it, gentlemen," said
Colonel Starbottle, who had been known in Sacramento
as a gentleman of the old school, "there's some lovely
creature at the bottom of this." The gallant colonel then
proceeded to illustrate his theory by divers sprightly
stories, such as gentlemen of the old school are in the
habit of repeating, but which, from deference to the
prejudices of gentlemen of a more recent school, I refrain from transcribing here.

But it would appear that even the colonel's theory was
fallacious. The only woman who personally might have
exercised any influence over the partners was the pretty
daughter of old man Folinsbee of Poverty Flat, at whose
hospitable house—which exhibited some comforts and
refinements rare in that crude civilization—both York
and Scott were frequent visitors. Yet into this charming
retreat York strode one evening a month after the quarrel, and beholding Scott sitting there, turned to the fair

hostess with the abrupt query, "Do you love this man?"
The young woman thus addressed returned that answer
—at once spirited and evasive—which would occur to
most of my fair readers in such an emergency. Without
another word York left the house. Miss Jo heaved the
least possible sigh as the door closed on York's curls and
square shoulders, and then like a good girl turned to her
insulted guest. "But would you believe it, dear?" she
afterward related to an intimate friend, "the other creature after glowering at me for a moment got up on its
hind legs, took its hat, and left too; and that's the last
I've seen of either."

The same hard disregard of all other interests or feelings in the gratification of their blind rancor characterized all their actions. When York purchased the land
below Scott's new claim and obliged the latter, at a great
expense, to make a long detour to carry a tail-race
around it, Scott retaliated by building a dam that overflowed York's claim on the river. It was Scott who in
conjunction with Colonel Starbottle first organized that
active opposition to the Chinese which resulted in the
driving off of York's labor gang. It was York who built
the wagon road and established the express which rendered Scott's mules and pack trains obsolete. It was
Scott who called into life the vigilance committee which
expatriated York's friend, Jack Hamlin. It was York who
created the *Sandy Bar Herald*, which characterized the
act as "a lawless outrage" and Scott as a "border ruffian."
It was Scott, at the head of twenty masked men, who

one moonlight night threw the offending "forms" into
the yellow river and scattered the types in the dusty
road.

These proceedings were received in the distant and
more civilized outlying towns as vague indications of
progress and vitality. I have before me a copy of the
Poverty Flat Pioneer for the week ending August 12,
1856, in which the editor, under the head of "County
Improvements," says:

> The new Presbyterian Church on C Street, at Sandy
> Bar, is completed. It stands upon the lot formerly oc-
> cupied by the Magnolia Saloon, which was so mysteri-
> ously burnt last month. The temple, which now rises
> like a phœnix from the ashes of the Magnolia, is virtu-
> ally the free gift of H. J. York, Esq., of Sandy Bar, who
> purchased the lot and donated the lumber. Other build-
> ings are going up in the vicinity, but the most noticeable
> is the Sunny South Saloon, erected by Captain Mat.
> Scott, nearly opposite the church. Captain Scott has
> spared no expense in the furnishing of this saloon, which
> promises to be one of the most agreeable places of resort
> in old Tuolumne. He has recently imported two new
> first class billiard tables with cork cushions. Our old
> friend, Mountain Jimmy, will dispense liquors at the
> bar. We refer our readers to the advertisement in an-
> other column. Visitors to Sandy Bar cannot do better
> than give Jimmy a call.

Among the local items occurred the following:

> H. J. York, Esq., of Sandy Bar, has offered a reward of
> $100 for the detection of the parties who hauled away
> the steps of the new Presbyterian Church, C Street,

Sandy Bar, during divine service on Sabbath evening last. Captain Scott adds another hundred for the capture of the miscreants who broke the magnificent plate-glass windows of the new saloon on the following evening. There is some talk of reorganizing the old vigilance committee at Sandy Bar.

When for many months of cloudless weather the hard unwinking sun of Sandy Bar had regularly gone down on the unpacified wrath of these men, there was some talk of mediation. In particular, the pastor of the church to which I have just referred—a sincere, fearless, but perhaps not fully enlightened man—seized gladly upon the occasion of York's liberality to attempt to reunite the former partners. He preached an earnest sermon on the abstract sinfulness of discord and rancor. But the excellent sermons of the Reverend Mr. Daws were directed to an ideal congregation that did not exist at Sandy Bar, a congregation of beings of unmixed vices and virtues, of single impulses and perfectly logical motives, of preternatural simplicity, of childlike faith and grown-up responsibilities. As unfortunately the people who actually attended Mr. Daws's church were mainly very human, somewhat artful, more self-excusing than self-accusing, rather good-natured, and decidedly weak, they quietly shed that portion of the sermon which referred to themselves, and accepting York and Scott—who were both in defiant attendance—as curious examples of those ideal beings above referred to, felt a certain satisfaction—which, I fear, was not altogether Christianlike—in their "raking-down." If Mr. Daws expected York and Scott to shake hands after the sermon, he was disappointed. But he did not relax his purpose. With that quiet fearlessness and determination which had won for him the respect of men who were too apt to regard piety as synonymous with effeminacy, he attacked Scott in his own house. What he said has not been recorded, but it is to be feared that it was part of his sermon. When he had concluded Scott looked at him not unkindly over the glasses of his bar, and said, less irreverently than the words might convey, "Young man, I rather like your style; but when you know York and me as well as you do God Almighty, it'll be time to talk."

And so the feud progressed; and so, as in more illustrious examples, the private and personal enmity of two representative men led gradually to the evolution of some crude, half-expressed principle or belief. It was not long before it was made evident that those beliefs were identical with certain broad principles laid down by the founders of the American Constitution, as expounded by the statesmanlike A., or were the fatal quicksands on which the ship of state might be wrecked, warningly pointed out by the eloquent B. The practical result of all which was the nomination of York and Scott to represent the opposite factions of Sandy Bar in legislative councils.

For some weeks past the voters of Sandy Bar and the adjacent camps had been called upon, in large type, to

RALLY! In vain the great pines at the crossroads—whose trunks were compelled to bear this and other legends— moaned and protested from their windy watch towers. But one day, with fife and drum and flaming transparency, a procession filed into the triangular grove at the head of the gulch. The meeting was called to order by Colonel Starbottle, who, having once enjoyed legislative functions and being vaguely known as the Warhorse, was considered to be a valuable partisan of York. He concluded an appeal for his friend with an enunciation of principles, interspersed with one or two anecdotes so gratuitously coarse that the very pines might have been moved to pelt him with their cast-off cones as he stood there.

But he created a laugh, on which his candidate rode into popular notice; and when York rose to speak, he was greeted with cheers. But, to the general astonishment, the new speaker at once launched into bitter denunciation of his rival. He not only dwelt upon Scott's deeds and example as known to Sandy Bar, but spoke of facts connected with his previous career hitherto unknown to his auditors. To great precision of epithet and directness of statement, the speaker added the fascination of revelation and exposure. The crowd cheered, yelled, and were delighted; but when this astounding philippic was concluded, there was a unanimous call for Scott. Colonel Starbottle would have resisted this manifest impropriety, but in vain. Partly from a crude sense of justice, partly from a meaner craving for excitement, the assemblage was inflexible; and Scott was dragged, pushed and pulled upon the platform. As his frowsy head and unkempt beard appeared above the railing, it was evident that he was drunk. But it was also evident, before he opened his lips, that the orator of Sandy Bar—the one man who could touch their vagabond sympathies (perhaps because he was not above appealing to them)— stood before them. A consciousness of this power lent a certain dignity to his figure, and I am not sure but that his very physical condition impressed them as a kind of regal unbending and large condescension. Howbeit, when this unexpected Hector arose from this ditch, York's myrmidons trembled. "There's naught, gentlemen," said Scott, leaning forward on the railing, "as that man hez said as isn't true. I *was* run outer Cairo; I *did* belong to the Regulators; I *did* desert from the army; I *did* leave a wife in Kansas. But thar's one thing he didn't charge me with, and maybe he's forgotten. For three years, gentlemen, I was that man's pardner!" Whether he intended to say more, I cannot tell; a burst of applause artistically rounded and enforced the climax, and virtually elected the speaker. That fall he went to Sacramento, York went abroad, and for the first time in many years distance and a new atmosphere isolated the old antagonists.

With little of change in the green wood, gray rock and yellow river, but with much shifting of human landmarks and new faces in its habitations, three years passed over Sandy Bar. The two men, once so identified with its character, seemed to have been quite forgotten. "You will never return to Sandy Bar," said Miss Folins- bee, the Lily of Poverty Flat, on meeting York in Paris, "for Sandy Bar is no more. They call it Riverside now; and the new town is built higher up on the riverbank. By the way, Jo says that Scott has won his suit about the Amity Claim, and that he lives in the old cabin, and is drunk half his time. Oh, I beg your pardon," added the lively lady, as a flush crossed York's sallow cheek, "but bless me, I really thought that old grudge was made up. I'm sure it ought to be."

It was three months after this conversation, and a pleasant summer evening, that the Poverty Flat coach drew up before the veranda of the Union Hotel at Sandy Bar. Among its passengers was one, apparently a stranger, in the local distinction of well-fitting clothes and closely shaven face, who demanded a private room and retired early to rest. But before sunrise next morn- ing he arose, and, drawing some clothes from his carpet- bag, proceeded to array himself in a pair of white duck trousers, a white duck overshirt, and straw hat. When his toilet was completed, he tied a red bandana hand- kerchief in a loop and threw it loosely over his shoul- ders. The transformation was complete. As he crept softly down the stairs and stepped into the road, no one would have detected in him the elegant stranger of the previous night, and but few have recognized the face and figure of Henry York, of Sandy Bar.

In the uncertain light of that early hour, and in the

change that had come over the settlement, he had to pause for a moment to recall where he stood. The Sandy Bar of his recollection lay below him, nearer the river; the buildings around him were of later date and newer fashion. As he strode toward the river, he noticed here a schoolhouse and there a church. A little farther on, the Sunny South came in view, transformed into a restaurant, its gilding faded and its paint rubbed off. He now knew where he was; and running briskly down a declivity, crossed a ditch, and stood upon the lower boundary of the Amity Claim.

The gray mist was rising slowly from the river, clinging to the treetops and drifting up the mountainside until it was caught among these rocky altars, and held a sacrifice to the ascending sun. At his feet the earth, cruelly gashed and scarred by his forgotten engines had, since the old days, put on a show of greenness here and there, and now smiled forgivingly up at him, as if things were not so bad after all. A few birds were bathing in the ditch with a pleasant suggestion of its being a new and special provision of Nature, and a hare ran into an inverted sluice-box as he approached, as if it were put there for that purpose.

He had not yet dared to look in a certain direction. But the sun was now high enough to paint the little eminence on which the cabin stood. In spite of his self-control, his heart beat faster as he raised his eyes toward it. Its window and door were closed, no smoke came from its adobe chimney, but it was else unchanged. When within a few yards of it, he picked up a broken shovel, and shouldering it with a smile, he strode toward the door and knocked. There was no sound from within. The smile died upon his lips as he nervously pushed the door open.

A figure started up angrily and came toward him—a figure whose bloodshot eyes suddenly fixed into a vacant stare, whose arms were at first outstretched and then thrown up in warning gesticulation—a figure that suddenly gasped, choked, and then fell forward in a fit.

But before he touched the ground, York had him out into the open air and sunshine. In the struggle, both fell and rolled over on the ground. But the next moment York was sitting up, holding the convulsed frame of his former partner on his knee, and wiping the foam from his inarticulate lips. Gradually the tremor became less frequent and then ceased, and the strong man lay unconscious in his arms.

For some moments York held him quietly thus, looking in his face. Afar, the stroke of a woodman's ax—a mere phantom of sound—was all that broke the stillness. High up the mountain, a wheeling hawk hung breathlessly above them. And then came voices, and two men joined them.

"A fight?" No, a fit; and would they help him bring the sick man to the hotel?

And there for a week the stricken partner lay, unconscious of aught but the visions wrought by disease and fear. On the eighth day at sunrise he rallied, and opening his eyes, looked upon York and pressed his hand. Then he spoke:

"And it's you. I thought it was only whiskey."

York replied by only taking both of his hands, boyishly working them backward and forward as his elbow rested on the bed, with a pleasant smile.

"And you've been abroad. How did you like Paris?"

"So, so! How did *you* like Sacramento?"

"Bully!"

And that was all they could think to say. Presently Scott opened his eyes again.

"I'm mighty weak."

"You'll get better soon."

"Not much."

A long silence followed, in which they could hear the sounds of woodchopping, and of Sandy Bar, already astir for the coming day. Then Scott slowly and with difficulty turned his face to York and said:

"I might hev killed you once."

"I wish you had."

They pressed each other's hands again, but Scott's grasp was evidently failing. He seemed to summon his energies for a special effort.

"Old man!"

"Old chap."

"Closer!"

York bent his head toward the slowly fading face.

"Do ye mind that morning?"

"Yes."

A gleam of fun slid into the corner of Scott's blue eyes as he whispered:

"Old man, thar *was* too much saleratus in that bread!"

It is said that these were his last words. For when the sun, which had so often gone down upon the idle wrath of these foolish men, looked again upon them reunited, it saw the hand of Scott fall cold and irresponsive from the yearning clasp of his former partner. The feud of Sandy Bar was at an end.

The
Devotion
of
∾ Enriquez

In the chronicle which dealt with the exploits of Chu Chu, a Californian mustang, I gave some space to the accomplishments of Enriquez Saltello who assisted me in training her, and who was also brother to Consuelo Saltello, the young lady to whom I had freely given both the mustang and my youthful affections. I consider it a proof of the superiority of masculine friendship that neither the subsequent desertion of the mustang nor the young lady ever made the slightest difference to Enriquez or me in our exalted amity. To a wondering doubt as to what I ever could possibly have seen in his sister to admire he joined a tolerant skepticism of the whole sex. This he was wont to express in that marvelous combination of Spanish precision and California slang for which he was justly famous.

"As to thees women and their little game," he would

348

say, "believe me, my friend, your old oncle 'Enry is not in it. No, he will ever take a back seat when lofe is around. For why? Regard me here! If she is a horse you shall say, 'She will buck-jump,' 'She will ess-shy,' 'She will not arrive,' or 'She will arrive too quick.' But if it is thees women where are you? For when you shall say, 'She will ess-shy,' look you, she will walk straight; or she will remain tranquil when you think she buck-jump; or else she will arrive and, look you, you will not. You shall get left. It is ever so. My father and the brother of my father have both make court to my mother when she was but a senorita. My father think she have lofe his brother more. So he say to her, 'It is enofe; tranquilize yourself. I will go. I will efface myself. Adios! Shake hands! Ta-ta! So long! See you again in the fall.' And what make my mother? Regard me! She marry my father—on the instant! Of thees women, believe me, Pancho, you shall know nothing. Not even if they shall make you the son of your father or his nephew."

I have recalled this characteristic speech to show the general tendency of Enriquez's convictions at the opening of this little story. It is only fair to say, however, that his usual attitude toward the sex he so cheerfully maligned exhibited little apprehension or caution in dealing with them. Among the frivolous and light-minded intermixture of his race he moved with great freedom and popularity. He danced well; when we went to fandangos together his agility and the audacity of his figures always procured him the prettiest partners—his professed sentiments, I presume, shielding him from subsequent jealousies, heartburnings or envy. I have a vivid recollection of him in the mysteries of the *semi-cuacua*, a somewhat corybantic dance which left much to the invention of the performers and very little to the imagination of the spectator. In one of the figures a gaudy handkerchief, waved more or less gracefully by dancer and danseuse before the dazzled eyes of each other, acted as love's signal and was used to express alternate admiration and indifference, shyness and audacity, fear and transport, coyness and coquetry, as the dance proceeded. I need not say that Enriquez's pantomimic illustration of these emotions was peculiarly extravagant, but it was always performed and accepted with a gravity that was an essential feature of the dance. At such times sighs would escape him which were supposed to portray the incipient stages of passion; snorts of jealousy burst from him at the suggestion of a rival; he was overtaken by a sort of St. Vitus's dance that expressed his timidity in making the first advances of affection; the scorn of his ladylove struck him with something like a dumb ague, and a single gesture of invitation from her produced marked delirium. All this was very like Enriquez, but on the particular occasion to which I refer, I think no one was prepared to see him begin the figure with the waving of *four* handkerchiefs! Yet this he did pirouetting, capering, brandishing his silken signals like a ballerina's scarf in the languishment or fire of passion until, in a final figure where the conquered and submitting fair one usually sinks into the arms of her partner, need it be said that the ingenious Enriquez was found in the center of the floor supporting four of the dancers! Yet he was by no means unduly excited either by the plaudits of the crowd or by his evident success with the fair.

"Ah, believe me it is nothing," he said quietly, rolling a fresh cigarette as he leaned against the doorway. "Possibly I shall have to offer the chocolate or the wine to thees girls, or make to them a promenade in the moonlight on the veranda. It is ever so. Unless, my friend," he said suddenly turning toward me in an excess of chivalrous self-abnegation, "unless you shall yourself take my place. Behold, I gif them to you! I vamos! I vanish! I make track! I skedaddle!"

I think he would have carried his extravagance to the point of summoning his four gypsy witches of partners and committing them to my care, if the crowd had not at that moment parted before the remaining dancers and left one of the onlookers, a tall slender girl, calmly surveying them through gold-rimmed eyeglasses in complete critical absorption. I stared in amazement and consternation, for I recognized in the fair stranger Miss Urania Mannersley, the Congregational minister's niece!

Everybody knew Rainie Mannersley throughout the length and breadth of the Encinal. She was at once the envy and the goad of the daughters of those southwestern and eastern immigrants who had settled in the valley. She was correct, she was critical, she was faultless and observant. She was proper yet independent; she was highly educated; she was suspected of knowing Latin and Greek; she even spelled correctly! She could wither the plainest field nosegay in the hands of other girls by giving the flowers their botanical names. She never said, "Ain't you?" but "Aren't you?" She looked upon "Did I which?" as an incomplete and imperfect form of "What did I do?" She quoted from Browning and Tennyson and was believed to have read them. She was from Boston. What could she possibly be doing at a free-and-easy fandango?

Even if these facts were not already familiar to everyone there, her outward appearance would have attracted attention. Contrasted with the gorgeous red, black and yellow skirts of the dancers, her plain tightly fitting gown and hat, all of one delicate gray, were sufficiently notable in themselves even had they not seemed, like the girl herself, a kind of quiet protest to the glaring flounces before her. Her small straight waist and flat back brought into greater relief the corsetless, waistless, swaying figures of the Mexican girls, and her long, slim well-booted feet peeping from the stiff white edges of her short skirt, made their broad low-quartered slippers, held on by the big toe, appear more preposterous than ever. Suddenly she seemed to realize that she was standing there alone, but showed no fear or embarrassment. She drew back a little, glancing carelessly behind her as if missing some previous companion, and then her eyes fell upon mine. She smiled an easy recognition;

then a moment later her glance rested more curiously
upon Enriquez, who was still by my side. I disengaged
myself and instantly joined her, particularly as I noticed
that a few of the other bystanders were beginning to
stare at her with little reserve.

"Isn't it the most extraordinary thing you ever saw?"
she said quietly. Then, presently noticing the look of embarrassment on my face she went on, more by way of
conversation than of explanation: "I just left uncle making a call on a parishioner next door, and was going
home with Jocasta" (a peon servant of her uncle's)
"when I heard the music, and dropped in. I don't know
what has become of her," she added, glancing around
the room again. "She seemed perfectly wild when she
saw that creature over there bounding about with his
handkerchiefs. You were speaking to him just now. Do
tell me—is he real?"

"I should think there was little doubt of that," I said
with a vague laugh.

"You know what I mean," she said simply. "Is he quite
sane? Does he do that because he likes it, or is he paid
for it?"

This was too much. I pointed out somewhat hurriedly
that he was a scion of one of the oldest Castilian families, that the performance was a national gypsy dance
which he had joined in as a patriot and a patron, and
that he was my dearest friend. At the same time I was
conscious that I wished she hadn't seen his last performance.

"You don't mean to say that all that he did was in the dance?" she said. "I don't believe it. It was only like him." As I hesitated over this palpable truth she went on, "I do wish he'd do it again. Don't you think you could make him?"

"Perhaps he might if *you* asked him," I said a little maliciously.

"Of course I shouldn't do that," she returned quietly. "All the same, I do believe he is really going to do it— or something else. Do look!"

I looked and to my horror saw that Enriquez, possibly incited by the delicate gold eyeglasses of Miss Mannersley, had divested himself of his coat and was winding the four handkerchiefs tied together picturesquely around his waist, preparatory to some new performance. I tried furtively to give him a warning look, but in vain.

"Isn't he really too absurd for anything!" said Miss Mannersley, yet with a certain comfortable anticipation in her voice. "You know, I never saw anything like this before. I wouldn't have believed such a creature could have existed."

Even had I succeeded in warning him, I doubt if it would have been of any avail. For seizing a guitar from one of the musicians, he struck a few chords and suddenly began to zigzag into the center of the floor, swaying his body languishingly from side to side in time with the music and the pitch of a thin Spanish tenor. It was a gypsy love song. Possibly Miss Mannersley's lingual accomplishments did not include a knowledge of Castilian, but she could not fail to see that the gestures and illustrative pantomime were addressed to her. Passionately assuring her that she was the most favored daughter of the Virgin, that her eyes were like votive tapers, and yet in the same breath accusing her of being a "brigand" and "assassin" in her attitude toward "his heart," he balanced with quivering timidity toward her, threw an imaginary cloak in front of her neat boots as a carpet for her to tread on, and with a final astonishing pirouette and a languishing twang of his guitar, sank on one knee and blowing a kiss, threw a rose at her feet.

If I had been seriously angry with him before for his grotesque extravagance, I could have pitied him now for the young girl's absolute unconsciousness of anything but his utter ludicrousness. The applause of dancers and bystanders was instantaneous and hearty; her only contribution to it was a slight parting of her thin red lips in a half incredulous smile. In the silence that followed the applause, as Enriquez walked pantingly away I heard her saying, half to herself, "Certainly a most extraordinary creature!" In my indignation I could not help turning suddenly upon her and looking straight into her eyes. They were brown, with that peculiar velvet opacity common to the pupils of nearsighted persons, and seemed to defy internal scrutiny. She only repeated carelessly, "Isn't he?" and added, "Please see if you can find Jocasta. I suppose we ought to be going now, and I dare say he won't be doing it again. Ah!

There she is. Good gracious, child! what have you got there?"

It was Enriquez's rose which Jocasta had picked up and was timidly holding out toward her mistress.

"Heavens! I don't want it. Keep it yourself."

I walked with them to the door, as I did not fancy a certain glitter in the black eyes of the Senoritas Manuela and Pepita, who were watching her curiously. But I think she was as oblivious of this as she was of Enriquez's particular attentions. As we reached the street I felt that I ought to say something more.

"You know," I began casually, "that although those poor people meet here in this public way, their gathering is really quite a homely pastoral and a national custom, and these girls are all honest hardworking peons or servants enjoying themselves in quite the old idyllic fashion."

"Certainly," said the young girl, half abstractedly. "Of course it's a Moorish dance, originally brought over, I suppose, by those old Andalusian immigrants two hundred years ago. It's quite Arabic in its suggestions. I have got something like it in an old *cancionero* I picked up at a bookstall in Boston. But," she added, with a gasp of reminiscent satisfaction, "that's not like *him!* Oh, no! *he* is decidedly original. Heavens, yes."

I turned away in some discomfiture to join Enriquez, who was calmly awaiting me with a cigarette in his mouth outside the *sala*. Yet he looked so unconscious of any previous absurdity that I hesitated in what I thought was a necessary warning. He, however, quickly precipitated it. Glancing after the retreating figures of the two women he said, "Thees mees from Boston is return to her house. You do not accompany her? I shall. Behold me—I am there."

But I linked my arm firmly in his. Then I pointed out first, that she was already accompanied by a servant; secondly, that if I who knew her had hesitated to offer myself as an escort it was hardly proper for him, a perfect stranger, to take that liberty; that Miss Mannersley was very punctilious of etiquette which he, as a Castilian gentleman, ought to appreciate.

"But will she not regard lofe—the admiration excessif?" he said, twirling his thin little mustache meditatively.

"No; she will not," I returned sharply, "and you ought to understand that she is on a different level from your Manuelas and Carmens."

"Pardon, my friend," he said gravely. "Thees women are ever the same. There is a proverb in my language. Listen: 'Whether the sharp blade of the Toledo pierce the satin or the goatskin, it shall find behind it ever the same heart to wound.' I am that Toledo blade—possibly it is you, my friend. Wherefore let us together pursue this girl of Boston on the instant."

But I kept my grasp on Enriquez's arm and succeeded in restraining his mercurial impulses for the moment. He halted and puffed vigorously at his cigarette, but the next instant he started forward again.

"Let us, however, follow with discretion in the rear; we shall pass her house; we shall gaze at it; it shall touch her heart."

Ridiculous as was this following of the young girl we had only just parted from I nevertheless knew that Enriquez was quite capable of attempting it alone. I thought it better to humor him by consenting to walk with him in that direction, but I felt it necesary to say:

"I ought to warn you that Miss Mannersley already looks upon your performances at the *sala* as something *outré* and peculiar, and if I were you I shouldn't do anything to deepen that impression."

"You are saying she ees shock?" said Enriquez gravely.

I felt I could not conscientiously say that she was shocked and he saw my hesitation.

"Then she have jealousy of the senoritas," he observed with insufferable complacency. "You observe! I have already said. It is ever so."

I could stand it no longer.

"Look here, Harry," I said, "if you must know it, she looks upon you as an acrobat—a paid performer."

"Ah"—his black eyes sparkled. "The torero, the man who fights the bull, he is also an acrobat."

"Yes, but she thinks you a clown!—a *gracioso de teatro*,—there!"

"Then I have make her laugh?" he said coolly.

I don't think he had, but I shrugged my shoulders.

"Bueno!" he said cheerfully. "Lofe, he begin with a laugh, he make feenish with a sigh."

I turned to look at him in the moonlight. His face presented its habitual Spanish gravity, a gravity that was almost ironical. His small black eyes had their characteristic irresponsible audacity, the irresponsibility of the vivacious young animal. It could not be possible that he was really touched with the placid frigidities of Miss Mannersley. I remembered his equally elastic gallantries with Miss Pinkey Smith, a blonde western belle, from which both had harmlessly rebounded. As we walked on slowly I continued more persuasively:

"Of course this is only your nonsense, but don't you see, Miss Mannersley thinks it all in earnest and really your nature?" I hesitated, for it suddenly struck me that it *was* really his nature. "And hang it all! You don't want her to believe you a common buffoon or some intoxicated *muchacho.*"

"Intoxicated?" repeated Enriquez, with exasperating languishment. "Yes, that is the word that shall express itself. My friend, you have made a shot in the center—you have ring the bell every time! It is intoxication—but not of *aguardiente.* Look! I have long time an ancestor of whom is a pretty story. One day in church he have seen a young girl, a mere peasant girl, pass to the confessional. He look her in her eye, he stagger"—here Enriquez wobbled pantomimically into the road—"he fall!"—he would have suited the action to the word if I had not firmly held him up. "They have take him home where he have remain without his clothes and have dance and sing. But it was the drunkenness of lofe. And look you, thees village girl was a nothing, not even pretty. The name of my ancestor was—"

"Don Quixote de la Mancha," I suggested maliciously. "I suspected as much. Come along. That will do."

"My ancestor's name," continued Enriquez gravely, "was Antonio Hermenegildo de Salvatierra, which is not the same. Thees Don Quixote of whom you speak exist not at all."

"Never mind. Only for Heaven's sake, we are nearing the house; don't make a fool of yourself again."

It was a wonderful moonlight night. The deep redwood porch of the Mannersley parsonage under the shadow of a great oak, the largest in the Encinal, was diapered in black and silver. As the women stepped upon the porch their shadows were silhouetted against the door. Miss Mannersley paused for an instant and turned to give a last look at the beauty of the night as Jocasta entered. Her glance fell upon us as we passed. She nodded carelessly and unaffectedly to me, but as she recognized Enriquez she looked a little longer at him with her previous cold and invincible curiosity. To my horror Enriquez began instantly to affect a slight tremulousness of gait and a difficulty of breathing, but I gripped his arm savagely and managed to get him past the house as the door closed finally on the young lady.

"You do not comprehend, friend Pancho," he said

gravely, "but those eyes in their glass are as the *espejo ustorio,* the burning mirror. They burn, they consume me here like paper. Let us affix to ourselves thees tree. She will, without doubt, appear at her window. We shall salute her for good night."

"We will do nothing of the kind," I said sharply.

Finding that I was determined, he permitted me to lead him away. I was delighted to notice, however, that he had indicated the window which I knew was the minister's study, and that as the bedrooms were in the rear of the house, this later incident was probably not overseen by the young lady or the servant. But I did not part from Enriquez until I saw him safely back to the sala where I left him sipping chocolate, his arm alternating around the waists of his two previous partners in a delightful Arcadian and childlike simplicity and an apparent utter forgetfulness of Miss Mannersley.

The fandangos were usually held on Saturday night. The next day being Sunday I missed Enriquez; but as he was a devout Catholic I remembered that he was at mass in the morning and possibly at the bullfight at San Antonio in the afternoon. But I was somewhat surprised on the Monday morning following, as I was crossing the plaza, to have my arm taken by the Reverend Mr. Mannersley in the nearest approach to familiarity that was consistent with the reserve of this eminent divine. I looked at him inquiringly. Although scrupulously correct in his attire his features always had a singular resemblance to the national caricature known

as "Uncle Sam," but with the humorous expression left
out. Softly stroking his goatee with three fingers he began condescendingly:

"You are, I think, more or less familiar with the
characteristics and customs of the Spanish as exhibited
by the settlers here."

A thrill of apprehension went through me. Had he
heard of Enriquez's proceedings? Had Miss Mannersley
cruelly betrayed him to her uncle?

"I have not given that attention myself to their language and social peculiarities," he continued with a
large wave of the hand, "being much occupied with
a study of their religious beliefs and superstitions"—it
struck me that this was apt to be a common fault of people of the Mannersley type—"but I have refrained from
a personal discussion of them. On the contrary, I have
held somewhat broad views on the subject of their remarkable missionary work and have suggested a scheme
of cooperation with them quite independent of doctrinal
teaching, to my brethren of other Protestant Christian
sects. These views I first incorporated in a sermon last
Sunday week, which I am told has created considerable
attention." He stopped and coughed slightly. "I have
not yet heard from any of the Roman clergy but I am
led to believe that my remarks were not ungrateful to
Catholics generally."

I was relieved, although still in some wonder why he
should address me on this topic. I had a vague remembrance of having heard that he had said something on

Sunday which had offended some puritans of his flock, but nothing more.

He continued, "I have just said that I was unacquainted with the characteristics of the Spanish-American race. I presume, however, they have the impulsiveness of their Latin origin. They gesticulate—eh? They express their gratitude, their joy, their affection, their emotions generally, by spasmodic movements? They naturally dance—sing—eh?"

A horrible suspicion crossed my mind; I could only stare helplessly at him.

"I see," he said graciously. "Perhaps it is a somewhat general question. I will explain myself. A rather singular occurrence happened to me the other night. I had returned from visiting a parishioner and was alone in my study reviewing my sermon for the next day. It must have been quite late before I concluded, for I distinctly remember my niece had returned with her servant fully an hour before. Presently I heard the sounds of a musical instrument in the road, with the accents of someone singing or rehearsing some metrical composition in words that, although couched in a language foreign to me, in expression and modulation gave me the impression of being distinctly adulatory. For some little time, in the greater preoccupation of my task I paid little attention to the performance, but its persistency at length drew me in no mere idle curiosity to the window. From thence, standing in my dressing gown and believing myself unperceived, I noticed under the large oak in

the roadside the figure of a young man, who by the
imperfect light appeared to be of Spanish extraction.
But I evidently miscalculated my own invisibility, for
he moved rapidly forward as I came to the window,
and in a series of the most extraordinary pantomimic
gestures saluted me. Beyond my experience of a few
Greek plays in earlier days, I confess I am not an adept
in the understanding of gesticulation; but it struck me
that the various phases of gratitude, fervor, reverence
and exaltation were successively portrayed. He placed
his hands upon his head, his heart, and even clasped
them together in this manner."

To my consternation the reverend gentlemen here
imitated Enriquez's most extravagant pantomime.

"I am willing to confess," he continued, "that I was
singularly moved by them, as well as by the highly
creditable and Christian interest that evidently produced them. At last I opened the window. Leaning out,
I told him that I regretted that the lateness of the hour
prevented any further response from me than a grateful though hurried acknowledgment of his praiseworthy
emotion, but that I should be glad to see him for a few
moments in the vestry before service the next day, or
at early candlelight before the meeting of the Bible
class. I told him that as my sole purpose had been the
creation of an evangelical brotherhood and the exclusion of merely doctrinal views, nothing could be more
gratifying to me than this spontaneous and unsolicited
testimony to my motives. He appeared for an instant

to be deeply affected, and indeed quite overcome with emotion, and then gracefully retired, with some agility and a slight saltatory movement."

He paused. A sudden and overwhelming idea took possession of me, and I looked impulsively into his face. Was it possible that for once Enriquez's ironical extravagance had been understood, met and vanquished by a master hand? But the Reverend Mr. Mannersley's self-satisfied face betrayed no ambiguity or lurking humor. He was evidently in earnest; he had complacently accepted for himself the abandoned Enriquez's serenade to his niece. I felt an hysterical desire to laugh, but it was checked by my companion's next words.

"I informed my niece of the occurrence in the morning at breakfast. She had not heard anything of the strange performance, but she agreed with me as to its undoubted origin in a grateful recognition of my liberal efforts toward his co-religionists. It was she, in fact, who suggested that your knowledge of these people might corroborate my impressions."

I was dumbfounded. Had Miss Mannersley, who must have recognized Enriquez's hand in this, concealed the fact in a desire to shield him? But this was so inconsistent with her utter indifference to him, except as a grotesque study, that she would have been more likely to tell her uncle all about his previous performance. Nor could it be that she wished to conceal her visit to the fandango. She was far too independent for that, and it was even possible that the reverend gentleman in his desire to know more of Enriquez's compatriots would not have objected. In my confusion I meekly added my conviction to hers, congratulated him upon his evident success, and slipped away.

But I was burning with a desire to see Enriquez and know all. He was imaginative but not untruthful. Unfortunately, I learned that he was just then following one of his erratic impulses and had gone to a rodeo at his cousin's in the foothills, where he was alternately exercising his horsemanship in catching and breaking wild cattle, and delighting his relatives with his incomparable grasp of the American language and customs, and of the airs of a young man of fashion. Then my thoughts recurred to Miss Mannersley. Had she really been oblivious that night to Enriquez's serenade? I resolved to find out if I could without betraying Enriquez. Indeed it was possible, after all, that it might not have been he.

Chance favored me. The next evening I was at a party where Miss Mannersley by reason of her position and quality was a distinguished—I had almost written a popular—guest. But as I have formerly stated, although the youthful fair of the Encinal were flattered by her casual attentions and secretly admired her superior style and aristocratic calm, they were more or less uneasy under the dominance of her intelligence and education, and were afraid to attempt either confidence or familiarity. They were also singularly jealous of her, for although the average young man was equally afraid of her cleverness and candor he was not above paying a tremulous and timid court to her for its effect upon her humbler sisters. This evening she was surrounded by her usual satellites including, of course, the local notables and special guests of distinction. She had been discussing, I think, the existence of glaciers on Mount Shasta with a bespectacled geologist, and had participated with charming frankness in a conversation on anatomy with the local doctor and a learned professor, when she was asked to take a seat at the piano. She played with remarkable skill and wonderful precision, but coldly and brilliantly. As she sat there in her subdued but perfectly fitting evening dress, her regular profile and short but slender neck firmly set upon her high shoulders, exhaling an atmosphere of refined puritanism and provocative intelligence, the utter incongruity of Enriquez's extravagant attentions if ironical, and their equal hopelessness if not, seemed to me plainer than ever. What had this well-poised, coldly observant spinster to do with that quaintly ironic ruffler, that romantic cynic, that rowdy Don Quixote, that impossible Enriquez? Presently she ceased playing. Her slim narrow slipper, revealing her thin ankle, remained upon the pedal; her delicate fingers were resting idly on the keys; her head was slightly thrown back and her narrow eyebrows prettily knit toward the ceiling in an effort of memory.

"Something of Chopin's," suggested the geologist ardently.

"That exquisite sonata!" pleaded the doctor.

"Suthin' of Rubinstein. Heard him once," said a gentleman of Siskiyou. "He just made that pianner get up and howl. Play Rube."

She shook her head with parted lips and a slight touch of girlish coquetry in her manner. Then her fingers suddenly dropped upon the keys with a glassy tinkle; there were a few quick pizzicato chords, down went the low pedal with a monotonous strumming, and she presently began to hum to herself. I started, as well I might, for I recognized one of Enriquez's favorite and most extravagant guitar solos. It was audacious; it was barbaric; it was, I fear, vulgar. As I remembered it, as he sang it, it recounted the adventures of one Don Francisco, a provincial gallant and roisterer of the most objectionable type. It had one hundred and four verses, which Enriquez never spared me. I shuddered as in a pleasant quiet voice the correct Miss Mannersley warbled in musical praise of the *pellejo*, or wineskin, and a eulogy of the dicebox came caressingly from her thin red lips. But the company was far differently affected: the strange wild air and wilder accompaniment were evidently catching; people moved toward the piano; somebody whistled the air from a distant corner; even the faces of the geologist and doctor brightened.

"A tarantella, I presume?" suggested the doctor.

Miss Mannersley stopped, and rose from the piano.

"It is a Moorish gypsy song of the fifteenth century," she said dryly.

"It seemed sorter familiar, too," hesitated one of the young men timidly, "like as if—don't you know?—you had without knowing it, don't you know?"—he blushed slightly—"sorter picked it up somewhere."

"I 'picked it up' as you call it, in the collection of medieval manuscripts of the Harvard Library and copied it," returned Miss Mannersley coldly as she turned away.

But I was not inclined to let her off so easily. I presently made my way to her side.

"Your uncle was complimentary enough to consult me as to the meaning of the appearance of a certain exuberant Spanish visitor at his house the other night."

I looked into her brown eyes, but my own slipped off her velvety pupils without retaining anything.

Then she reinforced her gaze with a pince-nez, and said carelessly:

"Oh, it's you? How are you? Well, could you give him any information?"

"Only generally," I returned, still looking into her eyes. "These people are impulsive. The Spanish blood is a mixture of gold and quicksilver."

She smiled slightly. "That reminds me of your volatile friend. He was mercurial enough, certainly. Is he still dancing?"

"And singing sometimes," I responded pointedly.

But she only added casually, "A singular creature,"

without exhibiting the least consciousness, and drifted away leaving me none the wiser. I felt that Enriquez alone could enlighten me. I must see him.

I did, but not in the way I expected. There was a bullfight at San Antonio the next Saturday afternoon, the usual Sunday performance being changed in deference to the Sabbatical habits of the Americans. An additional attraction was offered in the shape of a bull and bear fight, also a concession to American taste which had voted the bullfight "slow," and had averred that the bull "did not get a fair show." I am glad that I am able to spare the reader the usual realistic horrors, for in the Californian performances there was very little of the brutality that distinguished this function in the mother country. The horses were not miserable worn-out hacks but young and alert mustangs, and the display of horsemanship by the picadors was not only wonderful but secured an almost absolute safety to horse and rider. I never saw a horse gored; although unskillful riders were sometimes thrown in wheeling quickly to avoid the bull's charge, they generally regained their animals without injury.

The Plaza de Toros was reached through the decayed and tile-strewn outskirts of an old Spanish village. It was a rudely built oval amphitheater with crumbling whitewashed adobe walls and roofed only over portions of the gallery, reserved for the provincial "notables" but now occupied by a few shopkeepers and their wives with a sprinkling of American travelers and ranchmen.

The impalpable adobe dust of the arena was being whirled into the air by the strong onset of the afternoon trade winds which happily, however, helped also to dissipate a reek of garlic and the acrid fumes of cheap tobacco rolled in cornhusk cigarettes. I was leaning over the second barrier waiting for the meagre and circuslike procession to enter with the keys of the bull pen, when my attention was attracted to a movement in the reserved gallery. A lady and gentleman of a quality that was evidently unfamiliar to the rest of the audience were picking their way along the rickety benches to a front seat. I recognized the geologist with some surprise, and the lady he was leading with still greater astonishment. For it was Miss Mannersley, in her precise well-fitting walking costume—a monotone of sober color among the parti-colored audience.

However, I was perhaps less surprised than the audience, for I was not only becoming as accustomed to the young girl's vagaries as I had been to Enriquez's extravagance, but I was also satisfied that her uncle might have given her permission to come as a recognition of the Sunday concession of the management, as well as to conciliate his supposed Catholic friends. I watched her sitting there until the first bull had entered, and after a rather brief play with the picadors and banderilleros, was dispatched. At the moment when the matador approached the bull with his lethal weapon I was not sorry for an excuse to glance at Miss Mannersley. Her hands were in her lap, her head slightly bent forward over her knees. I fancied that she too had dropped her eyes before the brutal situation; to my horror I saw that she had a drawing book in her hand and was actually sketching it. I turned my eyes in preference to the dying bull.

The second animal led out for this ingenious slaughter was, however, more sullen, uncertain and discomposing to his butchers. He accepted the irony of a trial with gloomy suspicious eyes, and he declined the challenge of whirling and insulting picadors. He bristled with banderillas like a hedgehog, but remained with his haunches backed against the barrier, at times almost hidden in the fine dust raised by the monotonous stroke of his sullenly pawing hoof—his one dull heavy protest. A vague uneasiness had infected his adversaries; the picadors held aloof; the banderilleros skirmished at a safe distance. The audience resented only the indecision of the bull. Galling epithets were flung at him, followed by cries of *"Espada!"* Curving his elbow under his short cloak the matador with his flashing blade in hand advanced and—stopped. The bull remained motionless.

For at that instant a heavier gust of wind than usual swept down upon the arena, lifted a suffocating cloud of dust and whirled it around the tiers of benches and the balcony, and for a moment seemed to stop the performance. I heard an exclamation from the geologist who had risen to his feet. I fancied I heard even a faint cry from Miss Mannersley, but the next moment, as the dust was slowly settling, we saw a sheet of paper in the air that had been caught up in this brief cyclone dropping, dipping from side to side on uncertain wings until it slowly descended in the very middle of the arena. It was a leaf from Miss Mannersley's sketchbook, the one on which she had been sketching.

In the pause that followed it seemed to be the one object that at last excited the bull's growing but tardy ire. He glanced at it with murky distended eyes; he snorted at it with vague yet troubled fury. Whether he detected his own presentment in Miss Mannersley's sketch or whether he recognized it as an unknown and unfamiliar treachery in his surroundings I could not conjecture, for the next moment the matador, taking advantage of the bull's concentration, with a complacent leer at the audience advanced toward the paper. But at that instant a young man cleared the barrier into the arena with a single bound, shoved the matador to one side, caught up the paper, turned toward the balcony and Miss Mannersley with a gesture of apology, dropped gaily before the bull, knelt down before him with an exaggerated humility, and held up the drawing as if for his inspection.

A roar of applause broke from the audience, a cry of warning and exasperation from the attendants, as the goaded bull suddenly charged the stranger. But he sprang to one side with great dexterity, made a courteous gesture to the matador as if passing the bull over to him, and still holding the paper in his hand, re-leaped the barrier and rejoined the audience in safety. I did not wait to see the deadly dominant thrust with which

the matador received the charging bull; my eyes were
following the figure now bounding up the steps to the
balcony, where with an exaggerated salutation he laid
the drawing in Miss Mannersley's lap and vanished.
There was no mistaking that thin lithe form, the narrow
black mustache and gravely dancing eyes. The audacity
of conception, the extravagance of execution, the quaint
irony of the sequel could belong to no one but Enriquez.

I hurried up to her as the six yoked mules dragged the
carcass of the bull away. She was placidly putting up
her book, the unmoved focus of a hundred eager and
curious eyes. She smiled slightly as she saw me.

"I was just telling Mr. Briggs what an extraordinary
creature it was, and how you know him. He must have
had great experience to do that sort of thing so cleverly
and safely. Does he do it often? Of course, not just that.
But does he pick up cigars and things that I see they
throw to the matador? Does he belong to the management? Mr. Briggs thinks the whole thing was a feint to
distract the bull," she added with a wicked glance at the
geologist who, I fancied, looked disturbed.

"I am afraid," I said dryly, "that his act was as unpremeditated and genuine as it was unusual."

"Why afraid?"

It was a matter-of-fact question, but I instantly saw
my mistake. What right had I to assume that Enriquez's
attentions were any more genuine than her own easy
indifference? And if I suspected that they were, was it

fair to give my friend away to this heartless coquette?

"You are not very gallant," she said with a slight laugh as I was hesitating, and turned away with her escort before I could frame a reply.

But at least Enriquez was now accessible, and I should gain some information from him. I knew where to find him, unless he were still lounging about the building, intent upon more extravagance; but I waited until I saw Miss Mannersley and Briggs depart without further interruption.

The hacienda of Ramon Saltello, Enriquez's cousin, was on the outskirts of the village. When I arrived there I found Enriquez's pinto mustang steaming in the corral, and although I was momentarily delayed by these servants at the gateway, I was surprised to find Enriquez himself lying languidly on his back in a hammock in the patio. His arms were hanging down listlessly on each side as if in the greatest prostration, yet I could not resist the impression that the rascal had only just got into the hammock when he heard of my arrival.

"You have arrived, friend Pancho, in time," he said in accents of exaggerated weakness. "I am absolutely exhaust. I am bursted, caved in, kerflummoxed. I have behold you, my friend, at the barrier. I speak not, I make no sign at the first because I was on fire; I speak not at the feenish—for I am exhaust."

"I see; the bull made it lively for you."

He instantly bounded up in the hammock.

"The bull! *Caramba!* Not a thousand bulls! And thees one, look you, was a craven. I snap my fingers over his horn; I roll my cigarette under his nose."

"Well then—what was it?"

He instantly lay down again, pulling up the sides of the hammock. Presently his voice came from its depths, appealing in hollow tones to the sky.

"He asks me—thees friend of my soul, thees brother of my life, thees Pancho that I lofe—what it was? He would that I should tell him why I am game in the legs, why I shake in the hand, crack in the voice and am generally wipe out! And yet he, my pardner—thees Francisco— know that I have seen the mees from Boston! That I have gaze into the eye, touch the hand, and for the instant possess the picture that hand have drawn! It was a sublime picture, Pancho," he said, sitting up again suddenly, "and have kill the bull before our friend Pepe's sword have touch even the bone of hees back and make feenish of him."

"Look here, Enriquez," I said bluntly, "have you been serenading that girl?"

He shrugged his shoulders without the least embarrassment and said:

"Ah, yes. What would you? It is of a necessity."

"Well," I retorted, "then you ought to know that her uncle took it all to himself—thought you some grateful Catholic pleased with his religious tolerance."

He did not even smile. "Bueno," he said gravely.

"That make something too. In thees affair it is well to begin with the duenna. He is the duenna."

"And," I went on relentlessly, "her escort told her just now that your exploit in the bull ring was only a trick to divert the bull, suggested by the management."

"Bah! her escort is a geologian. Naturally she is to him as a stone."

I would have continued, but a peon interrupted us at this moment with a sign to Enriquez, who leaped briskly from the hammock, bidding me wait his return from a messenger in the gateway.

Still unsatisfied of mind I waited, and sat down in the hammock that Enriquez had quitted. A scrap of paper was lying in its meshes, which at first appeared to be of the kind from which Enriquez rolled his cigarettes; but as I picked it up to throw it away I found it was of much firmer and stouter material. Looking at it more closely, I was surprised to recognize it as a piece of the tinted drawing paper torn off the "block" that Miss Mannersley had used. It had been deeply creased at right angles as if it had been folded; it looked as if it might have been the outer half of a sheet used for a note.

It might have been a trifling circumstance but it greatly excited my curiosity. I knew that he had returned the sketch to Miss Mannersley, for I had seen it in her hand. Had she given him another? And if so, why had it been folded to the destruction of the drawing? Or was it part of a note which he had destroyed? In the first impulse of discovery I walked quickly with it toward the gateway where Enriquez had disappeared, intending to restore it to him. He was just outside talking with a young girl. I started, for it was Jocasta—Miss Mannersley's maid.

With this added discovery came that sense of uneasiness and indignation with which we illogically are apt to resent the withholding of a friend's confidence, even in matters concerning only himself. It was no use for me to reason that it was no business of mine, that he was right in keeping a secret that concerned another—and a lady; but I was afraid I was even more meanly resentful because the discovery quite upset my theory of his conduct and of Miss Mannersley's attitude toward him.

I continued to walk on to the gateway where I bade Enriquez a hurried good-by alleging the sudden remembrance of another engagement but without appearing to recognize the girl, who was moving away, when to my further discomfiture the rascal stopped me with an appealing wink, threw his arms around my neck, whispered hoarsely in my ear, "Ah! you see—you comprehend—but you are the mirror of discretion!" and returned to Jocasta. But whether this meant that he had received a message from Miss Mannersley or that he was trying to suborn her maid to carry one was still uncertain. He was capable of either.

During the next two or three weeks I saw him frequently, but as I had resolved to try the effect of ignoring Miss Mannersley in our conversation I gathered little further of their relations, and to my surprise, after one or two characteristic extravagances of allusion, Enriquez dropped the subject too. Only one afternoon, as we were parting, he said carelessly:

"My friend, you are going to the casa of Mannersley tonight. I too have the honor of the invitation. But you will be my Mercury—my Leporello—you will take of me a message to thees Mees Boston, that I am crushed, desolated, prostrate and flabbergasted—that I cannot arrive, for I have of that night to sit up with the grand aunt of my brother-in-law, who has a quinsy to the death. It is sad."

This was the first indication I had received of Miss Mannersley's advances. I was equally surprised at Enriquez's refusal.

"Nonsense!" I said bluntly. "Nothing keeps you from going."

"My friend," returned Enriquez with a sudden lapse into languishment that seemed to make him absolutely infirm, "it is everything that shall restrain me. I am not strong. I shall become weak of the knee and tremble under the eye of Mees Boston. I shall precipitate myself to the geologian by the throat. Ask me another conundrum that shall be easy."

He seemed idiotically inflexible, and did not go. But I did. I found Miss Mannersley exquisitely dressed and looking singularly animated and pretty. The lambent glow of her inscrutable eye as she turned toward me might have been flattering but for my uneasiness in regard to Enriquez. I delivered his excuses as naturally as I could. She stiffened for an instant, and seemed an inch higher.

"I am so sorry," she said at last in a level voice. "I thought he would have been so amusing. Indeed, I had hoped we might try an old Moorish dance together which I have found and was practicing."

"He would have been delighted, I know. It's a great pity he didn't come with me," I said quickly. "But," I could not help adding with emphasis on her words, "he is such an 'extraordinary creature,' you know."

"I see nothing extraordinary in his devotion to an aged relative," returned Miss Mannersley quietly as she turned away, "except that it justifies my respect for his character."

I do not know why I did not relate this to him. Possibly I had given up trying to understand them; perhaps I was beginning to have an idea that he could take care of himself. But I was somewhat surprised a few days later when after asking me to go with him to a rodeo at his uncle's he added composedly, "You will meet Mees Boston."

I stared, and but for his manner would have thought it part of his extravagance. For the rodeo, a yearly chase of wild cattle for the purpose of lassoing and branding

them, was a rather brutal affair and purely a man's function; it was also a family affair, a property stocktaking
of the great Spanish cattle owners, and strangers, particularly Americans, found it difficult to gain access to
its mysteries and the *festa* that followed.

"But how did she get an invitation?" I asked. "You
did not dare to ask"—I began.

"My friend," said Enriquez with a singular deliberation, "the great and respectable Boston herself, and her
serene venerable oncle and other Boston magnificoes
have of a truth done me the inexpressible honor to solicit
of my degraded papistical oncle that she shall come—
that she shall of her own superior eye behold the barbaric customs of our race."

His tone and manner were so peculiar that I stepped
quickly before him, laid my hands on his shoulders, and
looked down into his face. But the actual devil which I
now for the first time saw in his eyes went out of them
suddenly, and he relapsed again in affected languishment in his chair.

"I shall be there, friend Pancho," he said with a preposterous gasp. "I shall nerve my arm to lasso the bull
and tumble him before her at her feet. I shall throw the
'buck-jump' mustang at the same sacred spot. I shall
pluck for her the buried chicken at full speed from the
ground and present it to her. You shall see it, friend
Pancho. I shall be there."

He was as good as his word. When Don Pedro Amador, his uncle, installed Miss Mannersley with Spanish courtesy on a raised platform in the long valley where the rodeo took place, the gallant Enriquez selected a bull from the frightened and galloping herd, and cleverly isolating him from the band, lassoed his hind legs and threw him exactly before the platform where Miss Mannersley was seated. It was Enriquez who caught the unbroken mustang, sprang from his own saddle to the bare back of his captive and with only the lasso for a bridle halted him on rigid haunches at Miss Mannersley's feet. It was Enriquez who in the sports that followed leaned from his saddle at full speed, caught up the chicken buried to its head in the sand without wringing its neck, and tossed it unharmed and fluttering toward his mistress. As for her, she wore the same look of animation that I had seen in her face at our previous meeting. Although she did not bring her sketchbook with her as at the bullfight, she did not shrink from the branding of the cattle, which took place under her very eyes.

Yet I had never seen her and Enriquez together; they had never to my actual knowledge even exchanged words. And now although she was the guest of his uncle, his duties seemed to keep him in the field and apart from her. Nor as far as I could detect, did either apparently make any effort to have it otherwise. The peculiar circumstance seemed to attract no attention from anyone else. But for what I alone knew, or thought I knew, of their actual relations, I should have thought them strangers.

But I felt certain that the *festa* which took place in the broad patio of Don Pedro's casa would bring them together. And later in the evening, as we were all sitting on the veranda watching the dancing of the Mexican women whose white-flounced *sayas* were monotonously rising and falling to the strains of two melancholy harps, Miss Mannersley rejoined us from the house. She seemed to be utterly absorbed and abstracted in the barbaric dances, and scarcely moved as she leaned over the railing with her cheek resting on her hand. Suddenly she arose with a little cry.

"What is it?" asked two or three.

"Nothing—only I have lost my fan."

She had risen and was looking abstractedly on the floor.

Half a dozen men jumped to their feet. "Let me fetch it," they said.

"No thank you. I think I know where it is, and will go for it myself." She was moving away.

But Don Pedro interposed with Spanish gravity. Such a thing was not to be heard of in his casa. If the senorita would not permit *him*, an old man, to go for it, it must be brought by Enriquez, her cavalier of the day.

But Enriquez was not to be found. I glanced at Miss Mannersley's somewhat disturbed face and begged her to let me fetch it. I thought I saw a flush of relief come

into her pale cheek as she said in a lower voice, "On the
stone seat in the garden."

I hurried away leaving Don Pedro still protesting. I
knew the gardens and the stone seat at an angle of the
wall, not a dozen yards from the casa. The moon shone
full upon it. There indeed lay the little gray-feathered
fan. But close beside it also lay the crumpled black,
gold-embroidered riding gauntlet that Enriquez had
worn at the rodeo.

I thrust it hurriedly into my pocket and ran back. As
I passed through the gateway I asked a peon to send
Enriquez to me. The man stared. Did I not know that
Don Enriquez had ridden away two minutes ago?

When I reached the veranda I handed the fan to Miss
Mannersley without a word.

"Bueno," said Don Pedro gravely; "it is as well. There
shall be no bones broken over the getting of it for Enriquez, I hear, has had to return to the Encinal this very
evening."

Miss Mannersley retired early. I did not inform her of
my discovery, nor did I seek in any way to penetrate her
secret. There was no doubt that she and Enriquez had
been together, perhaps not for the first time; but what
was the result of their interview? From the young girl's
demeanor and Enriquez's hurried departure, I could
only fear the worst for him. Had he been tempted into
some further extravagance and been angrily rebuked, or
had he avowed a real passion concealed under his exag-

gerated mask, and been deliberately rejected? I tossed uneasily half the night, following in my dreams my poor friend's hurrying hoofbeats, and ever starting from my sleep at what I thought was the sound of galloping hoofs.

I rose early and lounged into the patio; but others were there before me, and a small group of Don Pedro's family were excitedly discussing something, and I fancied they turned away awkwardly and consciously as I approached. There was an air of indefinite uneasiness everywhere. A strange fear came over me with the chill of the early morning air. Had anything happened to Enriquez? I had always looked upon his extravagance as part of his playful humor. Could it be possible that under the sting of rejection he had made his grotesque threat of languishing effacement real? Surely Miss Mannersley would know or suspect something, if it were the case.

I approached one of the Mexican women and asked if the senorita had risen. The woman started, and looked covertly around before she replied. Did not Don Pancho know that Miss Mannersley and her maid had not slept in their beds that night but had gone, none knew where?

For an instant I felt an appalling sense of my own responsibility in this suddenly serious situation and hurried after the retreating family group. But as I entered the corridor a vaquero touched me on the shoulder. He had evidently just dismounted and was covered with the dust of the road. He handed me a note written in pencil on a leaf from Miss Mannersley's sketchbook. It was in Enriquez's hand, and his signature was followed by his most extravagant rubric.

FRIEND PANCHO: When you read this line you shall of a possibility think I am no more. That is where you shall slip up, my little brother! I am much more—I am two times as much, for I have marry Miss Boston. At the mission church, at five of the morning, sharp! No cards shall be left! I kiss the hand of my venerable uncle-in-law. You shall say to him that we fly to the south wilderness as the combined evangelical missionary to the heathen! Miss Boston herself say this. Ta-ta! How are you now?

Your own
ENRIQUEZ.

M'LISS:

AN IDYLL OF

RED MOUNTAIN

Chapter 1

Smith's
∾ Pocket

Just where the Sierra Nevada begins to sub-
side in gentle undulations and the rivers grow less rapid
and yellow, on the side of a great red mountain stands
Smith's Pocket. Seen from the red road at sunset, in the
red light and the red dust, its white houses look like the
outcroppings of quartz on the mountainside. The red
stage, topped with red-shirted passengers, is lost to view
half a dozen times in the tortuous descent, turning up
unexpectedly in out-of-the-way places, and vanishing
altogether within a hundred yards of the town. It is
probably owing to this sudden twist in the road that the
advent of a stranger at Smith's Pocket is usually attended with a peculiar circumstance. Dismounting from
the vehicle at the stage office the too-confident traveler
is apt to walk straight out of town under the impression
that it lies in quite another direction. It is related that

389

one of the tunnel men, two miles from town, met one of these self-reliant passengers with a carpetbag, umbrella, *Harper's Magazine* and other evidences of civilization and refinement plodding along over the road he had just ridden, vainly endeavoring to find the settlement of Smith's Pocket.

Had he been an observant traveler he might have found some compensation for his disappointment in the weird aspect of that vicinity. There were huge fissures on the hillside and displacements of the red soil, resembling more the chaos of some primary elementary upheaval than the work of man. And halfway down, a long flume straddled its narrow body and disproportionate legs over the chasm like an enormous fossil of some forgotten antediluvian. At every step smaller ditches crossed the road, hiding in their shallow depths unlovely streams that crept away to a clandestine union with the great yellow torrent below. Here and there the ruins of some cabin, with the chimney alone left intact and the hearthstone open to the skies, gave such a flat contradiction to the poetic delusion of *lares* and *penates* that the heart of the traveler must have collapsed as he gazed. And afterward even the barroom of the National Hotel would have seemed festive and invested with preternatural comfort and domesticity.

The settlement of Smith's Pocket owed its origin to the finding of a "pocket" on its site by a veritable Smith. Five thousand dollars was taken out of it in one half-hour by Smith. Three thousand dollars was expended by

Smith and others in erecting a flume and in tunneling. And then Smith's Pocket was found to be only a pocket, and subject like other pockets to depletion. Although Smith pierced the bowels of the great red mountain, that five thousand dollars was the first and the last return of his labor. The mountain grew reticent of its golden secrets and the flume steadily ebbed away the remainder of Smith's fortune. Then Smith went into quartz mining. Then into quartz milling. Then into hydraulics and ditching, and then by easy degrees into saloon keeping. Presently it was whispered that Smith was drinking a good deal; then it was known that Smith was an habitual drunkard; and then people began to think, as they are apt to, that he had never been anything else. But the settlement of Smith's Pocket, like that of most discoveries, was happily not dependent on the fortune of its pioneer, and other parties projected tunnels and found pockets. So Smith's Pocket became a settlement with its two fancy stores, its two hotels, its one express office, and its two first families. Occasionally its one long straggling street was overawed by the assumption of the latest San Francisco fashions imported per express exclusively to the first families, and making outraged nature in the ragged outline of her furrowed surface look still more homely, and putting personal insult on that greater portion of the population to whom the Sabbath, with a change of linen, brought merely the necessity of cleanliness without the luxury of adornment. Then there was a Methodist church, and hard by a *monte* bank, and a little beyond, on the mountainside, was a graveyard; and then a little schoolhouse.

"The master," as he was known to his little flock, sat alone one night in the schoolhouse with some open copybooks before him, carefully making those bold and full characters which are supposed to combine the extremes of chirographical and moral excellence. He had got as far as "Riches are deceitful," and was elaborating the noun with an insincerity of flourish that was quite in the spirit of his text, when he heard a gentle tapping. The woodpeckers had been busy about the roof during the day and the noise did not disturb his work. But the opening of the door, and the tapping continuing from the inside, caused him to look up. He was slightly startled by the figure of a young girl, dirty and shabbily clad. Still her great black eyes, her coarse uncombed lusterless black hair falling over her sunburned face, her red arms and feet streaked with the red soil, were all familiar to him. It was Melissa Smith—Smith's motherless child.

"What can she want here?" thought the master. Everybody knew M'liss, as she was called, throughout the length and height of Red Mountain. Everybody knew her as an incorrigible girl. Her fierce ungovernable disposition, her mad freaks and lawless character, were in their way as proverbial as the story of her father's weakness, and as philosophically accepted by the townsfolk. She wrangled with and fought the schoolboys with keener invective and quite as powerful arm. She followed the trails with woodman's craft, and the master had met her before, miles away, shoeless, stockingless and bareheaded on the mountain road. The miners' camps along the stream supplied her with subsistence during these voluntary pilgrimages, in freely offered alms. Not but that a larger protection had been previously extended to M'liss. The Reverend Joshua Mc-Snagley, "stated" preacher, had placed her in the hotel as servant, by way of preliminary refinement, and had introduced her to his scholars at Sunday school. But she threw plates occasionally at the landlord and quickly retorted to the cheap witticisms of the guests, and created in the Sabbath school a sensation that was so inimical to the orthodox dullness and placidity of that institution that, with a decent regard for the starched frocks and unblemished morals of the two pink-and-white-faced children of the first families, the reverend gentleman had her ignominiously expelled. Such were the antecedents and such the character of M'liss as she stood before the master. It was shown in the ragged dress, the unkempt hair and bleeding feet, and asked his pity. It flashed from her black fearless eyes, and commanded his respect.

"I come here tonight," she said rapidly and boldly, keeping her hard glance on his, "because I knew you was alone. I wouldn't come here when them gals was here. I hate 'em and they hates me. That's why. You keep school—don't you? I want to be teached!"

If to the shabbiness of her apparel and uncomeliness

of her tangled hair and dirty face she had added the humility of tears the master would have extended to her the usual moiety of pity, and nothing more. But with the natural though illogical instincts of his species, her boldness awakened in him something of that respect which all original natures pay unconsciously to one another in any grade. And he gazed at her the more fixedly as she went on still rapidly, her hand on the doorlatch and her eyes on his.

"My name is M'liss—M'liss Smith! You can bet your life on that. My father's Old Smith—Old Bummer Smith —that's what's the matter with him. M'liss Smith—and I'm comin' to school!"

"Well?" said the master.

Accustomed to be thwarted and opposed, often wantonly and cruelly, for no other purpose than to excite the violent impulses of her nature, the master's phlegm evidently took her by surprise. She stopped. She began to twist a lock of her hair between her fingers, and the rigid line of upper lip, drawn over the wicked little teeth, relaxed and quivered slightly. Then her eyes dropped and something like a blush struggled up to her cheek and tried to assert itself through the splashes of redder soil and the sunburn of years. Suddenly she threw herself forward, calling on God to strike her dead, and fell quite weak and helpless, with her face on the master's desk, crying and sobbing as if her heart would break.

The master lifted her gently and waited for the paroxysm to pass. When with face still averted, she was repeating between her sobs the *mea culpa* of childish penitence—that "she'd be good, she didn't mean to," etc., it came to him to ask her why she had left Sabbath school.

Why had she left Sabbath school? Why? Oh, yes. What did he (McSnagley) want to tell her she was wicked for? What did he tell her that God hated her for? If God hated her, what did she want to go to Sabbath school for? *She* didn't want to be beholden to anybody who hated her.

Had she told McSnagley this?

Yes, she had.

The master laughed. It was a hearty laugh and echoed so oddly in the little schoolhouse, and seemed so inconsistent and discordant with the sighing of the pines without, that he shortly corrected himself with a sigh. The sigh was quite as sincere in its way, however, and after a moment of serious silence he asked about her father.

Her father. What father? Whose father? What had he ever done for her? Why did the girls hate her? Come, now! What made the folks say, "Old Bummer Smith's M'liss" when she passed? Yes, oh yes. She wished he was dead—she was dead—everybody was dead, and her sobs broke forth anew.

The master then, leaning over her, told her as well as he could what you or I might have said after hearing such unnatural theories from childish lips, only bearing in mind perhaps better than you or I the unnatural facts of her ragged dress, her bleeding feet and the omnipresent shadow of her drunken father. Then raising her to her feet he wrapped his shawl around her, told her to come early in the morning, and walked with her down the road. Then he bade her good night. The moon shone brightly on the narrow path before them. He stood and watched the bent little figure as it staggered down the road, and waited until it had passed the little graveyard and reached the curve of the hill. There it turned and stood for a moment, a mere atom of suffering outlined against the far-off patient stars.

He went back to his work. But the lines of the copybook thereafter faded into long parallels of never-ending road over which childish figures seemed to pass sobbing and crying to the night. Then, the little schoolhouse seeming lonelier than before, he shut the door and went home.

The next morning M'liss came to school. Her face had been washed and her coarse black hair bore evidence of recent struggles with the comb in which both had evidently suffered. The old defiant look shone occasionally in her eyes, but her manner was tamer and more subdued. Then began a series of little trials and self-sacrifices in which master and pupil bore an equal part and which increased the confidence and sympathy between them. Although obedient under the master's eye, at times during recess if thwarted or stung by a fancied slight M'liss would rage in ungovernable fury. Many a palpitating young savage, finding himself matched with his own weapons of torment, would seek the master with torn jacket and scratched face and complaints of the dreadful M'liss. There was a serious division among the townspeople on the subject, some threatening to withdraw their children from such evil companionship and others as warmly upholding the course of the master in his work of reclamation. Meanwhile, with a steady persistence that seemed quite astonishing to him on looking back afterward, the master drew M'liss gradually out of the shadow of her past life, as though it were but her natural progress down the narrow path on which he had set her feet the moonlight night of their first meeting. Remembering the experience of the evangelical McSnagley, he carefully avoided that Rock of Ages on which that unskillful pilot had shipwrecked her young faith. But if in the course of her reading she chanced to stumble upon those few words which have lifted such as she above the level of the older, the wiser and the more prudent—if she learned something of a faith that is symbolized by suffering, and the old light softened in her eyes, it did not take the shape of a lesson. A few of the plainer people had made up a little sum by which the ragged M'liss was enabled to assume the garments of respect and civilization. Often a rough shake of the hand and words of commendation from a red-shirted and burly figure sent a glow to the cheek of the young master and set him to thinking if it was altogether deserved.

Three months had passed from the time of their first meeting. The master was sitting late one evening over the moral and sententious copies when there came a tap at the door and again M'liss stood before him. She was neatly clad and clean-faced, and there was nothing perhaps but the long black hair and bright black eyes to remind him of his former apparition. "Are you busy?" she asked, "can you come with me?" And on his signifying his readiness, in her old willful way she said, "Come then, quick!"

They passed out of the door together and into the dark road. As they entered the town the master asked her whither she was going. She replied, "To see my father."

It was the first time he had heard her use that filial expression, or indeed allude to him in any other way than "Old Smith" or the "Old Man." It was the first time in many weeks that she had spoken of him at all. He had been missed from the settlement for the past fortnight and the master had credited the rumors of the townsfolk that Smith had "struck something rich" on the North Fork, about ten miles from the village. As they neared the settlement the master gathered from M'liss that the rumor was untrue and that she had seen her father that day. As she grew reticent to further questioning and as the master was satisfied from her manner that she had some definite purpose beyond her usual willfulness, he passively resigned himself and followed her.

Through remote groggeries, restaurants and saloons, in gambling hells and dance houses the master, preceded by M'liss, passed and repassed. In the reeking smoke and blasphemous outcries of noisome dens the child holding the master's hand pursued her search with a strange familiarity, perfect self-possession, and implied protection of himself that even in his anxiety seemed ludicrous. Some of the revelers, recognizing M'liss, called to her to sing and dance for them and would have forced liquor upon her but for the master's interference. Others mutely made way for them. So an hour slipped by and as yet their search was fruitless. The master had yawned once or twice and whistled—two fatal signs of failing interest—and finally came to a full stop.

"It's half past eleven, Melissa," said he, consulting his watch by a broad pencil of light from an open shutter—"half past eleven. And it strikes me that our old friends the woodpeckers must have gone to bed some hours ago, unless they are waiting up for us. I'm much obliged to you for the evening's entertainment but I'm afraid that even the pretext of looking for a parent won't excuse further dissipation. We'd better put this off till to-morrow. What do you say, Melissa? Why! What ails the child? What's that noise? Why, a pistol! You're not afraid of that?"

Few children brought up in the primeval seclusion of Smith's Pocket were unfamiliar with those quick and sharp notes which usually rendered the evening zephyrs of that locality vocal; certainly not M'liss, to have started when that report rang on the clear night air. The echoes caught it as usual, and carried it round and round Red Mountain and set the dogs to barking all along the streams. The lights seemed to dance and move quickly on the outskirts of the town for a few moments afterward, the stream suddenly rippled quite audibly behind them, a few stones loosened themselves from the hillside and splashed into the stream, a heavy wind seemed to suage the branches of the funereal pines, and then the silence fell again, heavier, deadlier than ever.

When the last echo had died away the master felt his companion's hand relax its grasp. Taking advantage of this outward expression of tractability, he drew her gently with him until they reached the hotel, which—in her newer aspect of a guest whose board was secured by responsible parties—had forgivingly opened its hospitable doors to the vagrant child. Here the master lingered a moment to assure her that she might count upon his assistance tomorrow. And having satisfied his conscience by this anticipated duty he bade her good night. In the darkness of the road—going astray several times on his way home and narrowly escaping the yawning ditches in the trail—he had reason to commend his foresight in dissuading M'liss from a further search that night, and in this pleasant reflection went to bed and slept soundly.

For some hours after a darkness thick and heavy brooded over the settlement. The somber pines encompassing the village seemed to close threateningly about it as if to reclaim the wilderness that had been wrested from them. A low rustling as of dead leaves and the damp breath of forest odors filled the lonely street. Emboldened by the darkness other shadows slipped by, leaving strange footprints in the moist ditches for people to point at next day, until the moon, round and full, was lifted above the crest of the opposite hill and all was magically changed.

The shadows shrank away, leaving the straggling street sleeping in a beauty it never knew by day. All that was unlovely, harsh and repulsive in its jagged outlines was subdued and softened by that uncertain light. It smoothed the rough furrows and unsightly chasms of the mountain with an ineffable love and tenderness. It fell upon the face of the sleeping M'liss and left a tear glittering on her black lashes and a smile on her lip, which would have been rare to her at any other time. It fell also on the white upturned face of Old Smith with a pistol in his hand and a bullet in his heart, lying dead beside his empty pocket.

Chapter 2

Which
Contains
a Dream
of the Just
❧ Aristides

THE opinion which McSnagley expressed in reference to a change of heart, as experienced by M'liss, was more forcibly described in the gulches and tunnels. It was thought there that M'liss had struck a "good lead." And when there was a new grave added to the little enclosure and—at the expense of the master—a little board and inscription put above it, the *Red Mountain Banner* came out quite handsomely and did the correct thing for the memory of one of "our oldest pioneers," alluding gracefully to that "bane of noble intellects," touching slightly on the "vicissitudes of fortune," and otherwise assisting our dear brother into genteel obscurity. "He leaves an only child to mourn his loss," said the *Banner*, "who is now an exemplary scholar, thanks to the efforts of the Rev. J. McMcSnagley." That reverend gentleman, in fact, made a strong point of

402

M'liss's conversion, and indirectly referring to her former bad conduct and the suicide of her father, made affecting allusions in Sunday school to the beneficial effects of the "silent tomb," and in that cheerful contemplation froze most of the children into speechless horror and caused the fair-complexioned scions of the first families to howl dismally and refuse to be comforted.

Of the homes that were offered to M'liss when her conversion became known, the master had preferred that of Mrs. Morpher, a womanly and kindhearted specimen of southwestern efflorescence, known in her maidenhood as the "Per-ra-rie Rose." By a steady system of struggle and self-sacrifice she had at last subjugated her naturally careless disposition to principles of order, which as a pious woman she considered, with Pope, as "Heaven's first law." But she could not entirely govern the orbits of her satellites, however regular her own movements, and her old nature asserted itself in her children. Lycurgus dipped in the cupboard between meals, and Aristides came home from school without shoes, leaving those important articles at the threshold for the delights of a barefooted walk down the ditches. Octavia and Cassandra were "keerless" of their clothes. So that with but one exception, however the Prairie Rose might have trimmed, pruned and trained her own natural luxuriance, the little shoots came up defiantly wild and straggling. That one exception was Clytemnestra Morpher, aged fifteen. She was the realization of her mother's most extravagant dream. I stay my hand with difficulty at this moment, for I long to describe this model of deportment. But the progress of my story just at present supplants Clytemnestra in the larger prominence it gives to another member of the family, the just Aristides.

The long dry summer had come. As each fierce day seemed to burn itself out in little whiffs of pearl gray smoke on the mountain summits, and as the upspringing breeze scattered what might have been its red embers over the landscape, the green wave which in early spring had upheaved above Smith's grave grew sere and dry and hard. In those days the master, strolling in the little churchyard of a Sabbath afternoon, was sometimes surprised to find a few wild flowers plucked from the damp pine forest scattered there, and oftener rude wreaths hung upon the little pine cross. Most of these wreaths were formed of a sweet-scented grass which the children loved to keep in their desks, entwined with the pompon-like plumes of the buckeye and syringa, the wood anemone, and here and there the master noticed the dark blue cowl of the monkshood or deadly aconite. One day during a walk, in crossing a wooded ridge, he came upon M'liss in the heart of the forest, perched upon a prostrate pine, on a fantastic throne formed by the hanging plumes of lifeless branches, her lap full of grasses and pine burs, and crooning to the just Aristides who sat humbly at her feet, one of the melodies of her younger life. It was perhaps the influence of the season or the memory of this sylvan enjoyment which caused Aristides, one midsummer day, to have a singular vision.

The just Aristides had begun that morning with a serious error. Loitering on his way to school, occasionally stopping to inspect the footprints of probable bears, or indulging in cheerful badinage with the tunnel men —to whom the apparition of a short-legged boy weighed down by a preternaturally large satchel was an object of boisterous solicitude—Aristides suddenly found that he was an hour and a half too late for school. Whether this circumstance was purely accidental or not is a question of some uncertainty, for Aristides upon finding himself occupying this criminal position at once resolved to play truant. I shall not stop to inquire by what system of logic this result presented itself to that just youth as a consistent deduction, or whether some indistinct apprehension of another and a better world beyond the settlement where there were no schools and blackberries were plenty, had not influenced him in taking this fatal step. Enough that he entered on his rash career by instantly eating the dinner which he carried with him. Having propitiated that terrible god whose seat is every small boy's stomach, and with a feeling of inexpressible guiltiness creeping over him, he turned his back upon the schoolhouse and ran into the woods.

Away from the glare of the red road how deliciously cool was the damp breath and twilight dimness of the stately pines. How they seemed to welcome him in their

deepest recesses, ranging themselves silently around
him as he ran, shutting out the world and its school-
houses and the pursuit of indignant parents and vindic-
tive teachers. How in the forest depths the blue jay
called to him mockingly, and the kingbird, spreading
his tail like a crimson pennant, beckoned him onward.
How there was recognition and greeting even in the
squirrel that scampered past him, mischievously whisk-
ing his ridiculous tail within an inch of his outstretched
fingers. And how Aristides, at last flinging away hat,
shoes and satchel, uttered a shrill whoop and dashed
forward like a youthful savage. But are not these things
written in the dog-eared pages of every boy's memory,
even though they seemed afterward to the just Aristides
a part and parcel of his own strange vision?

Yet even such delights had their hour of culmination
and Aristides found himself at high noon back on the
road again in a state of feverish excitement, carrying a
ravished jay's nest, two pine cones, a dead hare and a
plume of the white syringa. Somewhat overpowered by
the weight of these trophies, which he had collected in
the vague belief that they would be of future service to
him, he began to look about for some convenient place
to bestow his booty. It was nearly time for the great
Wingdam stage to go by. When it came at last with a
sharp rattle of wheels and prancing of horses, and a red
pillar of dust hanging over it that partook of both the
fiery and cloudy attributes of the Israelitish sign, Aris-

tides exchanged epithets with the driver, and although standing knee-deep in red dust, felt a thrill of joy in the recognition which no future honor or dignity might ever give him.

Retracing his steps, the truant presently came to a semicircular opening in the side of Red Mountain which enclosed, like the walls of some vast amphitheater, what had been the arena of the early struggles of the gladiators of fortune. There were terrible traces of that struggle still: in the rock blasted by fire, in the bank furrowed by water, and in the debris of Red Mountain scattered along the gulch two miles in extent. Their forgotten engines were lying half-buried in the ditches—the primeval structure which had served them for a banking house was roofless, and held the hoards of field mice and squirrels. The unshapely stumps of ancient pines dotted the ground.

Aristides remembered that under the solitary redwood, which of all its brothers remained still standing, one of those early pioneers lay buried. No wonder that as the gentle breeze of that summer day swept through its branches the just Aristides might have heard as part of his wonderful dream, some echo of its far-off brothers of Lebanon, saying, "Since thou art fallen, no feller has risen up against us!"

But the short legs of Aristides were aching and he was getting thirsty. There was a rough cavern close at hand, and as most of these openings condensed their general dampness somewhere in quiet pools, Aristides turned into the first one. When he had slaked his thirst, he looked around him and recognized Smith's Pocket.

It had undergone little change in the last two years. The winter rains had detached those portions of the wall which were not upheld by decaying timbers. It was certainly a dirty pocket—a pocket filled with rubbish—a shabby pocket—a worn-out and ragged pocket. It was so unpromising in its present exterior, so graphic in its story of misfortune, and so terrible in its recent memories, that the most sanguine prospector would have passed it by as though the hopeless sentence of Dante had been written over its ragged portal.

The active mind of Aristides, however, saw in the lurking shadows of its arches much promise as a future playroom, to which he intended to induct hereafter his classical brother Lycurgus. In this reflection he threw himself on the ground, and luxuriously burying his bare feet in the cool, loose soil, gave himself up to serene meditation. But the heat and exertion were beginning to exert a certain influence over him and once or twice his eyes closed. The water rippled beside him with a sleepy sound. The sunlight on the hill without made him blink. The long-drawn cawing of a crow on the opposite hillside and the buzzing of a bluebottle fly who had sought retreat in the cavern had a like effect, and he felt himself falling asleep. How long he slept or if he slept at all he could not remember, for he started suddenly, and listening a moment, sprang to his feet.

The low, heavy blows of a pick came deadened and muffled from the extremity of the cavern.

At first a terrible fear took possession of him; for an instant the white rigid face of Smith, as he had seen it on the day of the inquest, when an irresistible curiosity led him to creep into the room where the dead man was lying—for an instant only, this fearful remembrance seemed to rise before him out of the gloom of the pit. The terror passed away.

Ghosts were historically unknown to Aristides, and even had his imaginative faculty been more prominent, the education of Smith's Pocket was not of a kind to foster such weaknesses. Except a twinge of conscience, a momentary recollection of the evil that comes to bad boys through the severe pages of Sunday-school books— with this exception, Aristides was not long in recovering his self-possession. He did not run away for his curiosity was excited. The same instinct which prompted an examination of bear tracks gave a fascination to the situation and a nervous energy to his frame.

The regular blows of the pick still resounded through the cavern. He crept cautiously to the deepest recesses of the pocket, held his breath and listened. The sound seemed to come from the bowels of the mountain. There was no sign of opening or ingress. An impenetrable veil of quartz was between him and the mysterious laborer. He was creeping back between the displaced rafters when a light glanced suddenly in his face and flashed on the wet roof above him. Looking fearfully down,

Aristides beheld between the interstices of the rafters, which formed a temporary flooring, that there was another opening below, and in that opening a man was working. In the queer fantasy of Aristides's dream, it took the aspect of a second pocket and a duplicate Smith!

He had no time to utter his astonishment, for at that moment an ominous rattling of loose soil upon his back made him look up, and he had barely time to spring away before a greater portion of the roof of Smith's Pocket, loosened by the displacement of its supports in his search, fell heavily to the ground. But in the fall a long-handled shovel which had been hidden somewhere in the crevices of the rock above came rattling down with it, and seizing this as a trophy, Aristides emerged from Smith's Pocket at a rate of speed which seemed singularly disproportionate with his short legs and round stomach.

When he reached the road the sun was setting. Inspecting his prize by that poetic light, he found that the shovel was a new one, and bore neither mark of use nor exposure. Shouldering it again, with the intention of presenting it as a peace offering to propitiate the just wrath of his parents, Aristides had gone but a few rods when an unexpected circumstance occurred which dashed his fond hope and to the conscientious child seemed the shadow of an inevitable Nemesis. At the curve of the road, as the settlement of Smith's Pocket came into view with its straggling street and its church spire that seemed a tongue of flame in the setting sun, a broad-shouldered figure sprang, apparently from out of the bank, and stood in the path of that *infelix* infant.

"Where are you going with that shovel, you young devil?"

Aristides looked up and saw that his interlocutor was a man of powerful figure whose face, though partially concealed by a red handkerchief, even in that uncertain light was not prepossessing. Children are quick physiognomists and Aristides, feeling the presence of evil, from the depths of his mighty little soul then and there took issue with the giant.

"Where are you going with that shovel; damn you, do you hear?" said he of the red handkerchief impatiently.

"Home," said Aristides stoutly.

"Home, eh!" said the stranger sneeringly. "And where did you steal it, you young thief?"

The Morpher stock not being of a kind to receive opprobrious epithets meekly, Aristides slowly and with an evident effort lifted the shovel in a menacing attitude.

A single step was all that separated six feet of Strength from three feet of Valor. The stranger eyed Aristides with an expression of surly amazement and hesitated. The elephant quailed before the gadfly. As that precocious infant waved the threatening shovel, his youthful lips slowly fashioned this tremendous sentence:

"You let me pass and I won't hit you!"

And here I must pause. I would that for the sake of poetry I could leave my hero, bathed in that heroic light, erect and menacing. But alas, in this practical world of ours the battle is too often to the strong. And I hasten over the humiliating spectacle of Aristides, spanked, cuffed and kicked, and pick him from the ditch into which he was at last ignominiously tossed, a defeated but still struggling warrior and so bring him, as the night closes charitably around him, in contrite tears and muddy garments to his father's door.

When the master stopped at Mrs. Morpher's to inquire after his errant pupil that night, he found Aristides in bed, smelling strongly of soap and water and sinking into a feverish sleep. As he muttered from time to time some incoherent sentence, tossing restlessly in his cot, the master turned to those about him and asked what it was he said.

It was nothing. Aristides had been dreaming and that was his dream.

That was all. Yet a dream that foreshadowed a slow-coming but unerring justice, that should give the little dreamer in after years some credit to the title of Aristides the Just.

Chapter 3

Under
the
Greenwood
∾ **Tree**

I⟨T⟩ was an amiable weakness of Mrs. Morpher to imagine that of all her classical progeny Clytemnestra was particularly the model for M'liss. Following this fallacy she threw Clytie at the head of M'liss when she was bad, and set her up before the child for adoration in her penitential moments. It was not therefore surprising to the master to hear that Clytie was coming to school, obviously as a favor to the master and as an example for M'liss and others. For Clytie was quite a young lady. Inheriting her mother's physical peculiarities, and in obedience to the climatic laws of the Red Mountain region, she was an early bloomer. The youth of Smith's Pocket to whom this kind of flower was rare sighed for her in April and languished in May. Enamored swains haunted the schoolhouse at the hour of dismissal. A few were jealous of the master.

Perhaps it was this latter circumstance that opened

413

the master's eyes to another. He could not help noticing that Clytie was romantic, that in school she required a great deal of attention, that her pens were uniformly bad and wanted fixing, that she usually accompanied the request with a certain expectation in her eye that was somewhat disproportionate to the quality of service she verbally required, that she sometimes allowed the curves of a round plump white arm to rest on his when he was writing her copies, that she always blushed and flung back her blonde curls when she did so.

I don't remember whether I have stated that the master was a young man—it's of little consequence, however. He had been severely educated in the school in which Clytie was taking her first lesson, and on the whole withstood the flexible curves and facetious glance like the fine young Spartan that he was. Perhaps an insufficient quality of food may have tended to this asceticism. He generally avoided Clytie. But one evening when she returned to the schoolhouse after something she had forgotten—and did not find it until the master walked home with her—I hear that he endeavored to make himself particularly agreeable, partly from the fact, I imagine, that his conduct was adding gall and bitterness to the already overcharged hearts of Clytemnestra's admirers.

The morning after this affecting episode M'liss did not come to school. Noon came but not M'liss. Questioning Clytie on the subject, it appeared that they had

left for school together but the willful M'liss had taken
another road. The afternoon brought her not. In the
evening he called on Mrs. Morpher, whose motherly
heart was really alarmed. Mr. Morpher had spent all
day in search of her without discovering a trace that
might lead to her discovery. Aristides was summoned
as a probable accomplice, but that equitable infant suc-
ceeding in impressing the household with his innocence,
Mrs. Morpher entertained a vivid impression that the
child would yet be found drowned in a ditch, or—what
was almost as terrible—mud-dyed and soiled beyond
the redemption of soap and water. Sick at heart, the
master returned to the schoolhouse. As he lit his lamp
and seated himself at his desk, he found a note lying
before him addressed to himself in M'liss's handwriting.
It seemed to be written on a leaf torn from some old
memorandum book, and to prevent sacrilegious trifling
had been sealed with six broken wafers. Opening it almost tenderly, the master read as follows:

RESPECTED SIR: When you read this, I am run away.
Never to come back. *Never* NEVER NEVER. You can
give my beeds to Mary Jennings and my Amerika's Pride
[a highly colored lithograph from a tobacco box] to
Sally Flanders. But don't you give anything to Clytie
Morper. Don't you dair to. Do you know what my
opinnion is of her, it is this, she is perfekly disgustin.
That is all and no more at present from

MELISSA SMITH

The master mused for some time over this characteristic epistle. As he was mechanically refolding it his eye
caught a sentence written on the back in pencil, in another handwriting, somewhat blurred and indistinct
from the heavy incisive strokes of M'liss's pen on the
other side. It seemed to be a memorandum belonging to
the book from which the leaf was originally torn:

July 17th. 5 hours in drift—dipping west—took out 20
oz.; cleaned up 40 oz. Mem.—saw M. S.

"July 17th," said the master, opening his desk and taking out a file of the *Red Mountain Banner*. "July 17th,"
he repeated, running over the pages till he came to a
paragraph headed "DISTRESSING SUICIDE." "July 17th—
why, that's the day Smith killed himself. That's funny!"

In a strict etymological sense there was nothing so
very ludicrous in this coincidence, nor did the master's
face betray any expression of the kind. Perhaps the
epithet was chosen to conceal the vague uneasiness
which it produced in his mind. We are all of us more
affected by these coincidences than we care to confess
to one another. If the most matter-of-fact reader of these
pages were to find a hearse standing in front of his door
for three consecutive mornings, although the circumstance might be satisfactorily explained—shall I go further and say, *because* the circumstance might be satisfactorily explained—he would vaguely wish it hadn't
happened. Philosophize as we may, the simple fact of

two remote lines crossing each other always seems to us of tremendous significance and quite overshadows the more important truth that the real parallels of life's journey are the lines that never meet. It will do us good to remember these things and look more kindly on our brothers of Borrioboola-Gha and their fetish superstitions when we drop our silver in the missionary box next Sabbath.

"I wonder where that memorandum came from," said the master, as he rose at last and buttoned up his coat. "Who is M. S.? M. S. stands for manuscript and Melissa Smith. Why don't—" But checking an impulsive query as to why people don't make their private memoranda generally intelligible, the master put the letter in his pocket and went home.

At sunrise the next morning he was picking his way through the palmlike fern and thick underbrush of the pine forest, starting the hare from its form and awakening a querulous protest from a few dissipated crows, who had evidently been making a night of it, and so came to the wooded ridge where he had once found M'liss. There he found the prostrate pine and tessellated branches but the throne was vacant. As he drew nearer what might have been some frightened animal started through the crackling limbs. It ran up the tossed arms of the fallen monarch and sheltered itself in some friendly foliage. The master, reaching the old seat, found the nest still warm. Looking up in the intertwining branches, he met the black eyes of the errant M'liss.

They gazed at each other without speaking. She was first to break the silence.

"What do you want?" she asked curtly.

The master had decided on a course of action. "I want some crab apples," he said humbly.

"Shan't have 'em! Go away! Why don't you get 'em of Clytemnerestera?" It seemed to be a relief to M'liss to express her contempt in additional syllables to that classical young woman's already long-drawn title. "Oh, you wicked thing!"

"I am hungry, Lissy. I have eaten nothing since dinner yesterday. I am famished!" and the young man, in a state of remarkable exhaustion, leaned against the tree.

Melissa's heart was touched. In the bitter days of her gypsy life she had known the sensation he so artfully simulated. Overcome by his heartbroken tone but not entirely divested of suspicion, she said:

"Dig under the tree near the roots and you'll find lots; but mind you don't tell," for M'liss had *her* hoards as well as the rats and squirrels.

But the master of course was unable to find them, the effects of hunger probably blinding his senses. M'liss grew uneasy. At length she peered at him through the leaves in an elfish way and questioned:

"If I come down and give you some, you'll promise you won't touch me?"

The master promised.

"Hope you'll die if you do?"

The master accepted instant dissolution as a forfeit. M'liss slid down the tree. The duties of hospitality fulfilled, she seated herself at a little distance and eyed the master with extreme caution.

"Why didn't you eat your breakfast, you bad man?"

"Because I've run away."

"Where to?" said M'liss, her eyes twinkling.

"Anywhere—anywhere away from here!" responded that deceitful wretch with tragic wildness of demeanor.

"What made you?—bad boy!" said M'liss, with a sudden respect of conventionalities and a rare touch of tenderness in her tones. "You'd better go back where your vittals are."

"What are victuals to a wounded spirit?" asked the young man dramatically. He had reached the side of M'liss during this dialogue and had taken her unresisting hand. He was too wise to notice his victory, however, and drawing Melissa's note from his pocket, he opened it before her.

"Couldn't you find any paper in the schoolhouse without tearing a leaf out of my memorandum book, Melissa?" he asked.

"It ain't out of your memorandum book," responded M'liss fiercely.

"Indeed," said the master, turning to the lines in pencil. "I thought it was my handwriting."

M'liss, who had been looking over his shoulder, suddenly seized the paper and snatched it out of his hand.

"It's father's writing!" she said after a pause, in a softer tone.

"Where did you get it, M'liss?"

"Aristides gave it to me."

"Where did he get it?"

"Don't know. He had the book in his pocket when I told him I was going to write to you, and he tore the leaf out. There now—don't bother me any more." M'liss had turned her face away and the black hair had hid her downcast eyes.

Something in her gesture and expression reminded him of her father. Something, and more that was characteristic to her at such moments, made him fancy another resemblance and caused him to ask impulsively and less cautiously than was his wont:

"Do you remember your mother, M'liss?"

"No."

"Did you never see her?"

"No—didn't I tell you not to bother, and you're a-goin' and doin' it," said M'liss savagely.

The master was silent a moment. "Did you ever think you would like to have a mother, M'liss?" he asked again.

"No-o-o-o!"

The master rose. M'liss looked up.

"Does Aristides come to school today?"

"I don't know."

"Are you going back? You'd better," she said.

"Well!—perhaps I may. Good-by!"

He had proceeded a few steps when, as he expected, she called him back. He turned. She was standing by the tree with tears glistening in her eyes. The master felt the right moment had come. Going up to her, he took both her hands in his and looking in her tearful eyes said gravely:

"M'liss, do you remember the first evening you came to see me?"

M'liss remembered.

"You asked me if you might come to school and I said—"

"Come!" responded the child softly.

"If I told you I was lonely without my little scholar and that I wanted her to come, what would you say?"

The child hung her head in silence. The master waited patiently. Tempted by the quiet, a hare ran close to the couple, and raising her bright eyes and velvet forepaws gazed at them fearlessly. A squirrel ran halfway down the furrowed bark of the fallen tree and there stopped.

"*We* are waiting, Lissy," said the master in a whisper and the child smiled. Stirred by a passing breeze, the treetops rocked. A slanting sunbeam stole through their interlaced boughs and fell on the doubting face and irresolute little figure. But a step in the dry branches and a rustling in the underbrush broke the spell.

A man dressed as a miner, carrying a long-handled shovel, came slowly through the woods. A red handkerchief tied around his head under his hat, with the loose ends hanging from beneath, did not add much favor to his unprepossessing face. He did not perceive the master and M'liss until he was close upon them. When he did, he stopped suddenly and gazed at them with an expression of lowering distrust. M'liss drew nearer to the master.

"Good mornin'—picnickin', eh?" he asked, with an attempt at geniality that was more repulsive than his natural manner.

"How are you—prospecting, eh?" said the master quietly, after the established colloquial formula of Red Mountain.

"Yes—a little in that way."

The stranger still hesitated, apparently waiting for them to go first, a matter which M'liss decided by suddenly taking the master's hand in her quick way. What she said was scarcely audible but the master, parting her hair over her forehead, kissed her, and so, hand in hand, they passed out of the damp aisles and forest odors into the open sunlit road. But M'liss, looking back, saw that her old seat was occupied by the hopeful prospector, and fancied that in the shadows of her former throne something of a gratified leer overspread his face. "He'll have to dig deep to find the crab apples," said the child to the master as they came to the Red Mountain road.

When Aristides came to school that day he was confronted by M'liss. But neither threats nor entreaties could extract from that reticent youth the whereabouts of the memorandum book nor where he got it. Two or three days afterward during recess he approached M'liss and beckoned her one side.

"Well," said M'liss impatiently.

"Did you ever read the story of 'Ali Baba'?"

"Yes."

"Do you believe it?"

"No."

"Well," said that sage infant, wheeling around on his stout legs, *"it's true!"*

Chapter 4

Which
Has a
Good
Moral
⁊ Tendency

SOMEWHAT less spiteful in her intercourse with
the other scholars, M'liss still retained an offensive attitude toward Clytemnestra. Perhaps the jealous element was not entirely stilled in her passionate little
breast. Perhaps it was that Clytemnestra's round curves
and plump outlines afforded an extensive pinching surface. But while these ebullitions were under the master's control, her enmity occasionally took a new and
irresponsible form.

In his first estimate of the child's character he could
not conceive that she had ever possessed a doll. But the
master, like many other professed readers of character,
was safer in *a posteriori* than *a priori* reasoning, for
M'liss had a doll. But then it was a peculiar doll, a
frightful perversion of wax and sawdust, a doll fearfully
and wonderfully made—a smaller edition of M'liss. Its

424

unhappy existence had been a secret discovered accidentally by Mrs. Morpher. It had been the old-time companion of M'liss's wanderings, and bore evident marks of suffering. It's original complexion was long since washed away by the weather and anointed by the slime of ditches. It looked very much as M'liss had in days past. Its one gown of faded stuff was dirty and ragged as hers had been. M'liss had never been known to apply to it any childish term of endearment. She never exhibited it in the presence of other children. It was put severely to bed in a hollow tree near the schoolhouse, and only allowed exercise during M'liss's rambles. Fulfilling a stern duty to her doll—as she would to herself—it knew no luxuries.

Now Mrs. Morpher, obeying a commendable impulse, bought another doll and gave it to M'liss. The child received it gravely and curiously. The master on looking at it one day fancied he saw a slight resemblance in its round red cheeks and mild blue eyes to Clytemnestra. It became evident before long that M'liss had also noticed the same resemblance. Accordingly she hammered its waxen head on the rocks when she was alone and sometimes dragged it with a string round its neck to and from school. At other times setting it up on her desk, she made a pincushion of its patient and inoffensive body. Whether this was done in revenge of what she considered a second figurative obtrusion of Clytie's excellencies upon her; or whether she had an intuitive appreciation of the rites of certain other heathens and indulging in that fetish ceremony imagined that the original of her wax model would pine away and finally die, is a metaphysical question I shall not now consider.

In spite of these moral vagaries the master could not help noticing in her different tasks the workings of a quick, restless and vigorous perception. She knew neither the hesitancy nor the doubts of childhood. Her answers in class were always slightly dashed with audacity. Of course she was not infallible. But her courage and daring in venturing beyond her own depth and that of the floundering little swimmers around her, in their minds outweighed all errors of judgment. Children are no better than grown people in this respect, I fancy. Whenever the little red hand flashed above her desk there was a wondering silence, and even the master was sometimes oppressed with a doubt of his own experience and judgment.

Nevertheless certain attributes which at first amused and entertained his fancy began to affect him with grave doubts. He could not but see that M'liss was revengeful, irreverent and willful. But there was one better quality which pertained to her semi-savage disposition—the faculty of physical fortitude and self-sacrifice; and another, though not always an attribute of the noble savage, truth. M'liss was both fearless and sincere—perhaps in such a character the adjectives were synonymous.

The master had been doing some hard thinking on this subject and had arrived at that conclusion quite common to all who think sincerely, that he was generally the slave of his own prejudices, and determined to call on the Reverend Mr. McSnagley for advice. This decision was somewhat humiliating to his pride, as he and McSnagley were not friends. But he thought of M'liss and the evening of their first meeting; and perhaps with a pardonable superstition that it was not chance alone that had guided her willful feet to the schoolhouse, and perhaps with a complacent consciousness of the rare magnanimity of the act, he choked back his dislike and went to McSnagley.

The reverend gentleman was glad to see him. Moreover, he observed that the master was looking "peartish" and hoped he had got over the "neuralgy" and "rheumatiz." He himself had been troubled with a dumb "ager" since last conference. But he had learned to "rastle and pray."

Pausing a moment to enable the master to write this certain method of curing the dumb ager upon the book and volume of his brain, Mr. McSnagley proceeded to inquire after Sister Morpher. "She is an adornment to Christe*w*anity, and has a likely, growin' young family," added Mr. McSnagley. "And there's that mannerly young gal—so well behaved—Miss Clytie." In fact, Clytie's perfections seemed to affect him to such an extent that he dwelt for several minutes upon them. The master was doubly embarrassed. In the first place, there was an enforced contrast with poor M'liss in all this praise of Clytie. Secondly, there was something unpleasantly confidential in his tone of speaking of Morpher's earliest born. So that the master, after a few futile efforts to say something natural, found it convenient to recall another engagement and left without asking the information required, but in his after reflections somewhat unjustly giving the Reverend Mr. McSnagley the full benefit of having refused it.

But the master obtained the advice in another and unexpected direction.

The resident physician of Smith's Pocket was a Dr. Duchesne, or as he was better known to the locality, "Dr. Doochesny." Of a naturally refined nature and liberal education, he had steadily resisted the aggressions and temptations of Smith's Pocket and represented to the master a kind of connecting link between his present life and the past. So that an intimacy sprang up between the two men, involving prolonged interviews in the doctor's little back shop, often to the exclusion of other suffering humanity and their physical ailments. It was in one of these interviews that the master mentioned the coincidence of the date of the memoranda on the back of M'liss's letter and the day of Smith's suicide.

"If it were Smith's own handwriting, as the child says it is," said the master, "it shows a queer state of mind that could contemplate suicide and indite private memoranda within the same twenty-four hours."

Dr. Duchesne removed his cigar from his lips and looked attentively at his friend.

"The only hypothesis," continued the master, "is that

Smith was either drunk or crazy and the fatal act was in a measure unpremeditated."

"Every man who commits suicide," returned the doctor gravely, "is in my opinion insane, or what is nearly the same thing, becomes through suffering an irresponsible agent. In my professional experience I have seen most of the forms of mental and physical agony and know what sacrifices men make to preserve even an existence that to me would seem little better than death, as long as their intellect remained unclouded. When you come to reflect on the state of mind that chooses death as a preferable alternative you generally find an exaltation and enthusiasm that differ very little from the ordinary diagnosis of delirium. Smith was not drunk," added the doctor in his usual careless tone, "I saw his body."

The master remained buried in reflection. Presently the doctor removed his cigar.

"Perhaps I might help you to explain the coincidence you speak of."

"How?"

"Very easily. But this is a professional secret, you understand."

"Yes, I understand," said the master hastily, with an ill-defined uneasiness creeping over him.

"Do you know anything of the phenomena of death by gunshot wounds?"

"No!"

"Then you must take certain facts as granted. Smith, you remember, was killed *instantly!* The nature of his wound and the manner of his death were such as would have caused an instantaneous and complete relaxation of *all* the muscles. Rigidity and contraction would have supervened of course, but only after life was extinct and consciousness fled. Now Smith was found with his hand tightly grasping a pistol."

"Well?"

"Well, my dear boy, he must have grasped it after he was dead, or have prevailed on some friend to stiffen his fingers round it."

"Do you mean that he was murdered?"

Dr. Duchesne rose and closed the door. "We have different names for these things in Smith's Pocket. I mean to say that he didn't kill himself—that's all."

"But, doctor," said the master earnestly, "do you think you have done right in concealing this fact? Do you think it just—do you think it consistent with your duty to his orphan child?"

"That's why I have said nothing about it," replied the doctor coolly, "because of my consideration for his orphan child."

The master breathed quickly and stared at the doctor.

"Doctor! you don't think that M'liss—"

"Hush! Don't get excited, my young friend. Remember I am not a lawyer—only a doctor."

"But M'liss was with me the very night he must have been killed. We were walking together when we heard the report—that is—a report—which must have been the one—" stammered the master.

"When was that?"

"At half past eleven. I remember looking at my watch."

"Humph! When did you meet her first?"

"At half past eight. Come, doctor, you have made a mistake here at least," said the young man with an assumption of ease he was far from feeling. "Give M'liss the benefit of the doubt."

Dr. Duchesne replied by opening a drawer of his desk. After rummaging among the powders and mysterious looking instruments with which it was stored, he finally brought forth a longitudinal slip of folded white paper. It was appropriately labeled *"Poison."*

"Look here," said the doctor, opening the paper. It contained two or three black coarse hairs. "Do you know them?"

"No."

"Look again!"

"It looks something like Melissa's hair," said the master, with a fathomless sinking of the heart.

"When I was called to look at the body," continued the doctor with the deliberate cautiousness of a professional diagnosis, "my suspicions were aroused by the circumstance I told you of. I managed to get possession of the pistol and found these hairs twisted around the lock as though they had been accidentally caught and violently disentangled. I don't think that anyone else

saw them. I removed them without observation, and—
they are at your service."

The master sank back in his seat and pressed his hand
to his forehead. The image of M'liss rose before him
with flashing eye and long black hair and seemed to
beat down and resist defiantly the suspicion that crept
slowly over his heart.

"I forbore to tell you this, my friend," continued the
doctor slowly and gravely, "because when I learned that
you had taken this strange child under your protection
I did not wish to tell you that which—though I contend it does not alter her claims to man's sympathy and
kindness—still might have prejudiced her in your eyes.
Her improvement under your care has proven my position correct. I have, as you know, peculiar ideas of the
extent to which humanity is responsible. I find in my
heart, looking back over that child's career, no sentiment but pity. I am mistaken in you if this circumstance
aroused any other feeling in yours."

Still the figure of M'liss stood before the master as he
bent before the doctor's words, in the same defiant attitude, with something of scorn in the great dark eyes
that made the blood tingle in his cheeks and seemed to
make the reasoning of the speaker but meaningless and
empty words. At length he rose. As he stood with his
hand on the latch he turned to Dr. Duchesne who was
watching him with careful solicitude.

"I don't know but that you have done well to keep

this from me. At all events it has not—cannot, and should not alter my opinion toward M'liss. You will of course keep it a secret. In the meantime you must not blame me if I cling to my instincts in preference to your judgment. I still believe that you are mistaken in regard to her."

"Stay, one moment," said the doctor. "Promise me you will not say anything of this or attempt to prosecute the matter further till you have consulted with me."

"I promise. Good night."

"Good night," and so they parted.

True to that promise and his own instinctive promptings the master endeavored to atone for his momentary disloyalty by greater solicitude for M'liss. But the child had noticed some change in the master's thoughtful manner, and in one of their long post-prandial walks she stopped suddenly, and mounting a stump, looked full in his face with big searching eyes.

"You ain't mad?" said she with an interrogative shake of the black braids.

"No."

"Nor bothered?"

"No."

"Nor hungry?" (Hunger was to M'liss a sickness that might attack a person at any moment.)

"No."

"Nor thinking of her?"

"Of whom, Lissy?"

"That white girl." (This was the latest epithet invented by M'liss, who was a very dark brunette, to express Clytemnestra.)

"No."

"Upon your word?" (A substitute for "Hope you'll die!" proposed by the master.)

"Yes."

"And sacred honor?"

"Yes."

Then M'liss gave him a fierce little kiss, and hopping down, fluttered off. For two or three days after that she condescended to appear like other children and be, as she expressed it, "good."

When the summer was about spent, and the last harvest had been gathered in the valleys, the master bethought him of gathering in a few ripened shoots of the young idea, and of having his Harvest Home, or Examination. So the savants and professionals of Smith's Pocket were gathered to witness that time-honored custom of placing timid children in a constrained position and bullying them as in a witness box. As usual in such cases, the most audacious and self-possessed were the lucky recipients of the honors. The reader will imagine that in the present instance M'liss and Clytie were preeminent and divided public attention: M'liss with her clearness of material perception and self-reliance, and Clytie with her placid self-esteem and saintlike correctness of deportment. The other little ones were timid and blundering. M'liss's readiness and brilliancy, of course, captivated the greatest number and provoked the greatest applause and M'liss's antecedents had unconsciously awakened the strongest sympathies of the miners, whose athletic forms were ranged against the walls, or whose handsome bearded faces looked in at the window. But M'liss's popularity was overthrown by an unexpected circumstance.

McSnagley had invited himself and had been going through the pleasing entertainment of frightening the more timid pupils by the vaguest and most ambiguous questions, delivered in an impressive, funereal tone. M'liss had soared into astronomy and was tracking the course of our "spotted ball" through space, and defining the "tethered orbits" of the planets, when McSnagley deliberately arose.

"Meelissy, ye were speaking of the revolutions of this yer yearth and its movements with regard to the sun, and I think you said it had been a-doin' of it since the creation, eh?"

M'liss nodded a scornful affirmative.

"Well, was that the truth?" said McSnagley, folding his arms.

"Yes," said M'liss shutting up her little red lips tightly.

The handsome outlines at the windows peered further into the schoolroom and a saintly, Raphael-like face with blond beard and soft blue eyes, belonging to the biggest scamp in the diggings, turned toward the child and whispered:

"Stick to it, M'liss! It's only a big bluff of the parson."

The reverend gentleman heaved a deep sigh and cast a compassionate glance at the master, then at the children, and then rested his eye on Clytemnestra. That young woman softly elevated her round, white arm. Its seductive curves were enhanced by a gorgeous and massive specimen bracelet, the gift of one of her humblest worshipers, worn in honor of the occasion. There was a momentary pause. Clytie's round cheeks were very pink and soft. Clytie's big eyes were very bright and blue. Clytie's low-necked white muslin rested softly on Clytie's white, plump shoulders. Clytie looked at the master and the master nodded. Then Clytie spoke softly:

"Joshua commanded the sun to stand still and it obeyed him."

There was a low hum of applause in the schoolroom, a triumphant expression on McSnagley's face, a grave shadow on the master's, and a comical look of disappointment reflected from the windows. M'liss skimmed rapidly over her astronomy and then shut the book with a loud snap. A groan burst from McSnagley, an expression of astonishment from the schoolroom, and a yell from the windows, as M'liss brought her red fist down on the desk, with the emphatic declaration:

"It's a damn lie. I don't believe it!"

Chapter 5

"Open
☙ Sesame"

THE long wet season had drawn near its close. Signs of spring were visible in the swelling buds and rushing torrents. The pine forests exhaled a fresher spicery. The azaleas were already budding, the ceano-thus getting ready its lilac livery for spring. On the green upland which climbed the Red Mountain at its southern aspect, the long spike of the monkshood shot up from its broad-leaved base and once more shook its dark blue bells. Again the billow above Smith's grave was soft and green, its crest just tossed with the foam of daisies and buttercups. The little graveyard had gathered a few new dwellers in the past year. The mounds were placed two by two by the little paling until they reached Smith's grave and there, there was but one. General superstition had shunned the enforced companionship. The plot beside Smith was vacant.

It was the custom of the driver of the great Wingdam stage to whip up his horses at the foot of the hill and so enter Smith's Pocket at that remarkable pace which the woodcuts in the hotel barroom represented to credulous humanity as the usual rate of speed of that conveyance. At least Aristides Morpher thought so as he stood one Sunday afternoon, uneasily conscious of his best jacket and collar, waiting its approach. Nor could anything shake his belief that regularly on that occasion the horses ran away with the driver, and that that individual from motives of deep policy pretended not to notice it until they were stopped.

"Anybody up from below, Bill?" said the landlord as the driver slowly descended from his perch.

"Nobody for you," responded Bill shortly. "Dusenberry kem up as usual and got off at the old place. You can't make a livin' off him, I reckon."

"Have you found out what his name is yet?" continued the landlord, implying that "Dusenberry" was simply a playful epithet of the driver.

"He says his name is Waters," returned Bill. "Jake said he saw him at the North Fork in '50—called himself Moore then. Guess he ain't no good, nohow. What's he doin' round here?"

"Says he's prospectin'," replied the landlord. "He has a claim somewhere in the woods. Gambles a little too, I reckon. He don't travel on his beauty anyhow."

"If you had seen him makin' up to a piece of calico inside, last trip, and she a-makin' up to him quite confidential-like, I guess you'd think he was a lady killer. My eye but wasn't she a stunner! Clytie Morpher wasn't nowhere to begin with her."

"Who was she, Bill?" asked half a dozen masculine voices.

"Don't know. We picked her up this side of Coyote. Fancy? I tell you! Pretty little hat and pink ribbings, eyes that ud bore you through at a hundred yards, white teeth, brown gaiters, and such an ankle! She didn't want to show it—oh, no!" added the sarcastic Bill with deep significance.

"Where did you leave her, Bill?" asked a gentle village swain who had been fired by the glowing picture of the fair unknown.

"That's what's the matter. You see after we picked her up, she said she was goin' through to Wingdam. Of course there wasn't anything in the stage or on the road too good to offer her. Old Major Spaffler wanted to treat her to lemonade at every station. Judge Plunkett kep' a-pullin' down the blinds and a-h'istin' of them up to keep out the sun and let in the air. Blest if old Mc-Snagley didn't want to carry her travelin' bag. There wasn't any attention, boys, she didn't get—but it wasn't no use—bless you! She never so much as passed the time of day with them."

"But where did she go?" inquired another anxious auditor.

"Keep your foot off the drag and I'll tell you. Arter we left Ring Tail Canyon, Dusenberry, as usual, got on.

Presently one of the outsides turned round to me and says he, 'Durned if Ugly Mug ain't got the inside track of all of you this time!' I looked down and durn my skin if there wasn't Dusenberry a-sittin' up alongside of the lady quite comfortable as if they had ben children together. At the next station Dusenberry gets off. So does the lady. 'Ain't you goin' on to Wingdam,' says I. 'No,' says she. 'Mayn't we have the pleasure of your kempany further?' says the judge, taking off his hat. 'No, I've changed my mind,' says she and off she walked arm in arm with him as cool as you please."

"Wonder if that wa'n't the party that passed through here last July?" asked the blacksmith, joining the loungers in front of the stage office. "Waters brought up a buggy to get the axle bolted. There was a woman setting in the buggy but the hood was drawn down and I didn't get to see her face."

During this conversation Aristides, after a long, lingering glance at the stage, had at last torn himself away from its fascinations. He was now lounging down the long straggling street in a peculiarly dissipated manner with his hat pushed on the back part of his head, his right hand and a greater portion of his right arm buried in his trousers pocket. This might have been partly owing to the shortness of his legs and the comparative amplitude of his trousers, which to the casual observer seemed to obviate the necessity of any other garment. But when he reached the bottom of the street and further enlivened his progress by whistling shrilly between his fingers, and finally drew a fragment of a cigar from his pocket and placed it between his teeth, it was evident that there was a moral as well as physical laxity in his conduct. The near fact was that Aristides had that afternoon evaded the Sunday school and was open to any kind of infant iniquity.

The main street of Smith's Pocket gradually lost its civilized character, and after one or two futile attempts at improvement at its lower extremity terminated impotently in a chaos of ditches, races and trailings. Out of this again a narrow trail started along the mountainside and communicated with that vast amphitheater which still exhibited the pioneer efforts of the early settlers. It was this trail that Aristides took that Sunday afternoon and which he followed until he reached the hillside a few rods below the yawning fissure of Smith's Pocket. After a careful examination of the vicinity, he cleared away the underbrush beside a fallen pine that lay near and sat down in the attitude of patient and deliberate expectancy.

Five minutes passed—ten, twenty, and finally a half hour was gone. Aristides threw away his cigar which he had lacked determination to light, and peeled small slips from the inner bark of the pine tree and munched them gravely. Another five, ten and twenty minutes passed. The sun began to drop below the opposite hillside. Another ten minutes and the whole of the amphitheater above was in heavy shadow. Ten minutes more and the distant windows in the settlement flamed redly. Five minutes and the spire of the Methodist church caught the glow—and then the underbrush crackled.

Aristides, looking up, saw the trunk of the prostrate pine slowly lifting itself before him.

A second glance showed the fearless and self-possessed boy that the apparent phenomenon was simply and easily explained. The tree had fallen midway and at right angles across the trunk of another prostrate monarch. So accurately and evenly was it balanced that the child was satisfied, from a liberal experience of the application of these principles to the game of seesaw, that a very slight impulse to either end was sufficient to destroy the equilibrium. That impulse proceeded from his end of the tree, as he saw when the uplifted trunk disclosed an opening in the ground beneath it and the head and shoulders of a man emerging therefrom.

Aristides threw himself noiselessly on his stomach. The thick clump of an azalea hid him from view though it did not obstruct his survey of the stranger, whom he at once recognized as his former enemy—the man with the red handkerchief—the hopeful prospector of Red Mountain and the hypothetical "Dusenberry" of the stage driver.

The stranger looked cautiously around and Aristides shrank close behind the friendly azalea.

Satisfied that he was unobserved, the subterranean proprietor returned to the opening and descended, reappearing with a worn black-enameled traveling bag which he carried with difficulty. This he again enveloped in a blanket and strapped tightly on his back. A long-handled shovel brought up from the same mysterious storehouse completed his outfit. As he stood for a moment leaning on the shovel, it was the figure of the hopeful prospector in the heart of the forest. A very slight effort was sufficient to replace the fallen tree in its former position. Raising the shovel to his shoulder he moved away, brushing against the azalea bush which hid the breathless Aristides. The sound of his footsteps retreating through the crackling brush presently died out and a drowsy Sabbath stillness succeeded.

Aristides rose. There was a wonderful brightness in his gray eyes and a flush on his sunburned cheek. Seizing a root of the fallen pine he essayed to move it. But it defied his endeavors. Aristides looked around.

"There's some trick about it but I'll find it yet," said that astute child.

Breaking off the limb of a buckeye, he extemporized a lever. The first attempt failed. The second succeeded and the long roots of the tree again ascended. But as it required prolonged effort to keep the tree up, before the impetus was lost Aristides seized the opportunity to jump into the opening. At the same moment the tree slowly returned to its former position.

In the sudden change from the waning light to complete darkness, Aristides was for a moment confounded. Recovering himself he drew a match from his capacious pocket, and striking it against the sole of his shoe, by the upspringing flash perceived a candle stuck in the crevices of the rock beside him. Lighting it, he glanced curiously around him. He was at the entrance of a long gallery at the further extremity of which he could faintly see the glimmering of the outer daylight. Following this gallery cautiously he presently came to an antechamber, and by the glimmering of the light above him at once saw that it was the same he had seen in his wonderful dream.

The antechamber was about fourteen feet square with walls of decomposed quartz mingling with flaky mica that reflected here and there the gleam of Aristides' candle with a singular brilliancy. It did not need much observation on his part to determine the reason for the stranger's lonely labors. On a rough rocker beside him were two fragments of ore taken from the adjacent wall, the smallest of which the two arms of Aristides could barely clasp. To his dazzled eyes they seemed to be almost entirely of pure gold. The great strike of '56 at Ring Tail Canyon had brought to the wonderful vision of Smith's Pocket no such nuggets as were here.

Aristides turned again to the wall, which had been apparently the last scene of the stranger's labors and from which the two masses of ore were taken. Even to his inexperienced eye it represented a wealth almost incalculable. Everywhere through the loose red soil glittering star points of the precious metal threw back the rays of his candle. Aristides turned pale and trembled.

Here was the realization of his most extravagant

fancy. Ever since his strange dream and encounter with the stranger he had felt an irresistible desire to follow up his adventure and discover the secrets of the second cavern. But when he had returned to Smith's Pocket a few days after, the wreck of the fallen roof had blocked up that part of the opening from which he had caught sight of the hidden workman below. During his visit he had picked up from among the rubbish the memorandum book which had supplied M'liss with letter paper. Still haunting the locality after school hours, he had noticed that regularly at sunset the man with the red handkerchief appeared in some mysterious way from the hillside below Smith's Pocket and went away in the direction of the settlement. By careful watching, Aristides had fixed the location of his mysterious appearance to a point a few rods below the opening of Smith's Pocket. Flushed by this discovery, he had been betrayed from his usual discretion so far as to intimate a hinting of the suspicion that possessed him in the few mysterious words he had whispered to M'liss at school. The accident we have described above determined the complete discovery of the secret.

Who was the stranger and why did he keep the fact of this immense wealth hidden from the world? Suppose he, Aristides, were to tell? Wouldn't the schoolboys look up at him with interest as the hero and discoverer of this wonderful cavern and wouldn't the stage driver feel proud of his acquaintance and offer him rides for nothing? Why hadn't Smith discovered it—who was poor and wanted money, whom Aristides had liked, who was the father of M'liss for whom Aristides confessed a secret passion, who belonged to the settlement and helped to build it up—instead of the stranger? Had Smith never a suspicion that gold was so near him, and if so, why had he killed himself? But did Smith kill himself? And at this thought and its correlative fancy again the cheek of Aristides blanched, and the candle shook in his nerveless fingers.

Apart and distinct from these passing conjectures one idea remained firm and dominant in his mind: the man with the red handkerchief had no right to this treasure! The mysterious instinct which directed this judicial ruling of Aristides had settled this fact as indubitably as though proven by the weight of the strongest testimony. For an instant a wild thought sprang up in his heart and he seized the nearest mass of ore with the half-formed intention of bearing it directly to the feet of M'liss as her just and due inheritance. But Aristides could not lift it and the idea passed out of his mind with the frustrated action.

At the farther end of the gallery a few blankets were lying. With some mining implements, a kettle of water and a few worn flannel shirts they were the only articles this subterranean habitation possessed. In turning over one of the blankets Aristides picked up a woman's comb. It was tortoise shell, and bright with some fanciful ornamentation. Without a moment's hesitation Aristides pocketed it as the natural property of M'liss. A pocketbook containing a few old letters found in the breast pocket of one of the blue shirts was transferred to that of Aristides with the same coolness and sentiment of instinctive justice.

Aristides wisely reflected that these unimportant articles would excite no suspicion if found in his possession. A fragment of the rock, if he had taken it when he felt impelled to, would have precipitated the discovery that Aristides had decided to put off until he had perfected a certain plan.

The light from the opening above gradually faded and Aristides knew that night had fallen. To prevent suspicion he must return home. He re-entered the gallery and reached the opening of the egress. One of the roots of the tree projected into the opening.

He seized it and endeavored to lift it, but in vain. Panting with exertion he again and again exerted the fullest power of his active sinews, but the tree remained immovable—the opening remained sealed as firmly as with Solomon's signet. Raising his candle toward it, Aristides saw the reason for its resistance. In his hurried ingress he had allowed the tree to revolve sufficiently to permit one of its roots to project into the opening, and this held it firmly down. In the shock of the discovery the excitement which had sustained him gave way, and with a hopeless cry the just Aristides fell senseless on the floor of the gallery.

Chapter 6

The
Trials of
☙ Mrs. Morpher

"Now, where on earth can that child be?"
said Mrs. Morpher, shading her eyes with her hand
as she stood at the door of the "Mountain Ranch," looking down the Wingdam road at sunset. "With his best
things on, too. Goodness! What *were* boys made for?"

Mr. Morpher, without replying to this question apparently addressed to him as an adult representative of
the wayward species, appeared at the door and endeavored to pour oil on the troubled waters.

"Oh, *he's* all right, Sue! Don't fuss about *him*," said
Mr. Morpher with an imbecile sense of conveying comfort in the emphasized pronoun. "He's down the gulch,
or in the tunnel, or over to the claim. He'll turn up by
bedtime. Don't you worry about *him*. I'll look him up

in a minit," and Mr. Morpher, taking his hat, sauntered down the road in the direction of the National Hotel.

Mrs. Morpher gazed doubtfully after her liege. "Looking up" Aristides, in her domestic experience, implied a prolonged absence in the barroom of the hotel, the tedium whereof was beguiled by seven-up or euchre. But she only said: "Don't be long, James," and sighed hopelessly as she turned back into the house.

Once again with her own castle walls. Mrs. Morpher dropped her look of patient suffering and glanced defiantly around for a fresh grievance.

The decorous little parlor offered nothing to provoke the hostility of her peculiar instincts. Spotless were the white curtains, the bright carpet guiltless of stain or dust. The chairs were placed arithmetically in twos, and added up evenly on the four sides with nothing to carry over. Two bunches of lavender and fennel breathed an odor of sanctified cleanliness through the room. Five daguerreotypes on the mantelpiece represented the Morpher family in progressive stages of petrifaction, and had the Medusalike effect of freezing visitors into similar attitudes in their chairs. The walls were further enlivened with two colored engravings of scenes in the domestic history of George Washington, in which the Father of his Country seemed to look blandly from his own correct family circle into Morpher's and to breathe quite audibly from his gilt frame a dignified blessing.

Lingering a moment in this sacred enclosure to readjust the tablecloth Mrs. Morpher passed into the dining room, where the correct Clytie presided at the supper table at which the rest of the family were seated. Mrs. Morpher's quick eyes caught the spectacle of M'liss with her chin resting on her hands and her elbows on the table, sardonically surveying the model of deportment opposite to her.

"M'liss!"

"Well?"

"Where's your elbows?"

"Here's one and there's the other," said M'liss quietly, indicating their respective localities by smartly tapping them with the palm of her hand.

"Take them off the table instantly, you bold forward girl—and you, sir, quit that giggling and eat your supper, if you don't want to be put to bed without it!" added Mrs. Morpher to Lycurgus, to whom M'liss's answer had afforded boundless satisfaction. "You're getting to be just as bad as her, and mercy knows you never were a seraphim!"

"What's a seraphim, mother, and what do they do?" asked Lycurgus with growing interest.

"They don't ask questions when they should be eating their supper and thankful for it," interposed Clytie authoritatively, as one to whom the genteel attributes and social habits of the seraphim had been a privileged revelation.

"But, mother—"

"Hush, and don't be a heathen. Run and see who is

coming in," said Mrs. Morpher as the sound of footsteps was heard in the passage.

The door opened and McSnagley entered.

"Why, bless my soul! How do you do?" said Mrs. Morpher with genteel astonishment. "Quite a stranger, I declare."

This was a polite fiction. M'liss knew the fact to be that Mrs. Morpher was reputed to set the best table in Smith's Pocket, and McSnagley always called in on Sunday evenings at supper to discuss the current gossip, and nag M'liss with selected texts.

The verbal McSnagley as usual couldn't stop a moment, had just dropped in "in passin'." The actual McSnagley deposited his hat in the corner and placed himself in the flesh on a chair by the table.

"And how's Brother James and the fammerly?"

"They're all well—except Risty; he's off again—as if my life weren't already pestered out with one child." And Mrs. Morpher glanced significantly at M'liss.

"Ah, well, we all of us have our trials," said McSnagley. "I've been ailin' again. That ager must be in my bones still. I've been rather onsettled myself today."

There was the appearance of truth in this statement. Mr. McSnagley's voice had a hollow resonant sound and his eyes were nervous and fidgety. He had an odd trick, too, of occasionally stopping in the middle of a sentence and listening as though he heard some distant sound. These things which Mrs. Morpher recalled afterward did not, in the undercurrent of uneasiness about Aristides which she felt the whole of that evening, so particularly attract her notice.

"I know something," said Lycurgus, during one of these pauses, from the retirement of his corner.

"If you dare to—Kerg!" said M'liss.

"M'liss says she knows where Risty is but she won't tell," said the lawgiver, not heeding the warning. The words were scarcely uttered before M'liss's red hand flashed in the air and descended with a sounding box on the traitor's ear. Lycurgus howled, Mrs. Morpher darted into the corner, and M'liss was dragged defiant and struggling to the light.

"Oh, you wicked, wicked child—why don't you say where if you know?" said Mrs. Morpher, shaking her as if the information were to be dislodged from some concealed part of her clothing.

"I didn't say I knew for sure," at last responded M'liss. "I said I thought I knew."

"Well, where do you think he is?"

But M'liss was firm. Even the gloomy picture of the future state devised by McSnagley could not alter her determination. Mrs. Morpher, who had a wholesome awe for this strange child, at last had recourse to entreaty. Finally M'liss offered a compromise.

"I'll tell the master but I won't tell you—partikerly him," said M'liss, indicating the parson with a bodkin-like dart of her forefinger.

Mrs. Morpher hesitated. Her maternal anxiety at

length overcame her sense of dignity and discipline.

"Who knows where the master is or where he is to be found tonight?" she asked hastily.

"He's over to Dr. Duchesne's," said Clytie eagerly. "That is," she stammered, a rich color suddenly flushing from her temples to her round shoulders, "he's usually there in the evenings, I mean."

"Run over, there's a dear, and ask him to come here," said Mrs. Morpher, without noticing a sudden irregularity of conduct in her firstborn. "Run quick!"

Clytie did not wait for a second command. Without availing herself of the proffered company of McSnagley she hastily tied the strings of her school hat under her plump chin and slipped out of the house. It was not far to the doctor's office and Clytie walked quickly, overlooking in her haste and preoccupation the admiring glances which several of the swains of Smith's Pocket cast after her as she passed. But on arriving at the doctor's door, so out of breath and excited was this usual model of deportment that on finding herself in the presence of the master and his friend, she only stood in embarrassed silence, and made up for her lack of verbal expression by a succession of eloquent blushes.

Let us look at her for a moment as she stands there. Her little straw hat trimmed with cherry-colored ribbons rests on the waves of her blonde hair. There are other gay ribbons on her light summer dress, clasping her round waist, girdling her wrist and fastening her collar about her white throat. Her large blue eyes are very

dark and moist—it may be with excitement or a tearful
thought of the lost Aristides—or the tobacco smoke
with which I regret to say the room is highly charged.
But certainly as she stands leaning against the doorway,
biting her moist scarlet lip and trying to pull down the
broad brim of her hat over the surging waves of color
that *will* beat rhythmically up to her cheeks and
temples, she is so dangerously pretty that I am glad
for the master's sake he is the philosopher he has just
described himself to his friend the doctor, and that he
prefers to study human physiology from the inner sur-
faces.

When Clytie had recovered herself sufficiently to
state her message the master offered to accompany her
back. As Clytie took his arm with some slight trepida-
tion Dr. Duchesne, who had taken sharp notes of these
"febrile" symptoms, uttered a prolonged whistle and
returned thoughtfully to his office.

Although Clytie found the distance returning no
farther than the distance going, with the exhaustion
of her first journey it was natural that her homeward
steps should be slower and that the master should
regulate his pace to accommodate her. It was natural,
too, that her voice should be quite low and indistinct
so that the master was obliged to bring his hat nearer
the cherry-colored ribbons in the course of conversation.
It was also natural that he should offer the sensitive
young girl such comfort as lay in tenderly modulated

tones and playful epithets. And if in the irregularities of
the main street it was necessary to take Clytie's hand
or to put his arm around her waist in helping her up
declivities, the master saw no impropriety in the act as
was evident from the fact that he did not remove his
arm when the difficulty was surmounted. In this way
Clytie's return occupied some moments more than her
going and Mrs. Morpher was waiting anxiously at the
door when the young people arrived.

As the master entered the room M'liss called him to
her. "Bend down your head," she said, "and I'll whisper.
But mind, now, I don't say I know for truth where Risty
is. I only reckon."

The master bent down his head. As usual in such
cases, everybody else felt constrained to listen and
McSnagley's curiosity was awakened to its fullest extent.
When the master had received the required information
he said quietly:

"I think I'll go myself to this place which M'liss wishes
to make a secret of and see if the boy is there. It will
save trouble to anyone else if she should be mistaken."

"Hadn't you better take someone with you?" said
Mrs. Morpher.

"By all means. I'll go!" said Mr. McSnagley, with
feverish alacrity.

The master looked inquiringly at M'liss.

"He can go if he wants to, but he'd better not," said
M'liss looking directly into McSnagley's eyes.

"What do you mean by that, you little savage?" said McSnagley quickly.

M'liss turned scornfully away. "Go," she said, "go if you want to," and resumed her seat in the corner.

The master hesitated, But he could not withstand the appeal in the eyes of the mother and daughter. After a short inward struggle he turned to McSnagley and bade him briefly "Come."

When they had left the house and stood in the road together, McSnagley stopped.

"Where are you goin'?"

"To Smith's Pocket."

McSnagley still lingered. "Do you ever carry any weppings?" he at length asked.

"Weapons? No. What do you want with weapons to go a mile on a starlit road to a deserted claim? Nonsense, man, what are you thinking of? We're hunting a lost child, not a runaway felon. Come along," and the master dragged him away.

Mrs. Morpher watched them from the door until their figures were lost in the darkness. When she returned to the dining room Clytie had already retired to her room, and Mrs. Morpher, overruling M'liss's desire to sit up until the master returned, bade her follow that correct example. "There's Clytie now, gone to bed like a young lady, and do you do like her," said Mrs. Morpher, with this one drop of balm in the midst of her trials, trimmed the light and sat down in patience to wait for Aristides, consoling herself with the reflection of Clytie's excellence. "Poor Clytie!" mused that motherly woman. How excited and worried she looks about her brother. I hope she'll be able to get to sleep."

It did not occur to Mrs. Morpher that there were seasons in the life of young girls when younger brothers ceased to become objects of extreme solicitude. It did not occur to her to go upstairs and see how her wish was likely to be gratified. It was well in her anxiety that she did not and that the crowning trial of the day's troubles was spared her then. For at that moment Clytie was lying on the bed where she had flung herself without undressing, the heavy masses of her blonde hair tumbled about her neck and her hot face buried in her hands.

Of what was the correct Clytie thinking?

She was thinking, lying there with her burning cheeks pressed against the pillow, that she loved the master! She was recalling step by step every incident that had occurred in their lonely walk. She was repeating to herself his facile sentences, wringing and twisting them to extract one drop to assuage the strange thirst that was growing up in her soul. She was thinking—silly Clytie—that he had never appeared so kind before, and she was thinking—sillier Clytie—that no one had ever before felt as she did then.

How soft and white his hands were! How sweet and gentle were the tones of his voice! How easily he spoke—

so unlike her father, McSnagley, or the young men whom she met at church or on picnics! How tall and handsome he looked as he pressed her hand at the door! Did he press her hand or was it a mistake? Yes, he must have pressed her hand, for she remembers now to have pressed his in return. And he put his arm around her waist once and she feels it yet, and the strange perfume as he drew her closer to him. (Mem.—The master had been smoking. Poor Clytie!)

When she had reached this point she raised herself and sat up and began the process of undressing, mechanically putting each article away in the precise methodical habit of her former life. But she found herself soon sitting again on the bed, twisting her hair, which fell over her plump white shoulders, idly between her fingers, and patting the carpet with her small white foot. She had been sitting thus some minutes when she heard the sound of voices without, the trampling of many feet, and a loud rapping at the door below. She sprang to the door and looked out in the passage. Something white passed by her like a flash and crouched down at the head of the stairs. It was M'liss.

Mrs. Morpher opened the door.

"Is Mr. Morpher in?" said a half-dozen strange hoarse voices.

"No!"

"Where is he?"

"He's at some of the saloons. Oh tell me, has anything happened? Is it about Aristides? Where is he—is he safe?" said Mrs. Morpher, wringing her hands in agony.

"*He's* all right," said one of the men with Mr. Morpher's old emphasis, "but—"

"But what?"

M'liss moved slowly down the staircase and Clytie from the passage above held her breath.

"There's been a row down to Smith's old pocket—a fight—a man killed."

"Who?" shouted M'liss from the stairs.

"McSnagley—shot dead."

Chapter 7

The People
vs.
John Doe Waters:
Before
Chief Justice
ᐁ Lynch

The hurried statement of the messenger was corroborated in the streets that night. It was certain that McSnagley was killed. Smith's Pocket, excited but skeptical, had seen the body, had put its fingers in the bullet hole and was satisfied. Smith's Pocket, albeit hoarse with shouting and excitement, still discussed details with infinite relish in barrooms and saloons and in the main street, in clamorous knots that in front of the jail where the prisoner was confined seemed to swell into a mob. Smith's Pocket, bearded, blue-shirted and belligerent, crowding about this locality, from time to time uttered appeals to justice that swelled on the night wind, not infrequently coupling these invocations with the name of that eminent jurist—Lynch.

Let not the simple reader suppose that the mere taking off of a fellow mortal had created this uproar. The

460

tenure of life in Smith's Pocket was vain and uncertain at the best, and as such philosophically accepted. The blowing out of a brief candle here and there seldom left a permanent shadow with the survivors. In such instances, too, the victims had received their quietus from the hands of brother townsmen socially, as it were, in broad day, in the open streets and under other mitigating circumstances. Thus, when Judge Starbottle of Virginia and French Pete exchanged shots with each other across the plaza until their revolvers were exhausted and the luckless Pete received a bullet through the lungs, half the town witnessed it and were struck with the gallant and chivalrous bearing of these gentlemen. To this day they point with feelings of pride and admiration to the bullet holes in the door of the National Hotel, as they explain how narrow was the escape of the women in the parlor. But here was a man murdered at night in a lonely place and by a stranger—a man unknown to the saloons of Smith's Pocket—a wretch who could not plead the excitement of cards or the delirium of whiskey as an excuse. No wonder that Smith's Pocket surged with virtuous indignation beneath the windows of his prison and clamored for his blood.

And as the crowd thickened and swayed to and fro, the story of his crime grew exaggerated by hurried and frequent repetition. Half a dozen speakers volunteered to give the details with an added horror to every sentence. How one of Morpher's children had been missing

for a week or more. How the schoolmaster and the parson were taking a walk that evening, and coming to
Smith's Pocket heard a faint voice from its depths which
they recognized as belonging to the missing child. How
they had succeeded in dragging him out and gathered
from his infant lips the story of his incarceration by the
murderer, Waters, and his enforced labors in the mine.
How they were interrupted by the appearance of
Waters, followed by a highly colored and epithet-
illustrated account of the interview and quarrel. How
Waters struck the schoolmaster, who returned the blow
with a pick. How Waters thereupon drew a derringer
and fired, missing the schoolmaster but killing Mc-
Snagley behind him. How it was believed that Waters
was one of Joaquin's gang, that he had killed Smith,
etc., etc. At each pause the crowd pushed and panted,
stealthily creeping around the doors and windows of
the jail like some strange beast of prey, until the climax
was reached and a hush fell, and two men were silently
dispatched for a rope, and a critical examination was
made of the limbs of a pine tree in the vicinity.

The man to whom these incidents had the most
terrible significance might have seemed the least concerned as he sat that night but a few feet removed
from the eager crowd without, his hands lightly clasped
together between his knees and the expression on his
face that of one whose thoughts were far away. A
candle stuck in a tin sconce on the wall flickered as the
night wind blew freshly through a broken pane of the

window. Its uncertain light revealed a low room whose cloth ceiling was stained and ragged, and from whose board walls the torn paper hung in strips, a lumber room partitioned from the front office, which was occupied by a justice of the peace. If this temporary dungeon had an appearance of insecurity, there was some compensation in the spectacle of an armed sentinel who sat on a straw mattress in the doorway and another who patrolled the narrow hall which led to the street. That the prisoner was not placed in one of the cells in the floor below may have been owing to the fact that the law recognized his detention as only temporary. And while providing the two guards as a preventive against the egress of crime within, discreetly removed all unnecessary and provoking obstacles to the ingress of justice from without.

Since the prisoner's arrest he had refused to answer any interrogations and since he had been placed in confinement he had not moved from his present attitude. The guard finding all attempts at conversation fruitless had fallen into a reverie, and regaled himself with pieces of straw plucked from the mattress. A mouse ran across the floor. The silence contrasted strangely with the hum of voices in the street.

The candlelight, falling across the prisoner's forehead, showed the features which Smith's Pocket knew and recognized as Waters, the strange prospector. Had M'liss or Aristides seen him then they would have missed that sinister expression which was part of their fearful remembrance. The hard, grim outlines of his mouth were relaxed, the broad shoulders were bent and contracted, the quick searching eyes were fixed on vacancy. The strong man—physically strong only—was breaking up. The fist that might have felled an ox could do nothing more than separate its idle fingers with childishness of power and purpose. An hour longer in this condition and the gallows would have claimed a figure scarcely less limp and impotent than that it was destined to ultimately reject.

He had been trying to collect his thoughts. Would they hang him? No, they must try him first legally, and he could prove—he could prove— But what could he prove? For whenever he attempted to consider the uncertain chances of his escape he found his thoughts straying wide of the question. It was of no use for him to clasp his fingers or knit his brows. Why did the recollection of a schoolfellow long since forgotten blot out all the fierce and feverish memories of the night and the terrible certainty of the future? Why did the strips of paper hanging from the wall recall to him the pattern of a kite he had flown forty years ago? In a moment like this, when all his energies were required and all his cunning and tact would be called into service, could he think of nothing better than trying to match the torn paper on the wall, or to count the cracks in the floor? An oath rose to his lips but from very feebleness died away without expression.

Why had he ever come to Smith's Pocket? If he had

not been guided by that hellcat, this would not have happened. What if he were to tell *all* he knew? What if he should accuse *her?* But would they be willing to give up the bird they had already caught? Yet he again found himself cursing his own treachery and cowardice, and this time an exclamation burst from his lips and attracted the attention of the guard.

"Hello, there! Easy, old fellow. Thar ain't any good in that," said the sentinel, looking up. "It's a bad fix you're in, *sure,* but rarin' and pitchin' won't help things. 'Tain't no use cussin'—leaseways, 'tain't that kind o' swearing that gets a chap out o' here," he added, with a conscientious reservation. "Now, ef I was in your place, I'd kinder reflect on my sins and make my peace with God Almighty, for I tell you the looks o' them people outside ain't pleasant. You're in the hands of the law and the law will protect you as far as it can—as far as two men can stand agin a hundred, *sabe?* That's what's the matter and it's as well that you knowed that now as any time."

But the prisoner had relapsed into his old attitude and was surveying the jailor with the same abstracted air as before. That individual resumed his seat on the mattress and now lent his ear to a colloquy which seemed to be progressing at the foot of the stairs. Presently he was hailed by his brother turnkey from below.

"Oh, Bill," said *fidus* Achates from the passage, with the usual Californian prefatory ejaculation.

"Well?"

"Here's M'liss! Says she wants to come up. Shall I let her in?"

The subject of inquiry, however, settled the question of admission by darting past the guard below in this moment of preoccupation and bounded up the stairs like a young fawn. The guards laughed.

"Now, then, my infant phenomenon," said the one called Bill as M'liss stood panting before him, "wot's up? And nextly, wot's in that bottle?"

M'liss whisked the bottle which she held in her hand smartly under her apron and said curtly, "Where's him that killed the parson?"

"Yonder," replied the man, indicating the abstracted figure with his hand. "Wot do *you* want with him? None o' your tricks here, now," he added threateningly.

"I want to see him!"

"Well, look, make the most of your time, and *his* too, for the matter of that. But mind now, no nonsense, M'liss, he won't stand it!" repeated the guard with an emphasis in the caution.

M'liss crossed the room until she was opposite the prisoner. "Are you the chap that killed the parson?" she said, addressing the motionless figure.

Something in the tone of her voice startled the prisoner from the reverie. He raised his head and glanced quickly with his old sinister expression at the child.

"What's that to you?" he asked, with the grim lines setting about his mouth again and the old harshness of his voice.

"Didn't I tell you he wouldn't stand any of your nonsense, M'liss?" said the guard testily.

M'liss only repeated her question.

"And what if I did kill him?" said the prisoner savagely. "What's that to you, you young hellcat? Guard! Damnation!—what do you let her come here for? Do you hear? Guard!" he screamed, rising in a transport of passion, "take her away! Fling her downstairs! What the hell is she doing here?"

"If you was the man that killed McSnagley," said M'liss without heeding the interruption, "I've brought you something." And she drew the bottle from under her apron and extended it to Waters, adding, "It's brandy. Cognac—A-1."

"Take it away and take yourself with it," returned Waters without abating his angry accents. "Take it away! Do you hear?"

"Well, that's what I call ongrateful, doggone my skin if it ain't," said the guard, who had been evidently struck with M'liss's generosity. "Pass the licker this way, my beauty, and I'll keep it till he changes his mind. He's naturally a little flustered just now but he'll come round after you go."

But M'liss didn't accede to this change in the disposition of the gift and was evidently taken aback by her reception and the refusal of the proffered comfort.

"Come, hand the bottle here!" repeated the guard. "It's agin rules to bring the pris'ner anything, anyway, and it's confiscated to the law. It's agin the rules, too, to ask a pris'ner any question that'll criminate him, and on the whole you'd better go, M'liss," added the guard, to whom the appearance of the bottle had been the means of provoking a spasm of discipline.

But M'liss refused to make over the coveted treasure. Bill arose half jestingly and endeavored to get possession of the bottle. A struggle ensued, good-naturedly on the part of the guard but characterized on the part of M'liss by that half-savage passion which any thwarted whim or instinct was sure to provoke in her nature. At last with a curse she freed herself from his grasp. And seizing the bottle by the neck she aimed it with the full strength of her little arm fairly at his head. But he was quick enough to avert that important object, if not quick enough to save his shoulder from receiving the strength of the blow, which shattered the thin glass and poured the fiery contents of the bottle over his shirt and breast, saturating his clothes and diffusing a sharp alcoholic odor through the room.

A forced laugh broke from his lips as he sank back on the mattress, not without an underlying sense of awe at this savage girl who stood panting before him and from whom he had just escaped a blow which might have been fatal. "It's a pity to waste so much good licker," he added with affected carelessness, narrowly watching each movement of the young pythoness, whose rage was not yet abated.

"Come, M'liss," he said at last, "we'll say quits. You've lost your brandy and I've got some of the pieces of yonder bottle sticking in my shoulder yet. I suppose brandy is good for bruises, though. Hand me the light!"

M'liss reached the candle from the sconce and held it by the guard as he turned back the collar of his shirt to lay bare his shoulder. "So," he muttered, "black and blue. No bones broken, though no fault of yours, eh, my young cherub? There—why, what are you looking at, M'liss—are you crazy? Hell's furies, don't hold the light so near! What are you doing? Help!—ho, there! Help!"

Too late, for in an instant he was a sheet of living flame. When or how the candle had touched his garments saturated with the inflammable fluid Waters, the only inactive spectator in the room, could never afterward tell. He only knew that the combustion was instantaneous and complete, and before the cry had died from his lips not only the guard, but the straw mattress on which he had been sitting, the loose strips of paper hanging from the walls and the torn cloth ceiling above were in flames.

"Help! Help! Fire! Fire!"

With a superhuman effort M'liss dragged the prisoner past the blazing mattress, through the doorway into the passage, and drew the door, which opened outwardly, against him. The unhappy guard, still blazing like a funeral pyre, after wildly beating the air with his arms for a few seconds, dashed at the broken window which gave way with his weight and precipitated him, still flaming, into the yard below. A column of smoke and a licking tongue of flame leaped from the open window at the same moment, and the cry of fire was re-echoed from a hundred voices in the street. But scarcely had M'liss closed the open door against Waters, when the guard from the doorway mounted the stairs in time to see a flaming figure leap from the window. The room was filled with smoke and fire. With an instinct of genius M'liss, pointing to the open window, shouted hoarsely in his ear:

"Waters has escaped!"

A cry of fury from the guard was echoed from the stairs, even now crowded by the excited mob who feared the devastating element might still cheat them of their intended victim. In another moment the house was emptied and the front street deserted, as the people rushed to the rear of the jail—climbing fences and stumbling over ditches in pursuit of the imagined runaway. M'liss seized the hat and coat of the luckless Bill, and dragging the prisoner from his place of concealment hurriedly equipped him and hastened through the blinding smoke of the staircase boldly on the heels of the retiring crowd. Once in the friendly darkness of the street, it was easy to mingle with the pushing throng until an alley crossing at right angles enabled them to leave the main thoroughfare. A few moments' rapid flight, and the outskirts of the town were reached. Here the tall pines opened their abysmal aisles to the fugitives, and M'liss paused with her companion. Until daybreak at least they were safe!

From the time they had quitted the burning room to

that moment, Waters had passed into his listless abstracted condition, so helpless and feeble that he retained the grasp of M'liss's hand more through some instinctive prompting rather than the dictates of reason. M'liss had found it necessary to almost drag him from the main street and the hurrying crowd, which seemed to exercise a strange fascination over his bewildered senses. And now he sat down passively beside her and seemed to submit to the guidance of her superior nature.

"You're safe enough now till daylight," said M'liss when she had recovered her breath, "but you must make the best time you can through these woods tonight, keeping the wind to your back until you come to the Wingdam road. There! Do you hear?" said M'liss, a little vexed at her companion's apathy.

Waters released the hand of M'liss and commenced mechanically to button the coat around his chest with fumbling purposeless fingers. He then passed his hand across his forehead as if to clear his confused and bewildered brain. All this, however, had no better result than to apparently root his feet to the soil and intensify the stupefaction which seemed to be creeping over him.

"Be quick, now! You've no time to lose! Keep straight on through the woods until you see the stars again before you, and you're on the other side of the ridge. What are you waiting for?" And M'liss stamped her little foot impatiently.

An idea which had been struggling for expression at last seemed to dawn in his eyes. Something like a simpering blush crept over his face as he fumbled in his pocket. At last, drawing forth a twenty-dollar piece, he bashfully offered it to M'liss. In a twinkling the extended arm was stricken up, and the bright coin flew high in the air, and disappeared in the darkness.

"Keep your money! I don't want it. Don't do that again!" said M'liss, highly excited, "or I'll—I'll—bite you!"

Her wicked little white teeth flashed ominously as she said it.

"Get off while you can. Look!" she added, pointing to a column of flame shooting up above the straggling mass of buildings in the village. "The jail is burning. If that goes the block will go with it. Before morning these woods will be filled with people. Save yourself while you can!"

Waters turned and moved away in the darkness. "Keep straight on, and don't waste a moment," urged the child, as the man seemed still disposed to linger. "Trot now!" and in another moment he seemed to melt into the forest depths.

M'liss threw her apron over her head and coiled herself up at the root of a tree in something of her old fashion. She had prophesied truly the probable extent of the fire. The fresh wind, whirling the sparks over the little settlement, had already fanned the single flame into the broad sheet which now glowed fiercely, defining the main street along its entire length. The breeze which fanned her cheek bore the crash of falling timbers and the shouts of terrified and anxious men. There were no engines in Smith's Pocket, and the contest was unequal. Nothing but a change of wind could save the doomed settlement.

The red glow lit up the dark cheek of M'liss and kindled a savage light in her black eyes. Relieved by the background of the somber woods, she might have been a red-handed Nemesis looking over the city of Vengeance. As the long tongues of flame licked the broad colonnade of the National Hotel and shot a wreathing pillar of fire and smoke high into the air, M'liss extended her tiny fist and shook it at the burning building with an inspiration that at the moment seemed to transfigure her.

So the night wore away until the first red bars of morning light gleamed beyond the hill, seeming to emulate the dying embers of the devastated settlement. M'liss for the first time began to think of the home she had quitted the night before and looked with some anxiety in the direction of Mountain Ranch. Its white walls and little orchard were untouched, and looked peacefully over the blackened and deserted village. M'liss rose, and stretching her cramped limbs, walked briskly toward the town. She had proceeded but a short distance when she heard the sound of cautious and hesitating footsteps behind her, and facing quickly about, encountered the figure of Waters.

"Are you drunk?" said M'liss passionately, "or what do you mean by this nonsense?"

The man approached her with a strange smile on his face, rubbing his hands together and shivering as with cold. When he had reached her side he attempted to take her hand. M'liss shrank away from him with an expression of disgust.

"What are you doing here again?" she demanded.

"I want to go with you. It's dark in there," he said, motioning to the wood he had just quitted. "I don't like to be alone. You'll let me be with you, won't you? I won't be any trouble." And a feeble smile flickered on his lips.

M'liss darted a quick look into his face. The grim outlines of his mouth were relaxed and his lips moved again impotently. But his eyes were bright and open—bright with a look that was new to M'liss—that imparted a strange softness and melancholy to his features—the incipient gleam of insanity!

Chapter 8

The Author
to the Reader:
∾ Explanatory

IF I remember rightly, in one of the admirable tragedies of Tsien Tsiang at a certain culminating point of interest an innocent person is about to be sacrificed. The knife is raised and the victim meekly awaits the stroke. At this moment the author of the play appears on the stage, and delivering an excellent philosophical dissertation on the merits of the "situation," shows that by the purest principles of art the sacrifice is necessary, but at the same time offers to the audience the privilege of changing the denouement. Such, however, is the nice esthetic sense of a Chinese auditory, and so universal the desire of bloodshed in the heathen breast, that invariably at each representation of this remarkable tragedy the cause of humanity gives way to the principles of art.

I offer this precedent as an excuse for digressing at a moment when I have burned down a small settlement, dispatched a fellow being, and left my heroine alone in the company of an escaped convict who has just developed insanity as a new social quality. My object in thus digressing is to confer with the reader in regard to the evolution of this story—a familiarity not without precedent, as I might prove from most of the old Greek comedies, whose *parabasis* permits the poet to mingle freely with the *dramatis personæ*, to address the audience and descant at length in regard to himself, his play and his own merits.

The fact is that during the progress of this story I have received many suggestions from intimate friends in regard to its incidents and construction. I have also been in the receipt of correspondence from distant readers, one letter of which I recall signed by an "Honest Miner," who advises me to "do the right thing by M'liss," or intimates somewhat obscurely that he will "bust my crust for me," which, though complimentary in its abstract expression of interest and implying a taste for euphonism evinces an innate coarseness which I fear may blunt his perceptions of delicate shades and Greek outlines.

Again, the practical nature of Californians and their familiarity with scenes and incidents which would be novel to other people have occasioned me great uneasiness. In the course of the last three chapters of M'liss

I have received some twenty or thirty communications from different parts of the state corroborating incidents of my story, which I solemnly assure the reader is purely fictitious. Someone has lately sent me a copy of an interior paper containing an old obituary of Smith of Smith's Pocket. Another correspondent writes to me that he was acquainted with the schoolmaster in the fall of '49, and that they "grubbed together." The editors of the serial in which this story appears assure me that they have received an advertisement from the landlord of the National Hotel contingent upon an editorial notice of its having been at one time the abode of M'liss; while an aunt of the heroine, alluding in excellent terms to the reformed character of her niece M'liss, clenches her sincerity by requesting the loan of twenty dollars to buy clothes for the desolate orphan.

Under these circumstance I have hesitated to go on. What were once the bodiless creatures of my fancy—the pale phantoms of thought, evoked in the solitude of my chamber, and sometimes even midst the hum of busy streets—have suddenly grown into flesh and blood, living people, protected by the laws of society and having their legal right to actions for slander in any court. Worse than that, I have sometimes thought with terror of the new responsibility which might attach to my development of their characters. What if I were obliged to support and protect these Frankenstein monsters? What if the original of the principal villain of my story should feel impelled through esthetic principles of art to work out in real life the supposititious denouement I have sketched for him?

I have therefore concluded to lay aside my pen for this week, leaving the catastrophe impending, and await the suggestion of my correspondents. I do so the more cheerfully as it enables the editors of this weekly to publish twenty-seven more columns of Miss Braddon's "Outcasts of Society" and the remainder of the "Duke's Motto"—two works which in the quiet simplicity of their homelike pictures and household incidents are attended with none of the difficulties which beset my unhappy story.

Chapter 9

Cleaning
∾ Up

As the master, wan-eyed and unrefreshed by
slumber, strayed the next morning among the blackened
ruins of the fire he was conscious of having undergone
some strange revulsion of sentiment. What he remembered of the last evening's events, though feverish and
indistinct as a dream—and like a dream, without coher-
ency or connected outline—had nevertheless seriously
impressed him. How frivolous and trifling his past life
and its pursuits looked through the lightning vista
opened to his eyes by the flash of Water's pistol! Suppose I had been killed, ruminated the master, what
then? A paragraph in the *Banner*, headed "Fatal Affray,"
and my name added to the already swollen list of victims to lawless violence and crime! Humph! A pretty

scrape, truly! And the master ground his teeth with vexation.

Let not the reader judge him too hastily. In the best regulated mind thankfulness for deliverance from danger is apt to be mingled with some doubts as to the necessity of the trial.

In this frame of mind the last person he would have cared to meet was Clytie. That young woman's evil genius, however, led her to pass the burnt district that morning. Perhaps she had anticipated the meeting. At all events, he had proceeded but a few steps before he was confronted by the identical round hat and cherry-colored ribbons. But in his present humor the cheerful color somehow reminded him of the fire and of a ruddy stain over McSnagley's heart, and invested the innocent Clytie with a figurative significance. Now Clytie's reveries at that moment were pleasant if the brightness of her eyes and the freshened color on her cheeks were any sign, and as she had not seen the master since before the fire, she naturally expected to take up the thread of romance where it had been dropped. But it required all her feminine tact to conceal her embarrassment at his formal greeting and constrained manner.

"He is bashful," Clytie reasoned to herself.

"This girl is a tremendous fool," growled the master inwardly.

An awkward pause ensued. Finally, Clytie *loquitur*: "M'liss has been missing since the fire!"

"Missing?" echoed the master in his natural tone.

Clytie bit her lip with vexation. "Yes, she's always running away. She'll be back again. But you look interested. Do you know," she continued with exceeding archness, "I sometimes think, Mr. Gray, if M'liss were a little older—"

"Well?"

"Well, putting this and that together, you know!"

"Well?"

"People will talk, you know," continued Clytie, with that excessive fondness weak people exhibit in enveloping in mystery the commonest affairs of life.

"People are damned fools!" roared the master.

The correct Clytie was a little shocked. Perhaps underneath it was a secret admiration of the transgressor. Force even of this cheap quality goes a good way with some natures.

"That is," continued the master, with an increase of dignity in inverse proportion to the lapse he had made, "people are apt to be mistaken, Miss Morpher, and without meaning it to do infinite injustice to their fellow mortals. But I see I am detaining you. I will try and find Melissa. I wish you good morning." And Don Whiskerandos stalked solemnly away.

Clytie turned red and white by turns and her eyes filled with tears. This denouement to her dreams was utterly unexpected. While a girl of stronger character and active intelligence would have employed the time in digesting plans of future retaliation and revenge,

Clytie's dull brain and placid nature were utterly perplexed and shaken.

"Dear me!" said Clytie to herself, as she started
home, "if he don't love me, why don't he say so?"

The master, or Mr. Gray, as we may now call him as
he draws near the close of his professional career, took
the old trail through the forest which led to M'liss's
former hiding place. He walked on briskly, revolving
in his mind the feasibility of leaving Smith's Pocket.
The late disaster, which would affect the prosperity
of the settlement for some time to come, offered an
excuse to him to give up his situation. On searching
his pockets he found his present capital to amount to
ten dollars. This increased by forty dollars due him from
the trustees would make fifty dollars; deduct thirty dollars for liabilities, and he would have twenty dollars left
to begin the world anew. Youth and hope added an indefinite number of ciphers to the right hand of these
figures, and in this sanguine mood our young Alnaschar
walked on until he had reached the old pine throne in
the bank of the forest. M'liss was not there. He sat
down on the trunk of the tree and for a few moments
gave himself up to the associations it suggested. What
would become of M'liss after he was gone? But he
quickly dropped the subject as one too visionary and
sentimental for his then fiercely practical consideration.
To prevent the recurrence of such distracting fancies,
he began to retrace his steps toward the settlement. At

the edge of the woods, at a point where the trail forked toward the old site of Smith's Pocket, he saw M'liss coming toward him. Her ordinary pace on such occasions was a kind of Indian trot. To his surprise she was walking slowly, with her apron thrown over her head—an indication of meditation with M'liss and the usual way in which she excluded the outer world in studying her lessons. When she was within a few feet of him he called her by name. She started as she recognized him. There was a shade of seriousness in her dark eyes and the hand that took his was listless and totally unlike her old frank, energetic grasp.

"You look worried, M'liss," said Mr. Gray soothingly, as the old sentimental feeling crept over his heart. "What's the matter now?"

M'liss replied by seating herself on the bank beside the road and pointing to a place by her side. Mr. Gray took the proffered seat. M'liss then, fixing her eyes on some distant part of the view, remained for some moments in silence. Then, without turning her head or moving her eyes, she asked:

"What's that they call a girl that has money left her?"

"An heiress, M'liss?"

"Yes, an heiress."

"Well?" said Mr. Gray.

"Well," said M'liss, without moving her eyes, "I'm one —I'm a heiress!"

"What's that, M'liss?" said Mr. Gray laughingly.

M'liss was silent again. Suddenly turning her eyes full upon him, she said:

"Can you keep a secret?"

"Yes," said Mr. Gray, beginning to be impressed by the child's manner.

"Listen, then."

In short quick sentences, M'liss began. How Aristides had several times hinted of the concealed riches of Smith's Pocket. How he had last night repeated the story to her of a strange discovery he had made. How she remembered having heard her father often swear that there was money "in that hole," if he only had means to work it. How, partly impressed by this statement and partly from curiosity and pity for the prisoner, she had visited him in confinement. An account of her interview, the origin of the fire, her flight with Waters. (*Questions* by Mr. Gray: What was your object in assisting this man to escape? *Ans.* They were going to kill him. *Ques.* Hadn't he killed McSnagley? *Ans.* Yes, but McSnagley ought to have been killed long ago.) How she had taken leave of him that morning. How he had come back again "silly." How she had dragged him on toward the Wingdam road, and how he had told her that all the hidden wealth of Smith's Pocket had belonged to her father. How she had found out from some questions that he had known her father. But how all his other answers were "silly."

"And where is he now?" asked Mr. Gray.

"Gone," said M'liss. "I left him at the edge of the wood to go back and get some provisions, and when I returned he was gone. If he had any senses left, he's miles away by this time. When he was off I went back to Smith's Pocket. I found the hidden opening and saw the gold."

Mr. Gray looked at her curiously. He had, in his more intimate knowledge of her character, noticed the unconcern with which she spoke of the circumstances of her father's death and the total lack of any sentiment of filial regard. The idea that this man whom she had aided in escaping had ever done her injury had not apparently entered her mind, nor did Mr. Gray think it necessary to hint the deeper suspicion he had gathered from Dr. Duchesne that Waters had murdered her father. If the story of the concealed treasures of Smith's Pocket were exaggerated he could easily satisfy himself on that point. M'liss met his suggestion to return to the Pocket with alacrity, and the two started away in that direction.

It was late in the afternoon when Mr. Gray returned. His heightened color and eager inquiry for Dr. Duchesne provoked the usual hope from the people that he met "that it was nothing serious." No, nothing was the matter, the master answered with a slight laugh, but would they send the doctor to his schoolhouse when he returned? "That young chap's worse than he thinks," was one sympathizing suggestion. "This kind of life's too rough for his sort."

To while away the interim, Mr. Gray stopped on his way to the schoolhouse at the stage office as the Wing-dam stage drew up and disgorged its passengers. He was listlessly watching the passengers as they descended when a soft voice from the window addressed him, "May I trouble you for your arm as I get down?" Mr. Gray looked up. It was a singular request as the driver was at that moment standing by the door, apparently for that purpose. But the request came from a handsome woman, and with a bow the young man stepped to the door. The lady laid her hand lightly on his arm, sprang from the stage with a dexterity that showed the service to have been merely ceremonious, thanked him with an elaboration of acknowledgment which seemed equally gratuitous and disappeared in the office.

"That's what I call a dead set," said the driver, drawing a long breath as he turned to Mr. Gray, who stood in some embarrassment. "Do you know her?"

"No," said Mr. Gray laughingly, "do you?"

"Nary time! But take care of yourself, young man. She's after you, sure!"

But Mr. Gray was continuing his walk to the schoolhouse, unmindful of the caution. From the momentary glimpse he had caught of this woman's face, she appeared to be about thirty. Her dress, though tasteful and elegant, in the present condition of California society afforded no criterion of her social status. But the figure of Dr. Duchesne waiting for him at the schoolhouse door just then usurped the place of all others and she dropped out of his mind.

"Now then," said the doctor, as the young man grasped his hand, "you want me to tell you why your eyes are bloodshot, why your cheeks burn, and your hand is dry and hot?"

"Not exactly! Perhaps you'll understand the symptoms better when you've heard my story. Sit down here and listen."

The doctor took the proffered seat on top of a desk, and Mr. Gray, after assuring himself that they were entirely alone, related the circumstances he had gathered from M'liss that morning.

"You see, doctor, how unjust were your surmises in regard to this girl," continued Mr. Gray. "But let that pass now. At the conclusion of her story I offered to go with her to this Ali Baba cave. It was no easy job finding the concealed entrance. But I found it at last, and ample corroboration of every item of this wild story. The pocket is rich with the most valuable ore. It has evidently been worked for some time since the discovery was made but there is still a fortune in its walls, and several thousand dollars of ore sacked up in its galleries. Look at that!" continued Mr. Gray, as he drew an oblong mass of quartz and metal from his pocket. "Think of a secret of this kind having been entrusted for three weeks to a penniless orphan girl of twelve and an eccentric schoolboy of ten, and undivulged except when a proper occasion offered."

Dr. Duchesne smiled. "And Waters is really clear?"

"Yes," said Mr. Gray.

"And M'liss assisted him to escape?"

"Yes."

"Well, you are an innocent one! And you see nothing in this but an act of thoughtless generosity? No assisting of an old accomplice to escape?"

"I see nothing but truth in her statement," returned Mr. Gray stoutly. "If there has been any wrong committed I believe her to be innocent of its knowledge."

"Well, I'm glad at least the money goes to her and not to him. But how are you to establish her right to this property?"

"That was my object in conferring with you. At present the claim is abandoned. I have taken up the ground in my own name (for her), and this afternoon I posted up the usual notice."

"Go on. You are not so much of a fool, after all."

"Thank you! This will hold until a better claim is established. Now, if Smith had discovered this lead, and was, as the lawyers say, 'seized and possessed' of it at the time of his death, M'liss, of course, as next of kin, inherits it."

"But how can this be proved? It is the general belief that Smith committed suicide through extreme poverty and destitution."

Mr. Gray drew a letter from his pocket.

"You remember the memorandum I showed you,

which came into my possession. Here it is. It is dated the day of his death."

Dr. Duchesne took it and read:

"July 17th. Five hours in drift—dipping west. Took out 20 oz.—cleaned up 40 oz.—Mem. Saw M. S."

"This evidently refers to actual labor in the mine at the time," said Dr. Duchesne. "But is it legally sufficient to support a claim of this magnitude? That is the only question now. You say this paper was the leaf of an old memorandum, torn off and used for a letter by M'liss. Do you know where the original book can be found?"

"Aristides has it, or knows where it is," answered Mr. Gray.

"Find it by all means. And get legal advice before you do anything. Go this very evening to Judge Plunkett and state your case to him. The promise of a handsome contingent fee won't hurt M'liss's prospects any. Remember, our ideas of abstract justice and the letter of the law in this case may be entirely different. Take Judge Plunkett your proofs. That is," said the doctor, stopping and eying his friend keenly, "if you have no fears for M'liss if this matter should be thoroughly ventilated."

Mr. Gray did not falter.

"I go at once," said he gaily, "if only to prove the

child's claim to a good name if we fail in getting her property."

The two men left the schoolhouse together. As they reached the main street the doctor paused:

"You are still determined?"

"I am," responded the young man.

"Good night and God speed you, then," and the doctor left him.

The fire had been particularly severe on the legal fraternity in the settlement. Judge Plunkett's office together with those of his learned brethren had been consumed with the courthouse on the previous night. The judge's house was on the outskirts of the village, and thither Mr. Gray proceeded. The judge was at home but engaged at that moment. Mr. Gray would wait, and was ushered into a small room evidently used as a kitchen but just then littered with law books, bundles of papers and blanks that had been hastily rescued from the burning building. The sideboard groaned with the weight of several volumes of *New York Reports* that seemed to impart a dusty flavor to the adjacent victuals. Mr. Gray picked up a volume of supreme court decisions from the coal scuttle and was deep in an interesting case when the door of the adjoining room opened and Judge Plunkett appeared.

He was an oily man of about fifty, with spectacles. He was glad to see the schoolmaster. He hoped he was not suffering from the excitement of the previous evening. For his part, the spectacle of sober citizens rising in a body to vindicate the insulted majesty of the laws of society and of man had always something sublime in it. And the murderer had really got away after all. And it was a narrow escape the schoolmaster had, too, at Smith's Pocket.

Mr. Gray took advantage of the digression to state his business. He briefly recounted the circumstances of the discovery of the hidden wealth of Smith's Pocket and exhibited the memorandum he had shown the doctor. When he had concluded Judge Plunkett looked at him over his spectacles and rubbed his hands with satisfaction.

"You apprehend," said the judge eagerly, "that you will have no difficulty in procuring this book from which the leaf was originally torn?"

"None," replied Mr. Gray.

"Then, sir, I should give as my professional opinion that the case was already won."

Mr. Gray shook the hand of the little man with great fervor and thanked him for his belief. "And so this property will go entirely to M'liss?" he asked again.

"Well—ah—no, not exactly," said Judge Plunkett, with some caution. "She will benefit by it undoubtedly—undoubtedly," and he rubbed his hands again.

"Why not M'liss alone? There are no other claimants!" said Mr. Gray.

"I beg your pardon—you mistake," said Judge Plunkett, with a smile. "You surely would not leave out the widow and mother?"

"Why, M'liss is an orphan," said Mr. Gray in utter bewilderment.

"A sad mistake, sir, a painful though natural mistake. Mr. Smith, though separated from his wife, was never divorced. A very affecting history—the old story, you know—an injured and loving woman deserted by her natural protector but disdaining to avail herself of our legal aid. By a singular coincidence that I should have told you, I am anticipating you in this very case. Your services, however, I feel will be invaluable. Your concern for her amiable and interesting daughter Narcissa—ah, no, Melissa—will, of course, put you with us. You have never seen Mrs. Smith? A fine-looking noble woman, sir—though still disconsolate—still thinking of the departed one. By another singular coincidence that I should have told you, she is here now. You shall see her, sir. Pray, let me introduce you." And still rubbing his hands Judge Plunkett led the way to the adjoining room.

Mr. Gray followed him mechanically. A handsome woman rose from the sofa as they entered. It was the woman he had assisted to alight from the Wingdam stage.

Chapter 10

The
Red
～ Rock

In the strong light that fell upon her face, Mr. Gray had an opportunity to examine her features more closely. Her eyes, which were dark and singularly brilliant, were half closed, either from some peculiar conformation of the lids, or an habitual effort to conceal expression. Her skin was colorless with that satinlike luster that belongs to some brunettes, relieved by one or two freckles that were scarcely blemishes. Her face was squared a little at the lower angles but the chin was round and soft, and the curves about the mouth were full and tender enough to destroy the impression left by contemplation of those rigid outlines. The effect of its general contour was that of a handsome woman of thirty. In detail, as the eye dwelt upon any particular feature, you could have added a margin of ten years either way.

"Mrs. Smith—Mr. Gray," said the lawyer briskly. "Mr.
Gray is the gentleman who, since the decease of your
husband, has taken such a benevolent interest in our
playful Narcissa—Melissa, I should say. He is the preceptor of our district school, and besides his relation as
teacher to your daughter has, I may say in our legal
fashion, stood *in loco parentis*—in other words, has been
a parent, a—a—father to her."

At the conclusion of this speech Mrs. Smith darted a
quick glance at Mr. Gray, which was unintelligible to
any but a woman. As there were none of her own keen-
witted sex present to make an ungracious interpreta-
tion of it, it passed unnoticed, except the slight embarrassment and confusion it caused the young man from
its apparent gratuity.

"We have met before, I believe," said Mrs. Smith,
with her bright eyes half-hidden and her white teeth
half-disclosed. "I can easily imagine Mr. Gray's devotion to a friend from his courtesy to a stranger. Let me
thank you again for both my daughter and myself."

In the desperate hope of saying something natural,
Mr. Gray asked if she had seen Melissa yet.

"Oh, dear, no! Think how provoking! Judge Plunkett says it is absolutely impossible till some tiresome
formalities are over. There are so many stupid forms to
go through with first. But how is she? You have seen
her, have you not? You will see her again tonight, perhaps? How I long to embrace her again! She was a

mere baby when she left me. Tell her how I long to fly to her."

Her impassioned utterance and the dramatic gestures that accompanied these words afforded a singular contrast to the cool way with which she rearranged the folds of her dress when she had finished, folding her hands over her lap and settling herself unmistakably back again an the sofa. Perhaps it was this that made Mr. Gray think she had, at some time, been an actress. But the next moment he caught her eye again and felt pleased—and again vexed with himself for being so— and in this mental condition began to speak in favor of his old pupil. His embarrassment passed away as he warmed to his subject, dwelling at length on M'liss's better qualities. It did not return until in a breathless pause he became aware that this woman's bright eyes were bent upon him. Then the color rose in his checks, and with a half-muttered apology for his prolixity he offered his excuses to retire.

"Stay a moment, Mr. Gray," said the lawyer. "You are going to town, and will not think it a trouble to see Mrs. Smith safely back to her hotel. You can talk these things over with our fair friend on the way. Tomorrow at ten I trust to see you both again."

"Perhaps I am taxing Mr. Gray's gallantry too much," interposed the lady with a very vivid disclosure of eyes and teeth. "Mr. Gray would be only too happy." After he had uttered this civility there was a slight consciousness of truth about it that embarrassed him again. But Mrs. Smith took his proffered arm and they bade the lawyer good night and passed out in the starlit night together.

Four weeks have elasped since the advent of Mrs. Smith to the settlement, four weeks that might have been years in any other but a California mining camp, for the wonderful change that has been wrought in its physical aspect. Each stage has brought its load of fresh adventurers. Another hotel, which sprang up on the site of the National, has its new landlord and a new set of faces about its hospitable board, where the conventional bean appears daily as a modest vegetable or in the insincerer form of coffee. The sawmills have been hard at work for the last month, and huge gaps appear in the circling files of redwood where the fallen trees are transmuted to a new style of existence in the damp sappy tenements that have risen over the burnt district. The great strike at Smith's Pocket has been heralded abroad. Above and below, and on either side of the crumbling tunnel that bears that name, other tunnels are piercing the bowels of the mountain, shafts are being sunk, and claims are being taken up even to the crest of Red Mountain, in the hope of striking the great Smith lead. Already an animated discussion has sprung up in the columns of the *Red Mountain Banner* in regard to the direction of the famous lead—a discussion assisted by correspondents who have assumed all the letters of the alphabet in their anonymous arguments, and have formed the opposing "angle" and "dip" factions of Smith's Pocket. But whatever be the direction of the lead, the progress of the settlement has been steadily onward, with an impetus gained by the late disaster. That classical but much abused bird, the phoenix, has been invoked from its ashes in several editorials in the *Banner* to sit as a type of resuscitated Smith's Pocket, while in the homelier phrase of an honest miner "it seemed as if the fire kem to kinder clean out things for a fresh start."

Meanwhile the quasi-legal administration of the estate of Smith is drawing near a termination that seems to credit the prophetic assertion of Judge Plunkett. One fact has been evolved in the process of examination, viz., that Smith had discovered the new lead before he was murdered. It was a fair hypothesis that the man who assumed the benefit of his discovery was the murderer, but as this did not immediately involve the settlement of the estate it excited little comment or opposition. The probable murderer had escaped. Judicial investigations even in the hands of the people had been attended with disastrous public results and there was no desire on the part of justice to open the case and deal with an abstract principle when there was no opportunity of making an individual example. The circumstances were being speedily forgotten in the new excitement. Even the presence of Mrs. Smith lost its novelty. The *Banner,* when alluding to her husband, spoke of him as the "late J. Smith, Esq.," attributing the present activity of business as the result of his lifelong example of untiring energy, and generally laid the foundation of a belief, which thereafter obtained, that he died comfortably in the bosom of his family, surrounded by disconsolate friends. The history of all pioneer settlements has this legendary basis and M'liss may live to see the day when her father's connection with the origin of the settlement shall become apocryphal, and contested like that of Romulus and Remus and their wolfish wet nurse.

It is to the everlasting credit and honor of Smith's Pocket that the orphan and widow meet no opposition from the speculative community and that the claim's utmost boundaries are liberally rendered. How far this circumstance may be owing to the rare personal attractions of the charming widow or to M'liss's personal popularity, I shall not pretend to say. It is enough that when the brief of Judge Plunkett's case is ready there are clouds of willing witnesses to substantiate and corroborate doubtful points to an extent that is more creditable to their generosity than their veracity.

M'liss has seen her mother. Mr. Gray, with his knowledge of his pupil's impulsiveness, has been surprised to notice that the new relationship seems to awaken none

of those emotions in the child's nature that he confidently looked for. On the occasion of their first meeting, to which Mr. Gray was admitted, M'liss maintained
a guarded shyness totally different from her usual frank
boldness—a shyness that was the more remarkable from
its contrast with the unrepressed and somewhat dramatic emotions of Mrs. Smith. Now, under her mother's
protection and care, Mr. Gray observes another radical
change in M'liss's appearance. She is dressed more
tastefully and neatly—not entirely the result of a
mother's influence, but apparently the result of some
natural instinct now for the first time indulged, and exhibited in a ribbon or a piece of jewelry worn with a
certain air of consciousness. There is a more strict attention to the conventionalities of life: her speech is
more careful and guarded; her walk, literally, more
womanly and graceful. Those things Mr. Gray naturally attributes to the influence of the new relation,
though he cannot help recalling his meeting with
M'liss in the woods on the morning of the fire, and dat-
ing many of these changes from thence.

It is a pleasant morning and Mr. Gray is stirring
early. He has been busied in preparation the night
previous, for this is his last day in Smith's Pocket. He
lingers for some time about the schoolhouse, gathering
up those little trifles which lie about his desk which
have each a separate history in his experience of
Smith's Pocket and are a part of the incrustations of

his life. Lastly, a file of the *Red Mountain Banner* is taken from the same receptacle and packed away in his bag. He walks to the door and turns to look back. Has he forgotten anything? No, nothing. But still he lingers. He wonders who will take his place at the desk. For the first time in his pedagogue experience, perhaps, he feels something of an awful responsibility as he thinks of his past influence over the wretched little beings who used to tremble at his nod, and whose future, ill or good, he may have helped to fashion. At last he closes the door almost tenderly and walks thoughtfully down the road. He has to pass the cabin of a miner whose little boy is toddling in the ditch, his pinafore, hands and face in a chronic state of untidiness. Mr. Gray seizes him with an hilarious impulse, and after a number of rapid journeys to Banbury Cross in search of an old woman who mounted a mythical white horse he kisses the cleanest place on his broad expanse of cheek, presses some silver into his chubby fist, tells him to be a good boy and deposits him in the ditch again. Having in this youthful way atoned for past sins of omission, he proceeds with a sense of perfect absolution on his way to the settlement.

A few hours lie between him and his departure, to be employed in friendly visits to Mrs. Morpher, Dr. Duchesne, M'liss and her mother. The Mountain Ranch is nearest, and thither Mr. Gray goes first. Mrs. Morpher, over a kneading trough with her bare arm whitened with flour, is genuinely grieved at parting with the master and in spite of Mr. Gray's earnest remonstrances insists upon conducting him into the chill parlor, leaving him there until she shall have attired herself in a manner becoming to "company." "I don't want you to go at all—no more I don't," says Mrs. Morpher, with all sincerity, as she seats herself finally on the shining horsehair sofa. "The children will miss you. I don't believe that anyone will do for Risty, Kerg and Clytie what you have done. But I suppose you know best what's best. Young men like to see the world and it ain't expected one so young as you should settle down yet. That's what I was telling Clytie this morning. That was just the way with my John afore he was married. I supposed you'll see M'liss and *her* before you go. They say that she is going to San Francisco soon. Is it so?"

Mr. Gray understands the personal pronoun to refer to Mrs. Smith, a title Mrs Morpher has never granted M'liss's mother, for whom she entertains an instinctive dislike. He answers in the affirmative, however, with the consciousness of uneasiness under the inquiry. And as the answer does not seem to please Mrs. Morpher, he is constrained to commend M'liss's manifest improvement under her mother's care.

"Well," says Mrs. Morpher, with a significant sigh, "I hope it's so. But bless us, where's Clytie? You mustn't go without saying good-by to her," and Mrs. Morpher starts away in search of her daughter.

The dining room door scarcely closes before the bed-room door opens, and Clytie crosses the parlor softly with something in her hands. "You are going now?" she says hurriedly.

"Yes."

"Will you take this?" putting a sealed package into his hand, "and keep it without opening it until—"

"Until when, Clytie?"

"Until you are married."

Mr. Gray laughs.

"Promise me," repeats Clytie.

"But I may expire in the meantime, through sheer curiosity."

"Promise!" says Clytie gravely.

"I promise, then."

Mr. Gray receives the package. "Good-by," says Clytie softly.

Clytie's rosy cheek is very near Mr. Gray. There is nobody by. He is going away. It is the last time. He kisses her just before the door opens again to Mrs. Morpher.

Another shake of hands all around and Mr. Gray passes out of the Mountain Ranch forever.

Dr. Duchesne's office is near at hand. But for some reason that Mr. Gray cannot entirely explain to himself he prefers to go to Mrs. Smith's first. The little cottage which they have taken temporarily is soon reached, and as the young man stands at the door he re-knots the bow of his cravat and passes his fingers through his curls—trifles that to Dr. Duchesne or any other critical, middle-aged person might look bad.

M'liss and Mrs. Smith are both at home. They have been waiting for him so long. Was it that pretty daughter of Mrs. Morpher—the fair young lady with blonde curls—who caused the detention? Is not Mr. Gray a sly young fellow for all his seeming frankness? So he must go today? He cannot possibly wait a few days and go with them? Thus Mrs. Smith, between her red lips and white teeth, and under her half-closed eyes; for M'liss stands quietly apart without speaking. Her reserve during the interview contrasts with the vivacity of her mother as though they had changed respective places in relationship. Mr. Gray is troubled by this and as he rises to go, he takes M'liss's hand in his.

"Have you nothing to say to me before I go?" he asks.

"Good-by," answers M'liss.

"Nothing more?"

"That's enough," rejoins the child simply.

Mr. Gray bites his lips. "I may never see you again, you know, Melissa," he continues.

"You will see us again," says M'liss quietly, raising her great dark eyes to his.

The blood mounted to his cheek and crimsoned his forehead. He was conscious, too, that the mother's face had taken fire at his own as she walked away toward the window.

"Good-by, then," said Mr. Gray pettishly, as he stooped to kiss her.

M'liss accepted the salute stoically. Mr. Gray took Mrs. Smith's hand. Her face had resumed its colorless satinlike sheen.

"M'liss knows the strength of your good will and makes her calculations accordingly. I hope she may not be mistaken," she said, with a languid tenderness of voice and eye. The young man bent over her outstretched hand, and withdrew as the Wingdam stage noisily rattled up before the National Hotel.

There was but little time left to spend with Dr. Duchesne, so the physician walked with him to the stage office. There were a few of the old settlers lounging by the stage who had discerned, just as the master was going away, how much they liked him. Mr. Gray had gone through the customary bibulous formula of leave-taking. So with a hearty shake of the doctor's hand and a promise to write he climbed to the box of the stage. "All aboard!" cried the driver, and with a preliminary bound, the stage rolled down Main Street.

Mr. Gray remained buried in thought as they rolled through the town, each object in passing recalling some incident of his past experience. The stage had reached the outskirts of the settlement when he detected a well-known little figure running down a bytrail to intersect the road before the stage had passed. He called the driver's attention to it and as they drew up at the crossing Aristides's short legs and well-known features were plainly discernible through the dust. He was holding in his hand a letter.

"Well, my little man, what is it?" said the driver impatiently.

"A letter for the master," gasped the exhausted child.

"Give it here!—Any answer?"

"Wait a moment," said Mr. Gray.

"Look sharp, then, and get your billet-duxis before you go next time."

Mr. Gray hurriedly broke the seal and read these words:

Judge Plunkett has just returned from the county seat. Our case is won. We leave here next week. J. S.

P. S. Have you got my address in San Francisco?

"Any answer?" said the driver.

"None."

"Get up!"

And then the stage rolled away from Smith's Pocket, leaving the just Aristides standing in the dust of its triumphal wheels.

About
❧ Bret Harte

About
BRET HARTE

It was as a boy of eleven that the writer known today as Bret Harte published his first original work, a poem. The time was just one year before the discovery that ushered in the great California Gold Rush.

No one at that time could possibly have connected these two facts. For young Francis Brett Harte was the city-bred, bookish son of a schoolmaster, whose boyish yen for travel and adventure had been completely vicarious. Born in 1836 in Albany, New York, Harte grew up there and in New York and Brooklyn, devoted to books. He was particularly enthralled by the novels of Dickens, Dumas, Irving and Cooper, writers whose humorously ironic phrasing, melodramatic plots and vivid characterizations he was later to emulate so brilliantly in creating a new kind of fiction, the "western."

In 1854, he joined his mother and new stepfather in California. By then the Gold Rush was in full swing. The raw

509

new country and the strange assortment of fortune-seekers which Harte met in San Francisco had a tremendous impact on the sensitive, urbane young man. He was shocked by the racial violence he saw manifested toward the Indians, Mexicans and Chinese; but he saw also the drama of adventure and the hazards of fortune or luck. And he met a gallery of characters more picturesque than Dickens' own.

In a series of jobs as miner, messenger for Wells Fargo Express, country schoolmaster, then typesetter, newspaper contributor and finally magazine editor and writer, Harte recorded all these types in his memory: the illiterate miners, the ranchers, the outlaws, the luck-dealing gamblers, the self-styled colonels and judges, the pert, hardy daughters of frontiersmen, the Wells Fargo expressmen, and the real and the false ladies.

His keen reporter's eye and sensitive ear caught their speech and mannerisms, and his sophisticated mind interpreted their thinking with irony and wit. Yet he also wrote with passion against injustice. When citizens massacred a village of Indians near the town where he was editor of the local newspaper, the diatribe he printed forced him to leave for San Francisco.

There he became editor of the famous *Overland Monthly* that also gave Mark Twain and Jack London their start. With its publication in 1868 of "The Luck of Roaring Camp," Bret Harte was immediately hailed as a new literary genius. His fame quickly spread to the East and across the Atlantic to England. Walter Van Tilburg Clark in his foreword to this book has eloquently described Harte's instant and phenomenal popularity.

For the next three years Harte's fame continued to mount, as he turned out hundreds of stories, sketches, poems and parodies that treated with warm pathos and humor this altogether new life of the far West. In the words of the day he had "struck it rich," and like many another man who had mined a rich vein he went back East in triumph.

But like many a miner's fortune, Harte's also soon dwindled. His money went in extravagant living and his immense popularity was short-lived. Once the novelty of his stories had worn off, the American reading public tired of Harte's repetition of the same theme. And perhaps, too, his readers by now preferred a less realistic image of their Golden West. Harte, although highly talented, seemed unable to change his style and theme. His disciples of "local color"—Mark Twain and even Rudyard Kipling—soon outran him.

Unable to fulfill a major writing contract with *The Atlantic Monthly* and in need of funds, Harte took a State Department consulship first in Germany, then in Glasgow, Scotland. He finally settled in London where he continued to turn out his western stories for a still appreciative audience. His wit and notable social gifts made him welcome in various circles in London where he continued to live until his death in 1902.

In England, Harte is still one of the most widely read American short story writers. "The Luck of Roaring Camp," "Tennessee's Partner" and "The Outcasts of Poker Flat" are regarded there and in the United States as authentic treasures of American literature. There are, however, many readers who through the years have preferred the stylized "westerns," patterned after Bret Harte but lacking his perception, wit and realism.

Now the tide again is turning. Discerning critics and western writers like Walter Van Tilburg Clark recognize that Bret Harte not only lived in and knew the old West at first hand, but also that he wrote with rare understanding of that unique and unbelievable period. This was not the black and white world of good versus bad portrayed in the modern "western," but a harsh, hostile world where luck or the weather spelled life or death, where bad men were sometimes softhearted and good men often unjust, unfeeling and violently prejudiced against helpless minority groups.

A newer generation, with a fuller knowledge of his life and times, is coming to see Bret Harte for what he really was—the unique, perceptive and highly literate interpreter of a colorful time now past, when greed for gold pushed America to the Pacific coast and closed her old frontier forever.